KNIFE MUSIC

KNIFE MUSIC

DAVID CARNOY

New York

Cover photo by David Carnoy

www.knifemusicbook.com

www.parkmadisonpress.com

ISBN: 0-615-24325-8
ISBN-13: 978-0-615-24325-2

First ParkMadison Press paperback printing:
November 2008

Acknowledgments

A big debt of gratitude goes to Dr. Rick Bloom, who let me trail him through his hospital's corridors and operating rooms and gave me a glimpse into the life of a surgeon. Thanks to Commander Terri Molakides of the Menlo Park Police Department for taking the time to answer my questions, particularly as they pertain to a homicide investigation of this peculiar nature. Book Doctor Jerry Gross critiqued and edited the manuscript and continually offered sage advice and encouragement. Agent John Silbersack made a couple of key suggestions that required me to perform additional surgery but made the book much better in the end. And finally, I'd like to thank my family and especially my wife Lisa, who somewhat patiently tolerated me holed up in a home office, tapping away on a keyboard late at night and on weekends.

KNIFE MUSIC

PART 1

GALL AND GLORY

1/ Code three

Nov. 9, 2006—p.m. 11:16

The trauma alert went off in Parkview Medical Center's emergency department. Four miles from the hospital there had been an accident.

"I have a sixteen-year-old female involved in an MVA," a paramedic informed the triage nurse at Parkview by CB radio. "She is awake at the scene, arousable. But she appears to have some head and neck injuries as well as chest and abdominal injuries involving the steering column."

The girl's Volkswagen Jetta had jumped the curb and hit a telephone pole at high speed. Although she was wearing a seat belt, the front end of the car was crushed and the steering wheel driven back into her, pinning her to her seat. Rescue personnel had tried to move the seat back, but the tracks were jammed and they were forced to squeeze her out the best they could. Using all his strength, a fireman pulled the wheel a few inches away from the girl while paramedics carefully tugged on her until she was freed.

"We're arriving code three in four minutes," the paramedic said.

Ted Cogan, the senior trauma surgeon in the hospital that evening, came down to the emergency department from his on-call room on the second floor just as the paramedics were wheeling the victim into the hospital. Cogan was a tall man of medium build made to look even taller by the clogs he was wearing, which, when he walked on the hard, bare floors of the hospital, came out sounding like the slow clip-clop of a horse pulling a tourist carriage.

Only a few minutes earlier, he'd been resting comfortably in bed, dozing. One side of his hair, graying at the temples, was standing on end and his green scrub shirt was not tucked into his pants in the front. Rumpled as he was, though, the look didn't add years to him. Instead, it gave him a boyish charm, as if he were late for school, rather than on time for work.

The paramedics steered the victim into the trauma room. White and young with blond hair, she was looking up at the ceiling, her mouth covered by an oxygen mask. In the room, the head trauma nurse, Pam Wexford, started barking orders at an intern: "We need you on that side. No, there. OK, on three, we lift."

They transferred the girl, who was strapped to a hard-board stretcher, her neck stabilized by a cervical collar, from the paramedics' gurney to the trauma-room gurney. Cogan moved into the room, but stood off to the side, trying to stay out of the way of the emergency workers. Although he was at the top of the pyramid and technically in charge, there were few, if any, instructions he had to give in these early moments because standard procedure was in effect. The team would make sure the victim had an airway, they'd take her vital signs, start an IV, draw a blood sample, and strip off her clothes. Then they'd take preliminary X-rays of her neck, chest, and pelvis.

"Dr. Cogan, so nice of you to join us."

This was John Kim, the chief surgical resident, talking and working on the girl at the same time. Kim was thirty but he looked twenty. A baby-faced Korean-American. Cogan liked him, if only because he possessed the two qualities that made just about anybody tolerable: he was competent and had a good sense of humor.

"Wouldn't miss it for the world," Cogan said. "What happened?"

"She hit a telephone poll doing about 50."

"Ouch."

"90 over 60, Doctor," Pam Wexford said. "Pulse 120. Hemoglobin 15."

The girl's blood count was normal. *But her blood pressure was lower than normal and her heart was running fast, which probably meant she was losing blood—the question was from where. She didn't appear to have any major external lacerations, so they were probably looking at a fracture, some sort of chest trauma, or the laceration or rupture of an organ,* Cogan thought.

"We're going to have to cut your clothes off," Wexford said to the girl. "So please try to remain still."

The girl responded by opening and shutting her eyes and groaning. She was wearing jeans, which made the cutting more difficult, but Wexford, a real-life version of Edward Scissorhands, still managed to shred her pants, mock-turtle neck shirt, bra, and panties, in under a minute. When she was finished, Cogan went over to a counter, where there was a latex-glove dispenser, and pulled out a couple of gloves. He stretched a glove over each hand, then turned his attention to the victim, who was lying naked on the gurney, her legs spread slightly apart. He noted that she was a thin, well-proportioned girl with muscular legs and a flat stomach. She had four or five superficial wounds—cuts and scratches—on her arms and face, then a deeper cut and bruise on her right shin that an intern was attending to.

"How're we doing, Cynthia?" Cogan said to the X-ray technician.

"Ready when you are, Doctor."

"Pam?"

"BP 90 over 60. Pulse 130."

"OK, Cynthia. Gimme a Kodak moment."

The X-ray technician moved the portable X-ray machine over to the victim. When it was in place, she told everybody to clear the room except for one intern, who was putting on a lead apron, preparing himself for the unenviable task of pulling the patient taut (by the feet) during the cervical shot. Cynthia took several X-rays, repositioning the machine for each new shot, always making sure to remind everybody to "clear" before she pressed the remote switch from where she stood behind the lead screen that prevented her from being exposed to the radiation.

As soon as she was done, the rest of the trauma team came back into the room and resumed their duties. A couple of zealous interns whose names Cogan always got mixed up started firing questions at the girl, who mainly responded with groans and grimaces.

Intern #1: "Do you know where you are? Do you know how you got here?"

Intern #2: "Miss, are you allergic to any medication?"

Intern #1: "Are you allergic to antibiotics? Penicillin?"

Intern #2 (touching her leg with the needle): "Can you feel that?"

Intern #1: "Miss, I'm going to have to give you a rectal exam. OK?"

"80 over 60, Doctor," Pam Wexford said. "Pulse 150."

"All right," Cogan said. "Do we have a name for her yet?"

The nurse glanced at the paramedics' paperwork. "Kristen," she said. "Kristen Kroiter."

"Kristen," Cogan said, speaking to the girl. "Is that your name?"

She didn't answer. She just opened and closed her eyes.

"OK. I'm Dr. Cogan and this is Dr. Kim and we're here to help you. We're all here to help you. You've been in a car accident and you're in a hospital. Do you understand that?"

With the oxygen mask still covering her mouth, the answer came out sounding like a grunt but it was affirmative enough for Cogan to continue.

"I'm going to ask you a few questions and give you a

quick examination so we can determine your condition. OK?"

She groaned. Then, squirming a little in the restraints, she murmured through the mask: "It hurts so much."

"I know it hurts," he said, taking her hand. "And I'd like to make it so it doesn't hurt. But I can't give you anything just yet because if we give you something you might not be able to tell us where it hurts and we need you to tell us where it hurts so we can make it better."

He examined her eyes, then said: "Eyes are equal and reactive."

Lungs were next.

"Kristen," he said, "I want you to try to take some deep breaths."

As he listened with his stethoscope, a wave of pain appeared on her face every time she took a breath. But her lungs appeared to be clear. "Breath sounds equal and present bilaterally," he announced to the team. Then to her: "Does it hurt when you breathe?"

She had trouble answering him so he told her if she didn't want to speak that she could just squeeze his hand. She could squeeze his hand, couldn't she?

She could.

Next, with his free hand—his right—he began to examine her chest. Her skin was warm and moist—she was sweating; Cogan noticed sweat building up on her forehead. He worked his way slowly across her chest, pressing gently on her rib cage, feeling for tender spots. All of a sudden, she screamed, and Cogan felt one of her fingernails dig into his hand. He quickly let up on the spot.

"OK," he said. "I'm sorry."

He pressed down again, this time more gently on the left side of her abdomen. She didn't scream but groaned instead, then closed her eyes and said, "Please."

"Tender left upper quadrant with possible crepitance of left lower ribs," he announced.

Just then Cynthia, the X-ray technician, came back into the room and said: "Film's ready, Doctor."

"Thanks. Kristen, can you hear me?"

The girl opened her eyes.

"You're doing good," he said. "I have to go away for a minute but Pam here is going to take care of you while Doctor Kim and I take a look at what's going on inside of you. But we'll be right back."

Cogan got one more reading on her vital signs—her blood pressure and pulse were holding steady—then he went to the other side of the room, where Kim had put the X-rays up on the light box and was looking at her chest X-ray. He was looking at her lungs. White was air. Black was nothing, emptiness, a non-functioning lung.

They were looking at white.

"No pneumothorax," Kim said, informing Cogan of what he, too, saw: neither lung had collapsed. "But she's got rib fractures. Left ribs 9-11. That's why she's having trouble breathing."

Rib fractures were extremely painful. They turned grown men into babies.

"I think that's it," the younger doctor went on after a moment, looking at her neck and pelvic X-rays. "C-spine is clear and her pelvic films are normal."

"Doctor," Wexford said, her voice more urgent than it had previously been. "Her blood pressure is falling. She's getting more tachycardic."

Both surgeons turned around and looked at the machines. She was 80 systolic. Her heart rate was up to 170. Her hemoglobin down to 12.

Kim looked at him, his face tense. They both were thinking the same thing.

"Do you want me to do a wash?" Kim asked.

"I'd better do it," Cogan said.

He went back over to the patient and asked a nurse for a peritoneal lavage tray. "Quickly, please," he said. His voice remained calm but the whole team immediately went on alert, for everybody knew that Cogan, unlike some surgeons, made such demands only when the situation truly called for it.

A "wash" was short for a peritoneal lavage, a procedure in which a saline solution is injected into the peritoneum, the membrane lining the abdominal cavity, then aspirated back into the syringe. If the saline solution comes back bloody, it means there is blood where there shouldn't be.

Cogan made an incision in the girl's belly button, then carefully pushed a narrow piece of plastic tubing into the hole he'd made. Next, he attached the tubing to a syringe filled with saline solution and, with his thumb, slowly squeezed the plunger on the syringe, gradually pushing the saline solution into the girl. When the syringe was almost empty, he carefully began to pull up on the plunger, aspirating the fluid back into the syringe.

What came back was a deep red.

"Grossly bloody," he said, handing the syringe to a nurse. Then, after a brief pause: "OK, ladies and gentlemen. I think she's got splenic rupture. Hang more fluid, cross her for six units, and let's get her to the OR stat."

With that order, the whole team began to focus its efforts on transferring the girl, along with her IVs, from the fixed gurney she was lying on to one that had wheels and was mobile.

"Kristen," Cogan said to the girl, taking her hand. "You're doing good but we're going to take you upstairs so we can take a look at what's going on inside you if we have to. Do you know where your parents are? We need to get their consent if we have to operate. Is there a number where we can reach them?"

He knew she probably wouldn't be able to answer him but the rules said he had to at least make an attempt to contact the parents of a minor before he operated on her.

Her eyes were vacant; she looked at him, then closed

them.

"OK, let's go," Wexford said loudly. "Head or feet, Dr. Kim?"

Kim took the feet at the front end of the gurney and pulled, while Pam pushed from the back where the girl's head was. The team's job was finished. The girl was officially Cogan's patient.

2/ Why today?

March 31, 2007—p.m. 4:25

Standing by the visitor's dugout, Detective Hank Madden wipes his brow in the late Saturday afternoon sun. It's hot, too hot for March, and Madden's head is throbbing—from the heat and the fresh-cut grass of the outfield. His allergies have been wreaking havoc on him all week, but that hasn't kept him away from the newly refurbished La Entrada Middle School field in Menlo Park where his son is pitching in his team's opening game of the Alpine/West Menlo Little League.

The batter steps back into the batter's box. The kid thinks he's Barry Bonds. Same stance. Same cool cockiness. It makes Madden smile because there's his son, standing on the mound just like Greg Maddux. He knows that Henry, whom the other boys call Chico because of the hint of his mother's Hispanic features, is imitating Maddux. All he can talk about when he's at home is Maddux. Twelve years old. He knows every statistic, has every baseball card. He has the motion. The leg-kick.

The umpire's hand goes up in a fist. The pitch is a strike.

He never lets it show, but Madden takes immense pleasure in watching that motion. The sheer power it generates. Sometimes he smiles after a good inning or if one of the other parents comes up to him and compliments his son.

But mostly he stands there with his hands in his pockets, silently watching the game, looking decidedly unpartisan, a man in his late fifties with a small head of receding gray hair combed carefully back, a thin man who wears glasses and keeps a neat, trim mustache.

Many years ago, when he was his son's age, he'd also stood off to the side of the Little League field near his home, watching the games, not able to play himself. It pains him to think of those days. As a boy, he had polio. The illness had left him with a short right leg and a drop foot. At school they'd called him Chester. He was that character on *Gunsmoke* who walked with a limp. Marshall Dillon's deputy, Chester.

It took him fourteen years to make detective. Just fourteen, he likes to tell people. The amount of time has not made him bitter; on the contrary, it has made him feel superior, for he feels he's worked harder, studied more, and is better prepared than any of his counterparts. And if there's anything he's tried to instill in his son, it's his work ethic.

In the off-season, they watch videotapes of the Padres' and A's pitching staffs, among the best in the league, then drive over to La Entrada, where the game is today, and his son pitches to him. The only problem is Madden isn't a good catcher. Anything a few feet too far to the left or right of him he has trouble getting to, which frustrates Henry because it embarrasses him to watch his father scramble awkwardly for the ball. He thinks he looks goofy.

"I know I look goofy," Madden admits. "So don't make me move. That should be your priority."

The advice has paid off. Today, his son is pitching strike after strike. The catcher barely has to move his mitt. After each out, Henry glances over at his father, who nods in approval. No words, not even a smile, just a nod. Then, in the middle of the third inning, Madden's beeper goes off.

He winces. It's the number of another detective, Jeff Billings. He waits a moment, then takes out his cell phone, turns it on, and speed-dials the number.

When Billings answers, he asks, "What's up?"

"Where are you?"

"I'm at my kid's Little League game. It's opening day."

"Pete's looking for you," he says, referring to their boss, Detective Sergeant Pete Pastorini. "Why aren't you answering your phone?"

"I didn't want to be reached."

"Funny."

"It's true."

"Well, he got a call a little while ago from someone in the DA's office and had to go out and meet some people."

"What people?"

"The parents of a girl who say she was raped by her doctor."

Madden feels his throat tighten and his heart jump a little. It always happens, the moment he hears a doctor is involved. He can't help it. He hates that he can't, and he hates that Billings knows he can't, which only makes his heart race faster. Taking a breath, he looks at the mound. Another strike. Henry still hasn't allowed a hit. *Damn*, he thinks. *Why today? Why now?*

"You're the one on-call," he says. "Why don't you take it?"

Technically they're all on-call, but they have an official schedule where each detective is assigned to specific off-hours blocks. That ensures that at least one detective will be able to respond quickly and soberly.

"He wants you, Hank," Billings says, hiding his envy well. There's only a faint hint of resentment in his voice. "Don't ask me why. But he sounded anxious."

If the sergeant had requested him it must be important. It must be something he didn't feel Billings, the youngest and least experienced in the group, could handle.

"OK," he says. "Where am I going?"

3/ Parting the Red Sea

Nov. 10, 2006—a.m. 12:34

Cogan walked out of the operating room.

"Beautiful, Dr. Kim," he said as he left. "If you don't make it as a surgeon, you have a bright future as a tailor."

"Believe me," said Kim, who was closing the girl, "I've considered it."

By the scrub sink, Cogan pulled down his mask, stripped off his gloves, and removed his gown. Then he washed his hands and face, first with hot, then cold water. After he was finished, he checked his shoes for blood and wiped them clean with a paper towel, which he always did before meeting with a patient's family.

"They're outside, in the waiting room," the desk nurse, Julie, informed him. "Mother and father."

At this late hour, the OR was practically deserted. Just a skeleton staff remained.

"She insured?" Cogan asked.

"Through the father's company."

"Hey, you wouldn't have any of your famous herbal tea stashed away there, would you?"

The nurse smiled. "What's in it for me?"

"I've got cookies."

"What kind?"

"Homemade chocolate chip. Remember O'Dwyer, the

guy who was in the fight the other night? His wife hooked me up."

She thought about it. Then, looking inside her desk drawer, she said, "It's your lucky night, Cogan. I've got apricot."

"I'll be back."

He pushed a button on the wall that opened the automatic OR doors and walked through them, down the hall to where the couple was seated on a vinyl couch.

"Mr. and Mrs. Kroiter?"

They stood up, anxiously. "Yes."

"Hello, I'm Dr. Ted Cogan. I'm a surgeon. Please. Sit down."

The couple probably would have been glad to continue standing but Cogan was the one who wanted to sit. He'd been standing for the last two and a half hours.

"Your daughter was in a car accident," he began. "We're not exactly sure what happened—we don't know what caused the accident—but the paramedics said her car jumped the curb and she hit a telephone poll." He paused briefly to let them absorb what he said, then continued: "She came into the hospital and we realized she was bleeding internally so we took her to the operating room. It turned out she'd ruptured her spleen and we had to do a splenectomy. The operation was uneventful and she's doing very well. She has a few broken ribs and some minor cuts and scratches but otherwise there's nothing wrong with her. She's on her way to the recovery room as we speak."

"Does that mean she's OK?" the girl's mother asked.

Cogan looked at Mrs. Kroiter. More and more, he noticed, his initial impressions of people were rooted less in looks but in temperament. Beauty registered, certainly, but his primary concern—the first question he invariably asked himself—was, "Is this person going to be difficult?"

The couple didn't look difficult. She was dressed in a nylon warm-up suit, purple and green, Nike—something she might wear for a quick trip to the mall or Safeway. The husband had on a jacket and tie. Business looking. Nothing flashy. *Funny*, Cogan thought, *he prefers to face the public in his standard uniform, even at two o'clock in the morning.* Mrs. Kroiter was slender, in her early forties, as was the husband. She had short hair, dark eyebrows, and blue eyes that were puffy and red, presumably from crying. The husband was bald but it didn't hurt his looks, for he had a military air to him, good strong bone structure in his face, and blue eyes like his wife, but brighter, more alert, and seemingly more patient. *One of those guys who played football in high school even though he probably shouldn't have*, he thought.

"Mrs. Kroiter," he said, "your daughter has sustained a very serious injury but if all goes well she should recover from it."

"So she's going to be OK?"

"Again, you have to understand, your daughter's just come out of surgery. We had to remove her spleen. Everything went very well. She's doing very well."

The husband put his arm around the wife, who was seated next to Cogan, and extended his right hand across her. "Bill Kroiter," he said in a deep, confident voice.

Cogan shook the hand.

"Cogan, you said your name was?"

"Yes."

"You performed the operation?"

"That's right."

"The spleen, that's an organ?"

"Yes. The spleen filters your blood and protects against bacterial infection. The body—especially the adult body—can function fine without it, but a major infection will always be a possibility. We gave your daughter an injection in the operating room to protect her from the bacteria to which she will be most susceptible, streptococcal pneumonia. She'll have to take antibiotics until she's twenty-one and she'll have to be very careful when she has a cold or feels at all fluish."

It went like that for a while. The couple asking questions and Cogan trying to answer them as clearly and succinctly as he could. But he kept having to repeat himself. It was the same with most families. They didn't trust you at the start (they didn't trust doctors), but if you could manage to give the same answers and tell the same story over and over, they started to believe you. And then, of course, there was always one final question: *could they see her?*

"Sure," Cogan said. "But just for a minute, OK?"

He explained that they preferred not to have people visiting with patients in the recovery room. In the morning, she'd go to the floor—she'd be put in a room where they could visit with her as much as they wanted.

"If you could hold on a moment, I'd just like to make sure she's settled in," he said. "And if you have any more questions, I'll be available during the day. The nurses will know how to track me down."

Cogan walked back to the OR. Posted at the entrance, just above the button for the automatic doors was a large sign that read: "AUTHORIZED PERSONNEL ONLY. PROPER OPERATING ROOM ATTIRE REQUIRED."

"She out yet?" he asked Julie, the desk nurse, a woman in her late thirties who was strikingly good looking above the waist but had inherited her father's short, stocky or—as she sometimes called them—"fugly" legs.

"Not yet," she said. "Here." She handed him a mug of steaming tea. "Don't burn yourself."

"Thanks."

He sat down in a chair next to her. As he took tiny sips of tea, he stared down at the floor. He was thinking about how much sleep he could get. If he went to sleep in fifteen minutes, after he was through with the girl's parents, he could probably get three, maybe three and a half hours—

"You ever been to a spa, Ted?"

He looked up. "What?"

"You ever been to a spa?"

"Yeah. With my ex. She was a firm believer in paying to be pampered."

"You never went alone, though?"

"No."

"But what if you wanted to meet someone?"

"Would I go to a spa?"

"Yeah."

He shrugged. "I think you'd be better off at Club Med."

"But everybody's looking there. It's a meat market."

"I'd tend to think that would increase your odds."

"But I don't want to go to a place where everybody's looking. It's, you know—"

"Unromantic," he said.

"Exactly."

He told her she was going to have to get over that part. The fact was after you got married, it doesn't matter where you met your husband. Wherever you met him was going to seem romantic. Or not, depending on how you are getting on.

"I met my ex-wife on a chairlift, skiing at Heavenly Valley," he said. "Not bad, right? But what does it count for now?"

She looked at him sympathetically and nodded. "So you really don't think a spa is the way to go?"

He laughed. She'd already decided.

"Sure," he said. "Why the hell not?" Then, standing: "Hey, what's going on in five?"

They both looked over at the door to operating room number five. Through a small window that was cut into the door, they could see glimpses of a commotion.

"Who's in there?" he asked.

"Dr. Beckler. Emergency gall bladder."

"Really. How's the bug up her ass doing?"

"Thriving, last I checked."

"I'm going take a closer look."

"Be careful."

Cogan took another sip of tea, set the mug down, then put his mask on and went into the operating room. There were four people in the room: resident surgeon Dr. Anne Beckler, an anesthesiologist, a nurse, and the patient, an extremely fat woman who was sprawled out on the table, the right side of her belly split open where Beckler had made a six-inch incision.

"Can you hold her open or can't you?" Beckler was shouting at the resident, who was trying to keep the hole open so Beckler could get her hand inside the patient and see what she was feeling at the same time. The resident was trying to reattach a small retractor that had slipped off a contraption called a Bookwalter retractor, a steel halo that was affixed to the gurney and positioned over the patient. Several small bear-claw retractors were clipped onto the halo, their claws hooked into the tissue around the sides of the wound, pulling it back and creating a generous entrance into the body.

In the old days, when Cogan was in medical school, the Bookwalter didn't exist. You had to hold wounds open "manually," pulling the retractors apart yourself, which, in this instance, would have posed a particularly difficult challenge, because the patient was so fat that it would have taken the Incredible Hulk to hold her open for more than a few minutes without a rest. And the resident, Evan "DocToBe" Rosenbaum, was no Incredible Hulk. He was a skinny, five-foot-eight, twenty-nine-year-old from Long Island whose parents, the story went, had bought him a personalized license plate for his first car that read "DOCTOBE." Rosenbaum spent all his free time playing golf, desperately trying to make up for his inadequacies as a surgeon. He was a 20-handicap surgeon but a superb golfer, a skill that impressed some of his fellow surgeons far more than anything he could have accomplished in the operating room.

"I got it," DocToBe Rosenbaum answered, finally getting

the retractor properly attached. Cogan estimated the woman weighed close to four hundred pounds. Each flap of fat had to be a foot thick. Rosenbaum might as well have been trying to part the Red Sea, which, in this case, happened to be more white than red.

"What do you want, Cogan?" Beckler said without looking at him.

"Oh, I'm fine, Anne, and how are you this evening?"

"Take the peanut gallery somewhere else. I've got my hands full."

Beckler always seemed to have her hands full. Cogan thought it was the only way she was able to function. The only problem was that in order to maintain her superiority she had to intimidate everybody into a more frazzled state than hers. The method worked well with her underlings—nurses and suck-ass residents like Rosenbaum. But it had less satisfactory results with her fellow surgeons, with whom she was forced to use more vicious tactics, the last of which was charm.

Cogan always wondered whether he would have forgiven her behavior if she'd been better looking. Not that she was bad looking—she was tall, thin, and had nice green eyes and alabaster skin. But out of uniform she dressed badly and was decidedly unsexy, almost androgynous. Cogan thought the longer she'd been one of the boys—been part of the club of surgeons—the more her exterior, from her mannerisms to her language, had become male. But on the inside she was still fiercely female or, at least, a fierce defender of feminist principles. And in that sense, Cogan, the Harvard man and an old boy if ever there was an old boy, represented to her all that was evil.

He, of course, disagreed with her assessment.

"What's going on?" he asked.

"Dammit," Beckler said, ignoring him, "get the light in here. Are you sure she hasn't had it out already?"

"I checked, Doctor," the anesthesiologist said. "It's not

on her chart."

"Check it again. She's got scars all over the fucking place."

Cogan took the patient's chart from the anesthesiologist and looked at it. He could see why Beckler was concerned. The woman already had four scars on her belly from previous operations. Two were from C-sections, one was an appendix, and the other could have been from any number of other procedures.

"What's the problem, Anne?" he asked.

"Let me see her chart," said Beckler.

He held up the chart. "There's nothing here about a gall bladder being removed."

"Shit."

"She can't find it, can she?" Cogan whispered to the nurse.

"No," the nurse whispered back, "she can't."

"Anne, why don't you get a laproscope in there," he said.

"I wouldn't need a camera if Rosenbaum wasn't such a lightweight."

"Well, Rosenbaum is a lightweight. And I'm not scrubbing in. So you better get a scope in there."

She shot him a piercing glance. Then she looked at the others, who were all waiting for her to respond. She was cornered and she knew it.

"OK," she said after a moment, "let's do it. Get her on TV."

Usually, the camera, which looked liked a stainless steel wand, was used for laproscopic surgery, which was much less invasive than open surgery. Four small holes were cut into the belly. In one went the camera wand, and in the others, the surgical instruments. The surgeon could do the whole operation looking at a television screen and the patient would, in theory, be out of the hospital in two days instead of five.

"To the left," Beckler said.

They all looked at the television screen. Rosenbaum was maneuvering the wand into position under the liver, where the gall bladder was supposed to be. He moved the camera around the area, once, twice, then a third time. Cogan didn't see the gall bladder. But if the chart said it was there, it had to be there. And then he saw it.

"There," he said pointing.

"Where?" Beckler asked.

"On the liver."

Rosenbaum moved the camera to where he was pointing and pushed the liver to one side, flipping it up a little. And there, indeed, it was. A brown, pathetic looking mass attached to the liver.

"Wow, look at that," Rosenbaum said. "It's literally fused to the liver."

"Disgusting," said Beckler.

Cogan smiled—a smile no one could see through his mask. But the pleasure showed in his eyes.

"Well, this surgeon's got an appointment with his bed. It's been fascinating as always. Good night, all."

" 'Night, Ted," the nurse said.

"Goodnight, Anne."

Beckler didn't answer him. "Kelly, clamp please," she said to the nurse.

He thought of saying goodnight to her again—but then thought better of it. He'd had enough fun with her for one evening. And she was definitely not amused.

4/ Domestic dispute

March 31, 2007—p.m. 4:38

The home is just off Middlefield Road, in a development called Vintage Oaks, a gated community in Menlo Park a few blocks from Menlo-Atherton High School. Madden knows the place well. The land it's on isn't exactly sacred, but in the early 90s some residents predictably accused nearby St. Patrick's Seminary, which once owned the property, of making a "deal with the devil" when it sold forty-two acres of vacant land to Vintage Oaks' developers for $22 million to escape financial crisis.

The general area between San Francisco and San Jose is known as the Midpeninsula, and Menlo Park, twenty-five miles from each city, sits smack-dab in the middle of it. During the 60s and 70s this stretch of suburban sprawl grew at a tempered rate as residents warily guarded open space with an eye toward preserving their views and avoiding traffic jams. But with the rise of Silicon Valley and the dotcom boom—and all the wealth and publicity they brought with them—the Midpeninsula went upscale in a hurry. Property values skyrocketed, few open parcels near residential areas remained off-limits to development, and once modest Menlo Park, wedged between staid, old-money Atherton to the north and left-leaning, university-tied Palo Alto to the south, took on a bit of both its neighboring towns' personalities. Maybe that's why today Madden thinks the slightly snobbish yet remotely down-to-earth residents of Vintage Oaks are perfect representations of their geographical location.

As he drives onto the block he's looking for, he sees that a group of kids has gathered in front of a house at the end of the street. They're decked out in street-hockey gear, but clearly something has distracted them enough to table their game because he just passed their abandoned goals.

"Hey, guys," he calls out through the half-open passenger-side window, pulling up alongside them. "What's going on?"

They eye him curiously, squinting in the face of the late afternoon sun.

"This lady was screaming," says a boy wearing a San Jose Sharks teal-colored road jersey, an expensive, kid-sized replica of the real thing. He's the tallest of the bunch but is still probably no more than ten or eleven.

"It sounded like Mrs. Kroiter," offers another, this one in Phoenix Coyotes regalia.

"We think they're having a domestic dispute," says the goalie of the group, appropriately short and stocky.

The way the kid says it, so matter-of-factly, makes Madden smile. His ten-year-old daughter sometimes mimics him, using words reserved for adults, and he can't help but find it amusing, even if the words she uses are sometimes disconcerting.

"You a cop, too?" the first boy asks, nodding in the direction of the patrol car that's parked in front of Pastorini's unmarked Chevy Impala. "They call for backup?"

Madden doesn't answer. Instead, he says: "Any of you guys know Timmy Gordon?" They shake their heads. "Well, Timmy Gordon was about your age when he got hit by a car three blocks from here and lost his leg. You kids should go play down at the park," he says, hoping to scare them off.

They look at him like he's crazy. He knows what they're thinking: *This is a gated community, and it isn't a through street—*

who's going to drive fast into a cul-de-sac in a gated community in broad daylight?

"Who are you?" the goalie demands.

"A concerned citizen," he says, edging his car forward. "Now, move along."

Instead of parking on the sidewalk he turns into the driveway and pulls his unmarked Ford Crown Victoria in behind the less expensive of the two cars parked there, an older Audi A4 sportwagon. Next to it is a big 7-series BMW. *Probably the husband's car,* he thinks.

The home is at the end of a cul-de-sac, a large two-story, ranch-style house with a generous front yard, though nothing that could be described as a "spread." For that, you have to head north another mile or two to Atherton. That's where the homes of the truly wealthy begin—and have always begun, dating back to the late 1800s, when rich San Franciscans like Faxon Dean Atherton built estates there (then it was called Fair Oaks) to escape the city's cold summers. Billings likes to call them "inset homes." And it isn't because they're the homes of the "set" that's "in" at the moment. No, these are homes that you can't see from the road. They're set back, hidden from view by tall bushes, cement walls, or both.

These people have bushes, too: a short row that lines a walkway leading up to the house and cuts through a perfectly manicured lawn. At first, there's no hint of the commotion the boys alluded to. But in the middle of the walkway, Madden hears something that makes him stop in his tracks. It's muffled, but there's no mistaking what it is: a horrible moaning, guttural and anguished, mixed with inconsolable sobbing. And he knows then why Pastorini was looking for him. The domestic dispute, whatever its origins, had ended badly. Very badly indeed.

He raps lightly on the front door. The door's unlocked, so he pushes it open slowly and enters a spacious foyer with a high, vaulted ceiling. A modest but graceful crystal chandelier hangs over an impressively real looking silk floral arrangement sitting in the middle of a round mahogany table. Peering down a short hallway, he can make out the back of man's balding head—he's sitting on a couch in the living room—and Pastorini nearby pacing back and forth, holding a can of Diet Coke in one hand, talking on his cell phone with the other. Somewhere off to the right, a police radio squawks. The officer responds in a hushed tone, and the woman's wailing, which seems to be coming from the same place, suddenly stops. A moment of eerie silence, then he hears her mutter something: "I told him no police," he thinks she said. "Godammit, I told him . . ."

As her voice trails off, Pastorini looks up and sees Madden standing in the foyer. The sergeant flashes a foreboding look, then, finishing his conversation, closes the flip on his cell phone and gestures to someone out of frame to approach. When the uniformed officer appears, Pastorini leans over to the man on the couch and says in a gentle voice, "Excuse me, Mr. Kroiter, one of my detectives is here. I'm going to step away for a minute. Your pastor is on his way."

Madden takes a couple steps toward the living room, but before he gets there Pastorini intercepts him. "Come on," he says, taking him by the arm and turning him around. "Let's talk outside."

Madden's not used to seeing Pastorini like this, sullen and ominous. He's a big man, imposing, but usually very neurotic, which takes some of the bite out of him. People say he's missed his calling as an opera singer. Rotund and barrel-chested, he has short legs and wears his dark, wavy hair slicked back. Whenever he yells across the office in his booming tenor's voice, Billings, the resident comedian, responds in an Italian accent and addresses him as "Luciano" or "Maestro," which amuses everybody but Pastorini. "I'll Luciano you," he says, whatever that means.

He's forever talking about cutting down on his caffeine. "You think I'm edgy, Hank?" he'll ask the always calm Madden, whom he considers his right hand. "You think I gotta cut down?"

He tries, all the time. But his way of cutting down is switching from one form of caffeine to another—from espresso to regular coffee, for instance, or, in this, his latest phase, from iced coffee to Diet Coke. He'll go from drinking four to five iced coffees a day to eight to ten Diet Cokes. In the end, everything evens out.

"What's going on, Pete?" Madden asks when they get outside.

Pastorini, spotting a small white wrought-iron bench in the entryway, decides to sit. The bench is meant to accommodate two, but the sergeant almost fills it.

He exhales deeply and says in a low voice: "I'll tell you what's going on. A couple of hours ago, I get a call from the DA's office—from Crowley himself—asking to do him a favor. He says, 'I know these people, they're friends of mine, and they say their sixteen-year-old daughter was raped by her doctor back in late February.' "

He pauses, anticipating a reaction, but Madden, prepared this time, doesn't let his apprehension show.

"I heard."

"Well, he tells me that a couple of uniforms are going over to their house to make a report and would I mind making sure everything is handled correctly. No big deal, right? But when I show up, this guy, Kroiter, immediately starts giving me the third degree. You know, throwing names around, and telling me about all his experience he's had with detectives. He's in the insurance business. Investigates insurance fraud. That's how he knows Crowley."

Madden doesn't care about the politics. He just wants to know whether they have a body or not. Yet he knows Pastorini well enough to know he's telling the story the way he is for a reason. He figures the process is somehow therapeutic. So he plays along. He asks: "Why did it take him over a month to report that his daughter had been raped?"

"I'm getting to that."

The sergeant takes a sip of Diet Coke, jiggling the can to rustle the last remaining drops from it.

"The girl kept a diary," he says. "Her grades were down, and her mother was poking around her room, looking for reasons why and discovered it a few days ago."

Madden's momentarily confused. Then it strikes him: "She wrote about it in her diary but didn't tell anyone," he says.

"Not exactly. She wrote about having sex with the doc but nothing about rape."

Now Madden's really confused.

"Thing is she was drunk," Pastorini goes on. "The parents think this guy took advantage of her. Maybe, maybe not. Either way, I tell them, we're looking at it as a rape case."

In California, statutory rape doesn't exist. If an adult has sex with a minor, it's prosecuted as a rape case. That's all Pastorini meant.

"She sexually active prior?"

"Virgin. And the parents had a doctor confirm she ain't anymore."

"Wonderful. And the incident took place in the hospital?"

"No, the guy's home."

Pastorini draws the can of soda to his mouth again—even though it's empty.

"Anyway," he continues, "we finally get done with the parents and it comes time to talk to the girl and confirm all this, right? So the father goes upstairs to get her. But she won't come out of her room."

At first, Kroiter—Bill is his first name—tried to sweet-talk his daughter into opening the door. *Come on down, honey, and talk to the nice officers.* That sort of thing. But when she didn't respond, he started to get angry. Went right to: "OK, I've had enough of this crap, shut off the music, and come out right now!" When his voice hit a certain octave, Pastorini decided he'd better go up and try to coax her out. He was pretty good at that type of negotiation, having two teenage daughters himself. But when he didn't get anywhere, he got a bad feeling something was wrong. He told one of the uniforms to break the lock.

The room was empty. There was some music playing over her computer's speakers, but no sign of the girl. They figured she flew the coop, slipped out the window or something. But then one of the uniforms looked in the bathroom attached to the room.

"When I heard him say 'Holy Christ,' I knew it was bad," Pastorini says.

"How bad?"

"She hung herself from the showerhead, Hank."

"Jesus."

The sergeant shakes his head slowly, staring blankly ahead.

"Turned seventeen a couple of weeks ago," he says, and takes another phantom sip of Diet Coke from the empty can. Madden notices then that the street-hockey gang is looking at them. They're not on the sidewalk in front of the house anymore, but they're milling around in the street, doing a bad job of pretending they're not interested.

"Pete?"

"What?"

"Tell me she left a nice note explaining everything."

Pastorini nods, only half-hearing what he said. "On the desk. I saw something. A poem, I think."

"A poem?"

"Yeah, it was typed out. Computer printout. But something was written on the bottom. Something odd."

"What'd it say?"

Pastorini looks up at him, his mouth slowly breaking into an ironical smile.

"You're going to love this," he says.

"What?"

"It said, 'I will not be a victim.' "

5/ Keanu Reeves's aura

Nov. 10, 2006—a.m. 5:45

Morning came not with light but with the ring of the telephone. Sometimes, because the room was dark, he didn't know whether it was night or day or whether he'd slept fifteen minutes or three hours. So he answered the phone like this:

"What time is it?"

"5:45 in the a.m. Rise and shine, big boy."

It was Julie, thank God, and not the triage nurse downstairs.

"Gimme a minute," he said, his eyes still closed.

"I'm telling you, Cogan, you should think about that spa."

"Find me one where they submerge you in a vat of coffee and I'm there."

"I'm perking as we speak."

"I'm glad one of us is."

"Get up. I let you sleep fifteen minutes extra."

"How kind."

After he hung up, he willed himself out of bed and went to the window and drew the shades. It was just getting light out. A dull gray day. But you never knew with Northern California weather. Things had a way of burning off. By noon it could be sunny and seventy.

"Beckler's looking for you," Julie said when he walked into the OR twenty minutes later, clean-shaven and showered.

"What's she want?"

"She didn't say. Hey, Cogan, have you ever heard of a comb?"

"Is that a new surgical instrument?"

"The latest. Makes you look pretty with no side effects."

"Sounds promising. I'll be back. I'm just going to check on the girl."

He walked over to the recovery room, which was just across the hall from the OR. It had been a slow night. There were five patients in the room, including the fat woman, who was three times as big as Cogan's patient. They were lying directly across from each other, in separate curtained-off spaces.

Both the fat lady and the girl were asleep. Cogan picked up the girl's chart. He was mainly interested in her vitals. Her blood pressure was running 110 over 60. Her heart rate was in the 80s. And her urine output near 100cc per hour. Everything was good.

"Hey, Ted."

"Morning, Josie."

This was the recovery nurse, Josie Ling. Asian-American. Short and serious. Very dry sense of humor.

"They let you off pretty easy, huh? Only one vic."

One victim too many, as far as he was concerned. "What are her post-op labs?" he asked.

"Post-op hemoglobin 13 and most recent 13.6."

"Good."

He reached down and gently pulled down the blanket that was covering the girl. It wasn't gentle enough, however, because she stirred.

"Hi, Kristen," he said quietly. "It's Dr. Cogan again. How are you doing? Are you feeling any pain?"

She opened and closed her eyes. She was very groggy.

"You're not in any pain, are you, Kristen?"

"Not really," she said.

"Are you aware of what happened? Do you know where you are?"

"I was in a car accident," she answered. "I'm in the hospital."

"Do you remember the accident?"

"Yeah."

"What happened?"

"Someone turned in front of me."

"Someone cut you off?"

She nodded. She was fully awake now. Drowsy but awake. He explained to her that she'd had an operation. She'd been bleeding internally, which was very dangerous. The impact of the accident had ruptured her spleen, so they had to take it out.

She wanted to know whether that was bad.

"Well, there are much worse things that could have happened to you," he said. "But it's still an operation and we have to watch you very carefully for the next few days. That's why my friend, Josie, is here. She's here to monitor you for the next few hours before we send you to a room."

The girl's eyes took in the nurse briefly then fell back on Cogan.

"Your parents were here earlier," he said. "They saw you right after the operation. But I suggested they go home because I knew you'd be sleeping for a while."

"Were they mad?"

"No. Upset but not mad."

She looked away, distraught. "They'll never let me get a car now," she murmured.

"I wouldn't worry about that right now."

"You don't know my Dad."

"I'm just going to check your dressing," he said, trying to take her mind off the car. "Then I'll let you go back to sleep."

"OK."

He lowered the blanket a little more, so it was just below her waist, then lifted her pajamas until her bandage was exposed. The bandage was clean, dry, and intact. It seemed fine. Next, he felt her stomach, pressing lightly, making sure it wasn't excessively firm. Then, covering her up, he said, "Everything looks good."

"Is it going to be a big scar?"

"No, not too big. Just about this long." He spread his fingers apart about four inches. "And very thin. You know Keanu Reeves?"

"Not personally."

Cogan smiled. "You like him?"

"He's OK."

"Well, he was in a motorcycle accident and they had to remove his spleen. Same as you, and he looks pretty good in a bikini, right?"

"I guess." She paused, closing her eyes. Then, opening them again, she said: "But he's a movie star. He has an aura. He could have five scars and it wouldn't matter."

Cogan laughed.

"Well, maybe you have an aura, too, and you just don't know it."

"I better," she said. "Because I'm not going to have a car."

6/ A moment of fatal impulsiveness

<u>March 31, 2007—p.m. 4:57</u>

They'd found the girl facing forward, a leather belt around her neck, suspended with her back to the wall of the shower stall. What struck Pastorini was how close her feet had been to touching the floor. They were no more than a couple of inches above the tiles. It turned out she'd worn a pair of platform sandals into the shower and kicked them off. One sandal was in one corner of the shower, the other just in front of her. They must have had four-inch heels. Orange, decorated with retro flower-power flowers.

Pastorini didn't notice any of that right away, though. When he first saw her, there was something about how close her feet were to the floor that made him think they weren't too late, that maybe they could bring her back. So, he dove into the shower stall and lifted her up and tried to unhook the belt from the showerhead. But at five-seven he had trouble lifting her high enough. That's when the bigger of the two uniforms had to step in and help.

They gave her CPR on the floor of her room. They tried to resuscitate her for almost ten minutes, even though Pastorini knew the moment he put his mouth to hers that it was hopeless. Her body was still warm, but he thought she must have been dead for at least fifteen minutes and probably longer. Both of the parents were screaming. *No, God. No, no, no.* And then, when it was clear that nothing could be done for her, everybody and everything just stopped for a moment. Pastorini, on his knees, looked across the room at Bill Kroiter, who'd pulled his wife's head to his chest, impossibly trying to shield her from the unfathomable. To say anything was pointless.

After he gave them a moment with her, he had the uniforms take them downstairs. Then he himself lifted the girl onto her bed and covered her with a sheet he found in a linen closet down the hall. He was sorry he moved the body, he told Madden. But he just couldn't bear to see her lying on the floor like that. And since he'd already moved her once, it didn't seem to matter that he put her up on the bed.

"Can't blame him," Greg Lyons, an investigator from the San Mateo County Coroner's Office, now says. "I probably would have done the same thing given the circumstances."

Lyons is standing by the side of the bed, stretching latex gloves over his hands. Not far behind him, Vincent Lee, one of the county crime-scene photographers, is in the bathroom doing his job, and the bursts of light from his flash and the sound of it recharging between shots leak into the bedroom at regular intervals.

"He's pretty shaken," says Madden, already gloved. "Been sipping an empty can of Diet Coke for ten minutes."

"Better that than a full bottle of Jack."

"True."

With his blond hair pulled back in a ponytail, neatly trimmed goatee, and round, designer glasses, you'd guess Lyons was an artist of sorts long before you'd say coroner's investigator. He unclips his penlight from his shirt pocket and goes to work examining the body. The girl's face is ashen, her lips a faint blue. Her eyes are closed but her mouth is slightly open, just enough to appear disturbing. Lyons, a former paramedic, starts with the neck, where the classic V-shaped line of a ligature runs across the front just above the larynx. While the natural light streaming into the room isn't intense, Madden can make out the mark just fine. Still, Lyons plays the flashlight over the line to bring out its detail, then touches her chin and lifts it up, pushing her lips closed. The moment he lets go her mouth springs back to its original position and the gap returns.

"Rigor's already setting in," he comments. "How long you been here?"

"Twenty, twenty-five minutes—tops."

"Where's Burns?" Lyons asks.

Burns is his partner. He's in Lake Tahoe for the weekend.

"Skiing at Squaw," Madden says.

"I didn't know he skied. The guy can't stand the cold."

"His girlfriend's into it. But he only goes in the spring, when it's fifty and slushy."

Lyons nods, then lifts the girl's left eyelid, shines the light at the eye for a few seconds, then does the same for the right. He shows Madden what they both suspect will be there: the whites of the eyes are blotched with tiny red dots—pinpoint hemorrhages (or petechiae) that are the physical evidence of ligature strangulation. He looks at her cheeks and inside her nose for more, takes a look inside her mouth and ears, then pulls the sheet back and examines the rest of her body—or the parts he can without removing her clothes.

Making a circle with the flashlight, Lyons highlights a discoloration on her right arm—a small bruise in the bicep area.

"Someone could have grabbed her hard there," he says. "Looks pretty fresh." He moves the flashlight down to her wrists. "No signs of self-mutilation. And her hands look OK."

Madden nods. "I'll bag 'em when you're through."

They put paper, not plastic, bags on victims' hands to preserve any trace evidence. Usually, but not always, if there was some sort of struggle, you could pick it up from the victim's hands. If you were lucky, you'd find them clutching a hair or two. But the girl's hands look clean; her nails appear to be in pretty good shape, though her nail polish, an opalescent color, is chipping in places. Later, in the crime lab, the coroner will scrape the underside of her nails for debris, then clip them and package each hand's nails separately.

Madden watches Lyons turn the girl on her side and take a cursory look at the back of her neck and arms, paying a little extra attention to the area where the bruise is. The skin is discolored almost all the way around the arm, though not quite. That's the only thing that gives the appearance of a struggle—that, and the heel of her right foot, which is also bruised.

"She might have kicked it back against the shower wall," Lyons says, fishing a rectal thermometer out of his bag to take the body temperature and make a rough estimate of time of death. However, before he lowers the girl's light blue, terry-cloth-style sweatpants, Madden says:

"How 'bout we make sure there isn't any trace evidence first? We've got the time of death pretty nailed down anyway."

Lyons nods. "You got some reason to suspect foul play?"

"Just being cautious, Greg. There are some extenuating circumstances."

Without elaborating, Madden turns away and looks out the window, which faces the front of the house. Outside, another squad car has pulled up and a few curious neighbors are loitering on the sidewalk in front of the residence. But Pastorini's efforts to limit the spectacle—for the sake of both the family and their investigation—seem to be paying off. He's told officers to stay off their radios and he used his cell phone to call in a minimum number of personnel. If this was a homicide, he might call in all four general-crimes detectives and even the department's two narcotics-enforcement detectives, who are primarily assigned to drug- and gang-related cases but are also trained to assist in homicide investigations. The narcotics sergeant might show up, and even the division commander. However, in a situation like this, where they're looking to avoid any media attention, the fewer people traipsing around the premises the better. It also doesn't hurt that Vintage Oaks is gated and can be easily sealed off.

"Anybody interesting out there?" Lyons asks, making some notations in his notebook.

Madden glances at his watch. "Not really. Ambulance won't be here for another fifteen," he says, and just then Vincent Lee comes out of the bathroom. He's a tiny man, no more than five-three, who has a crew-cut and a diamond stud in his left ear. He went to the same high school as Madden, Woodside—or Weedside, as locals sometimes call it, deferring to the nickname that stuck from the peak pot years of the 70s. But Lee, who's in his early thirties, had graduated twenty-five years after Madden.

"I'm done in the bathroom, Hank," he says. "You ready for me in here?"

Madden nods. "We've got a couple of bruises. And since the body was moved, let's get some shots with the belt next to the ligature marks on her neck. I want to make sure everything matches up. Oh, and give me a couple of Polaroids of the bruises. Close-ups, OK?"

"If you don't mind, I'm going to take a few shots as well," Lyons says.

With digital SLR cameras becoming affordable, it had become easier—and a lot cheaper—to document crime scenes. Everybody these days seemed to have a decent camera. Even Madden had one out in the car, a Canon, that he kept around for backup.

After Lee shoots the body, Madden tells him to shoot the rest of the room, starting with the desk, where the poem, along with the girl's cell phone, is resting to the left of the computer's keyboard. To describe the room as that of your typical suburban teen girl wouldn't be a stretch, but on certain levels it feels more mature than that. Perhaps Madden's getting that vibe because on one wall there's a giant French movie poster with an almost life-size image of the actress Renée Zellweger in black boots and a mini-skirt. It's a poster for the movie *Bridget Jones's Diary*, which translates in French into *Le Journal de Bridget Jones*, and running down the left side of the print is a bulleted list of seven of Bridget's dos and don'ts from her diary, with the last item reading "J'arrête de faire des listes," or "I will stop making lists," as Vincent Lee, who did four years of French at Woodside High, informs him.

Yes, there are some girlish items—a small collection of dolls and stuffed animals on a shelf, a giant stuffed Sulley from *Monsters, Inc.* in a corner, a couple of homemade collages with pictures of friends, a flowery bedspread, and a violet Chinchilla beanbag that goes well with the aqua- and purple-colored Sulley. But overall, the room is pretty neat and relatively uncluttered. Her books are stacked three rows high on a bookshelf along with a row of DVDs that appear to be in alphabetical order. Her desk, too, only has a few things on it: a flat-panel Apple iMac, printer, iPod, portable DVD player, small stack of CDs, and some framed photos.

"Shame," says Lee, who's stopped taking pictures and is looking at one of the girl's photo collages. "Attractive girl—and not a bad photographer."

Madden shoots him a look. He's never comfortable talking about a victim's looks, but especially when she's lying dead in the room.

"What?" Lee says defensively. "Am I wrong?" Then, turning to Lyons, who's putting his camera away. "Greg? Am I?"

"No," Lyons says.

He isn't. The truth—or what Madden's gut tells him is the truth—is that she's a pretty girl but not a dangerous girl. Not a seductress. He's seen a few of those in his time. Fourteen-, fifteen-, sixteen-year-old girls who'd sat there smiling back at him, knowing they held some power over boys but preferred to covet men. They were adults in a children's world—to a degree. Always to a degree. But Kristen Kroiter, judging from the pictures on the walls and on her desk, is—or rather, was—not one of these girls.

"I tell ya, though," Lyons says, coming up next to Madden, who's standing at the desk, "she doesn't seem like the type to off herself."

Madden picks up the cell phone now that it's been shot. "They don't always," he says as he toggles through the menu system until he hits on the call-history icon.

"With the girls," Lyons goes on, "it's usually pills or wrists. They don't hang themselves too often. Not their thing."

"I heard about one in the East Bay last year," Lee says, in the middle of switching lenses. "A little older. Nineteen, I think."

"Well, maybe it's getting more popular," Lyons says. "She leave a note?"

Madden's still staring at the phone's screen. The girl appears to have made several calls that afternoon, though it looks to be seven calls to only two numbers, which could mean she didn't get through every time. "Some sort of poem," he says out of the side of his mouth, concentrating on correctly transcribing the numbers and the times they were called into his notebook. " 'Anthem for a seventeen-year-old girl' is the title."

Lyons looks at the sheet of paper.

"*Anthems* for a seventeen-year-old," he corrects him. "And it's not a poem. It's lyrics—to a song."

Madden stops writing and looks at him.

"You know it?"

"It's from a few years ago. By a Canadian band. Broken Social Scene."

"They're good," Lee approves from across the room.

"Now you're all gone got your makeup on and you're not coming back," Lyons mutters, reading from the sheet. "Bleaching your teeth, smiling flash, talking trash, under your breath. Park that car, drop that phone, sleep on the floor, dream about me." He pauses briefly, then recites the handwritten words at the bottom: "I will not be a victim. I can't. I'm sorry. Don't hate me, but you should have listened. You all should have listened."

"Mean anything to you?" Madden asks Lyons.

The investigator shrugs. "The song? Just the general angst of being a teenager, I guess."

"How 'bout this?" Madden says, hitting the space bar on the computer, waking the screen up. He points to an icon of a CD on the display. Then he hits the eject button on the keyboard and the tray slides out from the front of the computer's bulbous base. There's a disc in the tray, a CD-R. On the disc, neatly handwritten in permanent black ink, in all caps, are the words, "KNIFE MUSIC II."

"Ring any bells for you?"

Lyons stares at the disc, contemplating it. From directly behind them, Lee fires off a shot of the gold-colored Maxell CD-R. The burst of the flash appears to trigger one in Lyons's head as well, for he says suddenly: "You know, this is probably way off, but that's a term surgeons sometimes use to describe the music they play in the operating room."

"Surgeons?" Madden says, startled.

"Yeah. Why? *That* mean something?"

Madden looks at the numbers in his notebook. He puts the girl's phone down on the desk and pulls his Motorola out of its belt holster and flips it open.

"Hey, Donna," he says when he gets the weekend dispatcher on the phone. "Hank Madden. Can you do me a favor and run a couple phone numbers? I'm not at my car."

"Gimme a minute, Hank," she says. "Let me get my computer back on. I was just restarting it."

When she's ready, he reads the second number, the one the girl dialed four times. A short silence on the line, then her voice comes back.

"Belongs to one Carrie Pinklow."

He reads her the first number, the one the girl dialed three times, the last time around three hours ago, at 1:36.

"That one's T. Cogan."

"That a *Mr.* Cogan?" he asks.

Another silence, this one shorter.

"Actually, that's a doctor, Hank. *Dr.* T. Cogan."

7/ Seaver goes the distance

<u>Summer, 1973</u>

Cogan was nine when he first visited a hospital. His mother had something wrong with her brain, she kept forgetting things, and no one could tell her why, so they took her to the University of Chicago Medical Center to see someone called a *specialist.* He remembered walking into the hospital and seeing people in white coats and his father telling him these people were going to try to make his mother better. That was his first impression of doctors and his introduction to medicine.

His mother died in 1983, when he was nineteen. But she'd been institutionalized in a Jewish nursing home for the previous six years. She died at sixty. Initially, she was very forgetful. She couldn't remember, for instance, where she'd left things around the house. Or his father would take her shopping downtown, and he'd say, *Phyllis, meet me in front of such and such store at five o'clock.* But when he'd show up at five o'clock, she wouldn't be there. And he'd end up looking for her everywhere. When he finally found her he'd say, "What the heck's going on?" And she'd say, "I don't know. I don't remember a thing." There was obviously something wrong. And later there were personality changes. Today, people recognize these as symptoms of Alzheimer's disease, but back then no one really knew what was wrong.

His brother, who was almost eleven years older, grew up in a more traditional setting. His father would come home around six after a hard day at work in the bakery and his wife would meet him with a prepared dinner and would wait on him and her boy. She waited on everybody. She saw that as the role she had to play. And in that generation that *was* the role you had to play. There wasn't a lot of outward affection, hugging and kissing and so forth. And there wasn't a lot of Ward Cleaver, *Hello, Dear,* and all that. But there was at least some semblance of a family with dinner on the table.

By the time Cogan was nine it was all gone. They took his mother away for good when he was eleven. A few years earlier, his older brother had gone to 'Nam. He was in the Marines. It made for a strange adolescence. His father worked long hours then went out at night sometimes, leaving him home alone. It was at night, after he finished his homework, that he played ball. He would stand outside in the driveway, pitching old tennis balls into a wooden box filled with Styrofoam in the back of the garage. The hole in the box was the exact height and size of the strike zone. For hours, he'd throw balls into the box. Once, he threw fifty straight strikes.

"Who's pitching tonight, Teddy?" one of the neighbors, a widower named Sid Feinberg, would always ask when he took his dog out for his nightly walk.

"Seaver," he said.

"I thought he pitched Sunday."

"We're going for the pennant. I had to send him on one day's rest."

"Is that wise?"

"Well, it's the top of the seventh and he's pitching a two-hitter with thirteen strikeouts."

"Pull him," Feinberg said. "Pull him before it's too late."

"No way. He's going the distance."

Tom Seaver was his favorite pitcher. And Seaver always went the distance.

"We'll see," Feinberg called out as his dog dragged him away. "I'll be back for the ninth."

His mother's illness had made him a pitcher. Had it made him a doctor, too? He often wondered about that. All those visits to the hospital. All those men in white coats. Surely there'd been a transference.

In the beginning of the tenth grade, he met a girl, Melissa McCumber, at a high school science competition that was held at Northwestern University. She was tall, gawky, a year older than Cogan, and went to Frances Parker, a small private school that Cogan's friends said was for "rich bitches." And although Melissa McCumber was rich—or at least her stockbroker father was—she was not a bitch. In fact, she was one of the few truly nice girls Cogan had met.

On Sundays, when it was warm, she would invite him to her house in Lincoln Park to go swimming. It took a bus, a train, and some walking to get there, but he always thought it was worth it. Her friends would come over and they would play games and Mrs. McCumber would interrupt them, bringing them sandwiches and drinks by the pool. The McCumbers' refrigerator was always full—full of sodas, meats, pickles, and leftovers—and Cogan could take whatever he wanted. Mrs. McCumber encouraged him to. "Please, Teddy, eat this," she'd say. "It's just going to go bad otherwise. The girls won't eat it."

The first time he visited the McCumbers, he took the train and bus back home. But when Mrs. McCumber found out he'd taken public transportation across town after dark, the next time she insisted that he stay for dinner and that Mr. McCumber—Bill—would take him home when they were finished eating. Nothing was ever said, but Melissa must have told her parents what his situation was like at home: That his father worked long hours and often came back late (he never talked about dating, but Cogan had heard the rumors). And that he was basically going home to a Swanson frozen dinner. That had to be why Mrs. McCumber always had an extra steak or plenty of chicken for him. "Please, join us, Teddy," was how she asked. And when he sat down, he looked around the table and said to himself, *This is the way it's supposed to be. This is what I want to have when I get to this stage in my life.*

Bill McCumber was a heavyset man who'd had the lower part of his right leg blown off in the Korean War. He wore a prosthetic and walked with an awkward limp but it didn't stop him from playing golf most weekends. Usually, he wasn't around during the day; he'd come home just before dinner and sit down in the living room, prop his legs up on the coffee table, and have a cocktail and a cigar and read the newspaper. He was jovial and loud, almost the opposite of Cogan's father. But Cogan admired Bill McCumber, for he felt he was a man who truly knew how to enjoy life, and would continue to enjoy it no matter what misfortunes befell him. Cogan saw that as true strength. A real virtue.

Riding home in Mr. McCumber's Cadillac, they talked about sports and geography. Cogan had a foreign coin collection and knew something about the countries whose coins he'd acquired and more about the countries he hadn't, like Mongolia and those African republics that no Americans except the CIA ever visited. Someday, of course, he wanted to go there. He wanted to travel, and traveling was a passion of Mr. McCumber's. Every year, he'd take the family somewhere new. That year, they were going to Egypt to see the pyramids. The next year, maybe Scandinavia. As he drove, Mr. McCumber described previous trips and planned new ones. Cogan never said much. He nodded a lot or said, "Wow, that's great," though secretly he wished Mr. McCumber would take him along on the family's next trip.

Whenever they arrived in Cogan's neighborhood, the conversation would invariably die down. Budlong Woods was Jewish and middle class; it was made up of small houses and drab brick apartment buildings. Every time they pulled into the narrow, single-car driveway that served as his pitching mound, Cogan felt his cheeks flush with embarrassment. He wanted to escape the Cadillac as quickly as possible.

"Thank you for taking the time out to drive me home," he'd tell Mr. McCumber. "I appreciate it." Then he'd step out of the car and dash inside the house. It must have happened seven or eight times before one day Mr. McCumber stopped him.

"Hold on a second," he said. "I've been meaning to ask you something."

Cogan looked at him, a little petrified.

"Have you considered college at all? Did you have one in mind?"

Cogan said, no, not exactly. He liked Northwestern a lot. It was good academically and a Big Ten school, which was good for sports. He'd considered going there, but it depended on what money he could get—on whether, really, he could get a scholarship, because, frankly, his father couldn't afford to send him to a private school. His brother had gone to a state university.

Mr. McCumber nodded.

"You and Melissa have become good friends, haven't you?"

Cogan didn't know how to respond. He wasn't sure what Mr. McCumber was trying to get at. Did he think he had the hots for his daughter?

"I guess we have," he answered timidly. "We have similar interests."

"She thinks very highly of you. She says you're a good ball player and quite the student. Near the top of your class."

"She's been very nice to me. You and Mrs. McCumber, too."

"You know, I tried to send her away to school last year," Mr. McCumber went on, seeming to ignore his response. "But she didn't want to go. She's very close to her mother and she didn't want to leave her friends here."

There was a short silence. Cogan still didn't know what he was driving at.

"I thought with your mother having passed away, and your father—I understand he isn't around that much. I thought you might be interested in going away to school. To a boarding school."

"I don't know. I don't really know anything about boarding schools."

"Well, I think you'd be a good candidate for a scholarship. I could sponsor you—I could put in a word at my alma mater, the school I went to in Massachusetts. I give them a nice contribution each year. We could put in an application. Would you like to do that?"

Cogan shrugged. "Sure."

Mr. McCumber smiled. "OK, then," he said, becoming more himself. "We'll get to work on it. Good man."

They shook on it.

He didn't think much about Mr. McCumber's offer until Melissa, a week later, showed up at his baseball practice to angrily and tearfully condemn her father.

"He says we're getting too involved," she said. "That's why he wants to send you away."

Cogan looked at her, dumbfounded.

"What do you mean, involved?" he asked. "We're friends."

"He doesn't want us to go out."

"But we're not going out. We're just friends."

"Sure. But you know, Teddy—you know how close we've gotten. And you know—I think you do—that I like you more than as a friend."

Cogan, standing there behind the backstop on that sunny day suddenly realized he was at the center of some larger drama that was taking place completely in his absence. He'd assumed he was such a tiny part of the McCumber family's life. Another weekend visitor. Another of Melissa's many friends. And here he'd somehow become elevated to this exalted status, having to be sent away. *Sent away*—it seemed far too serious. Sure, she may have liked him. That didn't shock him. There had always been hints of that, though less than she was trying to make him believe now. But to have to be sent away because of it seemed awfully drastic, especially since her parents seemed to like him. He couldn't understand that. How could they want to send him away after they'd always welcomed him into their home and said nothing but good things about him?

"I don't get it," he said. "I thought your parents liked me."

"They do," she said.

"So what do they care whether we're friends or involved or whatever?"

Melissa fell silent.

"What do they care?" he pressed her.

She couldn't look him in the eye when she told him.

"You're Jewish, Teddy," she said. "And they don't want me dating Jewish boys."

"But we're not dating."

She fell silent again. Then, after a moment, she said: "They don't even want me to have feelings for Jewish boys."

"Well, stop them for Christ's sake."

"I can't."

Later, when he got home, he told his father about the incident. He told him about Mr. McCumber's offer and how it was some strange ruse to keep him from seeing his daughter, whom he didn't want to see anymore anyway.

His father took in all his bewilderment without saying a word. Then, after, a moment, he said: "You know, they sent your great uncle Adam to die in a concentration camp for a similar offense. The family who was hiding him gave him up to the Gestapo because he became involved with one of the daughters." He paused, then added: "Things have improved for your generation. Now there is guilt before. They know what they are doing is wrong, but they want to make it right."

His father said the McCumbers liked him.

"But why didn't they talk to me?" Cogan asked. "Why didn't they ask me how I felt?"

"Because your feelings are irrelevant."

That only made him feel worse.

"Do you like this girl?" his father asked.

Sure, he liked her. But he didn't want to date her. And he certainly didn't want to marry her, which is what her parents probably thought.

"Well, then maybe you should consider her father's offer. Is it a good school?"

Yes, it was. Very good, supposedly.

"And it won't cost anything?"

"Mr. McCumber gives a lot of money to the school. He says he can get me a scholarship."

"Then be nice to Melissa. Keep spending time with her."

"But her father's an anti-Semite."

"Yes. But he doesn't want to be. So you may as well take advantage of that."

So he did. And that's how he ended up at Andover. Then Yale.

Toward the end of college, when he was trying to decide what he wanted to do with his life, he spoke with his brother, Phil, whom he looked up to, and who, after the war, had become a high school teacher. He told his brother that he liked biology but studying human behavior was what really interested him. He was taking a lot of psychology classes. He was a double major, biology and psych. And he'd heard some people up at Harvard were looking at the biological basis of mental illness, which he thought might be a good way to combine the two disciplines. He told his brother he was seriously considering getting a doctorate in psychology.

"Teddy," his brother said, "there are one hundred and one guys out in the street with PhDs in psychology who are today driving taxis. They can't get a job. It's real fun, it's interesting to watch or to read about human behavior. But big fucking deal. You like psychology, go into psychiatry. You'll have a job. Make a living. Why don't you go to school for something that you can make a living at? Do yourself a favor and apply to medical school."

He'd thought a little about applying to medical school but had decided against it because a lot of the pre-meds he knew at Yale were real a-holes. They were high-strung tightwads. They wouldn't share their notes for class. They wouldn't tell you what books they were reading to prepare for a test. They were real borderline personalities, and he just couldn't see spending the next four years with them.

But reflecting on his brother's advice, it didn't sound like such a stupid idea. It was the Reagan years, the economy was good for some people, but as things stood, if he went into psychology and got a PhD, he probably would have a hard time getting a job when he got out. So he applied to medical school.

In his application and in interviews, he talked about how his mother had Alzheimer's and how he wanted to pursue a course of study in that direction. But once he got to medical school and did a couple of rotations in psych, he realized he was seeing very few Alzheimer's patients because Alzheimer's, it turned out, was a neurological condition, not a mental condition. What he ended up with instead was a lot of burnt-out schizophrenics who heard voices, talked to televisions, and were kept heavily medicated on Thorazine and other major tranquilizers.

The resident he was working for would jack his prescriptions up to the highest "acceptable levels," then leave the hospital to meet with a married woman. "Best thing for them, best thing for us," he'd say as he left. At first, Cogan found his philosophy reprehensible, but as the weeks passed he gradually began to see his point. No one seemed to be making any progress.

He began searching for something else to do. His next

stop was clinical medicine. He decided he wanted to be a cardiologist. But he got as far as doing the medicine clerkship when he realized he was seeing a lot of mundane, chronic problems that in the long run were going to bore him to death. Then came a rotation on surgery. And the surgeon—the resident he was involved with—was a cool guy, very bright. He'd done medicine already and hated it. He was fully trained, board certified and everything, and had gone back and trained in surgery, which told Cogan something.

They hung out together. When he was on call, Cogan would be on call with him. He'd tell Cogan he needed a pack of smokes, and Cogan would go out and get them and get kudos for it. That's sort of how you got in the club. You fetched cigarettes and did what you were told. Then, one day, you scrubbed on a case, the resident let you do something, he took you under his wing. And all the while he was doing that, he was building you up, making you feel enthusiastic about surgery. Until you began to think, "I like this stuff, I can do this stuff."

And that's how Cogan became a surgeon.

8/ Jenga

April 1, 2007—a.m. 8:09

From the beginning, Madden feels uneasy about the case. And it's not just because a doctor is involved or that the girl's father is so certain that the doctor's actions, not his, led to his daughter's death. Part of him can't help but empathize with the Kroiters. He, too, has a daughter. She's only ten, but he can easily imagine her to be Kristen's age. And he doesn't doubt he would have reacted just as the Kroiters had if he'd discovered she'd slept with the doctor, a man forty-three years old, even if she'd insisted the sex was consensual. He'd want to hammer the guy, too.

No, what's bothering him is how delicate the case seems. It reminds him of that game, Jenga, he plays with his family sometimes. You stack up the blocks and build a nice, stable tower. Then you take turns sliding out a block, hoping the tower doesn't topple on your turn. Usually, it's easy to pull blocks in the earlier rounds. But after your sixth or seventh go, things get pretty dicey. Pick the wrong block or fail to slide it out just right and the tower goes down with a loud clatter.

The problem with this case, Madden thinks, is that he already feels like he's on round seven. It's just after eight in the morning, and he's seated at his desk in his home office, his notes spread out on the desk in front of him. Yesterday, after they'd removed the girl's body, he'd spent another two hours at the house, searching her room for evidence and skimming the contents of her Mac before it was taken away for a computer forensic specialist to examine. He'd also spoken with her parents, which was easily the most painful part of the evening. They talked about their other children—an older daughter in law school at UCLA, and a son, a senior at Dartmouth, and how Kristen, their youngest, had expressed some interest in going back east for college. They showed him pictures: last year's family Christmas gathering, Kristen in a hospital bed recovering from her car accident, Kristen, much younger, on the beach at Half Moon Bay.

From the pictures, the girl looked more like her mother, a trim and proper woman with a streak of tomboy that made you think late thirties rather than early forties. She worked as a substitute French teacher and dabbled in interior design. Dressed simply and elegantly in silk khaki pants and a navy blue silk blouse, a string of pearls around her neck, her short hair neatly coifed, Elise Kroiter sat there silently at first, staring at the coffee table, reminding him of a stroke or advanced Alzheimer's victim who the nursing home staff had dressed and made up for a Sunday family visit. But when her husband began to recount the events leading up to that crushing afternoon, she broke from her shell and let her impressions be known. As she spoke, Madden detected a sense of challenge in her eyes; they were aimed squarely at her husband, and they seemed to say, *This is one conversation you won't monopolize. In fact, you will never monopolize a conversation again.*

No, Kristen hadn't seemed depressed, she said. Moody, yes—"like all teenage girls"—and maybe a little complacent. But the thing that had concerned them was that her grades had been suffering at school. Two teachers had alerted them that she'd nearly flunked two exams and failed to turn in several assignments on time. She wasn't her usual self, they said. Which is why Elise Kroiter took it upon herself to go poking around her daughter's room. She thought she might be on drugs or something. She found the diary instead.

And Madden's search? Had it turned up anything? Well, he told them, aside from the CD-R and the calls she'd made, he'd discovered a nearly empty bottle of Percoset with Cogan as the prescribing physician, as well as a more promising piece of evidence linking her to the doctor: a pair of scrub pants with a Parkview Hospital logo stamped on them. They were buried in a drawer and appeared to have a small stain with dried seminal fluid in the crotch area. Encouraging as that sounded, he didn't want to raise their expectations. Even if it came back positive for Dr. Cogan's DNA, he said, it didn't prove anything. They needed more.

It was then that the father said, "Please let us know how we can help, Detective. We're devastated, but we still want to see that son of a bitch brought to justice. He killed her."

The way he said it, so flatly and unemotionally but with utter conviction, disturbed Madden. He wasn't surprised that Kroiter believed Cogan was somehow responsible for Kristen's death (the alternative was too ghastly), but his tone just struck him as too assured.

"Well, Mr. Kroiter," he felt obligated to clarify, "we haven't determined that your daughter's death was a homicide."

"You will," he said.

Sitting at his desk now, Madden sighs deeply, takes off his glasses, and rubs his eyes. He's been up for two hours, working on the report. His children call the small spare bedroom that doubles as his office "the computer room" because he'd set up a pretty fancy computer, his one real toy, on the desk, along with a color printer and a scanner. There's little else in the room: A fold-out couch, one large bookshelf filled with mostly non-fiction books (Madden doesn't care much for novels and only goes to movies for his children's sake), and a line of family photos on the window sill. On the wall, there's a framed picture of him with the three other detectives from the general crimes unit, Billings, Burns, and Fernandez, as well as various diplomas and award plaques. Though there's space for it, a feature from the *San Jose Mercury News* that his wife, Maria, had framed for his birthday, sits on the floor, propped against the bookshelf, mostly hidden from view.

Only if you venture to that far corner of the room and face back toward the door will you see that the headline reads: "Handicap Doesn't Slow Detective in Race to Catch Criminals." Ask him why it hasn't found a place on the wall and he'll humbly mutter something about not feeling comfortable about tooting his horn, he's no show-off, and the frame would be in the closet if it hadn't been a gift from his wife. Nicaraguan by birth, she was Pastorini's housekeeper when they first met, and though they seemed an unlikely match—she barely spoke English, he barely spoke to women—their marriage had only gotten better as she became more fluent in English and he in Spanish. After thirteen years, he liked to tell people "it" worked because she thought he was too good for her and he thought she was too good for him—and that wasn't far from the truth.

The truth about the article is that it embarrasses him for a different reason. Buried in the middle of the piece is a reference to the sexual abuse he calculatingly divulged years ago to extract sympathy. At the time, the acknowledgment had been easily rationalized, a trifling revelation to which he was entitled, to help level the playing field and get the promotion he'd so badly wanted. But today it only represents pity. He looks at the headline and can't help adding a multiplier. "*Double* Handicap Doesn't Slow Detective . . ."

As a boy, while being treated for polio, a physician had sexually assaulted him. He told the reporter who'd interviewed him for the article that initially he hadn't known he was being abused. The doctor was crafty and, ironically, patient. Madden's mother liked reading the magazines in the waiting room, and after their first visit, the doctor suggested she might be more comfortable remaining there, particularly since the boy seemed embarrassed to have her in the room during parts of the check-up.

"I was nine," he told the reporter, "I didn't know what was required or not. But I'd had these exams before. I'd been to several doctors. So it seemed OK."

For instance, the doctor would hold his testicles and ask him to cough. Or he'd give him a rectal examination to make sure that his chronic constipation wasn't "flaring up." After a few visits, though, the man made incremental adjustments to the routine. His hand lingered a little longer. An extra finger was added to the rectal exam. Then it was not a finger at all.

"This may hurt a little," the doctor said, voicing the gentle warning he usually delivered before pricking him with a needle. "But not for long." Suddenly and excruciatingly, when he heard the man's zipper open behind him, he realized he'd been terribly betrayed; everything before had been a ruse. He let out a scream—or at least tried to—but the man covered his mouth, stifling the cry, as he raped him.

When he was through, the doctor pretended nothing happened; it had been as if he'd performed his regular examination. The only difference was, this time after he finished writing some notations in his chart, he handed Madden a box of tissues and said, "Henry, there's a bathroom next door. Why don't you take a moment and clean yourself up back there? There's nothing to be embarrassed about. Just use hot water." He remembered taking the tissues without saying anything. He was in a daze, certain he knew what had happened yet unable to totally believe it. Before he could get to the door, the doctor stopped him, gently squeezing his arm. "You know, Henry, whatever happens in a doctor's office is never discussed by the patient or the doctor with anyone else," he told him. "And that means your parents, too. It's the law."

He never said anything about the incident. And he never asked anybody whether it really was a law, because law or not, he thought his father would think it was his fault, that he deserved it. "The guy was an idiot, he had it coming to him," his father used to say about people who made bad decisions and had bad things happen to them as a result. He was ashamed that he hadn't seen it coming or reacted more quickly once he heard the man's fly open. He should have jabbed him with his elbow or tried to knock over the scale; the loud noise probably would have made him stop. And that was the part he knew his father would never understand—that he hadn't fought back. So he didn't say anything for a long time. Of course, years later, he realized he was completely wrong; he should've spoken out, for it would have prevented others from being abused.

"I truly regret that," he told the reporter, who would end up rewarding his candidness with a modicum of restraint. She provided enough detail without revealing too much.

"When asked why he was drawn to detective work," she wrote, "Madden reveals that his motive is partially personal. As a boy, while being treated for polio, a physician sexually abused him. He says that he was unable to confront the truth for many years, until he confided in a fellow officer who was working on a similar case. He regrets not saying anything earlier, for it could have prevented the physician, who was only brought to justice when Madden was in college, from abusing other patients.

" 'One day, he picked the wrong kid,' the detective said. 'I'm sorry I wasn't that kid. I won't let it happen again.' "

After the article came out, people behaved differently toward him. At times, he could tell they were being more cautious in how they chose their words. When certain topics came up, he no longer was a detective but a victim, which he found profoundly disturbing. Happily, Pastorini obliged his request that people "cut the bullshit" and relax and be "the insensitive bastards" they really were around him. But sometimes they took their comments a little too far. Maybe they were overcompensating, but most of them, especially guys like Billings and his partner, Fernandez—and even Pastorini occasionally—were just being pricks for the sake of being pricks. The Martin and Lewises of the office, Billings and Fernandez were constantly joking around. They had this shtick where they'd match up random people in fictional fights. "Madden versus the guy behind the deli counter at Luttiken's," they might say. Then they'd go around soliciting opinions and have people comment on the fighters' strengths and weaknesses. Each week there were two new fighters. And each week they'd declare a winner. For some reason, everybody found it amusing.

Madden isn't thinking about all that now, though. He puts his glasses back on, and starts typing on the computer. He's highlighted the main issues of the report and is now making a list of questions to ask the girl's friend, Carrie Pinklow, whom she called a few hours before her death and was with her the night the alleged rape took place. The report's based entirely on events that had transpired in the diary and the interview with the girl's parents. The rest of the file is the diary entries themselves—not the whole diary, just the entries that are relevant to the case, which adds up to twenty-five pages of the girl's clear, bubbly handwriting.

The selected pages chronicle a period of about five months. They start in November, when the girl had to have an emergency operation, and finished in late-March, about a month after she'd had sex with Cogan, the surgeon who'd performed the operation. It's a bizarre little story, Madden thinks. Months after being treated at the hospital, Kristen ends up at Cogan's home late one night after a party, drunk and practically unconscious. Her best friend, Carrie, had brought her there because she was worried about her condition but didn't want to take her to the emergency room out of fear both girls would get in trouble with their parents. Cogan agreed to let Kristen stay the night in his guest room. Then, according to the diary, he had sex with her while her friend slept in the living room.

Madden looks at the two photographs he has of Cogan. One is a driver's license picture, the other a photograph from the local newspaper announcing his marriage to Jennifer McFadden six years ago. The first he got from the DMV, the second from an Internet search.

Theodore Charles Cogan. Born December 10, 1963, in Chicago. Yale Undergrad. Harvard Med. Trauma surgeon at Parkview Med.

He's good-looking, Madden thinks. Intense eyes and a pleasant, confident smile. A doctor—a surgeon no less—with his looks can have any woman he wants, he thinks. Why, then, the girl?

No, Madden, he says to himself. *The question isn't why. It's why not?*

"Why" is intellectual. "Why not" is impulsive. And poor judgment is ninety percent impulsive.

His mind begins to drift. He imagines the scene that night—the girl in the doctor's guest room. Cogan sits down on the bed, starts talking to the girl. Then, lightly, he touches her. Maybe it's by accident. Maybe it's a test. But he touches her and she doesn't seem to mind. Then he lets his hand stray underneath her shirt. And while he's doing it, he isn't asking himself why he's doing it. The point is he can do it. So, why not?

"What are you doing, Daddy?"

Madden turns around. His daughter has walked into the room and is standing behind him.

"Daddy's doing his homework," he says.

She comes and sits in his lap.

"Who's that?" she asks, pointing at Cogan's picture.

"He's a doctor."

"Did he do something bad?"

"Maybe."

"What did he do?"

"Something you're too young to hear about."

"Is it X-rated?"

"Yes."

"Are you going to catch him?"

"I don't know. It's going to be very difficult to prove what he did. I'm not sure I can."

"That's why you're doing your homework?"

He smiles. "Yeah, that's why."

A short silence. She's buttered him up, now it's time for the kill.

"Can I play on the computer?" she asks.

"Did you eat breakfast?"

"Uh-huh."

"You sure?"

"Ask Mommy."

Madden looks at his watch. It's eight-fifteen.

"Just give Daddy ten minutes," he says. "Then you can play. But only for half an hour. You have to get ready for church."

"I can't get to the next level in a half an hour," she says.

"Sure you can."

"I didn't last time."

"That's not my fault, is it?"

"Can't we go to a later service?"

"The longer you keep Daddy from doing his homework, the less time you get to play," he says. "By my calculation, you're about to lose a minute."

She jumps off him.

"That's not fair," she says. "You didn't say anything before."

Madden looks at his watch. "There it is. You're down to twenty-nine."

"Cheater," she says, and runs out of the room.

9/ Three balls dancing

Nov. 10, 2006—a.m. 6:57

The girl was the first of several patients Cogan had to see that morning. Residents like Kim also did rounds, but when Cogan was in the hospital he had to see his patients twice a day—once in the morning and once in the afternoon.

There was O'Dwyer, the big, burly guy who'd gotten cracked in the back by a bar stool and almost lost a kidney. Sanchez, who'd been shot in the leg very close to his groin during a "dispute" over money with a friend. Hart, the Mr. Fix-it, who'd fallen off his roof at ten in the evening. And Traynor, an ungrateful son-of-a-bitch dot-commer who'd wrecked himself on his motorcycle for the second time in two years. When they brought him in four nights ago, Cogan didn't recognize him because he was so racked up. It took twelve hours of surgery and three surgeons to put him back together. But when he woke up a couple of days later in the ICU, Cogan realized he'd worked on him before.

"Hey, didn't I put you back together a couple of years ago?" he'd asked.

"Déjà vu, Doc," replied the kid, who was twenty-six and liked to boast to the nurses that he was worth ten million. "Déjà fucking vu."

The second accident only seemed to have made him more ungrateful and Cogan should have known not to joke with him, but this morning, after he finished his examination, he let one slip out: "You know, if you're going to continue to hurt yourself like this you might think about getting paid for it. Evel Knievel made a nice living breaking his bones."

"Is that supposed to be funny?"

"It's a polite way of saying maybe you should give the bike a rest for a while. Like indefinitely. You don't seem to have much luck with it."

"They pay you to give personal advice?"

"No, that's a freebie."

"Well, just do your fucking job and I'll do mine."

"And what would your job be?"

"To get the fuck out of here."

"Let me know when that position opens up, I'd like to interview for it. Does it come with stock options?"

"I wouldn't touch it if it didn't."

The list of people went on. These were his trauma patients. He would see them during their hospital stays then once or twice afterwards to make sure his work was holding up. But beyond that, they would see their regular doctors or be passed on to specialists.

He went to see his elective surgery patients next. Although he was trained as a trauma surgeon and performed that function four nights a week at Parkview, he was boarded as a thoracic surgeon, which meant he was a specialist in chest surgery. In some hospitals, the main reason trauma surgeons took elective cases was to make extra money because they were paid by the number of operations they did. But Cogan, who was on salary, took them for reasons that didn't offer an immediate pay-off: to stay sharp in his area of expertise, establish a reputation outside trauma, and to appear productive to hospital administrators. He wasn't planning on leaving Parkview tomorrow, but he knew he would someday, and he wanted to be able to pick his next destination.

Sometimes he wondered whether the extra work was

worth it, for there were days when he felt burnt out and longed to leave the profession altogether. When he was really fried, he prescribed himself a vacation and his attitude and outlook would improve. But in the last eighteen months he'd noticed that the medicine seemed to be having less and less of an impact. Even after he upped the dosage to a whole month away from the hospital, the all-too-familiar funk returned within a few days.

He tried not to let the little things get to him, like cocky dot-com douchebags who were making more than him. Or Mrs. Ellen Richter's hemorrhoids. But inevitably they did.

Mrs. Richter, age sixty-five, was the first of three lung-cancer patients he saw that morning. Cogan had removed a malignant tumor along with a third of her right lung two days earlier. Her prognosis was good. She might live five years. But this morning a complication had developed completely separate from the cancer. Mrs. Richter had hemorrhoids—she now had pain above and below—and she wanted to know what Cogan could do about it. She wanted him to operate on her again. Demanded it, in fact.

"Isn't there some laser surgery you could do?"

These were the moments that Cogan found most frustrating. A patient in Mrs. Richter's position should have been happy. She'd gotten through a life-threatening operation. He'd taken out her lung cancer. He might not have cured her, but she was far better off from where she'd started. And she should have been happy he'd done what he could for her. But here she was, demanding he fix her hemorrhoids at seven in the morning.

"I understand you're uncomfortable, Mrs. Richter," he said. "But right now, you don't need a surgeon. Right now, we need to get you through this without another operation. I'd rather see you use some cream for the hemorrhoids."

"I used the cream."

"Well, maybe we can try another one. I'm more concerned with the balls. How are you doing with the balls?"

Cogan was talking about the small device, an incentive spirometer, lying on the bed next to her. Made out of clear plastic, it housed three small balls that would, when you breathed hard enough into the device's mouthpiece, rise in their respective compartments.

"Show me what you can do," he said.

Mrs. Richter picked up the device and exhaled into it as hard as she could. One ball rose halfway up in its compartment, but the other two didn't rise at all.

"OK," he said. "That's better than yesterday."

He told her she had to breathe into the device for fifteen minutes every hour. They needed to get her lung capacity up and make sure she didn't get an infection.

"I'll be back this afternoon and I want to see those balls dancing."

"It's hard."

"I know it's hard. But it'll feel good when you get them all going. I promise."

His next patient was younger, a woman in her fifties named Greer, who was very aware of her body and constantly monitoring it.

"This seems more like the episodes I was having when you brought Dr. Fein to see me," she said, describing some pain she was having in her breasts. "With the exception of last night and the night before, my fever was 101 and my breasts felt really heavy and tender. I thought I was getting an infection."

She was wearing her own sleeping gown, a thin pajama top that was almost halfway open. She probably left it unbuttoned so she could more easily monitor herself, but unlike a patient he saw yesterday, a forty-two-year-old woman who'd been in a car accident five weeks earlier and hit the steering wheel with her chest, Greer was quite comfortable exposing herself and having doctors and nurses examine her.

Yesterday's patient had bruised her sternum and heart, a myocardial contusion, medically speaking. She had large, pendulous breasts that she clearly felt uncomfortable revealing. From the get-go, he'd noticed she was very uncomfortable with his examinations, which automatically put him on alert. He was always careful not to give any wrong impressions when he was examining his women patients, but with certain women he could sense that he really needed to take extra precaution.

When he examined women, he always had a female nurse or resident present at the examination. It was to protect him as well as the patient, because if anything went down—if the patient had a complaint—there was another woman there to act as a witness. In the three years Cogan had been at Parkview, two doctors had lost their jobs for allegedly doing inappropriate exams.

"I know you took some pain meds yesterday," he said to Greer without examining her. "Did you take anything today?"

"I took one pill last night. But other than my breasts, I feel fine. I got all three balls dancing."

"Really? Lemme see that."

She blew into the device.

"Wow," he said. "There's a woman down the hall who can barely get half of the first one."

"Well, when you first gave it to me, I thought you must be crazy."

"Very good. I'll be back."

His last patient was in the worst shape of the three and the youngest at thirty-six. An El Salvadorian, she had three children and Cogan felt very bad for her because she was going to "box." That was slang for die, and although he hadn't liked the phrase when he'd first heard it, over the years he'd found that it had become an integral part of his vocabulary, so much so that he rarely used the d-word anymore.

The woman had breast and lung cancer; they hadn't caught either early, and now they were carving her up in an attempt to save her. She'd had both breasts and an entire lung removed. She was very thin. She weighed only eighty-five pounds. If she were fifteen years older, Cogan wouldn't have operated on her but she was thirty-six and she had three kids and he wanted to try everything he could, even though he'd had to argue with administrators to get the OK. But now things had taken a turn for the worse. She had a lump on her shoulder that he was worried was a metastasis. He'd done the lung operation three weeks ago. Now the cancer was spreading. She was going to box.

"Hi, Mrs. Dominguez, how are you doing this morning?"

Mrs. Dominguez didn't say anything. She just made a face and gave a little shrug of her shoulders. Cogan wasn't sure whether she understood what he'd said or just didn't want to talk to him. Her English wasn't good, so he always brought along an interpreter. There were a couple of nurses on the floor who spoke Spanish and he would ask one of them to accompany him when he went to see Mrs. Dominguez.

"Ask her how her pain is," he said to the nurse, Claudia, who was standing next to him. "Is she in pain?"

Claudia translated what he said and Mrs. Dominguez immediately became more animated. She spoke quickly, rattling off an answer.

"She says she has trouble breathing. She has pain in her chest. In her arms. In her back."

"Ask if she took anything this morning."

"She took a pill about half an hour ago."

"Did it help?"

"A little, she says."

"OK. Well, tell her I don't want her to be afraid to say anything if she's in pain. She should ask one of the nurses to come find me and I'll up the dosage. OK?"

"OK," Mrs. Dominguez said after she heard the translation.

"Tell her I just want to examine the lump on her shoulder."

After Mrs. Dominguez nodded her consent, Cogan slid her pajama down her arm and pressed down lightly on the lump, which was just a little smaller than a golf ball. It felt spongy.

"I want you to tell her that I have to do some tests on that. I'm not going to do them now because I want her to rest. But this afternoon I'll come and do a test."

Claudia translated what he said.

"She wants to know if you are going to do another operation on her."

"Hopefully, we won't have to do a biopsy," he said to the nurse. "I'm just going to stick a needle in there and see what comes back. Hopefully, the lab will be able to tell just from the fluid. Don't translate it like that. But tell her something along those lines."

Whatever she said was good, because Mrs. Dominguez seemed relieved.

"Thanks, Claudia," he said to the nurse. Then to Mrs. Dominguez: "You hang in there, OK?"

Claudia translated what he said.

"OK," Mrs. Dominguez said.

"I'll be back this afternoon."

Whenever he met with patients who were in the advanced stages of cancer, he thought of Dr. Liu, an oncologist at the hospital who was known for his brutal honesty. Liu was Chinese, real Chinese, and although he spoke English well, he spoke with a harsh Chinese accent, which only seemed to add to the brutality of his medical analysis.

For instance, a patient who had lung cancer that had reappeared after a brief remission would ask with trepidation how things looked, and Liu, ever so bluntly, would respond: "You have lung cancer. You are going to die." Just like that. No sugar coating. No posturing.

Many left his office in tears, wondering how their doctors could have sent them to Dr. Liu. But remarkably, a few weren't angry. A few said thank you. They liked him because he was very up-front and knowledgeable about his field. He knew the literature. He knew his patients. He followed them very closely. And they appreciated it.

You have cancer. You are going to die.

Thank you for telling me. Thank you very much.

Cogan couldn't do it. Even if some people appreciated it. He couldn't shut the door like that, slam it in their faces. He always left it open a crack.

"If it was me," his ex-wife had once argued, "I'd want to know I was going to die. And I wouldn't want to waste my time or money on awful treatments that weren't going to work."

"Easy for a healthy person to say," he replied. But these people were desperate. Desperate to cling to any hope. And to extinguish that was cruel. "I tell them the truth," he said. "With certain types of cancer, I tell them there's little chance the treatment will work. But they don't want to hear it. They say, there must be something you can do. And the truth is, there's always something you can do. That is the cruelty of modern medicine."

"No," she said. "It's you who don't want to hear it, Ted. It's your denial. You know what's right but you let people convince you otherwise."

"Maybe," he said. "But it doesn't matter. The result is the same."

"Someday it might not be."

"Yeah, someday I'll be the one doing the dying."

"I didn't mean that."

"I know," he said. "I know what you meant."

10/ Shades of red

<u>April 1, 2007—p.m. 12:05</u>

Carrie Pinklow leads the way out to the backyard, to a glass metal table that's shaded by an umbrella. The house isn't as big as the Kroiters', but it's still nice, and looks like it's been renovated in recent years, with an extra room added behind the garage. Her parents are recently divorced, Carrie explains, and while she spends most of her time here, she does occasionally stay with her father, who's "temporarily" living in a two-bedroom apartment in Los Altos.

After they're seated, Madden takes out a small notepad from the inside pocket of his sports jacket and opens it in front of him on the table next to his coffee mug. Then he takes out a micro-cassette recorder and sets it on the table between them.

"Did you get shot?" she asks.

"Excuse me?"

"Your leg. Did you get shot?"

"Oh, no. I had polio as a boy," he explains. "Do you know what that is?"

She makes a face like, *Please, give me a break, I'm not an idiot.* Then she says: "Roosevelt had it."

"Yes, that's right."

"You don't look that old. I thought they had a vaccine."

"I'm fifty-eight," he says. "I was one of the last reported

cases."

"I'm sorry," she says, suddenly expressing heartfelt concern. "That's too bad."

"If you don't mind, I'd like to record you, Carrie. I don't like to miss anything. Is that OK with you?"

"OK. But if I start to break down or anything, you have to promise to turn it off. I've been crying all morning. I still can't believe it."

"Fair enough."

Madden looks at her. She's pretty but in a much different way than her friend. It's all up-front, there's nothing beneath the surface. She has dark straight hair, a nice complexion, a small nose, and bright blue eyes. But she's short and a little on the thick side—one of those girls whose bone structure will never allow them to be truly thin. Like her mother, who he met on the way in, she has a chest and from the cut of her tight, V-neck T-shirt, she's not afraid to make sure everybody knows it.

In her diary, in her less complimentary moments, Kristen had used such nouns as "flirt," "drama-queen," and "bigmouth," to describe her best friend. And although his reading may have colored his initial impressions of Carrie, nothing indicates Kristen was too far off in her assessments. Yes, Carrie's eyes look a little puffy from crying, but she's also taken the time to apply a healthy dose of makeup, along with a shade of lipstick that he considers unnecessarily red for this type of interview. If she does seem prepared for the likelihood that in the days ahead she's going to be at the center of a public drama, she is nervous. Her jaw is working hard on a wad of chewing gum and he's noticed her picking at the cuticles on her fingers.

"She called you a few times yesterday on her cell phone," he says.

"Yeah, I spoke to her. And we IM'd back and forth a little."

"And how'd she sound?"

"She was pretty upset, I guess."

"You guess?"

"Well, yeah. She wasn't a happy camper. She said the police were coming over to interview her and she'd been trying to reach Dr. Cogan to warn him."

"Did she reach him?"

"She said she spoke to him for, like, thirty seconds and he brushed her off as soon as he heard her voice. He told her he couldn't speak to her and to please stop calling him. He wasn't trying to be mean, he said, but he couldn't talk to her. Then he hung up."

"And that was what upset her?"

"Well, more like the combination of everything. With the police coming, she knew he was going to get in trouble, that he might lose his job. But at the same time she was angry at him for not listening—and her father, too."

You should have listened, Madden thinks. *You all should have listened.*

"She said she couldn't deal with it," Carrie goes on. "She didn't know what she was going to do. I mean, this had been going on for a couple of days—ever since her parents found her diary."

"But she didn't mention anything about wanting to kill herself."

The girl falls silent. She stops chewing her gum and looks down at the table, fidgeting in her seat.

"Carrie, did she say something?" he urges.

"She might have."

"What'd she say?"

"Well, it wasn't like she said she was going to kill herself, but she just made some comments."

She looks away again, tears welling up in her eyes. Then she covers her mouth with her hand and her expression becomes that of someone who's truly distraught.

"I have . . . this friend," she says.

Madden waits patiently for her to collect herself.

"I have this friend," she starts again. "Her older sister was living back East. In New York. When the whole 9/11 thing happened."

Madden looks at her, raising an eyebrow.

"Yeah."

"Well, the older sister knew this guy. He called her that morning and said, 'You won't believe this, but this plane just hit the tower next to me. It just plowed right into the building.' "

He nods, hoping the detour leads back to the main road.

"The thing is," she says, "they ended up chatting on the phone for like almost a half an hour. I mean, they were just kind of joking around like they normally would and he told her to turn on the TV and stuff."

"And she didn't encourage him to get out," he says, guessing the end.

"Yeah. And he ended up dying. And the thing was, all his friends and her family blamed her for it. I was just a kid then, but I always remembered that. And how it really messed her up. She was never the same."

At the Kroiter home yesterday, he didn't have any tissues with him. But this time he's stocked. He peels one off the travel Kleenex pack he has in his coat pocket and hands it to her.

"Thanks," she says, and dabs her eyes.

"I'm not here to blame anyone, Carrie. I'm only trying to piece together what happened."

"I know."

She puts the Kleenex to her nose and blows. He waits for her to continue. After a moment, she says: "She was talking about how she'd been watching *Officer and a Gentleman*. You know, that old movie with Richard Gere in it. Have you seen it?"

"I think so," Madden says, not sure he had.

"Well, it was like one of her favorite movies. And there's a scene toward the end where Mayo—the guy Richard Gere plays—there's this scene where Mayo's friend Sid kills himself because his fiancée rejects him. You know, it's very tragic, and we always cried when we watched it. Every time. And she was just talking about how she understood how he felt and why he'd do it. She never had before, but now she did."

A little astonished, Madden looks at her.

"How did Sid kill himself?" he asks.

"He hung himself in the shower."

Again, his eyes blink involuntarily; they can't hide the impact of her response.

"Why?" Carrie asks. "Is that how she did it?"

"Your mother didn't tell you."

"No." Her voice fills with panic. "Is that how? Is it?"

He nods.

"Turn it off," she says. "The tape. Please, turn it off."

11/ The countdown

Nov. 10, 2006—a.m. 7:30

After he was finished with rounds, Cogan went downstairs to the cafeteria for breakfast. He took oatmeal, two bananas, a yogurt, and orange juice, then carried his tray slowly out into the middle of the dining room, looking for someone to sit with. He saw Kim with a couple of other residents, then, further on, Bob Klein, a vascular surgeon, sitting alone reading *The San Jose Mercury News.* Klein saw him coming and waved him over.

"Rough night?" he asked, setting the newspaper aside.

"One MVA," Cogan said. "Sixteen-year-old. Drove Daddy's car into a telephone poll. Broke a couple of ribs, ruptured her spleen."

"White or black?"

"White girl. Cute."

"Heard you had a run-in with Beckler."

News traveled fast. No doubt thanks to Rosenbaum.

"Just gave her a little friendly advice."

"I'm sure."

A Jew with an all-American face, Klein looked ten years older than he should have. He was two years younger than Cogan but his hair was a shade grayer, and he had a permanent stressed look in his eyes. Cynical and self-deprecating, he'd once said: "I'm just one of those people who needs eight hours of sleep every night but who was stupid enough to pick a profession where that's impossible." For Klein, everything seemed to revolve around sleep and the conspiracy to deprive him of it. Everyone was a suspect, even—and especially—his family.

Klein yawned. "My wife and kid are killing me," he said bluntly. "I've got this presentation this afternoon. So last night, I say to Trish—since I put Sam down the night before, and I have some computer work to do—she should put him down. So she tries to put him down for a few minutes and then he starts screaming, 'Daddy, I want Daddy,' and she comes back and says, 'Bob, he wants you.' So I get up, and I go in, and she says, 'Oh, just put him down, it'll take a few seconds.' So I'm sitting in the bed with him and I'm reading Ninja Turtle books. Half an hour later, he's still knocking around the bed, so I walk into our bedroom and ask Trish, 'Did the babysitter give him a nap or something?' But she doesn't answer. She's lying there, snoring, out cold."

"That's what babysitters do, because a nap is good for them," Cogan said. "The kid sleeps and they just kick back for a while. But the kid's wired later and you're screwed."

"Exactly. But going back to the bed and laying down with him," Klein went on, determined to give a full report of his suffering. "Now it's eleven o'clock and he's still wired. Every time he'd try to get out of the bed, I'd say, 'Sam, if you get up out of this bed, Daddy's gonna lock you in this room.' "

"You gotta hammer them a little harder than that. Maybe he's a little young. But Christmas is always a good thing. You guys celebrate Christmas or Hanukkah, I forget?"

Klein's wife, Trish, wasn't Jewish.

"Hanukkah."

"All right. So you say, 'If you come into Mommy and Daddy's room one more time, you lose a day. No present on the fifth day.' Hammer him with that. That usually does the trick."

Klein nodded, impressed. "Since when did you become Mr. Child Psychologist?"

"Remember Jane, the school teacher with the kid?"

Klein mulled the name over. "Jane . . . Jane . . . dark hair? Big chest?"

"Bingo."

"I think I need one of those. But without the kid."

"No, what you need, my friend, is the countdown."

"Countdown to what?"

"To a better life. This is what you do: Next time you're participating in the whole sexual-act thing with Trish—and I know it happens every once in a while—when you're on the home stretch, you say, 'I'm going to count to ten, and when I get to zero, I'm going to come.' They love it. Drives 'em crazy."

Klein laughed. "You're shittin' me. She'll laugh."

"You think she'll laugh 'cause we're sitting here in this godforsaken cafeteria in the early morning hours after a sleep-deprived night. But in the heat of the moment, there is no laughter, only respect. You need to take command of your sexual situation—as limited as it may be. You'll sleep better at night, and more importantly, so will she."

"That's what you got for me? That's your solution to all my problems?"

"That's what I got."

Klein yawned again then took a sip of coffee. After a short silence, he said: "You on the market?"

"Why?"

"Trish has this new friend. She's looking to get fixed up. Thirty-six, recently divorced, works in the PR department at Sun Microsystems. Smart."

Cogan said he appreciated the offer but he'd already had his fill of smart, recently "liberated" divorcées. They'd worn him out both mentally and physically.

"What if I said she's got the body of a twenty-six-year-old?"

"I'd say I know a twenty-six-year-old with the body of an eighteen-year-old."

"Really?"

"Smart, too. And not always in a hurry, on some mission to make up for lost time."

"Just have a drink with her," Klein said. "An hour. It's no big deal."

"I know."

"She's not looking for any big, involved thing, if that's what you're afraid of. You know, she just wants to dip her toe back in the water. Have some fun."

Three months ago, he would have gladly taken Klein up on the offer. But he'd had a real run of late, dating seemingly a different woman every couple of weeks, looking for someone he wanted to stick with for a while but not quite finding her. He told himself he was looking for someone who could just hold his interest. But sometimes he was afraid he was looking for perfection. Whatever the case, he'd pushed hard for a while, and come away feeling he'd failed. Now he was tired of the feeling.

He explained this all to Klein but Klein really didn't get it, which Cogan had expected. It was hard for a married man to understand how a single man, with all the freedom in the world, could turn down a date with a woman the married man thought was attractive, because if the married man was in the single man's position he'd jump at the opportunity. The only explanation Klein could come up with was that there must be something truly wrong with Cogan.

"Must be nice," Klein said wistfully, picking up a small piece of paper next to his tray that noted the cafeteria's upcoming lunch specials. "To pick and choose like that from a new menu with new items every day. And if you're not hungry, well, you go light. Me, I'm looking at the same menu every day, rain or shine. Meatloaf."

"Come on, Trish is better than meatloaf. She's at least a cutlet."

"Yeah, when she feels like it. Hell, she can be filet mignon when she wants. But it's not like I can put in a request with the maitre d' and it shows up."

They ate in silence for a minute. Then Cogan said: "I went to see a patient this morning. A kid, twenty-six. Some dot-com dickhead. Pudgy face. Ponytail. Says he's worth ten mil. Thinks he's big shit. But the thing is, he keeps crashing his bike. Second time in two years he's been through trauma. And we're not talking little crashes. We're talking about this guy really fucking himself up. We're talking twelve hours in the OR. I mean, this last time, he barely made it. And he treats me like it's my job in life to put him back together. So today I told him, hey, maybe it was time he laid off the bike. And he says to me, 'Do they pay you to give advice too?' And I'm thinking, why did I save this motherfucker's life? To take this abuse?"

"Hey, we've all been there, Ted. We all get crappy patients every day. Between them, the administrators, and my wife, it's enough to put a guy over the edge."

"I know."

"Try coming home at seven o'clock after dealing with some of these schmucks and now your three-year-old boy needs to be entertained and watched and put to sleep. And you don't want to give because you've given all day. Trish is the same way. There's no give. If I say to her I'm getting hammered at the hospital she's going to say, 'Hey, I've got the same story.' "

Everybody had it worse, Cogan thought. It wasn't supposed to be this way. He wasn't supposed to be sitting here each morning, complaining. He should have been exhilarated. He should have been talking about how he'd saved that girl's life last night. But instead he was complaining about some asshole he shouldn't have saved. The good things somehow got lost. Overwhelmed. Outweighed.

Lowering his voice, he said: "This is between you and me. It doesn't leave this table, OK?"

He waited for Klein to agree to the terms, then quietly told him he'd been thinking more and more about splitting Parkview.

"And going where?" Klein asked.

"I don't know. To start my own business."

"Private practice? It's a haul, too, man. There isn't the kind of money there used to be in it."

"No. I mean a completely different business."

"Give up fixing people?"

"Yeah. Shit, between the Internet and the venture-capital firms looking at biotech companies, there's gotta be a ton of consulting out there."

"You mean, like Teddy Cogan, cyber-M.D.?" Klein said, laughing. He made it sound as if Cogan would be starring in his own new sitcom.

"I'm not kidding."

Klein considered it. He took a contemplative sip of coffee, then said: "Give up patient care. Sure, I've thought about it. I thought about going to B-school. Trish and I talked about it when Richardson left last year."

"Really?" It was the first Cogan had heard about it.

"But I don't want to be a regulator, Teddy. I don't want to be the director of some health plan. Even if there is more money in it and you have more control, none of the business-side stuff appeals to me. I didn't grow up wanting to be a bean counter."

"Me neither."

"We both know we're in too deep to let it go," Klein went on, seeming to relish his resignation. "We spent a third of our lives getting a degree to do what we do. So they changed the rules on us. We've still got too much time invested. To make it at something else would take . . . what? Five, ten years? Who knows? We'd both be pushing fifty by then."

"If I had to do it over again, Bob, I wouldn't. God, I wish I could start over."

"And that bothers you?"

"Sure."

"Welcome to midlife, pal."

They both sat in silence for a little while, then Cogan heard himself say unexpectedly: "I had this dream a couple of nights ago."

He was back in college, going out for the baseball team, he told Klein. It was tryouts, his senior year. The only thing was, he was the age he was now: forty-three. He'd just never graduated. He had one more year left of eligibility. And the coach introduced him to the players. He said, "This is Teddy Cogan, he played with the team a while back, then decided to take some time off. Now he's back and will be trying out with the rest of you."

He started doing the drills and the conditioning work. And he found himself running well, keeping up with everybody. He felt good. Then it was his turn on the mound—he was a pitcher—and he started to throw, and he realized he didn't have the velocity he used to. He couldn't strike anybody out. But he was craftier. He was getting guys to ground and fly out. And he made it through a couple of innings without allowing any runs. Walking off the mound, he thought, *Hey, maybe I have a shot here.*

After the last day of tryouts, they posted a list of the people who made the team. Cogan put his things away, all his equipment, then went over to where they'd posted the list—right next to the coach's office—and looked for his name. He went down the list. Down, down, he was looking at the names. Then, right near the end, he saw his. It said: Cogan T. But next to his name there was another name. And next to that it said: Chest Wall Mass. Suddenly, he realized he was reading a schedule for surgery. And that he was due in the OR in a few minutes.

Klein smiled. "I have the same dream. Only there's no team. It's just me and a couple of cheerleaders. And my beeper goes off."

"I'm telling you I was good," Cogan said. "I was pitching well."

"I'm sure you were. Bring your mitt to the OR next time and we'll toss a mass around after an operation. We'll see what you've got."

"I'd love to."

12/ Emergency visit

April 1, 2007—p.m. 12:12

Madden presses the record button on the micro-cassette recorder. It's the second time he's had to stop and restart the tape.

"That night. You went to a party. It was a college party?"

Carrie doesn't answer at first. She's still wrestling with the fear that people will think she could have prevented her friend's death. A few seconds pass. Then, finally, she says:

"Yeah. My brother goes to Stanford. He's in a frat there and they were having a big party."

"How'd you get in?"

"What do you mean?"

"Were they carding at the door or did you just walk right in."

"Well, we were there early. We went over to watch some basketball game."

"And you were drinking?"

"Yeah."

"What were you drinking?"

"I had a couple punches. I think it was rum punch. But I wasn't really drinking. That was sort of a deal we had. That one of us could drink and the other couldn't. I mean, it's not like we drank a lot. I don't even like to drink."

"But Kristen was drinking?"

"Yeah, you know, I guess she just sort of felt like it. She kind of had a bad week at school and she just wanted to have a good time."

"So then you're at the party."

"Yeah. It was fun. We were dancing and stuff. Then all of a sudden Kristen was gone. She went upstairs to the bathroom and threw up. I guess she'd also had a couple of beers during the party. You know, someone handed her a beer and she took it and after the punch she said it didn't seem strong at all. But that's what gets you sick. Mixing."

"Then what happened?"

"Then she was in pretty bad shape. They had to take her to a friend of Jim's room. That's my brother, Jim. And she was pretty out of it. We were slapping her and putting cold water on her face but she wasn't responding. So it got pretty scary. And that's when we decided to take her to Dr. Cogan's house. Because we didn't want to take her to the emergency room. Our parents would have killed us if they'd found out. And because Jim thought the frat might get in trouble because she was underage. So I suggested we drive over to Dr. Cogan's house and see if he was home before we went to the hospital."

"And how did you know where Dr. Cogan's house was?"

"Because we'd followed him a few times. I kind of had a crush on him. I think—"

He waits for her to finish the sentence, but she doesn't. So he says: "You think what?"

"It doesn't matter."

"Maybe it does."

"I was just going to say that I think she wrote about that—about how I had a crush. She told me she did."

Madden allows himself a smile. Kristen *had* written about it. *Nice and consistent,* he thinks.

"OK," he says, "then what happened?"

"Well, he was home. At first he didn't want to let us in, but we kind of begged him."

"So he did?"

"Yeah. He checked her out. He was mainly concerned she'd taken something else. You know, some drug or something."

"And she hadn't."

"I didn't think she had. And she said she hadn't. And so we mainly just started walking her around and trying to get her to drink water."

"Who was we?"

"Me, Dr. Cogan, and Gwen Dayton, who goes to the U. I think she's a junior."

"Do you remember how long that was?"

"Maybe an hour."

"And what time was it?"

"When we were walking her around?"

"When you finished."

"I think around one. Maybe a little later. At some point I know Jim called my mom to tell her I was staying in his room at school. My curfew was midnight."

"And what time was Kristen's curfew?"

"Hers was usually eleven. But she was going to stay over at my house."

"But she didn't?"

"No, because my mom always waits up for me. And she would have freaked if she'd seen her. I mean, she might not have freaked that bad but she would have told Kristen's parents and they definitely would have freaked. Jim told Mom that we were driving Kristen home and that I was going to stay with him. She was OK with that."

"And then you just stayed at Dr. Cogan's?"

"Yeah. I mean, Kristen was crashed out in his guest room. So we asked him if she could stay. He didn't want to at first. But then I promised I'd get her out of there early—by eight. My brother would come back and get us."

"And where'd you go?"

"I went to sleep in the living room. On the couch."

"And then what happened?"

She's silent.

"I think you already know," she says. "That's part of the reason why you're here, isn't it?"

"Yes, but I'd rather hear you say it."

"I'm not sure I should. I'm not sure that's what Kristen would have wanted."

"I don't think it's a question of what Kristen wanted at this point," he says.

She looks away. Then down at the ground.

"Carrie, did Kristen have sex with Dr. Cogan?"

13/ Dick-nar

Nov. 10, 2006—a.m. 10:04

After breakfast, Cogan went back up to the OR. He had two minor operations scheduled that morning, both bronchoscopies, which he could do in an hour with any luck. They were really pre-op ops: You ran a tube down the patient's trachea. Then you ran a camera and biopsy tools down the tube and took a sample of a suspected lung cancer. No cuts on the outside. And no anesthesia. The patient was awake during the whole operation, though heavily sedated.

He eased in to what he expected to be a fairly standard day. Once, he'd been asked to describe a typical day at the hospital to a group of high school students who'd come for a tour of the emergency department. At first, he hadn't been sure how to answer. Part of the problem was that his day—and he said this—was really a night and a day. He was almost always in the hospital for a twenty-four-hour shift. In the daylight hours, his work was very structured. He had operations scheduled, usually in the morning, and appointments to see patients. But at night, he never knew what to expect. He could sleep through the whole night without having to go to work. Or he could be up the whole night, treating one victim after another. Unfortunately, he didn't get to choose when people hurt themselves. But if he had his choice, everybody would hurt themselves between six and ten in the evening. He'd make it a law, if he were President.

The students laughed. Then one girl asked: "If you don't sleep at night, how do you keep awake during the day?"

"Coffee," he said. "Lots o' coffee."

And it was true. Cogan was a regular customer at the coffee cart out in the courtyard. On warm days, he'd go outside and sit at one of the half dozen or so umbrella-covered tables. It was almost like sitting at an outdoor café. He'd drink caffe latte, kibitz with other doctors, and flirt with nurses, who took as many cigarette breaks as he took coffee breaks. His fifteen minutes there were some of the most cherished moments of his job.

He didn't tell the high school students that, though. Nor did he talk about the petty squabbles that forever seemed to dog him. These kids didn't want to hear about office politics. They wanted to hear about blood and guts. How could he tell them that working in a hospital was just as much about stroking people's egos and gossiping behind their backs as it was about saving lives? Sometimes, he thought the problem was that during the years doctors were supposed to be developing personalities, they were holed up in libraries and labs. Too often, the result was a fully developed adult male or female of the species, performing a highly skilled profession with the social skills of a teenager.

Anne Beckler was just such a person. That morning, he didn't see her coming, he just heard her voice bearing down on him from behind.

"Hold up a minute, Cogan, I want to speak to you."

Her voice had an emotionless, authoritative tone to it, the kind a police officer uses when he asks you to step out of your car and show him your driver's license and registration. Cogan turned around slowly and faced her with a gracious, if somewhat phony, smile. He'd just come out of the OR after finishing the second bronchoscopy.

"What's up, Anne?"

"I notice you've managed to successfully avoid me the whole morning."

"It's ten o'clock. I don't think that qualifies as the whole morning. But I'll take it as a compliment. Successfully avoiding a bloodhound such as yourself for even an hour is an accomplishment."

"Why are you such a dick, Cogan?"

"Well, I've given it some thought," he said. "And this is what I've come up with. Really, I'm more of an ephemeral dick than a permanent dick. See, I'm only a dick when I sense someone is about to be a dick to me. I make a preemptive dick strike, so to speak."

"And what leads you to assume that someone is going to be a dick?"

"I have dick-nar."

"Dick-nar?"

"Dick sonar."

"Interesting. It's a shame that you don't also possess the ability to sense when your opinion is not needed in an operating room."

"That is a matter of opinion."

"For the record, I was just about to put the scope in when you dropped by. I would have gotten through the operation fine alone. I don't appreciate you making my surgical decisions in front of my resident."

"It was a friendly suggestion. I was just trying to help."

"Look, just because you're a trauma surgeon doesn't mean you can come waltzing into anybody's operating room and start calling the shots."

"I was lonely."

"I'm serious, Cogan."

That was the problem, he thought. She was serious.

"Look, Anne. Don't pull that trauma bullshit with me. We all decide what we want to be woken up for in the middle of the night. It's not my fault you get all the gall bladders and I get all the glory. You decided to be general. Not me."

"It's not about that. It's about attitude."

"I don't know what you want from me," he said, "but you're not going to get an apology. When I really do something wrong, I'll be glad to apologize. I'll get on my knees and beg for your forgiveness."

"I want you to stay out of my operating room."

"Show me the pink slip and I will."

"What?"

"The pink slip. The ownership papers. If it's yours, I want some proof of purchase."

That did it. That was the last straw. She wanted to hit him. He could see it in her eyes. Slap him right across the face. But she didn't. She just stuck her index finger in his face and said: "You—"

"Have a good day, Anne. If you'd like to discuss this in a more civilized manner over coffee in the courtyard, I'm buying."

She wanted to say something else, but before she could, he turned around and walked away, back in the same direction he was heading before she stopped him.

"Stay out of my OR," he heard her call after him.

Such a confrontation might have disturbed other surgeons but Cogan was unfazed. He had no intention of trying to rectify the situation with Anne Beckler. It was impossible, as far as he saw it, so he didn't let her worry him. That was the only way to win the game. You didn't let people like Beckler get under your skin. And you didn't let the little things bother you. You got good shock absorbers and rode the speed bumps like they were flat road: fast and smooth.

14/ Say it

<u>April 1, 2007—p.m. 12:16</u>

Madden waits. He must have waited a good five seconds, but Carrie still won't answer.

"Did Kristen have sex with Dr. Cogan?" he says again. Still nothing. No reaction. He can't figure out why she has reservations. Is she simply feeling overwhelmed? Or is she just playing some twisted version of the loyal friend?

"What do you think of Dr. Cogan today?" he asks, deciding to take a different tack.

"Today?"

"Yes, right now."

"I don't know," she says uncomfortably.

"I think you do. Kristen wrote about it. She said that you didn't think he was very nice to her."

"That was her problem, not mine."

He smiles inwardly. Now he's getting somewhere.

"Do you think Dr. Cogan made love to her or do you think he just wanted to have sex with her that one time for his own personal gratification?"

"I don't know. You'd have to ask him."

"Did she tell you she'd had sex with him?"

"She didn't have to tell me. I saw them."

He blinks.

"Excuse me?"

"I saw them."

"That night, you saw them having sex?"

"Yes," she says, and he thinks, *Jackpot, a witness, I've got a fucking eyewitness.* "I heard something—a sort of grunting—coming from the guest room. I mean, where I was sleeping—that couch—was right up against the guest room wall. So I tiptoed over and looked in the room. The door wasn't even closed all the way."

"And what'd you see?"

"He was on top of her, humping her."

"He was naked?"

"Yeah."

"And what was she doing?"

"She was just laying there kind of moaning, I guess. And then all of a sudden I heard her say, 'Fuck me. Fuck me like you mean it.' "

The remark floors Madden. Not because of the profanity, but because Kristen had written those exact words in her diary.

"I'll never forget that," Carrie goes on. "I was totally shocked. I mean, she was a virgin. It doesn't seem like something a virgin would say, does it?"

Madden doesn't know what to think.

"What happened after that?" he asks.

"Well, I went back into the living room and put a pillow over my head. I was very upset."

"Because your best friend was having sex with a guy you had a crush on?"

"Not that. I wasn't thinking about that. I wasn't into him anymore at that point. That was, like, a three-week thing."

He doesn't want to lead her too much, but he feels he's got to give her a nudge.

"So, it was just that they were having sex?"

"Yeah," she answers. "I mean, he was a man. You know, and pretty old, too—like my father's age. And there he is naked on top of my friend, grunting and stuff. I was kind of disgusted."

"And did you say anything to him the next morning?"

"To Dr. Cogan? No, I didn't see him. I called my brother at, like, seven-thirty and he came over and got us. We just kind of slipped out."

"And did Kristen say anything to you?"

"Not until the next day. I pretended to be surprised. I didn't want her to think I was a Peeping Tom or anything."

"And you didn't see Dr. Cogan again?"

"I didn't."

"But Kristen did?"

"She called him, and went over to his house, I think."

"But he brushed her off?"

"Yeah, he told her he couldn't see her anymore."

"Why?"

"Because he could lose his job."

Madden flips back a couple of pages in his notepad. He looks for the quote he wants. When he finds it, he says: "Kristen wrote: 'I can't tell if Dr. Cogan means to be hurtful but there have been moments during the past few weeks when I've felt completely rejected.' Did her mood reflect that?"

Tears begin to well up in Carrie's eyes. "Probably."

"Probably?"

"To be honest," she says, "at the time, I didn't really care. I could see she was hurting and I was kind of happy about it. You know, serves her right and all. She wanted it and she got what she deserved."

"Did she ever tell Dr. Cogan that when she had sex with him it was her first time?"

One tear, then more, stream down her face. It pains Madden to watch.

"No," she murmurs after a moment. "I don't think so."

"Why not?" he asks softly.

"Because she didn't want him to know."

Madden reaches into his pocket and hands her another

Kleenex. Her eyes move up to meet his. They seem to ask for some reassurance that she hadn't really screwed up.

"Was I a bad friend?" she asks.

Her words have an echo to them—they seem to hover over the yard long after she's said them.

"Was I?"

"Of course not," he says.

As she weeps, Madden looks over at the large windows of the living room. Standing there next to Carrie's mother, watching them with a drink in his hand, is Bill Kroiter. They exchange glances, then Kroiter turns around and walks away, out of Madden's line of sight.

15/ A minor act of recognition

Nov. 10, 2006—p.m. 4:49

Cogan had started afternoon rounds just before 4 p.m. They were a little less encompassing than morning rounds. Really, he was just coming by to say hi, and let everybody know he hadn't forgotten about them.

The girl was one of the last patients he saw that day. He hated finishing the day on a low note, so he saw his difficult patients first, then the ones he found more pleasant. He remembered as a boy facing dinner with a similar philosophy. Instead of pushing his vegetables to one side, he ate them first, then moved on to the food he really liked. It had seemed more satisfying that way, leaving nothing to lurk on the horizon to taint the taste of the chicken or beef, which he could then enjoy singularly and thoroughly. Maybe that was why he had no trouble doing his homework before he went out to play ball. He never wanted anything hanging over his head while he pitched.

The girl had been moved to her own room, but when he arrived she was not alone. There was another girl sitting in a chair next to her bed, which caught Cogan a little by surprise. He thought at least one of the girl's parents would be there, particularly the mother.

"Hello, Kristen," he said. "How are you feeling?"

"All right."

He flipped through her chart, looking at her vitals. Her urine output was up to 200, which was pretty standard for young patients. He'd have to tell the nurse to decrease her fluids.

"I'm just going to ask you a couple of questions and check your bandage," he said, setting the chart down at the foot of the bed. "Then I'll let you get back to your program."

"Oh, I don't care about that," the girl said quietly. "There's nothing good on TV at this hour."

He slipped his stethoscope under her gown from the top and gave her heart and lungs a quick listen. He told her to breathe deeply. When he was through, he lifted her gown a little from the bottom and examined her bandage. While he was examining it, she asked: "How long do you think I'll have to stay here?"

"Maybe three or four days," he said. "We have to make sure you don't get an infection."

"Do you think I could have my mom bring in my DVD player?"

He lowered her gown.

"I don't see why not. You like to watch movies?"

Her face reddened a little. "Sure," she said after a moment.

"She wants to be a director," the other girl chimed in.

"Really?" he said. "You're studying to be a director?"

"Well, we're in high school," Kristen explained. "You can't study to be a director in high school. They don't have any classes."

They were friends from school, he soon learned. But the other girl—her name was Carrie—had been shuttling between her parents' homes because they were separated. She eventually might go live with her dad, but then he was only in a two-bedroom apartment, and it was in a different school district. Kristen was on her way home from Carrie's dad's house when she had the accident, which had made Carrie feel guilty because they had sat around talking too long and Kristen had to rush to make her eleven o'clock curfew. Carrie felt it was her fault Kristen had been in the accident. But Kristen said it wasn't.

They were both pretty girls, Cogan thought. They reminded him of the girls he'd liked in high school. Thin, clean-cut, and a tad demure. They didn't have the cool confidence and hard faces that he remembered many of the most popular girls having. Carrie had short dark hair, big bright eyes, but a plain nose and slightly plump cheeks. The more ethereal of the two, Kristen had since the morning brushed her hair and pulled it back into a ponytail. She had fine light hair, more golden-brown than blond. With the ponytail, he could see her face better, and he realized she was more interesting than he'd previously thought. It was not a face that immediately struck you as beautiful. Perhaps because her skin was not perfect: she had a spattering of pimples on her forehead and a few scratches from the accident. But, when you took them away, there was something there.

Part of the allure, he thought, was how her personality played out on her face, because they seemed to complement each other perfectly. In her looks, he could feel a certain reticence—a sort of reluctance to let go and shine brightly. Her face was holding something back. And a similar theme seemed to run through her disposition. Both girls appeared nervous. But while Carrie revealed her tension with a steady stream of chatter, Kristen sat back and listened and kept her comments to a minimum, even though Cogan sensed she had strong opinions. Every time she made a comment, he felt her retreat, fearing she'd embarrassed herself. And he saw the same movement in her face and eyes.

"Is it true she almost died?" Carrie asked.

"Well, if we hadn't operated on her, yes, she would have died," he explained. "But we figured out pretty quickly what was wrong and took care of it."

Carrie seemed impressed. She looked at Kristen, and

Kristen gave her a look like *See, I told you.*

"I have to ask you a couple of questions," he said, cutting off the small talk. "This may seem silly, but have you passed gas?"

Kristen blushed. Her friend, meanwhile, had to look away and cover her face to keep from laughing.

"I told you it would sound silly, but it's actually very important. You see, when you have an operation like the one you had, where we go into your belly, your bowels and stomach go to sleep. They literally turn off. So it's very important for me to know whether you passed gas because that means they're back—"

"Yes," she said before he could finish, "I did."

Carrie started laughing.

"Stop it," Kristen told her friend, barely keeping a straight face herself. "It's not funny. It's important. You heard him."

"I'm sorry," Carrie said.

He told her she'd probably be able to start eating "clears" by the next morning. Clears were Jell-O, soup, and ginger ale.

"Is that something I should be trying to do?" she asked.

"What do you mean?"

"I mean, should I be trying to pass gas?"

"No, you don't have to. Just be aware whether it's happening or not, that's all."

"I can't believe I'm having this conversation."

He could have told her she was lucky, he could have been asking her a lot more embarrassing questions. He could have told her about the woman whom he'd just seen who was obsessed with her hemorrhoids. But he didn't. Instead, he said: "I think the most important thing for you to do now is to try to get out of bed and walk around a little bit. I'm going to tell the nurse to decrease your fluids and we'll probably take you off the IV. We'll switch your pain medication over from the morphine drip to Percoset, which is a milder painkiller but still very strong. And we'll take it from there. I won't be back until tomorrow afternoon but Dr. Kim, the other doctor who came to see you, will be around, and the nurses have my pager number if you need anything."

"OK," the girl said.

"I think that's it for now."

Just as he was about to go he looked down and saw a blue backpack sitting on the floor next to Carrie's chair. An emblem caught his eye. It was the head of a bear, the mascot of Menlo-Atherton High.

"Do you guys go to MA?" he asked.

"Yeah, uh-huh," Carrie said. "We're both juniors."

Months later, Cogan would look back on this moment, this minor act of recognition, and regret it more than almost any other. He'd wish he could turn back time and walk out of the room without saying another word. But instead, he said: "My next-door-neighbor's kid goes there. Josh Stein. Do you know him?"

The girls looked at each other questioningly.

"Dark hair," Cogan said, helping them. "Pretty tall. Glasses."

"Yeah," Carrie said after a moment. "I think I know who you mean." Then, turning to Kristen, "Remember that kid in our history class last year? Josh." Then, back to Cogan, "A little bit geeky, right? He has a laptop he carries around. He and his friends are always playing computer games."

"That's him."

"We don't really know him," Carrie said a little snobbishly. "But we know who you're talking about."

"Well, be nice to him. He may be a little geeky now, but when he shows up at your tenth reunion you're going to be surprised. Believe me, I know how these things turn out."

"Why?" Kristen asked. "Were you like that when you were in high school?"

"No. Not at all."

"What were you like?"

He smiled. “About ten pounds lighter.” Then, after a beat: “I’ll see you tomorrow. Remember, try to walk around a little.”

“I will,” she said.

PART 2

CROSSING THE LINE

16/ The accidental womanizer

April 1, 2007—p.m. 2:16

The frat house is a relatively simple looking structure, white, with a porch and two balconies, both on the second floor of the three-story building. Standing in the main parlor, Jim Pinklow, Carrie's older brother, age eighteen, is somberly offering the detective who's come to interview him a little history lesson: In the 1950s the house served as the University's admissions building, which is why today it's commonly referred to as Rejection House. Despite the moniker's negative connotation, according to Jim the house generally shares a positive standing among the women on campus—though a bad reputation tends to elicit more derogatory nicknames for both the brothers and the dwelling they inhabit.

Jim's fairly short, five-seven or so, a shade stocky like his sister but a decent looking kid with a tight haircut and intense blue eyes. He tells the detective he's never liked the smell of the house, *especially* on a Sunday after a big party, when the hardwood floors, sorely in need of a fresh coat of polyurethane, are still damp with beer. During the pledge period he and his fellow recruits, who live in freshmen dorms, would often spend the afternoons after blowouts trying to rid the floors of their stench. They would use Pine Sol and lemon-scented cleaners, even something that promised spring freshness. They tried everything, and by evening the odor would come back. Fainter, yes, but it would be there, lurking, waiting for the next batch of kegs to intensify it.

"Well, this is it," he says, leading the detective into a smaller side-room that has a large, heavily cushioned, black leather, half-moon sectional couch and big-screen TV.

"This is what?"

Jim looks at the detective. *He's a weird old bird this one*, he thinks. *Mr. Gimpy.*

"This is where it started, I guess."

That same Sunday afternoon, Cogan, wearing a pair of Ray Bans, sitting at an umbrella-covered table, drinking a lemon-flavored Calistoga sparkling water, is watching a blond get a tennis lesson on court five.

"What do you think?" asks his friend, Rick Reinhart, who's sitting to his left, across the table, facing the same direction.

Cogan looks again. As hard as he's studying the blond, Reinhart is studying him. It's a habit of Reinhart's. He'll tell a guy to check out a woman, then instead of looking at her himself he looks at the guy. Once Cogan had asked him about it, and Reinhart, discounting it, had said, "I'm just watching your reaction." But Cogan thinks it's weirder than that. He thinks Reinhart loves the moment so much, when he checks out an attractive woman he wishes he could see the expression on his own face.

"She's hot, isn't she?" Reinhart says. But it comes out sounding more like a lament than an exuberant declaration.

It's true, Cogan thinks. She *is* hot—in a certain way. Petite and slender, she has a perfect tan, the kind you really had to work on, that plays well with the white of her tennis skirt. If she has a weakness, it's her face. Not that she's bad looking. But she wears too much makeup, and it seems to affect the way she plays tennis, because she isn't moving much for the ball. It's as if she fears she may break into a sweat and threaten the perfect but delicate mask she's created.

"What do you want me to tell you?" he says. "She's good-looking."

"But you wouldn't go out with her, would you?"

Oh, shit, Cogan thinks. *Why does he set himself up like this? Why does he care?*

"What level of 'going' out are we talking about?"

"Whatever the fuck I'm doing."

"I don't know if I could handle that."

Reinhart doesn't really react. He just nods; he appears to chalk up the response, like he's taking a poll.

They watch her for a moment, then Reinhart says: "She does offer to pay for some meals." Cogan isn't sure whether he's talking to him or just thinking aloud. With his right hand, Reinhart nervously slicks back his dark, receding hair, then adjusts his Nike tennis shirt. He's neither as tall nor as athletic as Cogan: Reinhart's on the thick side, a heavy breather with big bones and a wide, handsome face. Thirty-eight and a plastic surgeon, his nickname is "The Rhino" partly because of his surname, partly because of his hard-charging style in whatever competitive activity he participates. As a kid, much to his dislike, he'd been called Rhino ("I was pretty heavy back then," he'll admit). He'd escaped the name when he went off to college, but then one day at the club he'd charged the net to get to a drop shot. He got to the ball but was unable to stop and ran straight through the net, snapping it from its moorings. Ever since then he'd become affectionately known as *The* Rhino, a name he accepted because Cogan had convinced him that, unlike Rhino, it had a singular, macho quality to it.

"Whenever we go out, she insists on splitting the check," he says. "And that's refreshing. But I've got to be the one to organize everything. I've got to pick the restaurant, the movie. She never says, 'Hey, why don't you come over and I'll make you dinner,' or anything like that. It's the little things, Teddy. She's in the game, but she doesn't move. She does nothing away from the ball to get open. There I am, scrambling in the backfield—"

Reinhart stands up and does his best Joe Montana imitation, dropping back a few steps with an imaginary football in his right hand, shifting back and forth, juking imaginary defenders. "There I am scrambling, and she's just standing there. And wham, I get creamed." He makes believe he's been hit by a 270-pound linebacker, rolls backward onto the grass, and lies down with his arms spread out at his sides. After feigning unconsciousness for a few seconds, he gets up and says: "Do you know what she did?"

"No, what?"

"She didn't get me anything for my birthday. Not even a card."

"Ouch."

"Didn't even offer to take me out."

"I thought she was out of town for your birthday."

"She was. But she could have set something up for when she got back."

"Sit down, will ya? You're making me nervous."

Reinhart sits down. But he can't stay down. As soon as he hits the chair, he bounces back up, as if the chair is electrified. He says, "Do you think she appreciates that I set this lesson up for her? I had to call her to remind her about it. She would have blown it off if I hadn't said anything."

"She's playing you, man. She likes you."

"She's got one wheel on the off-ramp."

Just as he makes the proclamation, the woman—Lisa is her name—comes to the fence and calls out to him. She motions for him to come over. Without so much as a glance at Cogan, Reinhart walks down to the tennis court and speaks to her. Then he heads back up toward the table.

"I'm going to get a drink," he says. "You want anything?"

"A *drink* drink?"

"Yeah."

"We're playing, man."

"Just a Bloody Mary. We've got time."

Cogan looks at his watch. It's just after two. "We're playing in fifteen minutes."

"I'll be OK."

"What're you getting for her?"

Reinhart murmurs something.

"What?"

"A bottle of Evian," he says louder. Then he points a warning finger at Cogan and says: "Not a word, Teddy. I don't want to hear it." He turns and walks away toward the pool and clubhouse.

"Are those whip marks on your back, Doctor?" Cogan calls after him. "It's amazing what kind of force the human vagina can generate. It's got tremendous torque. Very impressive, isn't it, Dr. Reinhart?"

"Shut up," says Reinhart.

Carrie and Kristen came around 4:30, just as the North Carolina–Clemson game was about to tip off. Jim remembers the time because he was crashed out on the couch in the parlor room, watching the game with five or six guys, when the girls walked in.

He and two other freshmen had spent the last hour lugging cases of Coors and Keystone Light up from the basement and dividing the cans into tubs. Afterward, they placed the tubs and some backup cases behind three fixed bars on the first floor and two they'd set up outside, in the backyard, where the pre-party was about to begin.

If they were having a smaller party, they'd go with kegs, but the frat president, Mark Weiss, preferred cans for big parties because it meant people could drink faster—you didn't get these long lines at the kegs. Cans were efficient. They also made it easier to measure how much people drank. And that was important for controlling a party, as well as for future planning.

These are the things that most outsiders don't understand, Jim tells the detective. A frat house isn't just a group of guys who get together to get shitfaced. It's a business—there are budgets to meet, funds to raise, and plenty of administration. And if you aren't careful—if you aren't efficient—the enterprise will fail.

Admittedly, his sister, Carrie, didn't quite see it that way. She looked at the house as a "PG-rated Chippendales, her own guy-land in the middle of Blahsville," and she had been ready to soak it all up the moment she walked in.

She didn't even wait to be introduced. She just walked into the TV room all jovial and asked in her loud voice, "Hey, who's playing?" as if she knew everybody. She'd met a couple of the guys before; that was true.

"But, man," Jim says, "I just wish she could be a bit more reserved and not try to dominate a room every time she enters it."

The other guys didn't seem to mind, though. They got right into it with her, jabbering away about which teams were going to make the Final Four in this year's tourney. As was her way, Carrie took the opposing view every chance she could, even though Jim doubted she had any idea what she was talking about. She kept mixing up players and teams. But the more mistakes she made, the more the guys seemed to take to her.

"Truth is," he says, "I barely noticed Kristen at first. Maybe it's because my sister's more outgoing. Also, she has pretty big tits and she was wearing a tight T-shirt. I saw some of the guys checking her out."

"And you were more concerned with that?"

"Yeah, I should've expected it, but I was kinda pissed she wore the shirt. Hey, can I ask you a question?"

"Shoot," the detective says.

"Did Kristen leave a note or anything?"

"I can't really speak to that right now."

Jim is silent a moment. Then he asks, "But she definitely killed herself?"

"An investigation is ongoing," the detective says. "At this point, her death hasn't been ruled a suicide or a homicide."

"My sister says that doctor's involved. That Kristen slept with him that night. Is that true?"

"I can't discuss that," he says.

"What can you discuss?"

"Not much. So, if you don't mind, I'll keep asking the questions and you keep answering them."

Cogan chuckles to himself as he watches Reinhart head past the lap pool toward the clubhouse. He can never understand how a person can be so together in his professional life and so messed up in his personal life. Not that he considers himself so together either. But the difference between how Reinhart runs his practice and how he manages his relationships with women is striking. As a doctor, he's logical, to the point, and sensitive with his patients. For a half an hour, he can sit down with a woman who's going to have an operation and calmly assuage her fears. Cogan has seen it. But in his social affairs he's almost the opposite: strangely irrational and combative.

They'd met a few years ago at the club, not long after Cogan's divorce had become final, and quickly became friends. Its official title is the Alpine Hills Tennis and Swim Club. But everybody who belongs simply calls it "the club." Set among oak trees and landscaped gardens, it's in Portola Valley on Alpine Road, one of the routes to the beach. The road, a favorite among bicyclists, winds up into the mountains, turns into Pescadero Road, and twenty-five miles later ends at Route 1 near Pescadero Beach at the Pacific Ocean. Most people see it for what it is: an incredibly scenic drive. But it always reminds Cogan of something else: who it brings to his hospital.

Alpine Road and some of the other favorite bike and motorcycle routes over the mountains are equidistant from Parkview and the university's ER, so Parkview regularly gets half of the accident victims, and sometimes more, depending on how busy the university is. Whenever he drives to the beach Cogan can't help but think of them. Well, not "them" actually. The victims, the ones who boxed, left less of an impression—took less out of him—than the ones he had to talk to afterward: the mothers and fathers, the sons and daughters, the husbands and wives, the boyfriends and girlfriends.

But the club is his refuge from all that. There are more exclusive clubs in the area—real country clubs with golf courses—but Alpine Hills, which costs $15,000 to join, is popular among the established younger set, particularly those who have families. This is, as Cogan likes to tell Reinhart, "Yummy Mummy Central"—the parade ground of young, attractive mothers whose blissful confidence in themselves and the secure position they've attained only made them seem more attractive.

"Hey, buddy, what's up?"

Klein had arrived.

"You just get here?" Cogan asks.

"Yeah, but I've been up since eight," he says, putting his racket on the table. "Trish has this thing about going to Café Barrone and reading the paper."

"I thought that was Saturdays."

"Now it's Sundays, too. She's got these friends she meets. You know, she'll say, 'Kate and her husband are going this morning. They asked us if we'd join them.' The next day it's someone else."

Cogan sees Trish standing over by the children's pool. She's putting floaters around her three-year-old-son's arms. Cogan waves at her but she doesn't wave back. She turns away, and he knows then that the report has come in from her friend, Deborah, whom he'd taken out for the second time on Thursday, and that it's bad.

"I wish they didn't get up so damn early, though," Klein goes on. "They're so fucking gung ho. Like going to a café was an expedition or something."

"Get with the program, buddy. You can't pursue leisure in a half-ass way around here."

"Tell me about it." Klein thinks about sitting, then decides against it, and begins stretching instead. As he goes into his routine, Cogan looks back up at the pool.

"How mad is she?"

"Who?"

"Your wife."

Klein doesn't say anything at first. He just shrugs.

"Come on," Cogan says. "I'm a big boy. I can take it."

"Well, what do expect? You traumatized her friend."

"I did her a favor."

"Some favor."

"What'd she say?"

"Look, as far as I'm concerned, it's none of our business. I told Trish that. It's the risk you take when you try to set someone up. That's all I have to say. I don't want to get involved. I'm here to play tennis."

"Who said anything about getting involved. Just give me a report."

"Nope. It's none of my business."

Cogan smiles. As much as he wants to, he knows it will do him no good to press Klein, who's already trying to change the subject by asking where the other guys are.

"Reinhart went to get a drink," he says perfunctorily. "He'll be back. Dr. Kim's going to be a few minutes late. I talked to him this morning."

While Klein stretches Cogan wonders how much time he and Trish have spent talking about Cogan's behavior the past couple of days. *Poor Klein,* he thinks. He'd probably taken Cogan's side at first—or at least insisted that it was none of her business. But then she'd forced him to see it her way.

Traumatized. That was pure Trish. And Klein knew it. He knew he'd been bullied, and worse yet, he knew there was nothing he could do about it. Cogan could hear the frustration in his voice.

But the thing about Klein is that he's a compartmentalist. It's how he copes. He puts different parts of his life in different compartments and doesn't let them mix. When he'd said "I'm here to play tennis," Cogan knew he'd gone into tennis mode, and he wasn't going to let anything distract him from that. It was his time to be away from his wife, to shoot the shit with the boys, play hard, and sweat. Anything else—his wife's complaints about Cogan, for instance—were temporarily off limits, filed and locked away in their separate drawer.

As he considers all this, Cogan's eyes stray to court five. The woman and the club pro are collecting balls, loading up the pro's basket for another go-round. Coming out of a bend, Klein notices what—or rather, who—Cogan is observing. "Wow," he says. "Serious tuna alert." He takes a few steps forward, trying to get a better look. "Who is she?"

"Reinhart's gal."

"Really? The one he wouldn't go public with because he was afraid he'd jinx the close?"

"All he does is complain about her. I think he likes her."

"How old do you think she is?"

"Why?"

"I can't tell anymore," Klein says. "I mean, if that woman told me she was twenty-two, it wouldn't surprise me. And if she told me she was thirty, that wouldn't either. It's disturbing, don't you think? I'm starting to lump people by decade. My father used to do that."

"How old do you want her to be?"

"What do you mean?"

"If you could have her, how old would you want her to be? What'd be your optimum age?"

"If I answer correctly, do I get her?"

"You'll have to take that up with The Rhino. I'm not in a bequeathing position."

Klein smiles. He likes hypothetical questions; the more absurd the question, the more he likes it. "I've always been partial to twenty-one," he says. "Senior year in college, I had a good year. Come to think of it, that may have been the last time I dated a girl who was twenty-one."

He'd met Trish when he was twenty-two, he says, though they hadn't officially started dating until she was twenty-four.

"I bet she's about that, twenty-four, twenty-five," Cogan guesses, nodding in the direction of the court.

"What's she do?"

"Sells gym memberships at 24-Hour Fitness."

"I don't know if I could do that."

"Sell memberships?"

"No, bring a young girl to the club, like Reinhart."

"She's not that young. All that sun, she's looking a little weathered in fact."

"I don't know," Klein says. "I'd be embarrassed."

"That's the beauty of The Rhino. He's cultivated an image that allows him to do that. People expect nothing less. In fact, I think they'd be disappointed if he showed up with a garden-variety highly educated professional woman. He'd lose his charm."

"What about you?"

"What about me, what?"

"What image are you cultivating?" he asks, a touch of antagonism in his voice.

"Well, I'll tell you, there's something to be said for going younger while you can—while you've still got your looks and people over at the next table aren't yet asking dad or sugar-daddy? We both know youth takes on a dimension all its own the older you get."

"I'm with you on that, bro," Klein says.

"I would say, however, that the last year or so I've felt myself slipping into an image and I haven't fought it. So I suppose that's a form of cultivation."

"What's that?"

"The accidental womanizer."

Klein raises an eyebrow.

"Yeah, you end up sleeping with a lot of women—or what your married friends think is a lot. But it's not something you aspire to do. It just happens. It's not something you control."

"But you tried with Trish's friend."

"Oh, no, I didn't try. Hard anyway. That's what upset her."

"But you didn't sleep with her."

"Not yet."

Klein laughs. "After how she reacted, you think she's going to sleep with you?"

"This isn't high school, buddy. I know you and Trish haven't been single since the Dark Ages, but we've all lived long enough to know that some strange shit happens with time. People think. They sit in traffic and mull over their lives. They lie in their designer beds with their designer sheets, and between sitcoms, they ponder their futures. Something that doesn't seem right one day can seem right the next. No one died here. No one's been hit by a car. No one's been diagnosed with cancer. What's the big fucking deal?"

Klein is silent. Cogan can see his mind working feverishly to digest, process, and analyze what he'd said. Klein can't just look at the big picture and leave it at that. He always has to break things down and look at all the parts. Then, inevitably, he pushes everything that isn't relevant to him aside and seizes on something that is.

"So," he says. "Do you call her or do you wait for her to call you?"

"I can't really remember how Kristen was dressed," Jim says

in a low voice, leading the detective up the stairs to the third floor. "I just remember it wasn't as provocative as my sister, but I still wasn't used to seeing her all dressed up and made up."

He vaguely recollects something simple: a black cotton skirt that stopped above her knees and a colored long-sleeve cotton ribbed shirt. Strictly Gap or Banana Republic. Basic but elegant.

"Could you tell how drunk she was?" the detective asks, also keeping his voice down.

"She was definitely tipsy," he answers. "But she wasn't, like, majorly stumbling or slurring her words."

"But she was drunk?"

"Yeah."

"Any idea how much she had to drink?"

"No. I didn't think it had been that much, though. I mean, she wasn't doing shots or anything. You know, I figured she'd had a few cups of punch and maybe a couple of beers."

"And that's not a lot?"

"Well, not necessarily over a four-hour period."

"And you say you took her to the third floor because there was a line for the bathrooms on the second."

"There wasn't a line. It was just that the stalls were occupied. Or at least she said they were. I didn't go in."

At the top of the stairs the detective stops to glance at his notepad—Jim thinks more to buy a few seconds to catch his breath than anything else—and just then a sleepy-eyed, well-built guy wearing boxers and a T-shirt emerges from the bathroom. It's Tom Radinsky. "Hey, P-Flam," he mutters to Jim in a throaty voice, puttering past them, seemingly indifferent to their presence.

"The guys aren't exactly early risers on weekends," Jim remarks, seeing Madden's frown. It's nearly three o'clock.

"P-Flam?"

Short for Pink Flamingo, he explains. It's his given R-

House name and a pathetic derivative of his family name, Pinklow. During hell week, whenever the pledgemaster called his name, he had to crane his neck and flap his arms and do what was labeled a "flamingo dance" but ended up looking more like a chicken dance.

"Sometimes, when I was inspired," he says, pulling open the bathroom door, "I'd give it a River Dance flare." It always cracked the guys up, earning him dog calls and high fives, the frat's currency of approval.

The third-floor bathroom is identical to the one on the second floor. There are two of everything—two shower stalls, two urinals, and two bathroom stalls, most of it seeming to date back a couple of decades.

The detective looks around the room.

"Not exactly the Four Seasons, huh," Jim says.

"And when you found her here, she was totally out?"

"I didn't find her. As I told you on the phone, I was standing outside the door, waiting for her. And she didn't come out after, like, five minutes, so I got worried and asked a girl I knew, Gwen Dayton, to go in and check on her."

"You found her in the condition you described her in."

"Yes, that would be accurate."

"Where was she exactly?"

Jim moves further into the bathroom and points to a spot just to the left of the radiator against the back wall.

"She was kind of propped up, with her legs on the floor and her back against the wall. She'd thrown up in the sink. It kind of looked like she'd sat down to take a rest."

"Then what'd you do?"

"I tapped her face a few times. I didn't really slap her—" He shows the detective how hard the blows had been by demonstrating on his own face. "Just kind of like that. Then I tried some water. And when that didn't do anything I went downstairs to find my sister."

He must have told the cop that same story three times, but this is the first time he's told it at the actual scene. He assumes it's the guy's interrogation technique. Ask each question over and over. He's been consistent, though. He's offered plenty of details—so many that sometimes he thinks he's boring the poor guy. He'd talked about Gwen Dayton, and how he had a crush on her. And how she'd introduced him to Kathy Jorgenson. And didn't it suck when the girl you liked introduced you to a girl who you felt nothing for?

"Then what happened?"

"Well, you might say we had an ugly scene on our hands."

The fourth time he looks at Trish, he finally catches her attention. Their eyes lock for an instant; she glares at him intensely, then turns away and calls out some instruction to her son, who's in the children's pool in front of her.

Cogan can't take it anymore. He isn't upset that Trish is pissed off at him. He doesn't need her approval. But he wants to hear what her friend had said. His curiosity is killing him.

"I'll be back in a minute," he tells Klein.

"It's not worth it, Teddy. She's just going to give you shit. And I don't want to be standing on the other side of the net with you in a bad mood."

"I've got a cup in my trunk. I'll let you wear it."

"That's not funny."

He heads over to the pool. Out of the corner of her eye, Trish sees him coming but pretends not to. *Incredible how juvenile people can get*, Cogan thinks as he marches up and sits down in the reclining beach chair next to her. He sits upright with the chair between his legs and his tennis shoes planted on the smooth gray pavement. For a few seconds, he sits there, watching the same group of kids splashing around in the pool that she is pretending to watch. Then, purposely, he pulls his chair a little closer to hers so the metal legs make a scraping sound, like he's clearing his throat.

"I'm not talking to you, Teddy," she says in a clipped

voice, continuing to stare straight ahead.

Her looks have always bothered him. Not because she's unattractive, but because he's always had a hard time describing her to people. He'd be on a date, for instance, and he'd be talking about Klein and Trish and their idiosyncrasies (for what better topic was there), and his date would ask what they looked like. Klein he could do, no problem. Attractive guy, prematurely gray—he could quickly give a pretty good picture. But Trish was tough. He had never thought she was attractive, but he knew other men who did. So, in an effort to be objective, he was always more generous than he instinctively wanted to be. She was fairly thin, he'd say, about five-four, with dark hair, dark eyes, and a somewhat prominent nose. Then he'd quickly move onto her personality, which he found more interesting anyway.

Looking at her now, he realizes why some men find her desirable. From certain angles she is. But he's always felt that her real allure is in the way she carries herself. She has a stiff, regal quality to her, which she mixes with a dry, sharp wit. It had taken them a while to warm up to each other, to get beyond first impressions, and see that underneath it all they were both decent, caring people. Once they had, they realized, much to their surprise, they actually enjoyed each other's company.

"Don't take it personally, Trish," he says, "I wasn't a shit to you."

That gets her attention. She turns and blinks a couple of times, surprised. "At least you admit it."

"I didn't admit anything. I just said I wasn't a shit to you."

It took a second for what he said to sink in; when it did, she let out something that sounded like a snort and called him a jerk.

"What's more of a dick maneuver: me telling her the truth or me just going through the motions so I can sleep with her?"

"That's beside the point," she says. "You were cruel. You knew she liked you."

"A couple of months down the road, I say, 'You know, the chemistry's just not quite right, I think we should move on.' What's worse?"

"It's the *way* you tell the truth, Ted."

"It's a gift."

"I'm serious."

"Well, usually I'm better at it. She just caught me at a bad moment. It touched a nerve or something, the way she said it."

"The way she said what?"

He sighs. He remembers her eyes the most, and the way they bore in on him but somehow stopped at the surface. It was as if someone had told her to look him directly in the eyes when she spoke but forgot to tell her to look for something. To really look. It all seemed like such a charade. She could have been reading from a script or a manual.

" 'All I want from you is to be honest with me,' " he quotes to Trish. " 'That's all I really want.' " It embarrasses him to repeat it because he can't understand how someone can say it and not feel embarrassed.

"What's wrong with her saying that?" Trish asks.

"She didn't want me to be honest. She just didn't want me to deceive her."

"So you were honest."

"Very."

"And when you said you'd be willing to sleep with her—"

"I didn't say willing. I said I found her attractive and wanted to sleep with her but I didn't foresee a relationship. Those were my words."

"And you didn't think she'd find that insulting?"

"I had a hunch she would. But I was kind of hoping she'd surprise me and show me a side that would make me want to have a relationship with her. I was kind of hoping she'd look me in the eyes and say very cooly, 'Let's get outta here,' and take me home and fuck me silly."

"That's what you're looking for? Really? I don't believe that, Ted. I think what she said touched another nerve."

He smiles. "And what nerve would that be?"

She hesitates a moment, seeming to decide whether to say what she wants to say—or how to say it. But then he watches her courage build as her expression turns angry. "I think it reminded you of your ex-wife," she declares resolutely, as if she'd been harboring the theory for a long time and was just waiting for the right moment to spring it on him.

He laughs. "Come on, Trish, you're reaching."

"I'm not saying it was totally conscious. But it triggered something."

"You can think what you want, if it'll make you feel better. But this has nothing to do with that. This was about going through the motions. About trying to make something out of nothing. It just wasn't real and I wanted it to get real. I've got to make some changes, Trish. I can't keep dialing it in like this."

"What kind of changes?"

He badly wants to tell her what's really going on in his head, that he's seriously considering leaving his job. But he knows it's better that he doesn't. He doesn't need her or Klein debating his future, particularly when they both have big mouths. Still, he's tempted to give her a hint, and in doing so he almost replies, too aggressively, "Big changes." But he stops himself and says instead, calmly, "Real changes, Trish."

"Well, it's not going to get real unless you give people more of a chance."

"I give people plenty of chances."

"Two dates," she scoffs. "You call that a chance?" She says something else, a slew of words he vaguely senses is the rumblings of a lecture. But he doesn't hear them because for some reason he finds himself thinking about a letter he'd received earlier in the week. Maybe it's the cries of the children splashing around in the pool that remind him of it. Or what he'd said about chances. But suddenly and briefly, he's somewhere else.

The letter was from a woman in Connecticut he'd slept with a couple of years ago and basically forgotten. A blond with thin, damaged hair who had a good body. "Hope all is going well for you," the letter read. "I seem to remember your birthday being around this time. Just wanted to wish you a happy birthday and let you know I'm thinking about you. I hope I'll get back there sometime soon and look you up."

The woman had two children but she hadn't told him about them until later, after she'd returned to Connecticut. He remembered that she'd made a big deal about it—she'd called him at the hospital and asked him if she could talk to him about "something important" when he got home from work. He spent the morning worrying about it; then, later, when she told him about having children, he was stunned and relieved. It was the last thing he'd expected her to say.

She told him she'd had such a difficult time with her divorce the past year she wanted to get away from her life. She said, "I wanted to get away from myself. That's why I didn't say anything. Do you think any less of me?"

The truth was he thought more of her. The idea of her taking a vacation from her life intrigued him. He understood that. So they kept talking for a few months until she stopped calling. Was it because he'd stopped calling? Or had she met someone? He can't remember.

A loud voice. Trish's. "Are you listening to me?"

He slowly turns his head to meet her gaze, squinting slightly behind his sunglasses as the sun peeks out from behind her head and shines directly in his eyes. "You know, I'm going to be forty-four this year."

"So?"

"I don't know."

"What's wrong, Teddy?"

The children. The letter. He felt like another Calistoga.

"I guess I just didn't think it would be like this."

"What's so bad about this?" she says, glancing around.

"Nothing," he says. "Nothing at all."

"Do you know how many people would kill for your life, Teddy? To be you?" Trish says.

"Well, if you know anybody who wants to trade, tell them I'm willing to part with everything but the car. And the fish tank. The car and the fish I'm keeping."

"I'm serious."

"So am I."

A shadow over them. Reinhart.

"Hey, what's going on?" he says, Evian in hand, a little red in the face from the drink—or probably drinks—he had. "Are we playing or what?"

"Yeah, sure," Cogan says. Then, standing up, to Trish: "I'll call Deborah when I get home. I'll make it better. I promise. She'll be good as new. Like it never happened."

"She's expecting it."

Cogan blinks. "Excuse me?"

Trish smiles. "You're so predictable. You think you aren't, but you are. Now go play tennis and do me a favor." She picks up a bottle of sunscreen and tosses it to him. "Tell Bob to put some of this on. That's the last thing I need, having him complain about a sunburn."

17/ Open Wide

April 1, 2007—p.m. 6:22

Madden sits at the table in the office lunchroom, staring at a diagram he's made on a pad of yellow legal paper, a plateful of half-eaten General Tso's chicken from Su Hong To Go and a can of Dr. Pepper nearby. The diagram, drawn horizontally across the page, is a flow chart with names and short descriptions of the various "players" involved in the alleged crime. Across the top, there's a time line, that goes from the time Kristen and Carrie arrived at the party—4:30 p.m.—to the time Jim picked up Kristen and Carrie at Cogan's home the next day—8:15 a.m.

"You want anything?" asks Pastorini.

"No, thanks."

A few feet away, the sergeant is standing in front of the vending machine, scanning its contents. There's a beep, then a thud as his selection drops into the bin. They refer to the small room as the lunchroom because it has a table, some chairs, and a couple of vending machines. But rarely does anybody actually eat their lunch in the room. During the day, most people go outside or eat at their desks. However, on Sunday nights, when they're working overtime like they are now, and there's practically no one in the office, the area becomes their conference room.

The general crimes detectives work out of an office in the

Menlo Park police department, which is located in the basement of City Hall at 701 Laurel Street. They work in an open office area, with no cubicles. Adjacent to their office area is an interview room, Pastorini's office, and the commander's office. The narcotics detectives, on the other hand, work out of an office in a police substation on Willow Road in East Menlo Park. It's in an area called Belle Haven, their little pocket of inner city, gangs and all, on the other side of the Bayshore freeway that's home to a significant number of Hispanics and Tongans. Like neighboring East Palo Alto, which in 1992 had the highest per capita murder rate in the nation with forty-two homicides, Belle Haven, also hard-hit by the crack epidemic of the early 90s, has seen its lot improve in recent years. While the real-estate boom has been much slower to touch these areas, a gradual and sometimes dramatic gentrification is underway. East Palo now has an IKEA, and a Four Seasons Hotel is under construction next to the freeway. Despite the upswing, however, trouble spots remain—and plenty of them.

"So the friend saw them having sex," Pastorini says. "The whole thing? That's beautiful."

"Well, she saw about twenty seconds' worth," Madden replies. "But she got a good look."

Pastorini sits down at the table and tears open the pack of Twizzlers he bought and peels off a strip of red licorice. "The friend," he says, pointing at the diagram with the drooping twine, "what's her name?"

"Carrie Pinklow. Parents are recently divorced. Lives mostly with her mother. Father's living in an apartment in Los Altos. That's where Kristen was coming from when she got into the initial accident that landed her at Parkview Medical."

"You sure *that* wasn't a suicide attempt?"

"Doesn't seem so from the diary. She wrote that someone cut her off and she swerved to avoid the car."

"Bizarre," Pastorini says. "And you think the bruise on

her arm is from the father?"

"He says he might have grabbed her arm pretty tightly at one point the day before. They were arguing. She tried to walk away and he didn't let her go."

"This Carrie girl, she credible?"

"She was pretty composed, all things considered."

"But there is a jealously factor."

"Sure. There are a lot of factors."

"You ever dealt with something like this before?" Pastorini asks.

"What?"

"Trying to squeeze a homicide out of a suicide?"

Pastorini made it sound like Madden was trying to get orange juice from apples.

The hint of a smile appears on Madden's lips. "Not really," he says. "Remember, we had that case a few years back where the kid decided to walk in front of a Caltrain and the parents sued the company that made his nasal spray? But nothing where an individual was involved."

"What's the term you used on the phone?"

"Foreseeable harm."

"Right."

"The intent doesn't have to be there," Madden explains again. "When Cogan slept with the girl, he didn't think his actions would cause her to later kill herself. But in committing the crime of statutory rape, he was aware—or at least, should have been aware—that his actions could potentially cause her emotional injury."

"And in its most extreme form," Pastorini finishes for him, "those emotional wounds could trigger her to kill herself."

"Exactly. All injuries flow from the initial injury. You stab a hemophiliac in the arm and she bleeds to death. So what if you didn't know she was a hemophiliac; I can charge you with killing her. Murder three."

"But you've got to prove I poked her first."

"Well, I'm not sure that's the word I'd use."

Pastorini smiles, taking pleasure in Madden's glum reaction. "Cheer up, Hank," he says. "You sound a whole lot better than you did when you called me this morning."

"I didn't know we had a witness then."

Pastorini nods in agreement, his seriousness returning.

"When did Kristen tell Carrie she had sex with Cogan?" he asks.

"The next day."

"That's good. That'll help. And she'll talk to the doc for us?"

"She'll talk."

"And you spoke to the frat?"

"I was over earlier today. Carrie's brother is a member."

At first, the brother was the only one who was talking. But with a little prodding from school officials, who promised even harsher penalties if the frat didn't cooperate, a couple of the guys confirmed what Carrie and the brother had said: the girl, Kristen, got hammered and threw up, then became a problem. The president of the frat told Carrie she had to get her friend out of there, he "didn't want any underage chicks dying on him."

"Nice," Pastorini says. "The brother was over at the doc's house, too, right?"

"No, but another girl from the university was. Gwen Dayton. I haven't contacted her yet. But I will."

He pulls out a photo from a folder that's sitting on the table under the yellow legal pad. It's a blown-up version of the young woman's driver's license photo. She's got long, dark hair, a small nose, and cheerleader looks. Her height is listed as five-eleven.

"Giddyup," Pastorini says expectedly, using his favorite *Seinfeld* expression. "Don't let Billings see that. He'll beg you to tag along."

"Don't worry."

Pastorini takes the photo in one more time, then, getting

back to business, says: "You think there's a chance Cogan's heard already?"

"Sure, there's always a chance."

"Well, I'd say we've got one more day before it really breaks. We're looking at Tuesday morning's papers. And then probably the evening news."

"If we're lucky."

Pastorini sits down and chews on a couple of Twizzlers while he thinks. Madden can't watch. There's something grotesque about the way he chews, with his mouth ajar, and that little smacking sound he makes.

"It's your call, Hank," he finally says. "I don't know. I talked to Gill. We could stick the friend on the phone with him and see what happens." Gill is actually short for Gillian—Gillian Hartwick—the commander of their division, a tall, attractive, and well-spoken woman who will field any questions from the media. Respected by officers for her warm, confident demeanor and straightforward management style, she's been with the force for over twenty years. "You'd have to get an OK from the DA's office first," Pastorini goes on. "It's tricky. It's always better to have the victim. Like Open Wide."

Madden feels himself grimace, then stops. He doesn't like the expression, though he's grown used to it, or at least thought he had.

"Open Wide" was a case from almost a year ago. It had been well covered by the press, the story of a dentist who'd molested at least one and probably several of his patients while they were under anesthesia. That patient—a thirty-one-year-old woman—had woken up prematurely and caught a glimpse of the guy putting his pecker back in his pants.

The sad thing was that if he'd been smart, he'd still be practicing. But when the woman called to accuse him of raping her, he panicked. Instead of denying the charge—there was, after all, no proof he'd done anything wrong—he begged her to meet with him and "work things out." A few days later, they got him on tape offering her ten grand, and it was over. He was finished.

Billings had nicknamed the case Open Wide for obvious reasons, and the name had stuck, much to Madden's displeasure. He hadn't been sexually assaulted in the same manner, but every time someone made the reference, he couldn't help but picture the detectives who'd finally caught *his* doctor sitting around, trying to come up with a nickname for the case and having a good chuckle with each new candidate ("The Big Prick" was the one that kept sticking in his head). If he'd complained, Pastorini might have put a stop to it. But he hadn't, it wasn't his practice to let people know they were getting under his skin, and Pastorini had let it go, quietly content to watch his number one detective squirm.

"I don't think we should put the friend on the phone," Madden says. "Not right away anyway."

"What do you want to do?"

"I've got a plan."

Pastorini chews a little slower.

"Really?"

"Really."

"Let's hear it."

18/ Visitors

April 2, 2007—p.m. 2:52

Monday afternoon. A little before three. Cogan's sitting out in the courtyard of the hospital, drinking coffee with Dr. Kim.

"I had my hand on her belly," he's saying to Kim. "And her boyfriend is giving me this look like: don't go any further or I'm going to kill you. Big black guy. And I say to the woman, 'Are you hungry?' And she says, 'Yeah.' And I say, 'I sure could go for a couple of Egg McMuffins right now. That sounds pretty good, doesn't it?' And her mouth's practically watering. I mean, they've been there all night, and they haven't given her anything to eat. So I ask her a couple more questions, and it turns out her brother and mother have had the flu recently. So I tell her it doesn't look like anything serious. If she had appendicitis, she wouldn't be hungry. That's one of the symptoms. And meanwhile, as I'm explaining all this, I want to kill fucking Allison."

Allison is an attending physician, a gastrointestinal surgeon a few years younger than Kim.

"Did you say something to her?"

"Hell yeah. Right after I got through with the woman I went up to Allison and I said, 'Why are you pulling me in on this bullshit stuff? If someone had taken five minutes to talk to this woman, I wouldn't be wasting my time. This is shit a first-year could handle and you've got me in on it because you're too fucking lazy to ask a couple of questions. The woman's hungry. She's ready to slam down five Big Macs. What does that tell you?' "

"Consider yourself lucky," says Kim. "She's got me in on shit like that all the time. I mean, all the fucking time."

"It's just lazy. I hate it."

"Dr. Cogan?"

Cogan looks over. It's Janine, a plump young nurse who only started last week.

"Yes."

"There are two men asking for you. Police officers."

"What are their names?"

She looks at him, a little puzzled. "Oh, I don't know. They said they were police officers."

"Are they wearing uniforms?"

"No. Just regular."

He turns to Kim. "Detectives," he says. "Probably Reed." Then to the nurse: "Did they say what they want?"

"To ask you a couple of questions."

"OK, thanks. Tell them I'll be right there."

Cogan reluctantly gets up, groaning a little as he does so. He hates to be interrupted during a nice, relaxed session of coffee and venting.

"You think they want to talk to you about that old lady?" Kim asks after the nurse has gone.

"Maybe. They caught the guy who did it, didn't they?"

"Yeah, two days ago."

The police occasionally interview him about victims he's treated, especially the ones who died ("Did she ever regain consciousness, say anything to you?"), and by now he knows many of the cops by name and has his favorites. Usually, they come to the hospital shortly after the victim arrives and sometimes at the same time. But every once in a while they show up later.

Cogan downs the little coffee he has left and walks over

to a garbage can and tosses the cup. "All right, Dr. Kim. We'll resume our bitching later. I'll see you tomorrow at the club."

"See ya."

The cops are sitting in the surgery waiting room. There are only five people in the room, including the receptionist, and it isn't hard to pick out the two detectives: both are wearing dark sport jackets and ties. What surprises Cogan is that he hasn't seen either of them before. For a second, he wonders if he has and just forgot. But he's good with faces and neither registers. One is older, a slight, balding guy with glasses and a neatly trimmed mustache. The other, an earnest, clean-cut black guy, looks like he could be a Jehovah's Witness. He has a warm, friendly smile.

"Hello, gentlemen. Ted Cogan."

They stand up and introduce themselves—Detectives Madden and Burns.

"Come on back," Cogan says. "My office isn't very big but I think we'll all fit."

As he leads them down the hall, he notices that the older guy, Madden, is limping. And then he notices he's wearing a special shoe—he has a dropfoot. Strange, Cogan thinks. He's never seen a handicapped cop. He has an urge to ask about it, but before the urge gets too strong they reach his office.

The room is small, about the size of a jail cell. It has a minimal amount of furniture: a desk, two chairs, filing cabinet, waste bin, and a desktop computer and printer. Really, all he uses the room for is to make phone calls, do paperwork, and check e-mail. He's rarely in his office for more than twenty or thirty minutes at a time, so it doesn't bother him that it's small. But it gets a little tight when he receives multiple visitors.

Cogan pulls in a third chair from Dr. Diaz's office, and when the cops are settled he closes the door and sits down behind his desk.

"What can I do for you gentlemen today?"

The older one, Madden, speaks. "Do you recall a young woman named Kristen Kroiter?"

Cogan blinks with surprise. The name registers—he knows it, well even—but he can't put a face with it. *Why do I know that name?* he thinks.

Madden continues, "You treated her about six months ago. She was in a car accident. Sixteen. Blond hair. I believe she ruptured her spleen."

Cogan remembers. And as soon as he remembers, he realizes he shouldn't remember too quickly.

"OK. Yeah. I think I know whom you're talking about. Thin girl, right? She's a student at Menlo-Atherton High. Why, did something happen to her?"

"Well, it's complicated," Madden says. "How do you know she goes to Menlo-Atherton?"

Cogan feels the heat rise in his face. But his voice remains steady. "Oh, I think she told me at some point. I think I asked her if she knew my neighbor's kid." As he speaks, he notices that the second detective is taking notes, scribbling on a small notepad. "I live in Menlo Park," he adds after a beat. "He goes to MA."

"Have you seen her since you treated her?"

"Well, she came in for a check-up about a month after the accident. That's standard. And then I may have run into her a couple times at Safeway. Or was it the mall? I can't remember exactly. Maybe one time at the mall and one time at Safeway."

"You spoke to her?"

"Yes, briefly. I asked her how she felt. How things were going. She seemed to be doing well."

"And those are the only times you spoke to her."

Cogan looks up at the ceiling, his heart pounding hard. The longer he waits, the greater their suspicions will be. So he says: "I think I may have spoken to her and her friend in front of my house a couple of times. They were visiting my neighbor's kid."

"And those are the only times you saw or spoke to her? The ones you've told us about?"

"Yes. Why, what's this all about?"

Neither detective speaks for a moment. Then Madden looks at his partner, Burns. Burns looks back at him, then turns to Cogan and asks: "Is there any reason Miss Kroiter would say she had sex with you?"

Cogan's eyes open wide. He laughs. "Sex. Are you kidding me?"

"No," Burns says, his warm smile gone, replaced by stern eyes.

Cogan looks at him dumbfounded. "You're fucking kidding me."

"We're not doing that either."

Cogan falls silent, a depressed look coming over his face. A hundred thoughts run through his mind at the same time. A dozen emotions. *They had promised not to say anything*, he thinks. *They were never there. It was weeks ago. Back in February, wasn't it? What had happened? Stay calm, Cogan. Stay calm.*

"What exactly did this girl say I did?" he says at last.

"Well, it's complicated," repeats Madden.

"How complicated could it be? What did she tell you?"

"Well, that's just it. She didn't tell us anything. She died. Saturday."

If the reference to sex had felt like a punch to the gut, this one is more like a Mike-Tyson-in-his-prime uppercut to the chin. The lights go out for a second; he's truly in shock. "Come again," he says.

"Looks like a suicide," Burns replies.

Cogan stares at them in utter horror.

"What police department are you guys from?"

Burns looks at Madden, and Madden says: "Menlo Park."

"No, I mean what unit?"

"Homicide."

* * *

By the time they met, Madden had known Cogan for two days. He didn't *know him* know him, of course. But he'd built an image of him: from a driver's license photo, from what two parents had thought, from what one girl had said and one had written, and from his own insights. In plotting Cogan's downfall, he'd taken that image and put it through the paces, running it over and over through a scene he'd carefully constructed in his mind. Take after take, he'd watched Cogan walk toward him into the hospital waiting room. Sometimes Cogan was apprehensive. Sometimes courteous. Sometimes jovial. And sometimes impatient. It didn't matter. For whichever Cogan showed up, Madden was prepared.

"What if he's hostile?" Burns had asked, driving to the hospital. Madden didn't think he'd be hostile. He thought he knew him well enough to know that. He counted on him to be calm. That's, after all, what he was paid to be: calm during a crisis. There was no reason to expect him to be overly jittery or nervous, especially since he didn't know why they wanted to see him. The alleged incident took place over a month ago, he reminded Burns. There was a reasonable chance Cogan would have concluded he was past it.

The plan was simple: get Cogan to answer as many questions as possible before he demanded to know what was going on. Madden knew from talking to Carrie that the one thing he feared the most was that people would find out he'd let the girl, a former patient, spend the night at his house. That was not a crime, but it looked bad, and he'd told both girls that he could lose his job if the hospital brass found out about it. So Madden doubted Cogan would be forthcoming about the girls' visit. And if they could get him to lie about that, they were in business. It would show he was hiding something.

Of course, they might never get there. As soon as they

mentioned Kristen Kroiter, Cogan might tell them he had no comment and they should speak to his lawyer. He might have thought long and hard about what transpired that night and what he would say if anybody ever asked him about it. Madden had met a few like that. The thinkers. The ones who'd rehearsed what they were going to say, knew exactly how they would react once they were confronted, even months after a crime. And sometimes it wasn't to deny their deeds, but to accept them.

He remembered the dentist, Parker. When they'd arrested him at his home, the guy hadn't looked the least bit perturbed. There was even the hint of a smile on his lips as they read him his rights. It was as if he knew this day had been coming and was resigned to it. Even when his wife broke down in shock, the guy's face had remained placid. He'd reached the end of a story that he knew the ending to—that he'd watched many times over—and he seemed to have found some release in finally living it out.

Now it was Cogan's turn. When Madden first saw him, the only thing that surprised him was how tall he was. Later, he realized his mistake. He was wearing clogs, which added a good two inches to his height. But the height had thrown Madden for a second. He had seemed bigger than he really was, and everything else—his looks, his demeanor, his smile, even the way he walked—seemed exaggerated as a result. As they walked down the hall toward Cogan's office, Madden felt a flush of anger: he understood exactly why those girls had gone to the trouble of befriending the kid next door just so they could create an opportunity to run into Cogan. For a second he hated him for that ability, and for his strong jaw and disarming smile. And then he hated himself for thinking that way, for being the least bit jealous.

To clear his mind, he looked over at Burns, who was already looking at him. Burns nodded, and looked away.

Whenever they went to a hospital, he could sense Burns was watching him. Madden had gotten over his fear of hospitals long ago, but every once in a while a smell or sound would get to him and he'd feel his throat tighten. Today, in the waiting room, it had happened. The tightness came and it must have showed on his face because Burns turned to him and asked, "You all right?"

"Yeah, fine," he said.

And as soon as he said he was fine, he was. They had a strange understanding, Burns and him. Burns took the lead on many of the cases that came out of Belle Haven. He had a chameleon-like quality that had always impressed Madden. "He has range," Pastorini once said. And it was true. In Belle Haven and East Palo Alto, Burns was black. But west of the freeway he was all white.

He'd been good today. *The perfect supporting player*, Madden thinks as they make their way out of the hospital. He keeps seeing the look on Cogan's face when Burns asked him about having sex with the girl. And when they told him about the diary. Had it been genuine disbelief? Hard to say, he thinks. Very hard. He doesn't know what kind of actor Cogan is. Doesn't know him well enough to know that. Not yet. But he will, he promises himself.

Neither of them speaks until they get outside. Then, at the bottom of the entranceway's steps, Burns asks: "What do you think, Hank?"

Madden doesn't say anything at first. He just stops at the curb and looks at his watch. His timer is at thirty-five seconds, ticking down from two minutes.

"I think we've got a ballgame," he finally says. Then he pulls out his cell phone and speed-dials the sergeant's number. "We're done," he tells Pastorini. "Wait thirty seconds and have the girl call."

Cogan is alone in his office no more than two minutes when the phone rings. For a moment, he sits there staring at it as if it's some mysterious foreign object that he's seeing and hearing for the first time. Nothing has changed: the room is exactly as it was when he entered it. And people are still moving around outside his office, doing their jobs as if nothing had happened. Yet everything seems intensely askew. He doesn't know where to begin, who to call or what exactly to do. He knows he has to get a lawyer, but which lawyer? Who's good? And who to call to find out who's good?

The phone rings again. His initial impulse is not to answer it, but suddenly he hopes it's Klein or Reinhart or anybody he knows. So on the fourth ring, just before the call slides into voice mail, he picks up.

"Cogan," he says.

"Hello, Dr. Cogan?"

"Yes?"

"This is Carrie Pinklow. I don't know if you remember me." Her voice wavers nervously: "Kristen's friend. I tried to reach you earlier today but you were out."

"Yes?"

"I don't know how to say this, but something terrible has happened."

"I know. The police were just here."

"Oh, my God. So you know. It's just awful," she says, speaking in an irritating staccato. "I can't believe she killed herself. The police talked to me, too."

"And what did you say when they came to talk to you?"

"I didn't know what to tell them. It was all in her diary. Everything that happened that night. You know about the diary, don't you?"

His tone suddenly turns sharp. "They said you made some comments. What did you tell them, Carrie?"

"I told them—I had to. I told them we went to your house. I'm sorry. I'm so sorry. Are you going to get in trouble?"

He lowers his voice. "Did you say anything about Kristen having sex with me?"

"They asked me about it."

"Shit."

"It was in her diary. There was nothing I could do. And then they said she called you Saturday afternoon. What did you say to her?"

"I didn't say anything. Why on earth would she kill herself? Over something I said? Is that what they were implying?"

"I know. It's just awful," she repeats.

"Christ. Why didn't you tell them she made the whole thing up?"

"I don't know," the girl says.

Cogan covers his face with his hand, exasperated. Rubbing his eyes, he lets out a long sigh.

"Do you think it would help if I did?" she says suggestively.

"It'd be a good start, don't you think?"

Just then he hears voices outside his door. A nurse talking to a doctor. "Look, I have to go," he says. "But this is bad, Carrie. Really fucking bad. I'm very sorry about your friend, but I'm in a heap of trouble here. A huge heap. And it's my own goddamn fault."

19/ Professional advice

April 2, 2007—p.m. 3:35

The first person Cogan calls is Klein, though he doesn't actually call him; he pages him. Klein gets back to him quickly, in less than a minute.

"Hey, buddy, you getting out of here?" he asks when Cogan picks up.

"Soon. You busy?"

"Just got a couple things to finish up. Why? What's up?"

"Can you come down? I need to talk to you."

"Sure. What's up? Girl troubles?"

"You could say that."

"Really. Which one? Do I know her?"

"This one's serious, Kleiny. Real serious."

"Oh," he says, taken aback. Then, after a beat: "I'll come right down."

When Klein arrives a few minutes later, he enters the office hesitantly, almost gingerly, as if he fears he's about to be reprimanded by a superior. Cogan knows he's scared him a little. As long as he's known him—about five years—he's never used the word "serious" to describe a situation he had with a woman, even his worst break-ups.

"Sit down," he tells Klein in a low voice. And then, when he's seated: "Look, I can't tell you everything right now, because I don't know where this thing's going. But I'll give you the truncated version. You remember that girl I was telling you about, the girl I treated, who was in the car accident? The one I kept running into?"

"Yeah, the one I met that day I stopped by."

Cogan had forgotten about that. "That's right. She and her friend were out in front of the house with my neighbor's kid when you drove up. Well, I never told you this but one night two or three months ago they stopped by my house late. The girl was drunk, practically unconscious. They'd been to a party—"

"The same girl you treated?"

"Yeah. Same one. It was the night of your birthday. After we went out."

Klein vaguely remembers something about it. "I called you after I came home. I heard them in the background and asked you who they were, and you said 'No one, just an old girlfriend and her friend.' That was them?"

"Actually, there were three."

Cogan explains why the girls had come—that Kristen's friend had brought her there because she remembered where he lived and hadn't wanted to take her to a hospital because they were afraid they would get in trouble with their parents.

They pleaded with him to help them. At first, he said no—he could get in trouble if he did. But they begged him to, and he gave in. Under normal circumstances he would have sent them on their way. But the truth was he was pretty buzzed himself after their outing that night. He'd actually had more to drink than he thought—even more than Reinhart—so his judgment wasn't a hundred percent.

"How bad was she?" Klein asks.

"She wasn't good. But compared to some of the shit that comes through here, she was OK."

He decided he'd take a quick look and if he couldn't handle it, he'd send them to the hospital. Well, they walked her around and gave her water. An older girl—a college girl—was there, too, helping. They basically babysat her for half an hour, and she started to get better. Then, at some point, they stuck her in the guest room and she went to sleep. At eight-thirty the next morning, the friend came back and picked her up and that was the end of that. He didn't hear anything about it until today.

"So the girl spent the night?"

"Yeah."

Klein makes a face and shakes his head.

"Look, it was incredibly poor judgment. I know it was. But at the time, I was just trying to help. I mean, we've all been in a situation like that when we were kids."

"The thing is," Klein says, "when you become a parent you stop thinking like a kid."

"Please, I don't need any of Trish's high-and-mighty crap right now. And if you tell her about this, I'll kill you. Not a word to anyone."

"Sorry, man. So, go on, what happened?"

It got worse. A lot worse. As he said, he hadn't heard anything about it until today. The girl, Kristen, who'd spent the night had come to see him once after that night. She thought she might have left her earrings in his house. She'd brought him a present, which he thanked her for, but told her he couldn't accept. Afterward, he told her she couldn't come to his house again, that he could get into trouble if she did. She seemed to understand his position. And when he ran into her at the Safeway the next week, everything seemed fine. They said hello. Everything was cordial.

That was back in March. Then about half an hour ago he got word there were two cops looking for him. He couldn't imagine they had anything to do with the incident. He'd worried about it for a couple of weeks, but when nothing came of it, he'd put it out of his mind. As far as he was concerned, it had never happened.

"How'd they find out about it?"

He looks at Klein. "You're not going to believe this," he says, not believing it himself. "The girl kept a diary. And her mother found it and read it."

"You're kidding. Online? On MySpace or something?"

"No. On paper. In a notebook, I guess."

"I didn't know kids did that anymore."

"Apparently so."

"And she wrote about how she was over at your house?"

He lowers his voice even more, almost to a whisper. "Not only that. She wrote about how she had sex that night—with me."

"Jesus."

"No, wait. It gets worse. Saturday she killed herself."

Now it's Klein's turn to be shocked.

"She's dead?"

"That's what they're telling me. And it just so happens she called me a few hours before it happened."

"And you spoke to her?"

"That's just it. I told her I couldn't speak to her. I think she was about to tell me what had happened—you know, warn me about her mother finding the diary—but I cut her off. I mean, I was nice about it. I told her she was a terrific girl and all but I really couldn't have any more contact with her. I wasn't an asshole, I swear. But I guess I was kind of abrupt. I had a call on the other line. Who knew? Who fucking knew?"

Klein sits there silently for a moment, staring at the ground. *Maybe he's thinking about what it would be like if the same thing had happened to him*, thinks Cogan. *Or maybe he's considering whether I slept with the girl.*

"I didn't do it," Cogan says, suspecting the latter. "This is something she fabricated. She made it up."

Klein looks up at him and nods. "So what are you going to do?"

"I'm not sure. I've got to get a lawyer."

"Have they charged you with anything?"

"Not yet."

"Is that enough proof, the diary?"

"I don't know. Apparently, the girl told her friend that it happened. And now the friend told the police that she saw us having sex."

"Christ."

"Do you know who represented Hanson?"

Hanson was a doctor who'd been accused of examining a patient's breasts unnecessarily. In the end, he hadn't been prosecuted, but the hospital let him go.

"I don't remember," Klein says. "That was like three years ago."

"Do you think Reinhart would know somebody?"

"Didn't you date a criminal lawyer?"

"Which one?"

"The one with the BMW convertible. Carol. Karen—"

"Carolyn," Cogan says.

"Yeah. Didn't she do sexual harassment–type cases?"

"You know," he says, pulling his Blackberry out of his pocket, "I think you're right."

"You still got her number?"

"I'm looking."

He does a listing by first name and sure enough, there it is: Carolyn Dupuy.

"Carolyn Dupuy," he says to Klein, who mutters something that sounds like, "Thank God for technology."

Cogan looks at his watch. It's a quarter to five. He may still be able to catch her. He picks up the phone and dials the number he has for her office.

Klein says, "When was the last time you spoke to her?"

"I don't know. Two, two and a half years ago."

"How'd you leave things?"

"She'd take a call," Cogan says. "I think." Just then the receptionist at Stevens, Clark, & Kirshner comes on and he raises his hand, signaling Klein to keep quiet.

"Does Carolyn Dupuy still work there?"

"Yes," says the receptionist. "Transferring."

A secretary picks up. "Carolyn Dupuy's office."

"Is she in?"

"Who's calling?"

"Ted Cogan. Tell her it's important."

The line goes silent. A few seconds later, he gets the secretary's voice again: "Hold on, she'll be with you in a moment." And in a moment, Carolyn comes on.

"Is this the world-renowned Dr. Ted Cogan?" she says in her smooth, deep broadcaster's voice.

"I think infamous is more apt at this point."

"To what do I owe the honor?"

"I need professional advice, Carolyn."

"I told you that a couple of years ago."

"I'm serious. I'm in a bit of trouble here. Actually, it may be a lot of trouble. And I'm looking for an attorney—a criminal attorney. I was hoping you might be able to recommend someone. Are you still doing sexual harassment cases?"

There's a short silence. "This is interesting," she says after a moment. He can practically see her smiling. "What have they got you on?"

"It's complicated," he says, echoing Madden's words. "But I'm basically about to be charged with having sex with a minor."

"How old was she?"

"Sixteen."

"Don't tell me you didn't know."

"I didn't do it. She was a patient."

"This really does sound interesting. Who's on the case? Did they send someone to talk to you yet?"

"Yeah, a couple of detectives. They showed up here about two hours ago." Cogan glanced at Madden's card, which was sitting on his desk next to the phone. "Some guy named Henry Madden."

"*Hank* Madden," she says. "You should be honored. They usual put him on the bigger stuff. Major crimes. Even homicides."

"Yeah, I know. I didn't tell you the other part. The girl's dead. They found her Saturday. They said it looks like she killed herself."

"Oh, boy."

Suddenly, she isn't so cheery.

"This Madden," he says. "You know him?"

"Sure. He's good. Very good. And he's not so keen on doctors."

"What do you mean?"

"There was an article about a year ago in the *Mercury*. I'll have to dig it up for you. Did you say anything to him?"

"Too much I'm afraid. Look, can I come talk to you? Or can you refer me to someone? I need to get the ball rolling here."

"Now?"

"Yeah. Or soon. Over the weekend. I've got to get someone by Monday."

Silence again. He hears her flip the page on her calendar. "What are you doing tomorrow?" she asks. "Say, around ten?"

He looks at Klein. They're supposed to play tennis at eleven. "Nothing," he says. "That's fine. Where do you want me to meet you?"

"Where else? Your favorite."

"The Creamery?"

"Why not?"

"I'll be there," he says. "Ten."

"Looking forward to it."

"I'm sure you are."

Cogan hangs up. After he does he puts his elbows on his desk and covers his face with his hands.

"You OK?" Klein asks.

"Yeah," he says, rubbing his eyes. "Do me a favor. Don't tell Kim why I can't make tennis. I'll talk to Reinhart tonight." Then, after a beat: "I'm sorry, man. I'm really sorry."

20/ Probable cause

<u>April 3, 2007—a.m. 10:06</u>

The next morning Cogan awakes weary and anxious after a night of the worst kind of sleep. He'd gone to bed early, around eleven, and though his body was exhausted his mind was full of energy, and it kept waking him even when his body had shut down. Once, he thought he'd slept several hours, but he looked at the clock and it only read twelve-thirty. He'd slept twenty minutes. Finally, at two, he turned on the television, and gradually drifted away to a roundtable of talking heads rehashing the political crisis *du jour*, only to wake again for good at six-thirty.

It begins raining around eight. The gray dreariness of the day seems completely appropriate, a sign of his plight, and when he looks outside all he can do is shake his head and say, "Just perfect." But as dismal as the day seems, all is not totally bleak. Due to the poor weather, the usually crowded Peninsula Creamery in downtown Palo Alto is only half full, and he's able to secure a booth in his favorite spot, near the window—a positive omen, he thinks.

Aggressively quaint yet thoroughly modern, Palo Alto's picturesque downtown is a small grid eleven blocks long and five wide that contains everything from fast-food joints to trendy eateries with French and Italian names to boutiques and art galleries. Trees line the streets and parking can be hard to find, especially on weekends when University Avenue, the city's main drag, gets an influx of out-of-towners dropping in on their way to and from Stanford Shopping Center, the other nearby shopping mecca.

Carolyn arrives fifteen minutes later. He looks up from his coffee and newspaper and there she is, standing over him, smiling, a small wet umbrella held out away from her jeans, dripping.

"Hello, Ted."

They look at each other a moment, each seeming to gauge how the other has faired against time.

"Hello, Carolyn," he says, getting up and kissing her on the cheek.

Whenever he runs into an old girlfriend he always wonders why he'd broken it off with her. Invariably, she seems attractive, and usually more attractive than he remembered. For a brief moment he forgets about all the things that had bothered him and returns to that initial impression he had—that initial thing that had attracted him in the first place.

Carolyn *is* attractive. She has a dark Mediterranean complexion and dark, fine hair that she tends to wear up in a bun, like she's wearing it now, with strands left hanging over her ears and a few over her forehead. Her eyes, also brown, are a little too small for her face, and she borders on taking too much sun, but he always liked how she put herself together. She tries to present a restrained, conservative image, but there are hints of a wilder, more passionate side that becomes even more apparent with a few drinks. He'd always thought she was sexiest when she was a little sloppy, when everything wasn't quite tucked in and her hair was tousled. He couldn't think of anybody who could wear a run in her stocking better.

They'd stopped seeing each other for a basic, mundane reason: he'd been unwilling to go to the next level, whatever that was. She'd broken it off with him, but he'd convinced himself that she'd really been bluffing and that he could have had her back if he'd made the effort. And he might have (or so he told himself) had her timing been better.

Sometime during their fifth month of dating she called him at work and asked him to come over that evening "to talk." He could tell from the tone of her voice that she was in action mode. Things weren't going exactly as she wanted them to go and now she was determined to right the course or abandon it altogether. The problem was he hadn't gotten much sleep over the previous week. He'd been working on a difficult case—a patient was boxing on him after a lung operation—and trauma had been unusually busy. So he asked her whether she could hold off for a couple of days until he was less stressed and more clear-headed. But she insisted they talk, she had her mind set, and they ended up breaking up over the phone.

"I'm not sure it's a good idea we see each other anymore," she said after he pressed her to reveal what she wanted to talk about. "I just don't think this is going anywhere, Ted. What do you think?"

"Let's just do it," he said. "Let's just get it over with."

They saw each other again, of course. They'd even slept together. But he could never forgive her for that day—he couldn't bring himself to forgive her for being so thoughtless. Maybe it was just an excuse. That's what Trish had said. But even if it was an excuse, he thought it was a good excuse.

Looking at her now, he still thinks it was a good excuse, but it takes him longer to remember. How old is she? They'd dated two and a half years ago, so that would make her what, thirty-four or thirty-five? Holding up well, he thinks. He wants to compliment her, but at the same time, doesn't want her to get the wrong impression. He decides on a perfunctory tone: "You look great—as usual."

Her reply is equally perfunctory. "Thanks," she says, angling into the booth across from him. "Here comes the waitress. I'm dying for a coffee."

* * *

They order; she takes an omelet, he the bagel and lox platter. Another server pours them coffee from a retro, silver coffee pot—a touch for which The Creamery, a 50s-style diner that has an Art Deco-meets-techno veneer, is known. Everything in the place seems to be either steel colored or black, except for the servers' t-shirts and the napkins, both of which are white. Empty, the room may have seemed cold and sterile, much like the trauma room. But filled with people the coldness is replaced by a sort of hip casualness. It's a place where you feel you can say profound things in a few words, effortlessly. That's what he'd once told Reinhart anyway. And on other days, under different circumstances, he might have been effortless. But today he finds himself laboring uncomfortably as he sets out to tell Carolyn what had led him to call her yesterday in a panic.

He starts from the beginning—from the time the girl came into the hospital—to the time the detectives showed up. She listens to him almost without commenting. Every so often she asks him to clarify something. She has a little trouble at first telling Kristen and Carrie apart, and it doesn't help that he's a little loose with his pronouns. But aside from a few interjections, she doesn't challenge him and reserves her judgment, even when he tells her he let the girl spend the night at his house. She just nods, takes a sip of orange juice, and goes back to eating.

After he finishes, there's a short silence. Then she says: "Why would the girl write and then tell her friend that she had sex with you, when she didn't? And why would the friend say she saw you having sex?"

He can't tell from her tone whether she believes him or finds his story hard to believe, and it bothers him that he can't.

"I have no idea," he says.

"In all your dealings with her, she seemed like a nice,

sane, stable sixteen-year-old girl?"

"Except for being accident-prone, yeah."

She nods. "You said she was attractive."

"She was."

"How attractive?"

He thinks about it for a second, forgetting both the animosity and sadness he has for the girl. "On a scale of one to ten she was about an eight, though she didn't think so. But if she'd decided to stick around, she would have been a knockout by senior year." His eyes become emotional with the thought. "I know she would have. I know these things."

The waitress comes. Carolyn doesn't say anything as she clears their plates. She just sits there, observing him. He can't tell what she's thinking. But she's wearing one of those *Well, I see you haven't changed* grins. *I see the same old Ted is alive and well.* And she seems glad he is. But then she remembers why they are here—or he thinks she does—and the smile fades and she suddenly says, "Oh, I have something for you. You should see this." She reaches into the back pocket of her jeans and fishes out a folded-up piece of paper.

The *San Jose Mercury* had done an article on the detective who'd come to see him, Henry Madden. "Handicap Doesn't Slow Detective in Race to Catch Criminals," the headline reads. It's an actual photocopy of the article, not something that had been pulled from the Internet or Lexis-Nexis, the research service.

"Look on the second page," she says. There, at the top, she'd highlighted a certain paragraph. Half-mumbling, he reads it aloud:

"When asked why he was drawn to detective work, Madden reveals that his motive is partially personal. As a boy, while being treated for polio, a physician sexually abused him. He says that he was unable to confront the truth for many years, until he confided in a fellow officer who was working on a similar case. He regrets not saying anything earlier, for it could have prevented the physician, who was only brought to justice when Madden was in college, from abusing other patients."

"Jesus," Cogan says after skimming the rest of the piece. "The guy's doing his therapy in the papers. What did people think of this when it came out?"

"In my office?"

"In general."

"I don't know. I think it was part of the department's attempt to give cops a human face. It was a few months after those Hispanic kids got beat up in Redwood City. People looked at it pretty cynically. But Madden's for real. He's a decent guy. Well respected."

He shakes his head, lost to a sudden rush of anxiety. "I'm done, Carolyn," he says morosely. "I'm fucked. The guy's clearly got a nasty chip on his shoulder for docs. I saw it in his eyes when he was interviewing me. He's tried and convicted me already."

She looks at him sympathetically—the first sympathetic look she'd given him the whole meal. She reaches out and takes his wrist and says, "Look, these cases are very difficult to prove. Yes, it's unfortunate they have an eyewitness. But that's far from a slam dunk."

"No bullshit." His tone is more confrontational than he intends it to be, but he's nervous. It makes her pull back. "If you were a doctor," he goes on, "what would you tell me? What would my prognosis be?"

She lets out a defensive laugh.

"I'm serious," he says.

"I'm sorry. Do you want me to use medical terms?"

"Use whatever terms you'd like."

She pauses and takes a breath. She appears as uneager to answer the question as he was uneager to ask it. "Well, from what you've told me, it looks like they have probable cause."

"Meaning?"

"They can arrest you."

"Why haven't they already?"

She explains that they could have. But it's possible they're gathering evidence for a grand-jury hearing. If they can get a grand jury to indict him, they can arrest and indict him at the same time. In some cases, they arrest the defendant, then go to the grand jury. But in delicate cases like this, prosecutors often go to a grand jury first to see whether they can get an indictment before arresting. If they can get one, it also means that the defendant won't be allowed to testify at his grand jury hearing.

She says that as a former prosecutor, that's how she'd proceed. "I wouldn't want you speaking before the grand jury—a respectable, well-spoken guy who's saved a lot of lives and is an upstanding citizen. It'd be a risk."

"So where does that leave me?" Cogan asks, not quite sure whose side she's on.

"I don't think they're going to arrest you in the next couple of days. They clearly don't want to make it appear that they knew they were going to arrest you when they went to see you at your office."

She explains that if they'd gone to his office, asked some questions, then arrested him, whatever he said could be thrown out in court. "I'd argue that, knowing they were going to arrest you, they should have read you your rights immediately."

"And now?"

"Now I could still argue that your remarks should be thrown out. But at least the detectives could say they hadn't gone to your office to arrest you; they'd gone just to question you. My bigger concern is that they're trying to build a murder case against you."

He stares at her, knowing he's heard her correctly but wishing he hadn't. "Murder? Why? Because I told her I couldn't speak to her anymore?"

"No. That in and of itself wouldn't be a crime. It's very

difficult to hold another person accountable for someone else's suicide. Even if you'd been nasty to her on the phone and said she was fat and unattractive and that she had no reason for living."

"Then what?"

"Well, the exception might be if you'd committed a crime previously that had impacted her. There's something called foreseeable harm. You may not have intended to cause her to commit suicide, but by sleeping with an underage girl, the law says you knowingly inflicted an emotional injury. And if it could be proven that initial injury led to her suicide, you could end up with a manslaughter charge. You'd probably be looking at two-to-five."

"You're serious? That could happen?"

She nods. "That's probably what Madden's after."

"Earlier, you said, 'I would argue.' Does that mean you want to represent me?"

She sits back in her chair, a look of anguish crossing her face. At first, she seems ready to say no, but then she bites her lip nervously and he knows she's in. "If you want," she says, "I'll take it—in the beginning, anyway. I'll make some inquiries, and we can see where things stand. I'll do that as a friend. But only if you want me to."

"Really, you'd represent me?"

She seems almost embarrassed. "What's wrong with that?"

"Nothing. I'm just surprised. Surprised in a good way."

"It's an interesting case. I think any criminal lawyer would want to take it."

"I'm not questioning your motivation."

"If I had some strange illness that was in your area of expertise, you'd help me, wouldn't you?"

"I'd do what I could. And if I didn't think I could handle it, I'd get the best person I knew to handle it."

"Just my point," she says.

He doesn't respond. He looks down and his eyes drift to

the check, which the waitress has placed closer to him. He wonders how much this all is going to cost. Not the lunch, but the attorney fees. At least if Carolyn represents him, he thinks, his money, or part of it anyway, will go to someone he knows. Two and a half years ago, he'd been at Bloomingdales's in the Stanford Shopping Center debating whether to spring for the two-hundred-dollar perfume ensemble or the four-hundred-dollar gold necklace for her birthday. And now he's looking at handing her firm fifty grand, probably more. Go figure.

When he looks up again, she's staring at him over her coffee mug. She's holding it in both hands, taking little sips. He stares back at her, not liking her confidence. It can only mean one thing: she's taken.

"Are you seeing someone?" he asks.

"Yes."

"Nice guy?"

"I think so."

"What will he—" Cogan stops himself.

"What will he what?"

"Nothing."

He was going to ask what her boyfriend would think if he knew that she was going to represent him. But then he thought better of it. He didn't want to give her the pleasure of answering.

"I should tell you something else," he says.

"What?"

"I was close to taking another job."

"Really?" She seems mildly surprised. "At which hospital?"

"Not at a hospital. At a venture-capital firm. A big one. The company has a number of biotech holdings. We'd just started talking numbers."

Now she's genuinely shocked—so much so that she doesn't seem to know quite what to say. "God, I remember you talking about doing some consulting. I mean, you were going to . . . but I didn't think—"

"Well, that's what I wanted to do—dip my toe in the water before I made the big leap. But they want a full-time guy."

"And you were close?"

"They made an offer. An attractive one."

"I don't know what to say, Ted. I'm sorry."

He smiles and shakes his head. "You know, it's funny. Business is all about risk and gain. Medicine is all about taking the safest course of action. They're such different worlds. A businessman knows risk and knows he can lose or gain in a huge way. In medicine, if there's a complication or a problem, you're often asked by your peers, 'Why did you do that? That was clearly the riskiest path to take.' The mental set is completely different. In medicine, you're chastised for taking the riskier path. But in business, if you're a risk taker, you can really score."

"Or really lose," she says.

"Well, yes. But mistakes aren't so frowned upon. They come with the territory."

After he finishes talking, he looks her in the eyes, almost daring her to say something about why he'd let those kids into his home that night. *Why had he taken that risk? Where was the possible gain there?* He wants to explain to her that back then, he didn't feel he had anything to lose. There was no new job sitting on the table that night. There was nothing.

She stares back, that faint smile of hers hovering ever so slightly on her lips. This time he doesn't like it. It's one of those smiles that an older woman bestows on a younger man when she's charmed by his innocence. He hadn't minded seeing it in his twenties, and even his early thirties, but now it only grates on him.

"So, when do you think they'll arrest me?"

"I don't know," she says. "But the important thing is that you remain calm when they show up, especially if they do it at the hospital. Don't say anything. I'm going to give you all my numbers. You can always page me. If I can't come right away, I'll have somebody else come."

He nods, clenching his jaw, suddenly reminded of the blunt Chinese doctor, Dr. Liu, who told people they were going to die. He looks out the window of the restaurant, depressed. Outside, it's still pouring, and there's a BMW sitting at a stoplight, its windshield wipers going full blast. With each swipe of the wipers, he hears the good doctor's voice. *You have lung cancer, you are going to die. You have lung cancer, you are going to die.* The blades are like metronomes.

21/ Blue Ford

April 11, 2007—p.m. 6:03

Two Wednesdays later, around six, standing at the kitchen window, Cogan notices a patrol car cruise past the house. It slows, and as it does, his chest tightens. When it doesn't stop, he breathes a sigh of relief and tells himself he's being paranoid, a patrol car usually checks the neighborhood twice a day—once in the morning and once late in the afternoon. But twenty minutes later, when the unmarked blue Ford sedan pulls up in front of his house, he has a sinking feeling his paranoia is justified.

Breathlessly, he watches Madden and his partner get out of the car. They're in no hurry. They stand for a moment next to the car and straighten their ties. Then they head slowly up the walkway to his front door.

The doorbell rings.

He knows what to expect when he opens the door, but for some reason when he finally does, his eyes open wide. He looks at the detectives as if they're complete strangers, even aliens.

"Dr. Cogan," Madden says. "Sorry to disturb you. But I'm afraid you're going to have to come down to the station with us. We have a warrant for your arrest. You've been charged with rape in the third degree and you should know that anything you say can and will be used against you . . ."

And so it is, just as he'd imagined it would be only no one's watching. He'd somehow expected a small crowd. Or the disbelieving stares of doctors and nurses as they led him out of the hospital. For that he's thankful: that they'd spared him the embarrassment and come here, not the hospital. The only person to see him leave his house that day with the detectives is a little girl who's out riding her new bike. And she doesn't even know what's happening.

"Hi, Dr. Cogan," she calls out to him gleefully, as she usually does.

"Hi, Katie," he calls back.

He doesn't think of it then, but later, when they're a few blocks from the station, he realizes that he was about her age the last time he'd taken a ride in the back of a cop car. It had been almost thirty years.

Back then, he'd cried, afraid of what his father would do to him when he found out he was a shoplifter.

Now he wishes his father were still alive to punish him.

PART 3

DISCOVERY

22/ Social logical

Excerpts from the diary of Kristen Kroiter:

Jan. 16

So Carrie finally did it! She went up to Josh Stein and talked to him. She's been talking about it for weeks but she never knew what to say. We'd be right about to go up to him but then she'd say, What am I going to say? And I'd be like I don't know. Just say something. And she'd be like I can't just say anything. And we'd go back and forth like that and afterwards we'd just laugh and feel really stupid because he and his friends are such dweebs.

Anyway, today at lunch we walked over to their little area on the outskirts of The Green and pretended to get a drink of water at the drinking fountain. Ever since the principal closed the parking lot during lunch, most kids eat in the grassy area in front of the library at the center of campus (the rich kids with cars used to hang out in the parking lot, I'm not kidding). Our school's kind of messed up because it's really two schools in one since around 70% are minorities from East Menlo Park and Redwood City, and the other 30% are from well off families from Atherton, Menlo Park, and Portola Valley, and the principal's always thinking up new ways to try to integrate everybody better. My brother and sister both went to private schools, but when we moved and got the bigger house, my Dad said he was "tapped out" and didn't have enough money to send me private. That was OK, though, I didn't want to go to an all-girls school like Castilleja and I can walk to school from where we live (can you say sleep in!).

Anyway, Josh and his friends sit on this bench in one corner of The Green. They're what you'd call a little fringe. So they're sitting there with this laptop, talking, and I don't think they noticed us at first, and Carrie just looked over their shoulders and saw something sort of strange on the screen. There were all these names. And she was like what are you guys doing? And they turned all red and got defensive and tried to cover up the screen.

They wouldn't show her at first, but then she leaned forward and showed them her boobs. I'm not kidding! Carrie's got pretty big boobs and she's always wearing V-cut T-shirts, so guys are always trying to look down her shirt. And I know she does it on purpose. She admitted it. And it was pretty funny because as soon as she leaned over their laptop I saw Josh's and the other kids' eyes go right to her boobs and it wasn't long before they were showing her what they were doing. Guys are so lame. Of course they were like you've got to promise not to tell anyone. They made us swear on our parents' lives, which I thought was pretty melodramatic until I saw what they were doing. I do admit it's cool. They've got a list of every kid's name in the school, like 2500 kids, and they've written a program whereby they can rank people by how popular they are. I'm not kidding. Then you can click on a button and a map of the school pops up and they've plotted where everybody hangs out at during lunch. Our bench is on there! And so are Carrie and me and Megan and Viv. You can click on a person's name and all this information comes up on them. And get this, I'm higher on the list than Carrie, which really pissed her off. I mean I think it's only like 10 places, but I'm ahead. I'm 92 and she's 97. Not bad, I must say.

She didn't want to show she was mad, but you could definitely tell she was. She was like, why do you think this is accurate? And Josh was like, it's not totally accurate right now. They were still in beta, which means the program and the list aren't final.

Carrie saw that as the perfect opportunity she was looking for. She was like, don't you guys think you should have some feminine input? She said she had to go, but she wanted to discuss it more with them in private, and asked Josh if we could come over to his house tomorrow after school. He was so surprised he didn't know what to say. He and his friends just looked at each other. I wonder what they expect. The whole thing's pretty stupid. She knows she's not going to do anything. She wouldn't know what to say to Dr. Cogan if she saw him. I know she wouldn't.

Jan. 21

Was beat the last few days so I didn't get a chance to write. Anyway, the real news is we went over to Josh's a couple of days ago to talk about the list. His house is actually really nice and so is his Mom, which kind of made me feel bad for him. I mean, I hope Carrie doesn't get too Machiavellian with him. He's basically a good kid, though he does stare at her boobs too much.

Carrie really wanted to discuss how people got rated. She actually said to me on the way over that they actually might have something interesting, and that she really wasn't going over just to find out where Dr. Cogan lived. Personally, I think she just wants to figure out what will get her higher on the list when it comes out.

The way it works is there are all these variables they assign numbers to. Where you hang out. Who you hook up with. Whether you have a car or not. What kind it is.

Whether you play sports. And then there are some more subjective ones. Like your looks and personality and that kind of stuff. That's how everything gets calculated.

At first Carrie was like, what makes you guys judge and jury? And they were like, because we did all the work, which was hard for her to disagree with. The truth is I think they're actually pretty accurate. But the thing that would bother me is the people on the bottom of the list. I mean, I'd feel bad for them. It would suck to find out you're a total loser. What if someone committed suicide over it or something. I don't know if I could deal with that kind of responsibility. Josh says they're going to put a disclaimer at the top of the list, you know, how this list should have no reflection on who you are as a person. And then they're going to put some names of famous people who were losers in high school. They're also going to say something good about each person.

Anyway, we stayed there a couple of hours discussing all the variables and a bunch of scenarios and frankly it wasn't as painful as I thought it would be. I almost totally forgot why we'd really gone there. And I think Carrie sort of forgot until she saw Dr. Cogan's car in the driveway next door. He was home! And then we got into Carrie's car and she started driving really slow past his house. And we looked into the window, and I was like, OH MY GOD there he is. And Carrie just freaked. I mean she almost peeled out. She was like, Oh my God, did he see us? Did he see us? And we were all squealing and laughing. What a joke. It was really juvenile. Really, really, juvenile. But kind of fun.

Jan. 27

Nothing much to report except that Carrie got a new phone. It's one of those Sidekicks with the built-in keyboard. It's really cute and I'm really jealous. Viv got one too, and now they send like these novels to each other instead of the shorthand texts we used to send. Like if we were going to meet at 7-Eleven, we'd just put in 7118, which meant we'd meet at 7-Eleven at 8. But now they're like, "Let's meet at 711 at 8 and what are you going to wear?" It sort of takes the fun out of it. Because the code was kind of fun. But this way's definitely better. Carrie's working on a new word code, so in case one of the guys grabs her phone during class or something, there won't be anything too incriminating. That could be totally dangerous.

I want one so bad but Dad won't let me have one. He's like you lost three phones already (I'm such a klutz sometimes, I swear), and this one costs more than just a standard phone. He said, if you want one so badly then pay for it yourself. He's been such a tightass lately. Since the accident he's definitely worse. I swear, he still thinks I was drunk. I just want to say, you know Dad, your problems aren't mine. Ever since Mom found out he had an affair, he's been on this saint kick.

He's trying to get me to join this church group, which would suck. There aren't even any cute guys in the group. They're such dorks, except for maybe Paul Germain, but he goes out with Ashley Vachs anyway. I'm hoping that if I just go to church every other week, he won't make me join.

I don't know. When I went every week, he didn't let me go to the lake with Carrie, which was so unfair. So I've stopped going certain weeks. He gives me grief each time, but I told him I wouldn't go at all if he kept making me, I don't care if I get grounded. He never used to make Mary and Rick go when they were my age, so why should I go. I told him that I thought that was pretty good that I was going every other week. And when I told Mary about it, she was like he's a lot easier than he was on me when I was a junior. Her curfew was 10. And I was like big deal, one hour difference. He gets on my case about so many other things. The point is he's different now than when she and Rick were still living here. He's like so much more Mr. Family Values it makes me sick.

In a way, when he and Mom were arguing it was better. It was like at least I knew where things stood. Now it all seems sort of phony. Them holding hands all the time. They never used to hold hands.

Sometimes I swear Carrie's lucky her parents are divorced. Her father's so much cooler about stuff. He talks to her like she's a person. And even if her mother's always waiting up for her, at least she doesn't freak if she's late. She's just like call if you're going to be late. That's why I gave you a cell phone. If I call, Dad's like get your ass home now, young lady.

God, I'm getting whiny! I hate being a whiner. I hate whiners, for that matter. It's getting late, so I have to go to sleep. Carrie called earlier to ask my advice about whether to tell Josh about Dr. Cogan having operated on me. I don't think Dr. Cogan ever said anything to Josh or else he probably would have said something. I'm not sure what telling him would do. I mean, what difference does it make? What's Josh going to say to Dr. Cogan. I think this girl in my class wants you, do you want her back? Some plan she's got. She's like maybe he'll take me out to dinner up in the city. He can't do it around here. But no one would know who she is up in the city. And people wouldn't know that she's almost 17.

She's living in a total fantasy world. I wish he'd just shoot her down and get it over with. That would teach her a lesson.

Feb. 4

Newsflash! We spoke to Dr. Cogan! Well, I actually did most of the talking because Carrie couldn't really speak. We went over to Josh's around two on Saturday. The plan was we'd drive by the house a few times and see if Dr. Cogan was home, and then, if he wasn't we wouldn't even bother checking if Josh was home. That was Carrie's genius plan anyway. Well, when we drove by to make the first pass, Dr. Cogan was standing outside talking to this other guy! As usual, Carrie was all freaked. She was like Oh, my God, Oh my God, what should we do. And she didn't stop! And I was like what are you doing, pull over and park. And she was like what are we going to say? I said, I don't know we'll just say something (I just wanted to get the whole thing over with, frankly she's such a big talker, I wanted to see what she'd really do).

Well, we went around the block and he was still there, talking, I don't think he'd noticed us go by the first time. And we parked across the street, half across from his house, half across from Josh's house. And I swear Carrie was trying to hide her face when she got out of the car. It was pretty funny. I wanted to see her squirm some more so I looked directly at Dr. Cogan and started crossing the street. He had this strange look on his face, like he recognized me but he didn't.

And I just walked right up and said hi, I don't know if you remember me but I'm Kristen Kroiter, you operated on me. And he was like, oh, yeah, how are you doing, is everything feeling all right? And then he turned to his friend and explained to him the whole story about how I'd been in this car accident and that I'd had to have a splenectomy. And he said, I was one of the "good" patients, though I'm not sure quite what that meant. And then he asked me whether my Dad had gotten me another car. He remembered all that stuff! I was totally surprised.

And I was like remember my friend, Carrie, she came to see me a few times in the hospital. And he smiled (what a great smile he has!), and he was like, sure. And that was like Carrie's big opportunity (yeah, right) but she didn't say anything. I swear I saw her turning red. Well, there was this little awkward silence, and I jumped in and said we actually stopped by to see if Josh was in. And he was like, so you took my advice. And I was like, huh? And he told his friend how we'd been talking about how Josh and his friends were geeky but that he said Josh and his friends would be rich studs in like 10 years and how we should be nice to them.

And his friend laughed. He was like geeks rule the world, especially around here. And then Carrie said Josh had this cool computer program he was working on, like a sociallogical experiment. The funny thing was she didn't say sociological (I looked it up in the dictionary), she actually said "social logical," which it kind of is in a way, but Dr. Cogan was like social logical, that sounds very scientific. And Carrie realized what she'd said and got all embarrassed.

So that was our big encounter. Afterwards, we went over to Josh's and checked if he was home (he wasn't, which was good, because Carrie was in a bad mood and she would have been mean). We had to go straight to the mall, where Carrie got this new pair of jeans (I swear her butt's getting bigger!).

Feb. 10

Another lame Saturday night. Just got back from The Creamery, which is like this faux diner that's been around forever. I swear sometimes I'd just rather sit home and watch a DVD (I just got two new movies—Wedding Crashers and Election. I could watch both of them like once a month, no problem). It's like the same thing every weekend. Carrie heard a rumor there was a party up in the hills, in Portola Valley, but she didn't have an exact address, and we spent like half an hour trying to find it. It's dark as hell up there, too. There are no streetlights. And by the time we got there we had like 15 minutes before the cops came. Usually, parties at houses in the hills take longer to break up, but it was just our luck that it didn't. So our next choice was either downtown Palo Alto or Café Barrone. I would have preferred going to Barrone and just getting some coffee, but there's this guy Carrie kind of likes that was going to The Creamery, so we went there instead. The thing about the Creamery is all the lame younger guys are there early, but the cooler people show up later since it's like the last stop. But by that time we have to leave, so what's the point? It's OK, I guess, it's not like the diner in Diner (I love that movie), even though it sort of tries to be.

Supposedly, in a couple weeks we're going to a Stanford party. Carrie's brother is going to take us, which should be pretty cool. Carrie's convinced she's going to date a college guy. Someone who can take her out to dinner, she says. I get the feeling she's losing interest in Dr. Cogan, which I knew she would. Lately, all she's been talking about is Eddie Bauer guy. That's this Eddie Bauer salesman at the mall who goes to junior college. I do admit he's pretty cute and Carrie claims she's going to set up a double date for us, though I told her I'm not going until I see the other guy.

On the way back from The Creamery, we were talking about who we'd lose it with, like what our ideal scenario would be. And I was like would you consider losing it with Eddie Bauer guy? And Carrie was like it depended, she might. She wants to lose it with an experienced guy. And I was like I'd rather lose it with a guy who was losing it with me, too. She was like, yeah, that might be OK, but she thought it would be better to do it with someone who knew what he was doing. It could really suck if he didn't know what he was doing. And if it really sucked it might give you a bad view of sex for a long time, and she didn't want to have a bad view of it. She'd talked to her cousin, who just graduated from college, and that's what she advised.

But I was like you want it to mean something, don't you? I mean what if you were just like another notch on some guy's bedpost. How would that make you feel?

As long as it was good, she said it didn't bother her that much. She said in a way she just wants to get it out of the way. I don't believe her, though. I mean, technically I have more experience than she does. I took a shower with a guy (she, of course, says it was totally innocent, and it was, but I did it). But the point is she doesn't have any experience to base her judgments on, so how's she supposed to know?

Feb. 11

You're not going to believe this, but I totally ran into Dr. Cogan at Stanford Shopping Center this afternoon. Carrie was over at Eddie Bauer talking to Eddie Bauer guy, and it wasn't as if I even existed, so I told her I was going over to the music store and to meet me there when she was through.

The store's really small and I walked up to this listening post, where this guy was standing, and when he turned around I realized it was Dr. Cogan. I was so surprised I didn't know what to say. I don't think he knew what to say either. He looked just as surprised. And I was like "hey." And he said hey back only he said it kind of loud cause he had the headphones on. I couldn't believe it, but he was listening to Maroon 5! I'm not kidding! That's the first thing I asked him when he took off his headphones. I was like, hey, what are you listening to? And he pointed to the button for Maroon 5, and I was like really, that's what I was coming over here to listen to. And he was like, it's decent, better than he thought it would be. And then we got into this whole discussion about bands that had great first albums but couldn't follow up with good second albums. He was totally knowledgeable. And then he was like, can you recommend anything, I need some new knife music. He plays music while he operates. I thought that was so cool. Knife music. I asked him who his favorite is to operate to. He said it depended on his mood and the type of operation. And sometimes he'd switch in the middle if it wasn't going the way he wanted it to.

And then he asked me about my DVD collection! He totally remembered! I was like, I can't believe you remember. And he said that he remembers everything, which is sort of a problem. And I was like, do you have a photographic memory? And he said, no, he didn't, he just had a very good memory. He never forgot a face.

We must have talked for like 15 minutes. He asked me what colleges I was looking into. I told him my brother was at Dartmouth and that my sister had gone to UCLA, but I hadn't decided whether I wanted to go East or not. And he was like you seem very smart, if your grades are good, you should consider going to school back East. He said I would definitely fit in there. I'd do well, which kind of surprised me. I was like, why, what makes you think that?

He said he could just tell that I wanted more from life and that I wanted to expand my horizons. He could tell that I didn't think California was all that it was cracked up to be, that it somehow made me feel uncomfortable.

I didn't know what to say. It was like he was reading my mind. I didn't tell him that of course. I just said, yeah, I was definitely thinking about the East because I was getting pretty bored here and SoCal didn't seem like an alternative even though most of my friends wanted to go to UCLA or Santa Barbara. Carrie totally wants to go to UCLA, though I'm not sure she'll get in. I personally think she'll end up at San Diego. That's her second choice. Dr. Cogan went to Yale. I told him I didn't think I had the grades to get in there, but my grades are pretty good, I'm in the top 10 of my class.

Anyway, I asked him why he was in California if he liked the East Coast better. And he was like, there's a mindset you have to go along with here. He was like everybody's into this quality of life stuff, it's first and foremost in everybody's mind, they're in such pursuit of it that they forget sometimes to really live. And he was like, I'm into it sometimes and sometimes I'm not. I totally agreed.

Anyway, Carrie finally showed up and she was in serious

shock when she saw who I was talking to. It was pretty funny. After Dr. Cogan left, she gave me a full grilling. And I was like, it was no big deal, he's a really nice guy (I wonder why he isn't married!?!). He plays Depeche Mode, Postal Service, and The Killers while he's operating. I don't know if I should have told her that, because all of a sudden she forgot about Eddie Bauer guy and all she could talk about was Dr. Cogan. She was like, did he say anything about me? And I was like, yeah, he asked me where my partner in crime was. And I was like she's over talking to Eddie Bauer guy. And she was like, you didn't. She was totally ready to hit me. And I was like, don't worry, I just said you were looking at some clothes in a store. As if it would matter!

Feb. 15

I started jogging again. Lately, I've been feeling kind of tired and blue in the afternoons, and I thought it might be because I'm not getting enough exercise. Last year I was playing a lot more tennis and swimming sometimes when it was warm. Of course as soon as I told Carrie I was going to start jogging again (I'm totally slow, which is why I call it jogging) she wanted to go with me which I'm not that into because I prefer to run with my iPod on and just kind of zone out. I don't need her babbling, although sometimes it does make it less painful when you run with someone. She did admit that her ass was getting fat, which I give her props for. She was totally down on herself yesterday. I think Eddie Bauer guy was supposed to call her but he didn't. The truth is I kind of like her better when she's a little down. She's a little more real. She's definitely my best friend but sometimes she gets on my nerves.

Dad said I could stay over at her house this Saturday as long as I got all my chores done and I finished my homework. He seems in a better mood these days because he got some big account which is going to make him a boatload. He definitely hasn't been as hard on me. But what sucks is he's talking about going to the Maroon 5 concert with us. I don't know if he's joking or not. He knows I have an extra ticket because I put them on the credit card. I was like are you for real? And he was like what's the problem I've taken you to a concert before. But that was when I was like 14 I said. Well, he said, since I'm paying for the tickets I can go if I want. I didn't really argue with him because I was more concerned about trying to stay over at Carrie's because of the party. So I didn't want to push it. God, it's one hurdle after another. My life. I swear.

23/ The quadfecta

May 1, 2007—p.m. 2:33

Three weeks after Cogan's arrest, Madden finds himself at The Dutch Goose in West Menlo Park, sitting in a booth with Pastorini to his left and Dick Crowley, the San Mateo County District Attorney, facing them across the table. It's about two-thirty, and the lunch crowd is mostly gone, leaving them with the place largely to themselves. They've all already eaten elsewhere, but The Goose, as it's more commonly known, along with the similarly grubby Oasis Beer Garden on El Camino, are the unofficial conference centers for law-enforcement officials, the place where they like to do their heavy meditation—ideally during Happy Hour, of course.

Though not much of a drinker himself, Madden has been a patron of the saloon from its early days. Part of its charm is that little has changed in the nearly forty years since its opening, including its menu, which features deviled eggs, steamed clams, burgers, of course, and pitchers of Anchor Steam beer. With its single pool table, two pinball machines, and jukebox in the back, thick wooden, butcher-block dining tables riddled with patrons' carvings, peanut shell–covered floors, and long wooden bar in front, the place has a classic hole-in-the-wall ambience that is in many ways the antithesis of the tidy, more pretentious yuppie restaurant/bars like The

Blue Chalk Café, Gordon Biersch, and Nola's, in downtown Palo Alto. And despite attracting the unavoidable assortment of young professionals and preppy college kids (it's long been a favorite watering hole for the Stanford football squad, with John Elway counted among those booted for disorderly conduct), The Goose draws a strong blue-collar contingent. Many, like Madden, are locals who've grown up in the area.

"What do you think, Hank?" Crowley asks, "She got it?"

The *it* Crowley is talking about is a combination of poise, gumption, consistency, and vulnerability—his ideal qualities in any witness involved in a sexual assault case. "The Quadfecta," he sometimes calls it.

"You saw her at the grand jury hearing," Pastorini answers for him. "She was composed. She presented sympathetically."

Pastorini and Madden have an understanding. Until Madden has something pertinent to add to the discussion, it's Pastorini's ball to drop, which he rarely does because he generally pitches it the moment he gets it.

"But she wasn't terribly descriptive. Yeses and noes are OK—to a point. She's got to tell a story. And is she going to be able to tell it in front of him?"

"Gut?"

Crowley nods.

"Hank?" Pastorini cues him.

"She'll do fine on the direct," he says, "But she'll need to be coached hard for the cross. She has a little bit of a flair for the dramatic. She should be OK, though."

Crowley doesn't respond immediately. Tall and lanky with big features and a full head of sandy brown hair that's flecked at the temples with gray, he towers over the table. Affable and outgoing, he has large hands that seem made for basketball, and indeed he played college ball for Cal in the late 70s. By his own admission, he was hardly a gifted player, a walk-on who cracked the starting five his senior year by coming earlier to practice and staying later than anyone.

However, the story isn't as inspiring as one would hope, for the team, hit by a rash of injuries, finished near the bottom of the conference that year. But that hasn't stopped Crowley from drawing parallels between his athletic and Madden's law-enforcement career. "I wasn't handicapped," he once remarked with the best of intentions. "But damn if I didn't *feel* handicapped."

At first glance, he doesn't appear to be a gifted prosecutor either. He's not a slick orator and his direct examination is often not the taut, tight line it should be; it meanders from lane to lane like a DUI on 280 late at night. As unpolished as he seems at times, he does bring a certain charm to the delivery that makes it seem deliberate, even overwrought, as if he's an actor warming up the jury for the real Dick Crowley, who will drop in when it really counts. And he usually does—he always seems to execute beautifully at critical junctures.

In the ten years they've known each other, Madden has observed him enough—and in enough different capacities—to think he has a handle on him. In his estimation, Crowley's a keen manipulator who's cultivated a persona that's unpredictable, contradictory (he's a part owner of the Country Sun Natural Foods store on California Avenue in Palo Alto yet he's regularly spotted at fast-food joints), self-deprecating, and easy to underestimate. "Well, that was lucky," is a favorite expression, yet most everybody's figured out that luck has little to do with his triumphs. What Madden finds intriguing—and he can't help admiring Crowley for it—is that even though most folks claim to have a handle on him, he still manages to keep them off balance. Madden thinks it's because they're always looking in the rear-view mirror, trying to anticipate when Crowley's going to flip the turbo boost, and they fail to concentrate on their own driving.

All that said, the Kroiter case has made him anxious—mainly, Madden thinks, because he sees too much room for luck, good and bad. Outside of getting a confession, so far most everything has gone their way, which is also making him a little nervous. The high point was three weeks ago, hours before Cogan's arrest, when tests came back on the three tiny semen stains they found in the crotch area of a pair of light green hospital scrub pants Madden had found tucked in the back of a drawer in Kristen's bureau. Cogan had given Kristen the scrubs to sleep in that night and she'd worn them home. The semen's DNA matched Cogan's.

In recent days, however, after Madden suggested that, upon further reflection, "The stains seem a little high in the crotch area, closer to the fly," Crowley's buoyancy has eroded a bit. Because of how minute both the semen and the girl's DNA sample (from a urine specimen), the defense will likely get an expert witness to testify that the discharge could simply have been "leakage" from the defendant and very well could have been present prior to that evening.

Crowley also doesn't love that he has a witness who's admitted to drinking alcohol that night. Though she didn't drink much, the defense would assuredly argue her memory was compromised. All these "intangibles," as he refers to anything open to interpretation, are contributing to Crowley's plaintiveness this afternoon. He stares down at the table, running a finger over the deep groove of the letter N, which someone presumably named Nick B. has carved into the table.

"Kristen was pretty, right?" he finally asks. "But nothing remarkable."

Madden would prefer not to discuss her looks, but he doesn't like the throwaway tone of Crowley's remark. He's underestimating her.

"I'm not sure about that," he ventures.

"Not sure about what?"

"That she was so unremarkable."

"Fair enough," Crowley says. "But is she the type of girl a jury will take one look at and say, yeah, we understand why this guy took the risk he did? We understand his temptation."

Madden pictures a juror sitting in the jurors' box, studying her photos and the video clips the DA's office would carefully produce. First, he's a male juror in the second row, then a female in the front row, center. Then he pictures himself in the box.

"One look, maybe not," he answers. "But eventually, yeah." He pauses a moment, then permits himself to add: "There's something very alluring about her. It's subtle. Do you remember that girl in your school who was pretty but hadn't been corrupted by popularity yet?"

Crowley smiles. "We called them catch-them-while-you-cans."

The comment is punctuated by a loud gurgling sound—Pastorini, sucking hard on a straw, is trying to bring up the last vestiges of Diet Coke from a bed of ice in a pint glass. Crowley shoots him a glance, cutting the quest short, but the dissonance is enough to throw him from his train of thought.

"What was I saying?" he asks.

"Catch them while you can," Pastorini parrots back, eager to redeem himself.

"Cans. Plural. I can live with that. But get me an ex-girlfriend, a one-night stand, his ex-wife—I don't care—to confirm what the girl said in that diary about the man's sexual proclivity."

"We're working on it," Pastorini assures him.

"I need it, boys."

"And Ms. Dupuy?" Madden asks, curious to know what lengths Crowley is willing to go to win.

"Ah yes, Ms. Dupuy. Our very hands-on defense attorney."

"Technically, she's on the list."

"I know," Crowley says. "How long did they date?"

"About five months. Going back a couple of years ago."

The DA shakes his head. Madden reads like he's talking

about a promising pupil who's inexplicably fallen in with the wrong crowd—and he's not quite sure what to do about it.

"Well, let's see how she behaves."

"You ever encounter something like this?" Pastorini asks.

"Like what?"

"Like an ex-girlfriend defending a guy in a rape case."

"Not that I'm aware of."

"Us neither. We were discussing it the other day, Hank and I. If you were him, would you have her defend you?"

Crowley thinks about it.

"You're asking the wrong question, Pete. The question is, would I have taken the case if I were her?"

"Well, both ways, I guess."

"She's a good lawyer," he says, as if that should explain not only her but also Cogan's choice. "I bet she's out there right now doing her best to dismantle all Hank's fine work."

"She's over at the university, conducting interviews," confirms Madden while contemplating the sturdiness—and trustworthiness—of his structure of the case. It's a building designed to look good from the outside, he thinks. Will anybody notice that the foundation's shoddy, the materials second-rate?

"We got a good head start," Crowley continues, "but the gap is going to quickly close. Perkins isn't going to give them everything, but she's going to give them something."

Joyce Perkins is the judge, and while she's generally a moderate with a slight liberal bent, she's been less protective of defendants' rights in rape cases. She's handled the diary cautiously, deferring to Crowley's request—ergo delay tactic—to keep it sealed and out of the defense's hands until she's permitted herself enough time to thoroughly analyze its contents.

Crowley believes she'll allow certain passages to be admitted, which would seem to bolster their case. However, he's justifiably worried that contradictions will arise when everybody starts to compare passages in the diary with deposition and live testimony.

Sitting there, his eye drifting down to a "Go Niners" carving in the table, Madden knows Crowley would like to have the most relevant and damaging passages read aloud in court.

"I wasn't sure what I should be doing," he envisages one of the young ADA's, or maybe even Carrie, reading from the diary, speaking softly so that everybody in the courtroom has to lean forward in their seats to catch everything she's saying. "So I said, 'Fuck me. Fuck me like you mean it,' because I'd once seen a woman do that in a movie."

"What is it, Hank?"

He looks up and sees Crowley, a look of concern on his face, staring at him.

"Nothing," he says. "Nothing important."

24/ *Like* like her

May 1, 2007—p.m. 2:46

"So you're standing outside the bathroom on the third floor," the lawyer asks. "Let's go back a minute."

"OK," Jim says.

"How long were you waiting for Kristen to come out?"

"I don't know. Maybe five minutes. And then I started to get concerned."

"And you knocked on the door?"

"Yeah, I knocked a few times. And like I said, I called to her."

"Pretty loud, right?"

"Yeah."

"Loud enough so that anybody would hear you?"

"Yeah, I mean, I wasn't shouting. But it was loud."

"So, why didn't you just go in? It isn't a hard door to open. It swings out. I tried it. Why didn't you just go in?"

Jim shrugs, glances at the microcassette recorder sitting on the table between them, and says, "I don't know. Like I told the detective, it just didn't seem right, going into the occupied bathroom. And then this girl I knew—Gwen Dayton —was coming up the stairs and I just asked her whether she could check."

The woman doesn't respond. Instead, with her perfectly manicured fingers, she tears off a small piece of bread from her half-eaten sandwich and tosses the crumbs to a blackbird that's looking up at her beseechingly from the ground, his head cocked to one side. *For an older woman, she's definitely hot*, he thinks. When he first saw her, thin with dark hair and olive skin, a well put-together woman who was wearing a navy blue pantsuit, he thought she could be a TV lawyer. Usually, he's nervous around good-looking women, but the idea of her being an actress puts him at ease, for it makes the interview seem less real. That, plus the four bong hits he'd done with his friend Dan Fleischman before he headed over to the meeting.

A brilliant, sunny day, they're sitting outside, in the plaza that's around back of Tressider Student Union, which serves, among other functions, as the home for a cafeteria, café, convenience store, arcade, barber shop, and a row of Wells Fargo ATM machines. Just past two-thirty, many of the black, wire-mesh weather-resistant tables and chairs, once filled with students during the lunch hours, now sit empty. But that hasn't deterred the scavengers—a couple dozen blackbirds and a handful of pigeons, which seem out of place among their suburban cousins—from making the rounds.

"At one point I left to find Carrie," he volunteers. "She was dancing with some guy. And I pulled her off the dance floor and told her that Kristen had passed out in the bathroom upstairs and that we had to get her out of there."

When they got up to the bathroom, he says, Kristen had been revived. Well, revived might be too strong a word. But she wasn't totally passed out. Her eyes would flutter open for a moment and she would mumble something.

"Did you hear what she said?" the lawyer asks.

"I know she said 'Leave me alone' a couple of times. And I think she said, 'I'll be all right in a minute.' "

"That's it?"

"It was hard to understand her. I mean, she was slurring her words and then she would nod off and Gwen was slapping her in the face. Not hard or anything. But, you know, just trying to keep her awake."

The woman breaks off another piece of bread and tosses it to the ground.

"Did you like Kristen, Jim?"

"How do you mean?"

"Did you like her?"

Another shrug. *How come they always ask the same questions?*

"*Like* like her?" His tone isn't defensive; he's not affronted. Rather, it sounds as if he's questioning himself and is genuinely curious to know the answer. "I mean she was nice," he continues, his voice steady. "I enjoyed talking to her. But she was my sister's friend. I'd known her for a long time. Since she was, like, ten. I felt responsible for her."

Looking down at the table, he shakes his head solemnly. "I mean, sometimes I think I'm to blame for everything that happened. If I'd just watched what she was drinking or made sure she ate more. I don't know."

"And you never thought of her in a sexual manner? You never looked over and said to yourself, 'Gee, she's kind of cute, I wouldn't mind fooling around with her'?"

"She may have been attractive, but I didn't think of her in a sexual manner," he explains, shifting his by-now-familiar introspective gear up a notch. "You just get to thinking about someone in a certain way. I mean, to me she was little Kristen, my sister's friend."

The lawyer looks away, silent a moment. Then, leaning forward, staring him down, she speaks in a low voice, as if letting him in on a secret. "A couple of witnesses have said they didn't see you for half an hour, Jim. How do you account for that?"

His jaw tightens. He hears C. J. Watkins's voice. *Vigorous defensive, Mr. P. When they come at you, you come right back. Firm but not angry. Got it?*

"What are you implying?"

"You're walking upstairs with a drunk girl. She's hammered. And you're pretty sloshed yourself—"

"It was a party," he says. "There are lots of people at parties. If someone didn't see me for thirty minutes, it doesn't mean I wasn't at the party. I could have been standing fifteen feet away from them and they might not know. Or I could have been outside with another girl."

"Jim, my client has spent nearly his entire adult life either studying to be a doctor or practicing as one."

"I'm aware of that."

"So if you're not telling me about something that happened, or something you may have heard happened, that would be very unfair to Dr. Cogan, wouldn't it?"

"Yes, it would."

In a gesture that's as deliberate as her bread tossing, he props his elbows up on the table and folds his hands in front of his mouth. He doesn't know whom he hates more, C. J. Watkins or the doctor.

"But what if nothing happened?" he says. "What if your client was drunk himself—hammered—and took advantage of a young girl's condition to have his way with her?"

She smiles and, without missing a beat, says, "What if you tell me about Kathy Jorgenson."

"What about her?"

"You said you were out back with her."

"I didn't say her specifically. I said 'another' girl—in the generic sense."

"But you were out back with her."

"Why, what'd she tell you?"

"That she went out back with you."

"OK, I was out back with Kathy Jorgenson. Yes, I admit it. And I regret it at the same time."

"Why don't you tell me how you ended up *out back* with Kathy Jorgenson."

"Well, it's kind of a long story."

"I've got time."

"I kind of figured you did."

25/ Sloppy kisses

May 1, 2007

It goes like this, he says. A few weeks before the party at the frat, he'd hooked up with a girl at a small birthday party in his dorm. She'd wanted to get stoned so he dug up a bong and some herb from a guy who lived down the hall, and took her back to his room.

Her name was Becky Goffman, and she wasn't bad, a little heavy but cute. Not that he thought that he was so hot, but normally he wouldn't have gone for her except for the fact that, with all the decent frosh girls being snapped up by upperclassmen, the first semester had been nearly a total bust on the female front—and this one wasn't shaping up any better.

In high school, he'd been a respectable athlete, he explains. Not one of the school's best, but he'd played on the varsity baseball team for two years, starting his senior year at second base. During his senior year, he'd grown almost two inches. But much to his consternation, the trend hadn't continued, and the only thing that had grown this year—and ironically, the exact inch he longed for—was his waist, he says, patting his stomach. All the drinking during the pledge period, which had seemed to last forever, had crept up on him. He'd seen it in the mirror that afternoon. His face was rounder than he had remembered it. Not bloated, but his jawlines had lost some of their cut.

So he decided to get stoned and see what would happen with Becky Goffman. Soon, they were making out. Their kisses were sloppy at first, but gradually they became tighter and more refined. Then a strange thing happened when he got her pants off. Her body went rigid—a tension enveloped it—and she stopped responding to his kisses.

"What's the matter?" he asked. "Are you a virgin or something?"

He said it half-jokingly, but when he got no answer, an alarm went off in his head.

"Are you?"

Again, silence. When she finally spoke, her voice was quiet, practically a whisper. "Would it be bad if I was?"

My God, he thought. "No, it's not bad. It's just something to take into consideration."

They lay next to each other, cramped in his single bed, staring up at the ceiling. Then Becky said: "We can do it if you want."

"I didn't do it," he tells the lawyer. "I didn't think it was fair because I knew I didn't want to date her. But here's the fucked up thing."

About two weeks later he found out Becky Goffman had slept with another guy, an upperclassman, the weekend after he'd fooled around with her. He doesn't tell the lawyer that guy was none other than C. J. Watkins, but he does say that his friend Stan Chen told him this upperclassman "fucked her and then supposedly called her a fat pig."

He was angry with Becky Goffman. If she'd given him the choice that night, he'd have slept with her. If she'd just said, "If you don't fuck me, I'm going to go out and fuck fill-in-the-blank dude." He might have blown her off afterward, but at least he would have been nice about it.

The lawyer flashes an impatient look.

"I'm sorry, am I making you uncomfortable?" he asks. "Am I being too personal?"

"Not at all," she says. "I'd just like to know what this has to do with you and Kathy Jorgenson?"

"I'm getting there. I just need you to know where I was at—what my mind-set was, Ms. Dupuy. That's how you say your name, right? *Doo-pwee*?"

The real party was a few days later, on Saturday, February 17. Like he said, Carrie and Kristen came around 4:30, just as the North Carolina game was about to tip off. At one point during the game, Kristen asked to use the bathroom, and he showed her where it was. And it was there, in a little alcove on the second floor, after she came out of the bathroom (not the bathroom she ended up passing out in, he stops to point out), that they had their one serious conversation of the night. He remembered them looking at some old photos of fraternity brothers that were framed on the wall. There were pictures all around the house. There, in the alcove, they were from the mid-70s.

She looked at the set from 1976 and said, "Someday you'll be on one of these walls, Jim. And in the middle of a party in like 2030 a couple of girls will walk up to your picture and say, 'Gee, that guy was pretty cute, I wonder what he's doing now. I wonder if he's bald and fat.' Do you ever think about that?"

He laughed. "Not really."

"I think about that stuff all the time. I'm always trying to guess what people will look like in twenty or thirty years. It'd be cool if you could just press a button and see for just a second what people looked like when they were a lot older. You know, your whole perspective of that person might change."

He wanted to ask her what she thought he might look like in twenty years, but then he thought of his father and got worried he wouldn't like her answer. His father wasn't fat, but he was definitely overweight and his hair was definitely receding.

"Carrie told me about your accident," he said, changing the subject. "She said you almost died."

"I *could* have died," she corrected him, enunciating her words carefully. "I didn't almost die. You know how dramatic Carrie can be."

"Even so, did it change the way you look at things at all?"

She shrugged. "Like am I more cautious? Like do I live every day like it's my last?"

"Yeah, I guess."

"No," she said, before pausing to think about it harder—or at least she seemed to be thinking about it harder. "I guess it just made me realize how boring things are around here. It was kind of exciting in a way. You want to see my scar?"

"OK."

The next thing he knew she'd hiked her shirt up a little and peeled back the top of her skirt. The whole thing caught him off guard and he wasn't quite sure how to react. He didn't want to stare, so he tried to avert his eyes at first, but then he realized he was supposed to look, so he did.

Jim says, "I didn't know whether she was showing me the scar because she saw me as an old friend or whether it was her way of flirting. But I think she was just comfortable. We were having a nice friendly conversation."

"Yeah, can you believe they got my whole spleen out through there?"

"It's pretty small," he said.

Just down the hall there was an open window, and he could hear girls' voices outside. He went to the window and looked down. Some girls from a nearby sorority, PiFis, had showed up for the pre-party barbecue. There, in the middle of the group, was Gwen Dayton.

Kristen came up behind him and looked over his shoulder.

"Who're those girls?" she asked.

"Them?" For a brief instant, he pictured Gwen twenty years older. He pushed the button and there she was coming out of the Macy's at Stanford Shopping Center, two children in tow, a boy and a girl, dark-haired and perfect. She was still beautiful but there was something completely average about her, and she knew it and hated it. He could see it in her eyes, that little shade of self-loathing.

"They're the bane of my existence," he said.

Gwen Dayton was a junior, one of those unpretentious tall, thin girls with long dark hair who reminded him a little of the actress Liv Tyler. Gwen had seen him during some of his difficult drunken moments and would always stop by at parties and say hello and ask how he was doing and how the guys were treating him. She was the only really attractive girl who was nice to him. No, not nice. Gwen was kind, and her kindness was genuine. When she asked him how it was going, she really wanted to know, and would listen attentively as he told her.

She dated Mark Weiss, the frat president. And maybe it was because she was unattainable that he felt so comfortable around her. She knew he had a crush on her, but she hadn't ever given him the cold shoulder or tried to pawn him off on someone else—until that night, anyway, with Kathy Jorgenson. At first, he thought it was just by chance that they'd come over together. But then he realized there was a purpose to the visit. Gwen was trying to set him up.

The thing was, he really didn't like Kathy Jorgenson. She was a thin mousey girl who wore her hair short and had slightly masculine features. He could've written her off as unattractive, but it was more complicated than that. He and his dorm-mate, a rail of a guy named Dan Fleischman who wore an earring and a buzz cut that made you think heroin-chic (though he'd tried nothing harder than Ecstasy), had a name for her precarious place in the looks hierarchy. She was residually attractive—a *rezi*. What that meant was that if you saw her alone you wouldn't give her a second glance. But since she managed to hang out with a group of good-looking girls, she appeared to be more attractive—their looks rubbed off on her.

She knew it, too. He and Fleischman had once scoped her out at a party, and they both made the same observation: The more "babe rays" she absorbed the more confident she became. They were her social Viagra. And she seemed to be getting a good dose of it standing next to Gwen.

"They still got you working, Jimmy?" Gwen asked.

"*They* don't have me working," he said, looking up from the job he was doing—pouring a bag of ice over a tub of beer. The girls weren't exactly twins, but they were both wearing jeans and t-shirts and had light sweaters wrapped around their waists. "Your boyfriend's got me working. It's a singular thing."

Weiss, the frat president, was a senior and would graduate this year. With any luck he'd go live someplace far, far away.

"We just came by to say hello," said Gwen. "Do you know Kathy?"

"Yeah." He half-extended a hand, which was wet. "I'd shake your hand, but I don't think you'd want to shake mine."

Kathy didn't say anything. She just flashed him a demure smile, which he felt under his skin. *My God*, he thought, *she* is *trying to set me up*, and in a moment of panic, he announced unexpectedly: "I'll have you know I've temporarily sworn off women, all forms of them."

"Going gay, are we?" Kathy said. "Don't think you're the first."

"I'm not going gay. I'm just taking a break."

Kathy made a face. "What's the matter, can't hack us?"

His usual urge was to go on the defensive. But today he

felt some potential in continuing on a self-deprecating tack.

"I'm just no good at it."

Gwen smiled. "Why don't I believe you?"

"Don't be fooled by the positive attitude."

That got a laugh out of Kathy, which, as much as he didn't like her, made him gush with pride. He was on a roll. The only thing to do now was to get out before he stalled.

"I'm going to check on the punch situation," he said. "Do you guys want any?"

"I'll take one," said Gwen.

Jim pointed at Kathy. "You?"

"Nothing right now, thanks. But maybe later."

He looked at his watch. It was seven-thirty. "Just be aware that my indentured servitude contract runs out in an hour."

"Right about when you stop giving up on women," said Kathy.

"You watch."

"I'm watching," she said.

So was C. J. Watkins. But Jim doesn't tell the lawyer that. He skips that part. *This part.*

"That's not for you, is it?" Watkins said.

Jim turned around from getting a cup of punch and there he was, standing there with a beer. Watkins wasn't looking at him, though. He had his back to him and was facing the small group who'd gathered around the barbecue, where Mark Garland, the resident chef, was cooking chicken and burgers. Jim glanced to his left, then his right—maybe Watkins had intended his comments for someone else. But there was nobody nearby.

"No," Jim said. "Gwen wanted one."

"G. D.," Watkins said. "I wonder what her middle name is. If it were say Olivia, her initials would be G. O. D. You ever ask her what her middle name is, Mr. P.?"

No, Jim hadn't. It had never occurred to him to ask her.

"Well, you want to know what I'd do if I liked her so much?"

"Ask her?"

"No. I'd nail her friend, that little butch chick that digs you."

"How do you know she digs me?"

Watkins looked at him for the first time. "Because I see everything, Mr. P. I can take one look around a room—or in this case, this poor excuse for a backyard—and I know what's going down. Just like Gretzky used to do on the ice. The world moves in slow motion for those guys. They know where everybody is. Got eyes in the back of their heads. It's the same for me."

"And just what sort of sport would you be playing?"

"The sport of sport fucking, sport," said Watkins.

Jim laughed. He always promised himself he wouldn't laugh, but there he was laughing again at something Watkins had said.

He couldn't help provoking him a little. "Got anybody in your sights?"

Watkins took a sip of beer then ran his hand through his dirty-blond hair, which was short on the sides but longer in front. A few strands always seemed to be hanging down, dangling in his eyes. It was a stylish, model's cut, but it required a lot of finger combing. Jim wouldn't have been able to stand it.

"I ain't playing yet," Watkins said. "This is just warm-ups. The skate-around. But I sense your need for guidance."

"I'm hopeless."

"I'm inclined to agree. But we are all not without a certain potential. Vitamin supplement?"

He extended a hand. Cupped in his palm was a small white and blue marble-colored pill, most likely an amphetamine, because that's what Watkins mostly ran in, though Jim had heard he could get anything—from X to crystal meth to Special K.

"Thanks, but I took my Flintstones this morning."

"Yabba dabba doo," Watkins said, and popped the pill in his mouth.

Jim knew that other C. J. Watkinses existed in the world. But he never thought he could exist—and even thrive—at a prestigious institution of higher learning such as Stanford. At a big state school, maybe. But here, it seemed absurd.

He wasn't quite sure why people tolerated Watkins, but Jim suspected it was because he had a certain undeniable charm and that his observations had a certain logic to them. That he was also good looking and had a perfectly sculpted body didn't seem to hurt either.

He reminded Jim of the disarmingly lecherous character Matthew McConaughey played in the movie *Dazed and Confused.* The movie had been a favorite among Jim and his high school friends. For almost a full year they'd recited lines from it whenever they were together. At parties, the movie's dialog was a kind of an internal code for the group. When one of them had had some success with one of the younger girls—a freshman or sophomore—he'd come back and say, "That's what I like about high school girls. I get older and they stay the same age." That was McConaughey's signature line in the movie.

Looking back on those days, Jim cringes. Their whole *Dazed and Confused* phase seemed lame, but even today he still admires the McConaughey character. The thing that had left the biggest impression on him was how comfortable that guy seemed to feel with himself. He hadn't gone to college. He had some menial job working for the city. And there he was, forever hitting on high school girls, and totally at ease with it.

Jim suspected that was C. J. Watkins's secret, too. Watkins had that same charm, that same ease, and that same twinkle in his blue eyes when he spoke, so when he said something inappropriate, it didn't come out sounding as bad as if someone else had said it.

"Could I alert you to one small impediment?" Jim said.

"I'm listening."

"I don't like Kathy Jorgenson."

"Weight problem?"

"No."

"Because if that's an issue I'll understand," said Watkins. "For a lot of guys it's an issue."

"She's not fat. She's just all full of herself for no reason."

"Sounds like a weight problem to me."

Jim laughed. Watkins was right. It *was* a weight problem. But he didn't know whether Watkins had meant it like that all along or not.

"Exteriors," Watkins went on before Jim could say anything. "Facades. Pay no attention. Inside there's a scared little girl who's incredibly insecure. Your job is to tap into that and expose it to the harsh glare of the male ego."

Beer in one hand, Watkins held his hands out in front of his face and cringed, pretending to cower to the heavens. He let out a little high-pitched scream, then laughed. Jim thought he was insane.

"And what's the point of that?"

"Right now you're a little boy. A harmless little boy. You're all nice and polite and sensitive, and when Miss Gwen Daytona 500 over there asked you to get her a cocktail, you looked like a twitch you zipped over here so fast." Watkins made his eye twitch several times.

"She didn't ask me. I asked her."

"Whatever you say. But you're a little boy to the 500. Why? Because of your inability to deliver pain."

Jim laughed. It sounded like something a football coach would say. *Son, you got to hit the man with authority. Let 'em know you're there.* The only difference was you didn't get to wear pads in the game Watkins was talking about.

"She's got a boyfriend," Jim said, looking for an exit ramp.

"He's a dick."

"He's our president."

"He's *your* president. No one presides over me."

Jim didn't say anything. He didn't know quite what to say. He'd never heard anybody rip Weiss that way, even though he'd done it himself on many occasions under his breath. Weiss was a decent enough guy, but he could be a borderline anus when it came time to participate in one of his "projects."

"The edge, Mr. P.," Watkins said out of the side of his mouth, turning his gaze once again upon the barbecue crowd. "Wouldn't you like to know what it's like to be sharp to the touch—a finely tuned instrument capable of giving yet taking?"

"Is that healthy?"

"The little butch chick."

"What should I do?"

"Go deliver your drink. I'll observe. Then report back to me in twenty."

"That's it?"

"For now."

"Then what happens?"

"We hone, Mr. P. And then we hone some more."

Jim says to Carolyn Dupuy: At around ten, at the height of the party, he told Kathy Jorgenson he needed some air, and asked her if she wanted to go outside for a few minutes.

He was going to call Gwen on her bluff. In a delusional moment, he thought he'd show her—show her just what she was missing. And in the back of his mind, after the whole Becky Goffman experience, he thought *If I'm not going to do it, someone else will.*

"Hey, I could use some fresh oxygen," he said. He was pretty cool about it. Real nonchalant. "I'm gonna step outside. Why don't you step with me?""

She said, sure, that'd be good. She needed some air herself.

He led her to the bench that flanked the frat's small basketball court, which was at the back end of the backyard in the shadows. He got his arm around her all right, but when he went to kiss her, she didn't return it, and flashed him this like-what-are-you-doing look. And then she said, "What are you doing?" And he said, "What does it look like I'm doing?" And she said: "I'm not going to kiss you in public, Jim."

He looked around. There were some people mingling around the back entrance, but he didn't think they could really see them from where they were standing. And he was pretty happy they couldn't.

"What's the big deal?" he said a little sloppily. He wasn't slurring his words, but he didn't exactly have complete control over them either. "No one can see us. And even if they could, they couldn't tell who we are."

"It's just a rule I have," she said.

"Well, let's go somewhere more private."

"I don't think so."

"Why not?"

"It's not on the agenda."

"Sorry, I didn't realize there was an agenda."

She smiled. "Don't be sorry." Her tone was almost mocking. "You're drunk anyway."

That set him off. "Not drunk enough to know you're lame. Not drunk enough to realize I didn't really want to do this."

He went back into the party. He saw them talking a few minutes later on, Gwen and Kathy. And then Gwen gave him a real dirty look. It was real wrath, and he'd never seen it before and it upset him. Not long after that he helped Kristen get up to the bathroom.

"If you want to know the truth, Ms. Dupuy," he says, "as much as I feel bad for what happened to Kristen that night, what really bothered me the next day was how badly I blew it with Gwen. First I'm a dick to her friend, then she finds me with a half passed-out high-school chick in the bathroom. She hasn't really talked to me since that night. And I don't blame her."

He pauses. Then, when Ms. Dupuy doesn't say anything, he says: "Anyway, that's how I ended up out back with Kathy Jorgenson."

26/ Who's the PI?

May 7, 2007—p.m. 1:30

About a week after the Crowley meeting, the DA's office sends over a packet containing two hours of voice recordings on microcassette and the transcript of the interviews Carolyn Dupuy conducted that afternoon at the university. Affixed to the top sheet is a yellow Post-It from the ADA that reads: "FYI, Hank. Let me know what you think."

A lot of what's there he's already heard, but, expectedly, each of the witnesses has embellished a little—or in the case of Jim, embarked on a long, detailed digression. No shocker, part of Dupuy's strategy is to raise ambiguities and strengthen assertions that Kristen was impaired at the party and plenty of opportunity was available for others to take advantage of her condition. The object is not to shift the blame but to shift the accountability. Her client may be on trial, but a lot of other people have some explaining to do, including Carrie. To cast doubt, she's going to prosecute each of them.

After a first read and listen (he skims the printed transcript and only consults the tape when it becomes necessary to further scrutinize select passages) he can't decide whether Jim's latest testimonial should bother him. He hadn't heard the backstory about the freshman in his dorm, but he knew about Kathy Jorgenson and the rendezvous "out back." Rereading the interview, he suspects Jim simply told the story to portray himself in a more favorable light. Though his voice dips into impatience at times, he mostly speaks in a confessional tone that, according to Billings' flash judgment, suggests the kid really "opened up" to the "babe."

As much as he'd like to dismiss the comment as an obnoxious jab, Madden knows Billings is probably right: Carolyn Dupuy has a hormonal advantage with frat boys like Jim. He can reconcile himself with that explanation for Jim's loquaciousness, but more vexing is the interview with Gwen Dayton, the college girl who ended up driving Kristen and Carrie from the party to Cogan's house.

She'd been forthright and descriptive with him. As an objective third party, he thought after interviewing her that she'd make a persuasive witness. And while he still thinks she will, he's perturbed that she seemed more animated under Dupuy's questioning and provided a couple of important extra details. He feels a pang or two of jealousy before arriving at the heartening conclusion that Dayton's revelations might actually end up hurting Cogan.

Ms. Dayton: "I told Kristen she had two choices. She could say that what she wrote in her diary was a fictional fantasy and deny that anything ever happened. Or she could say that what she wrote really happened."

Ms. Dupuy: "And how did she respond?"

Ms. Dayton: "Well, she didn't seem comfortable with either choice. She just wanted everybody to leave her alone. But ultimately she was more unwilling to say it didn't happen."

Ms. Dupuy: "Why did she come to you in the first place?"

Ms. Dayton: "Well, after that night—you know after we took her over to Dr. Cogan's house—I talked to her a few times to check how she was doing and whether everything was all right. And then she called me up one day—I guess it was about a month after the party—and told me what happened and that she needed someone to talk to."

Ms. Dupuy: "And in those times right after that night did she mention anything to you about having sex with Dr. Cogan?"

Ms. Dayton: "Not specifically. But she mentioned an older guy she'd hooked up with. She'd been trying to talk to him and he was blowing her off."

Ms. Dupuy: "In what context was she telling you this?"

Ms. Dayton: "Well, she was kind of asking for my advice. She did it in a hypothetical way. You know, what would you do if such and such happened?"

Ms. Dupuy: "And what did you say *you'd* do?"

Ms. Dayton: "Well, I don't really believe in forcing the issue. If someone doesn't want to talk to you, there isn't much you can do about it. I told her to be patient. She's a pretty girl. She's going to have lots of guys in her life. If this guy was worried he was going to lose his job by being in contact with her, that was a legitimate concern and she had to respect that."

Ms. Dupuy: "But it would have been pretty crappy if he slept with her knowing that he was going to blow her off?"

Ms. Dayton: "Well, not so much shitty. But pretty stupid."

Ms. Dupuy: "So, when you were there, in Dr. Cogan's house, did he do anything that might be perceived in any way as being inappropriate toward Kristen?"

Ms. Dayton: "No. I mean, he did a real basic examination. Just some stuff with her eyes, and mainly he was asking her a lot of questions. He was most worried that she'd done some other drugs. You know, whether someone had slipped her a roofie or LSD or something."

Ms. Dupuy: "But you said you smelled alcohol on his breath?"

Ms. Dayton: "Yeah, there was no doubt he'd been drinking. I think he even said at one point that he'd had a few cocktails himself that night."

Ms. Dupuy: "But he seemed in control as far as you could tell?"

Ms. Dayton: "Yeah. He was actually very calm. You know, Carrie was basically hysterical. She was all, 'Oh my God, I'm in so much trouble! I can't believe this is happening.' And at one point, he just told her to go sit in the living room and watch TV."

Ms. Dupuy: "And where were you?"

Ms. Dayton: "We were in the backyard, walking Kristen back and forth on the lawn. We'd do a few laps, then we'd get her to drink some water."

Ms. Dupuy: "But you didn't see Dr. Cogan give her any pills or inject her with anything?"

Ms. Dayton: "No. When she finally seemed semi-coherent, he gave her a glass of Alka Seltzer. And a spoonful of honey. He actually did the same for himself. He said that was his hangover medicine."

Ms. Dupuy: "What time was this?"

Ms. Dayton: "I'm not sure. Around one, I think."

Ms. Dupuy: "How long had you been there?"

Ms. Dayton: "About an hour, I guess."

Ms. Dupuy: "And then what happened?"

Ms. Dayton: "Well, I went back to campus."

Ms. Dupuy: "But you didn't take Kristen or Carrie?"

Ms. Dayton: "No, Kristen was asleep. And Carrie was going to stay on the couch. She said her mother was waiting up and she asked Dr. Cogan whether her brother could come pick them up in the morning. They would leave early, she promised."

Ms. Dupuy: "Where was Kristen at this point?"

Ms. Dayton: "She was already in the guest room. She went to the bathroom and when she came out she just curled up on the bed and fell asleep."

Ms. Dupuy: "Can you remember what she was wearing?"

Ms. Dayton: "What do you mean?"

Ms. Dupuy: "Did she go to sleep in the same clothes she came in?"

Ms. Dayton: "No, I think she had on some hospital pants. He gave them to her. As pajamas."

Ms. Dupuy: "But she seemed OK before that?"

Ms. Dayton: "Yeah, she was OK—relatively speaking."

Ms. Dupuy: "And Dr. Cogan agreed right away to let her stay there?"

Ms. Dayton: "He didn't put up a huge fight. I think he was tired, too. And Carrie was getting on his nerves. You know, her voice can be irritating."

Ms. Dupuy: "And then you left?"

Ms. Dayton: "Yeah."

Ms. Dupuy: "And how long was it before you spoke to her again?"

Ms. Dayton: "Two days later, I guess. Or three. I think it was a Tuesday."

What followed was a brief rehashing of when and how many times Dayton spoke with Kristen. It was hard for Gwen to determine exactly on which day each conversation took place, and they tried to narrow it down with "memory markers"—other events that took place on or near the same days. Then Carolyn's tone shifted a bit. Her voice turned louder, more pronounced on the tape. She said:

Ms. Dupuy: "I realize you're not an attorney, Gwen. So please don't take this the wrong way. I'm not judging what you did. I'm just trying to understand where this girl was coming from."

Ms. Dayton: "No, I understand."

Ms. Dupuy: "Well, what I want to know is, as you're giving Kristen some of this advice—I guess some of it from that friend of yours at the law school? As you're giving her this advice, did anybody say, 'Hey, by going down this path, you're opening a very harsh can of worms. This doctor is going to hire an attorney and that attorney is going to come after you with everything she's got, psychologists, medical experts, private investigators, anybody she can find who can help discredit your story'?"

Ms. Dayton: "I didn't say it exactly like that. But I certainly indicated that it wasn't going to be pretty. It's funny, my friend predicted Dr. Cogan would hire a woman attorney."

Ms. Dupuy: "Well, I wouldn't read too much into it. I'm not sure how calculated a move hiring me was."

Ms. Dayton: "I just mean it'd probably play better to—"

Ms. Dupuy: "Did you ever ask yourself whether Kristen might be lying?"

Silence on the tape. The abruptness of the question seemed to startle Dayton. After a moment, she said:

Ms. Dayton: "I did. I wasn't sure why she would, though. She seemed fairly levelheaded. Not like some girls. That's why I was so shocked when I found out she killed herself."

Ms. Dupuy: "But none of Dr. Cogan's actions during the time you spent with him would indicate that he was interested sexually in Kristen?"

Ms. Dayton: "Not to sound conceited, but the impression I got was that he was into me."

Ms. Dupuy: "What gave you that idea?"

Ms. Dayton: "Well, you know, I just got that vibe."

Ms. Dupuy: "Did he come onto you?"

Was Gwen blushing? Damn if he isn't, just listening.

Ms. Dayton: "Not exactly."

Ms. Dupuy: "Then what?"

Ms. Dayton: "Well, he asked me for my phone number."

Carolyn's turn to give pause.

Ms. Dupuy: "Did you give it to him?"

Ms. Dayton: "Yeah. I did, actually."

Ms. Dupuy: "And did he call you?"

Ms. Dayton: "No. No, he didn't. I did tell him I had a boyfriend, though."

Madden rewinds the tape and listens to the exchange again, wondering whether it might alter someone's impression of Cogan. Dupuy can argue that he was more interested in the Dayton girl (and, yes, the moment she takes the stand the jury will understand why he was interested). But Crowley would come back and say, look, the guy's a notorious hound dog, he's going to go after what's in front of him. The college girl leaves, look who's left.

Madden can't figure how Dupuy's going to make that little piece of information he'd failed to elicit work to her advantage. *Does she regret going at Dayton as hard as she did?* he wonders, and just then he hears Burns's voice behind him.

"Hey, Hank."

Madden swivels his desk chair around.

"Hey. How's the action on the other side of the freeway?"

"Little Ike and Tina," Burns says. "Wife says the husband stole a bunch of her stuff and raped her. They've been separated—or not, depending on who you talk to."

"Lovely."

"That the Kroiter case?" Burns asks, nodding in the direction of the transcript.

"Yeah. Dupuy's interview with that college gal."

"I got something for you there."

Madden eyes brighten. "The travel agent talk?"

"Sure. Just like the teacher. She admitted they'd had a relationship, but clammed right up when I mentioned the s-word. Refused to get into details, even after I hinted at a potential subpoena."

"Damn. Don't any of these women know it's healthy to hold a grudge?"

"There'll be one. There's always one. In the meantime, check this out."

Burns's hands him a sheet of paper. It's a call report.

"I got a call a little while ago from the admin I usually speak to at the Planned Parenthood," Burns says.

Someone was asking questions down there yesterday, on Sunday, he explains. A guy was inquiring whether a sixteen-year-old girl had been spotted coming through there close to two months ago. He had a printout with pictures of the girl. One of the photos was the same picture of Kristen Burns had showed the admin last month. The guy was perfectly nice, but after a day of mulling it over, she decided to notify the police as a precaution.

"Who's the PI?" Madden asks.

"Yeah, that's what I thought, too. But the thing is, the guy said he was a doctor and was checking on a former patient. He showed a Parkview Hospital ID. From the description, he sounded a lot like your boy, so I emailed over a photo and, sure enough, she ID'd him. It's your boy."

Madden stares at the sheet, which cites the administrator's name, time she called, and notes Burns had taken from the call.

"What's he up to?" Madden says, thinking aloud.

"Maybe he got bored, sitting home pitching tennis balls into his garage all day."

"Maybe. You did Planned Parenthood, right? This is Planned Parenthood?"

"Yeah, you did the free clinic."

"Can you do me a favor?"

"I checked already. No calls from anyone at the clinic."

Madden smiles. "You're a good man."

"It's a curse."

He turns to leave, but Madden stops him.

"Burns?"

"What?"

"He's not my boy."

"Figure of speech, man."

"He's not."

Now it's Burns's turn to smile. "Whatever you say, Hank."

27/ The writing exercise

Two days earlier (May 5)—p.m. 3:56

The first things that come to mind when a defendant shows up at a Planned Parenthood asking questions about his accuser are that he's a) too cheap to hire a private investigator, or b) got too much time on his hands and thinks he can do a better job than a professional detective, or c) watched too many movies in which the defendant—wrongly accused, of course—manages to solve his own case.

Madden will rack his brain over what took Cogan from point A to point B. He thinks back to the elderly couple who, about a week after his arrest, had called 911 to complain that there was a constant banging sound coming from the house across the street—the house "where that doctor lives who had sex with that dead girl."

It turned out the banging wasn't some sort of construction project but the sound of a tennis ball hitting a backstop. When the officers showed up, they found Cogan standing at the end of his driveway, with a baseball glove in his hand. He had apparently been pitching tennis balls into his garage for hours on end. They were impressed with the backstop: He'd fashioned it out of an old set of drawers that he'd flipped around, the handles facing away. A black square was painted on its flat back to mark the strike zone.

After the neighbors complained, Cogan went out and

got a couple of pieces of thick Styrofoam and either stapled or nailed them to the backstop, effectively muffling the impact of the ball. According to the officer who patrols the neighborhood, he's still out there almost every day, pitching. Cogan always waves to him when he drives past.

"He was very apologetic about the noise," the officer reported to Madden. He said he was just trying to kill some time and this was what he did as a kid to make himself feel better when his mother was sick. After the cop talked to the elderly couple, they seemed embarrassed to have involved the police.

"I'll tell you, Hank," the officer said, "people are funny. These folks were actually on good terms with this guy. The woman later told me she'd consulted him about a medical condition she had. But as soon as he gets arrested, they're afraid to talk to him, they gotta dial 911 to ask him to turn it down a notch."

Madden hasn't gone out of his way to keep tabs on Cogan, yet the snippets of info he gets give him enough material to sketch out a distinct portrait. This is a guy who rarely leaves his home now. But the odd thing is that while he seems withdrawn, he's friendly, even voluble whenever someone stops to speak with him. "Whenever I've talked with him," the officer remarked, "he's totally chill. He's a big fan of Tom Seaver, did you know that?"

Burns's explanation for why Cogan went to the Planned Parenthood seems the most logical. Guy becomes impatient sitting all day waiting for his case to progress and decides, why not poke around a little, see what I can dig up? But the more Madden thinks about it, the less sense it makes. Because if Cogan hadn't slept with the girl, why would he think she'd gone to the Planned Parenthood? And if he had slept with her, why would he want to find out and potentially risk drawing attention to the fact that she had?

Through all his deliberations, what never crosses his mind is that Kristen herself would be the impetus for the visit, that in going from point A to point B Cogan actually had made a very big stop at Point C.

He never imagines that what happened that Saturday, like the previous Saturday, was Cogan standing at the end of his driveway, toeing an imaginary rubber, looking in for an imaginary sign from an imaginary catcher. It's the middle of the fourth inning. There's one out, runners on second and third, and the count's three-and-two. The imaginary announcer announces, "A crucial moment in the game, folks. A hit breaks open this scoreless tie. The crowd rises with anticipation. The pitcher gets set, and—"

The pitcher does get set, but just as Cogan is about to go into his wind-up, the ump calls time. The phone is ringing. And it's not the bullpen phone. It's the actual phone inside his house, and since he's hoping Carolyn is calling with news—any news—he dashes inside to pick up before she gets the answering machine.

But instead of Carolyn's voice, he hears Josh's.

"Hey, what's up, kid?" he says, trying to catch his breath.

"Me and Steve, we're downtown. On University Ave."

"Are we playing later?"

He thinks Josh is calling to let him know what time they're gathering online for their nearly daily Gears of War session. Gears of War is a popular multiplayer video game for the Xbox 360, and shortly after Cogan's suspension from the hospital, Josh and Steve graciously had invited him to join their clan to help him kill time and allow his mind to take a break from the case. The boys, who claimed to have known Kristen (and Carrie) as well as anybody, are among the few people who inherently believe he didn't sleep with her. After discovering the real reason behind her visits to Josh's home, they consider Carrie "intensely manipulative" and think she's lying about witnessing the sex to deflect attention from her role in causing Kristen's suicide.

Josh isn't calling about a game time, though.

"I thought you'd like to know your friend's here. Getting

her hair cut," he says.

"What friend?"

"CP."

It takes a moment for Cogan to decipher the initials.

"Oh," he says.

"I just thought you'd like to know. You know, just in case you might want to accidentally run into her."

He's silent, not sure how to react to the information. He'd told Josh the court had imposed a full stay-away order. Josh knew Cogan wasn't supposed to go near her.

"You there, Ted?"

"Yeah, I'm here. Where is she?"

"In that fancy Yosh place. I bet she's going to be on TV. I can see her through the window. You want us to keep an eye on her?"

He hesitates. Part of him is angry with Josh for tempting him. But part of him appreciates the gesture.

"Do you have my cell number?"

"It's in my phone."

"Well, keep an eye on her and call me in five."

"You coming?" Josh asks.

"I don't know. I gotta think a minute."

"Well, don't think too long. I think they're almost finished."

"Call me in five."

Walking into the Borders Books, Music & Café, Cogan takes a quick look around, scanning the aisles, but he doesn't see Carrie. Josh and Steve had tracked her from the hair salon to the Apple store to her present location, the Borders store at the New Varsity Theater. Because the store, which sells books, music, and DVDs, inhabits what was once a classic mission-revival movie palace (done in by economics), it has more the feel of an independent bookstore than a chain, but it does have spacious dimensions, with multiple floors and an outdoor café, which makes the girl hard to locate.

He stops by the new fiction section and peruses a few titles, not sure whether to continue forward or position himself near the front of the store and wait for her. He then wanders off to the right, in the direction of where the old movie screen used to be.

"How're you doing today?"

He looks up. A young guy with a goatee and a friendly smile is standing in the next aisle over. His nametag reads J. D.

"Good, thanks."

"Need any help finding a DVD?"

"I'm OK for now."

"Well, picture and sound quality, I'm your man. I haven't watched all this shit but I've watched most of it. Plot's your problem. That's a taste thing. But I'll tell you whether the thing looks and sounds good, and whether it's got any extras that'll give you a hard-on."

"Thanks."

"Don't mention it."

He watches J. D. head down the aisle, where he stops to talk to an older woman who seems more willing to enlist his opinions. He wonders whether the guy will employ such colorful language with her. He somehow doubts it. He's so caught up in the thought that he doesn't immediately notice a figure standing in his peripheral vision. Because his mind is elsewhere, when he finally turns to look, the weight of the girl being there doesn't register. She's standing a few feet away, in the same aisle, staring at him as if he were her favorite movie star, her mouth slightly ajar.

Oh, there's Carrie, he says to himself. Then his back goes rigid, his heart races, and he thinks, *Oh, shit.*

"Hi," she says a little breathlessly.

"Hi."

"How are you?"

"Could be better. You?"

"Could be better."

"How's school?"

"School?" She seems a little surprised by the neutrality of the question. "I can't wait for summer."

"You think you're going to work or just hang out?"

She holds up a folded piece of paper. "I've been picking up job applications. But who knows. It's not as easy as it used to be to get a summer job."

"That's what I hear."

She looks down, and when she does, he takes the opportunity to scrutinize her more closely. She has a sort of a faux boho/70s look going, with slightly flared jeans, sandals and a tight green top that leaves an inch or so of her midriff exposed. Slung diagonally across her front and hanging on her hip: a small leather bag with south-of the-border roots. She seems thinner than he remembered. She wears the look well.

"I heard you were suspended," she says, still staring at the ground. "I'm sorry."

The ice broken, he takes a step forward. He could have come even closer, but he decides to keep his distance. Though he's easily old enough to be her father, he knows that's the last thing an observer would think he is. It doesn't help that he's dressed young—in jeans, a T-shirt, and running shoes.

"I'm not supposed to talk to you," he says.

She raises her eyes to meet his.

"I know."

"You're not afraid of me?"

"Should I be?"

"I'm pretty angry, Carrie."

"You don't seem angry."

She's right. He doesn't.

"Well, maybe not right this second. But I've been angry the past few weeks."

"So have I. My best friend's dead. And people think I'm partially responsible."

He smiles. "You? I thought I held that distinction."

"I was the last one to speak to her. I took her to your house. I'm dealing with a lot of what-ifs, you know."

He manages to keep the smile up, but it's forced now, its charm gone. Part of him had hoped for a more passive response, that she'd just stand there and quietly listen to his condensed tale of woe and feel not exactly guilt, but some kindred emotion that would make her reconsider the path she was taking. But clearly she's more concerned with her predicament.

"Is that why you told the police you saw me having sex with Kristen?" he continues in a calm voice, doing his best not to sound too antagonistic. "To deflect the blame?"

"No, I told them because it's the truth."

"I see. The truth. You're sure?"

"Of that, yeah."

"You're positive you're not just imagining something Kristen described to you at some point—something that maybe didn't really happen?"

"Don't be silly," she says.

The mocking tone of her response throws him. He starts to formulate an answer, but before he can get it out, she's already moved on.

She says, "Look, Kristen didn't want this. She didn't want you to get in trouble. All you had to do was talk to her."

"I couldn't."

"Well, you should have," she says.

"I agree. But that's easy to say now. At the time, I had an important call on the other line."

"What, some woman? Some hot date?"

Again, the mocking, he thinks. "No, a doctor. A specialist in Minnesota I was consulting about a patient."

"Well, she tried to talk to you before," she says, not allowing him the excuse. "Two months earlier. Or whenever it was when she left the CD. Remember that? She said she wrote you a note. There was something she needed to tell you. And you blew her off that time, too."

She had left a note. It was true. He'd come home one day and there was a small package lying on his welcome mat with a note attached.

Dear Doctor Cogan:

Thanks for all your help. I don't know how to thank you (again) but I thought you'd like this music mix I made. You can listen to it while you're operating on people. I hope it inspires you.

Kristen

P.S. Please call me on my cell phone when you get a chance at the number below. I have something I need to tell you.

For several hours, he'd debated whether he should return the gift or report to hospital officials that he'd received it, which was what he was supposed to do under regulations. Instead, he did what he felt was the safest thing: he called her cell phone and left a message, thanking her for her note and gently reiterating that he wasn't supposed to interact on a personal basis with his patients and that he risked losing his job if he did. He said he hoped she understood and wished her all the best. And that was the last he'd heard from her.

"I'm sorry," he says now to Carrie. "But I was hoping she understood my position."

"She understood it. You wanted to forget that night ever happened. I totally understand. That's fine. You made a mistake."

He goes to open his mouth to speak, but, somewhere between brain and tongue, his words hit a fork and don't know which way to turn. He smiles. She has him in a bind. If he answers that there's nothing to forget—nothing had happened—it would fit her theory that he wanted to forget. If he answers, yes, he had made a mistake, he'd be admitting that something had happened, which is what she seems to want. The only answer: not to answer.

"Is that what this is about?" he asks. "Forgetting and remembering?"

"No."

He moves a few paces down the aisle, goes to one of the bargain racks with $9.95 titles, and randomly picks a movie.

"Then what?"

No response. She looks down again, and when she does, he thinks: *We're standing in two parallel universes, two separate truths, and that instead of denying hers, I must embrace it or I'm dead.*

"That I didn't sleep with you?" he asks in a low voice, pretending to examine the DVD's case, which he notices is a Woody Allen film, *Sweet and Lowdown*.

"No."

"I didn't think so. Because if that's what this is about, that would be pretty petty, don't you think?"

He moves down the rack, selects another movie, *The Thomas Crown Affair*, and flips it around to look at its back.

"Can I ask you a question?" she says.

"What?"

"Why aren't you married?"

"Why?"

"I've just always wondered."

Great, he thinks. *This is her level of curiosity. A staple question.*

"I was," he says. "For two years."

"And what happened?"

"She left me for her ex-boyfriend."

"Why?"

"Better offer." His tone isn't condescending but he speaks as if the explanation should seem obvious. "She got a nice package: big house, platinum AmEx, convertible Mercedes. Benefits included devotion, emotional support, free psychological counseling."

Her face takes on a slightly puzzled look. "But doctors make good money."

"Some do, like my plastic surgeon friend Reinhart. He makes good money. But compared to what this guy came into, I might well have been earning minimum wage."

That gets a smile out of her. It's nothing special, but he's surprised by the charge it gives him. So much so that he has to look away. His eyes drop to the DVD case he's holding.

"This is the ultimate guy," he says. "Pierce Brosnan as Crown. Ask any woman over thirty and she'll tell you he's it. A nurse I know watched this movie something like twenty times. The *Titanic* for the over-thirty female set. It should be studied."

She laughs, a distant look in her eyes. It's one of those little laughs you let out when you remember something amusing from long ago, a precious moment.

"Gwen thought you looked like George Clooney," she says.

"Gwen?" he says, a little startled.

"She was there at your house that night. You remember her?"

"Sure."

All too well, he thinks. He'd gotten Gwen Dayton's phone number that night and slept with her a week later—a one-night fling, but it had certainly happened. He'd indexed her under "beautiful young women with boyfriends and interesting philosophies about cheating that you don't question." She'd told him that certain indiscretions were acceptable, even educationally necessary at this stage in her development, so long as they were isolated incidents. And he, an older, attractive man, a surgeon no less with zero ties to her collegiate life, had made the approved-for-trial list.

Although he was a little surprised she hadn't admitted to the tryst in her deposition, she'd obviously deemed it better to lie than risk losing her boyfriend. Not that he blamed her—or was so eager for her to tell the truth and make the tale any more sordid than it already was. But he wasn't sure it was the most prudent move given the likelihood that the information would eventually surface anyway.

"She mentioned it that night," Carrie goes on. "How you kind of looked like him."

"She probably watched a little too much *ER* as a kid."

"Probably. I never was into that show."

"I heard she gave Kristen some legal advice."

"Yeah," she says, surprised. "How'd you know?"

"I read her deposition."

"She has this friend who's a law student, I guess."

"And she never expressed any doubt about what happened?"

"What do you mean?"

"How'd she react when Kristen claimed she had sex with me?"

Carrie shrugs.

"I don't know. I guess she was shocked like everybody else. Why?"

"Nevermind. It's not important."

He puts the *Thomas Crown Affair* DVD back into its correct slot in the rack.

"Did you know?" she asks.

"Did I know what?"

"That your wife, she was cheating?"

He smiles. His brother had asked the same question. Reinhart and Klein, too. He had a hunch she was, he'd told them all. But that wasn't the complete truth. There was more. Just a bit. And Carrie, he decides, is going to hear it—and not because he expects his openness might elicit hers, but because he wants her to know what he's capable of enduring.

"Not for sure," he says. "But I was hoping she was."

He gets the reaction he wants. She blinks, taken aback. "Why?"

"Because I felt like a victim. Only I needed something to prove I was one. Something nice and concrete."

"Kristen felt just the opposite," she says, unimpressed.

"She didn't feel like a victim. Not at all. But everybody wanted to make her one."

"Her father?"

"Well, it started with her father. But her mother fed off him. You know, she was definitely influenced by him. I sometimes think her mom did it on purpose."

"Did what on purpose?"

"She was always creating little crises for Mr. Kroiter to deal with. You know, to get his attention. That's what Kristen said. Mrs. Kroiter knew Mr. Kroiter would flip when he saw what Kristen had written in her diary."

"So her mother should have gone to her first."

"Totally. That's what ticked Kristen off. Her mom could have totally kept her dad out of it."

"And what would she have told her mother?"

"The same thing she ended up telling her father. You know, that it was some stupid writing exercise she was doing."

"But her father didn't believe her?"

"He jumped all over her. Asked her what class she did it for. What teacher. What the exact assignment was. I mean, he's an investigator himself. Insurance stuff. He was hard to fool. He always knew when she was lying."

Now there's an ironic statement if there ever was one, Cogan thinks.

"He was like, 'OK, so you say it was for Miss Bracken,' " she goes on. " 'Well we're going to have a little meeting with Miss Bracken and see what she says.' "

The more he listens, the more depressed he becomes. He can't hold onto his indignation; it keeps slipping away. And for a brief second, in a strange out-of-body moment, he finds himself angry with the doctor for sleeping with the girl. The thought flusters him, and suddenly, without warning, his tone turns hostile.

"Well, she should have stuck to her story. She should have told him she made the whole thing up, that it *was* a writing exercise. Because that's what it was, wasn't it?"

"She defended you. She told him she wasn't raped. She told him she wanted to do it."

"By denying something, she was really admitting to something."

"She was defending you," Carrie repeats.

"She wasn't defending me. She was defending herself. And you, how can you say you saw us? Do you hate me that much?"

"I don't hate you. I wouldn't be talking to you if I hated you."

"Well, go ahead and fuck me. Fuck me right out of my career."

That does it. Finally, he's upset her. She looks at him a little helplessly, a pang of guilt in her eyes.

"It's not my fault," she says.

"Too easy," he shoots back. "Try again."

But before she can, one of their phones rings. He pulls his out to turn it off, but it's hers. She looks at the phone, checking the caller ID, and clicks the talk button on. "Hey, I'll call you right back," she says. "I'm picking up an application." After she hangs up, she turns to him and says: "I've gotta go. I was supposed to meet my mother ten minutes ago."

She puts the phone back in her bag and heads past him, toward the front of the store.

"Carrie, wait."

But she doesn't turn.

"Carrie, hold on."

He goes after her and takes her by the arm, not hard but hard enough to get her to turn around and face him. He's greeted by a defiant scowl.

"You won't tell anybody I talked to you, will you?"

"I talked to you first," she says, almost smirking.

"I take that as a 'no,' then."

"Take it for whatever you like. Can I go?"

He starts to loosen his grip on her arm, but at the last moment a thought from his subconscious makes him reverse course.

"When Kristen left that note for me, you mentioned she had something to tell me. What was it?"

"It doesn't matter now. I didn't even remember until you reminded me."

"Yes, it does."

She looks at him, seeming to weigh what she owes him, if anything.

"What was it?" he urges more gently, suddenly determined to get it out her, if only to wring some semblance of victory from what he's certain is a serious setback.

"She was going to tell you that you should go see a doctor."

He's stunned. "Excuse me?"

"I don't know exactly what for. She wouldn't tell me. I'm sure you know, though."

Whether she realizes the incapacitating effect of the remark or not, she takes it as her opportunity to make her break. She easily slips from his grasp and makes for the door.

"Carrie, wait."

"Sir, can I help you?"

He whirls around. J. D., the salesperson, is standing behind him, his welcoming smile replaced by the edgy, alarmed look of a security guard who hasn't seen action in a while and isn't supposed to.

"No. No, thanks. I'm fine."

"You're that guy, aren't you?"

"Which guy?" he replies, knowing full well whom he means.

"That guy in the papers."

"I don't know what you're talking about."

"The guy who slept with the girl who killed herself."

"I didn't sleep with any girl who killed herself."

"Well, you sure look like him."

"Well, I'm not him. I am fine, though," he repeats. "And you've been quite helpful. Really. Thanks."

He bolts for the door. But the delay costs him. By the time he gets outside, it's too late. Carrie's gone, disappeared around one corner or the other.

28/ Deleted scenes

May 5, 2007—p.m. 4:55

"She was going to tell you to go see a doctor."

The line, *Carrie's* line, is still reverberating through Cogan's head as he edges forward in traffic. He made the mistake of following the route he'd normally take home, taking University to Palm Drive, then turning right onto Arboretum and left onto Sand Hill Road next to Stanford Shopping Center. Like on most Saturday afternoons, Sand Hill, which became famous for its high commercial real estate prices during the tech boom of the 90s and runs for three and a half miles from the shopping center to the 280 freeway, is fully backed up. The traffic is actually worse than it was coming out toward the mall, yet it barely raises his ire. He might as well be in the fast lane on the freeway, doing eighty-five. His mind is racing, his fatalistic anxiety of the last several days replaced by nervous energy, a giddiness he hasn't felt in weeks.

What had she meant exactly? Carrie had intended to deliver the message to him weeks ago. Yet there he'd been fifteen minutes ago, standing before her in a store at the mall, physically, if not quite mentally, fit. The last time he'd been treated by a doctor was well over a year ago—for a foot injury sustained during a beach volleyball game, no less.

She was going to tell you to go see a doctor.

He keeps thinking that the only reason she could say such a thing was that something had been wrong with her. Something very wrong indeed. And wrong is good—of that he is certain.

He has a sudden desire to talk to someone. Carolyn? Maybe not, for despite his haste he's aware that whatever he reveals to her she'll have to pass on to the DA's office, and he needs time to consider the implications of such a move. But Klein—yes, Klein, the spineless wonder—will do.

"Hey, buddy," Klein answers his cell phone, recognizing the number on his caller ID.

"Where are you?"

"I'm over at the club. Why, what's up?"

Good. The club. It was closer than Klein's home. Once he got through the four-way intersection, it would be clear sailing, an eight-minute ride.

"Need to talk."

Klein sighs, sounding more rueful than irritated.

"Give me half an hour. I'm with Trish and the kid. We're eating. Why don't you meet me and Reinhart over at Blue Chalk in a little bit."

"*Now*, Kleiny. It's important. I saw her."

"Saw who?"

"The girl. Carrie."

"Ted, wait—"

But it's too late. He's already hung up.

Pulling into the swim and tennis club's parking lot, he's surprised by how distant the place feels, though it hasn't been that long since he's been there. He had a similar sensation rolling into a high school reunion years ago; the environs seem instantly familiar yet remote. And like that day, he's hit with a pang of nostalgia. Being relieved of his job had been hard, but sometimes he wonders whether he mourns the peripheral losses more—the simple pleasures of bantering with

Reinhart and Kim during matches or sitting around the pool, kibitzing and assessing the "talent." It's as if his DNA has been stripped of one of its strands.

Usually, when he arrives at the club, the girl behind the front desk doesn't even ask for his membership card. She just smiles and says, "Hi, Doctor, go ahead, I got you." But when he walks in today, this same girl, this little blond Miss Congeniality, looks startled to see him.

"Hey, Sandra," he says, handing her his membership card. "How are you?"

"OK," she says, and takes the card but seems unsure what to do with it.

Though he senses something's wrong, he thinks she's only acting strangely because she'd heard he'd been arrested. He asks her whether she's going to run it or should he just go through?

She looks at the card, then at him, then down at the card reader on the desk in front of her. It doesn't hit him immediately what she's afraid of, but when she finally goes ahead and runs the card, he knows from the look on her face what the problem is.

"I'm sorry," she says, "it says your membership is frozen." Then, after a beat: "Didn't they tell you?"

"Frozen? What's that mean exactly?"

"It's on hold."

"I didn't freeze it."

"No, I know. They did. Wait a sec. I better get Bill."

Bill, the manager, is a nice enough guy. Or at least he used to be. Middle-aged but very fit-looking, he turns up a couple of minutes later wearing his usual white polo shirt that shows off his physique. He's one of those guys who would have looked older had he worked in an office. But working—and working out—at the club five days a week has enabled him to retain a tenuously youthful luster, enhanced by a hair-care product that leaves his uniformly dark, slicked-back coif looking a shade unnatural.

"Hey, Ted. How are you?"

"I'm doing OK, Bill. I'm just having a little trouble getting past your crack security guard here."

He smiles at the girl, who smiles back, seeming to relax now that her manager is on hand to buffer the tension.

"I'm sorry, but your membership has been temporarily frozen," Bill says, adopting an official, impassive tone that he normally reserves for members who fail to pay their bar tabs.

"You froze it?"

"I didn't. The directors did. It's club policy."

"I didn't read that clause. Could you refresh me?"

"The club has the right to refuse anybody membership. In your case, they haven't terminated it, they've simply put it on hold until . . . until, well, your situation has been resolved."

"Why wasn't I informed?"

"You were. We sent a letter."

It was possible. After his arrest, he'd only been opening his mail sporadically and was quick to toss anything that looked irrelevant. He could have easily mistaken the envelope for one that contained the club's monthly newsletter.

"Aren't you on the board, Bill?"

"Yeah."

"And you voted with them. You didn't try to stop them."

"Well, I . . . you know . . . well, this was difficult for all of us."

"How's your mother?"

"What?"

Bill knows exactly what he's talking about, though he doesn't want to admit it. The guilt skulks about his face.

"She's fine," he says nearly in a whisper.

"The advice I gave you—pretty good, wasn't it?"

He looks down at the ground.

"Yeah."

"I didn't hear you."

"Yeah," Bill says more loudly—loud enough for those nearby to glance in their direction. "Look, Ted, it wasn't just the directors. We had parents complain. There are kids here."

"Christ. Give me a friggin' break."

Just then Klein comes out of the restaurant, and, spotting Cogan, makes a beeline for him.

"It's OK, Bill," he says. "He just came here to see me. I'll take it from here."

Klein takes his arm and says in a low voice: "Come on, man. It's not worth it. Let's go."

Minutes pass. In the car, Cogan's silent. He isn't super-pissed at Klein but he's pissed enough not to talk, which is the worst thing you can do with Klein because he's one of those guys who doesn't deal well with emotional nuances, the grays. He prefers things spelled out, like so many of the women Cogan dated. In fact, if Klein had been a woman, he would have been one of them, the kind who was always saying, "I can't read you," or asking, "What are you thinking right now?"

The funny thing is that as soon as he imagines the words coming out of Klein's mouth, Klein practically says them, though the echo has a more masculine ring: "What's up, man?" he asks. "What are you thinking?"

"I was thinking that you're going to ask me what I'm thinking."

"No, really."

He keeps staring at the road. "Really."

A brief silence.

"I'm sorry," Klein says. "I thought you knew."

"Don't worry about it."

"I was going to say something. I'm sorry, but we've been dealing with this new house all week. Our bid was accepted but Trish is suddenly on the fence. We've been going back and forth on it. She thinks prices are going to come down and that we could do better in six months or a year. Get something bigger for the same money. I don't know. It's all we talk about."

"Tough choice. I understand."

Klein won't let it go, though. He has to defend himself, has to explain that he only found out a few days earlier about the freeze when another member had asked him whether he knew how Cogan was taking it.

As he drones on, seeking his own pardon, Cogan finds himself thinking about how he'd handled the situation back at the club. He thinks he'd handled it well, he hadn't allowed Bill to humiliate him too badly. The bastard. He'd called Bill every day when his mother was in the ICU. Now here he was, selling him out at the first opportunity to cover his own ass.

"We went to a concert," Klein says.

Cogan looks over at him, not sure he's heard right, but aware that Klein is off the whole frozen membership rift.

"The Chemical Brothers," he goes on. "With Rosenbaum. A couple of nights ago. He got the tickets."

"DocToBe. That prick."

"Look, he may be inept, but he's not a bad guy."

"Don't get me started." The last guy he wants to discuss is Rosenbaum, who probably has been bad-mouthing him to anybody who will listen. He and Beckler were probably having a field day.

"Anyway, it was one of those electronica deals," Klein continues. "You know The Brothers, right?"

Cogan nods. Yeah, he knows The Brothers. He played them sometimes in the OR. *Where's he going with this?*

"It was basically like being in a giant club. And we're all pretty hammered and we're dancing behind this group of girls and my hand keeps knocking into one of them and she doesn't seem to mind. Then I actually put my hand on her waist. You know, nothing too advanced, but I just kept it there for a few seconds. And again, she doesn't do anything, doesn't turn around or anything. So I start to get a little bolder and a little bolder, and suddenly, I've got my hands on her stomach and she's leaning back into me. And you know, my hands kind of slip up a little from time to time and I can feel the wire in her bra and the base of her breasts and it's all really hot but somehow impersonal at the same time."

Cogan looks over at him, a little incredulous. It's the most intriguing story Klein has told in a while.

"And the other guys see you doing this?"

"Yeah, sure. They're encouraging me."

"So what happened?"

"Well, that's the weird thing. Nothing. As soon as the concert ends and the lights go on, she just says, 'See ya,' and walks away. You know, as if nothing had happened. It was as if we'd met at a party, talked for a few minutes, then went our separate ways."

"And you thought you were in."

"I didn't think anything. I mean, I doubt I would have done anything. But it occurred to me that something like that might have happened to you. Where maybe you had an exchange or something with this girl, maybe you were next to her on the bed like you said, and she made it out to be more than it was. Because I was having some pretty intense thoughts myself. It's not beyond the realm of possibility," Klein suggests feebly. "Am I right?"

"You think I did it, don't you?"

"I didn't say that."

"You're thinking, there she was, lying in the bed without any clothes on, why wouldn't Cogan cop a little feel? That's what he does. That's what he's good at. Getting women to take their clothes off and copping feels. So this one happened to be a little younger."

"A lot," Klein interjects.

"OK, a lot."

He waits for Klein to ask the inevitable, to press him for

the God's honest truth, his final testament, sworn on someone's life sacred to him. But instead he gets something more predictable: a taste of Klein's special brand of imperfectly timed righteousness.

"Hey, if you'd just said something when I had you on the phone that night, we wouldn't be having this conversation now. Instead of telling me you were with an old girlfriend and her friend, you should have told me who was really there. I would've knocked some sense into you. I would have told you to get them the hell out of there."

"I know," he says, slowing for traffic. "I know you would have, Kleiny."

Cogan smiles as he drives. Sometimes, after he's had a couple of glasses of wine at night, he'd lie back in his recliner and listen to the CD Kristen had given him. She'd burned the disc herself: it was a mix of twenty songs, most of them from movie soundtracks: *The Beach*, *Finding Forrester*, *10 Things I Hate About You*, *Beautiful Girls*, *Mean Girls*, *50 First Dates*, *Cruel Intentions,* and both *Bridget Jones* movies. She'd neatly listed all the songs on the CD case and even made a special label for the CD—*Knife Music* in bold red lettering.

The stereo set to the perfect volume—loud, but not too loud—he'd think back to that morning and remember sitting on the edge of the bed next to her, asking her how she felt as he wrestled with a light hangover of his own. *Had he held her hand?* He wasn't sure. But it wouldn't have surprised him if he did.

"You know, I can get into a lot of trouble if anybody finds out you were here," he said, looking her in the eyes. "I could lose my job."

Perhaps he'd stared too long. He'd looked to gauge her reaction, to make sure she understood he'd broken a major rule. But something about her expression, maybe the depth of her return gaze, caught him and drew him in, and his declaration hung there, suspended, instead of crashing down. He remembered silence, then the girl asking: "Where's Carrie?"

"On the couch in the living room. Sleeping."

"What time is it?"

He looked at a clock that was sitting on the little nightstand.

"Seven."

"You know, she likes you. Carrie—she has a crush on you."

"I know. You told me. Like three times."

"I did?" She turned her head, covered her mouth, and coughed. It wasn't a *cough* cough, but more the kind you let out to suppress nausea.

"You OK?"

"Yeah." She forced smile. "Would it be all right if I took a shower?"

"Sure. I'll get you a towel."

Yes, it is easy to imagine, he thought. Easy to think of how when he came back, she was standing in the bathroom that adjoined the guest room. The door to the bathroom was open, and she was naked, staring at herself in the mirror. He was so surprised he just stood there dumbly with the towel in his hand. She saw him in the mirror, but made no effort to cover herself. Instead, she calmly looked at him in the mirror and said, "I don't look so hot, do I?" When he didn't answer, she turned around and faced him, almost challenging him to assess her condition.

"Here," he said, handing her the towel. "Just hang it over the shower door when you're done. There should be some shampoo there. I don't know about conditioner. Do you need conditioner?"

He considers going into Blue Chalk to say hello to Reinhart, but when they can't find a parking space right away, he decides against it. Besides, he tells Klein, he has things to do.

"What things?" Klein asks. "Don't tell me you're playing video games with those kids."

"No games. Don't worry."

A short silence. Then:

"So what am I doing here, Ted? What's this about the girl? What did you want to tell me?"

He looks over at Klein, who's sitting there with part of his arm hanging out his window, looking a little peeved. He can see that he's tired of the new, unpredictably moody Ted, and wants the old aloof, good-humored Ted back.

"I did have something to tell you," he says.

As late as a few minutes ago, he'd considered telling him about talking to Carrie in the mall. But it strikes him that it would do no good, and is dangerous, for Klein can't keep a secret. He shouldn't have called him in the first place. He can't say that now, though. But he has to say something. So he says: "I wanted to tell you that I've been seeing this whole thing wrong."

"How so?"

"I've been too focused on the friend, Carrie. You know, thinking about why she would say she saw us having sex."

"Why would she?"

"Well, I think we'll have to pull in a psychiatrist to get to the bottom of that. I have a hunch it's some sort of weird transference. Or that she just feels terribly guilty. In either case, she seems pretty darn convinced."

"Wouldn't you say that's a big problem?"

"Absolutely. But it's not necessarily the root. Think about what Kristen was telling her parents."

He wants Klein to actually think, but he's too impatient.

"What was she telling them?"

"She was saying, 'I had consensual sex with Doctor Cogan. It was my choice to have sex with him. And yes, he was a dick for blowing me off afterward, but I'm OK with what I did. I made a decision and was willing to live with the consequences, regardless of what happened afterward. He was the guy I wanted to fuck, to lose my virginity to, and now bugger off, people, that's the story I'm sticking with, don't try to make me change it.' "

"Even if it's a lie?"

"Well, somehow it wasn't a lie to her. And given the choice between saying she was raped by me and saying it was consensual, she opted for consensual because, given only two choices, she was going with the one that was the closest to the truth, and that should have made everything OK."

"But wasn't the closest thing to the truth that nothing happened?"

"Yes, Doctor. But what if something did?"

"What do you mean?"

"What if someone else had sex with her?"

Klein blinked, genuinely startled. "Who?"

"I don't know. You ever watch the extras on a DVD?"

"Sure."

"You know how there are sometimes deleted scenes?"

"Yeah."

"Well, that's what I'm looking for. And I think I know where I can find one."

29/ King Kong

May 5, 2007—p.m. 6:15

There are two free clinics within a 15-mile radius. The first, a Planned Parenthood, is located two towns to the north in Redwood City, and the second, appropriately titled The Free Clinic, is in Palo Alto. A light green-colored building, the clinic is located in a lightly trafficked, predominantly residential area a few blocks from downtown. Though it's discreetly tucked back a little from the street, some visitors still choose to park a few blocks away.

The Palo Alto clinic would have been the more convenient choice, but Cogan thinks the girl may not have wanted to risk being spotted hitting the local clinic and opted instead for the Planned Parenthood.

After dropping off Klein, he phones Josh and asks him whether he has any photos of Kristen. He knows that he and Steve have assembled a collection of digital images for their most-popular database. But he needs good ones. Nothing grainy or even slightly out of focus.

Naturally, Josh is curious why he wants them. "You need somebody to ID her, don't you?"

"Very astute, Red Leader One."

"You want to tell me more?"

"Maybe later."

This is how they talk now. They have an understanding.

Cogan tells him something, but not everything, and Josh has to live with it. The slightest hint of prodding or pleading and he gets nothing; the conversation is over.

"Interesting," Josh says. "How do you want them?"

"What do you mean?"

"The format. Two per page? Four? Printed? Digital? Slide show for your handheld?"

He hadn't thought of that—going the more high-tech route. How will someone respond to the pictures on a handheld? It may seem more personal, but then again, it'd sure look bad if he got caught with them on the device.

"I'll tell you what," Josh says before Cogan can make up his mind. "I'll stick them on a memory card and show you what I got. When do you need them?"

"Tomorrow," he says. "Tomorrow morning. Early."

<u>May 7, 2007—p.m. 2:45</u>

"Pause it there," Madden says, looking at the small video monitor. "That's him pulling into the parking lot. That's his car."

"That's your boy alright," says Burns, holding the remote.

The time on the tape reads 11:32, which means he went to the Free Clinic after Planned Parenthood. When he walks into the clinic, it reads 11:33:21.

"He's talking to the same woman I spoke to," Madden says to Rebecca, the clinic's director, who's reluctantly agreed to let them look at the security tapes. "What's her name?"

"That's Heather. She was a volunteer last year but now she's paid. Part-time but paid."

"She in today?"

"This afternoon. Should be here in about twenty minutes."

"You see that?" Burns asks, pointing. "He's got a whole sheet of pictures. Looks like four different shots. That's more than we have."

Madden stares at the screen, mesmerized. He's observing Cogan's body language: the standoffish opening, the little flashes of that charming smile. The bastard, he's trying to seduce her—like he tries to seduce everything that crosses his path. *She must be twenty, twenty-one,* he says to himself, disgusted. And to think this guy was performing exams in the hospital, given *carte blanche* to touch young girls. It's preposterous.

"She shook her head," Burns says. "There, she did it again."

Madden doesn't respond, though. He's overcome by a wave of nausea.

"Hank, you alright?"

"Yeah." Feeling his partner's stare on him, he pulls out his handkerchief and wipes his brow. "I'm OK, don't worry."

As they watch (there's no audio), a second woman comes into the frame, and when she does, Madden starts to feel better. Heather gives her some forms. Then, she has another brief exchange with Cogan.

"This Heather," Madden says to the director after they've finished watching Cogan get in his car and drive away, "she say anything to you about this guy coming in?"

"No, she didn't mention it."

"It doesn't look like he got anything," Burns says.

"Let's see what she has to say. Twenty minutes, you said?"

The director nods. "You said he might be dangerous?"

"We don't know what he's up to. We'll be back in a bit. Come on, Mr. Burns. I'll buy you a latte at Peet's."

<u>May 6, 2007—a.m. 11:33</u>

Cogan takes one look at the girl behind the front desk of the

Adam and Jane Rosenberg Free Clinic and thinks: *This isn't good.* Her hair is shaved close on the sides, bleached on top, and she has at least five, and probably more, earrings running along the tops of her ears, plus two through her left eyebrow. He isn't intimidated by her style—in the hospital, he'd gotten along fine with his share of body piercing and tattoo enthusiasts. Rather, his pessimism is grounded more in her return gaze: At best, it approximates indifference; at worst, disdain. Her eyes seem to beg the question, *What sort of crap are you selling?*

"Hey," he says distantly, deciding to mirror the chilly reception. "Sorry to bother you."

"Hey," she says. "What's up?"

As he did at the Planned Parenthood earlier, he takes out his hospital ID—an old one, not the one they'd taken away from him when he was suspended.

"I'm a doctor over at Parkview," he says, flashing the ID in front of him just below chest level. "And I have a patient who may or may not have come through here a few months ago. She's in a bit of a jam now and we're just trying to determine whether she came in or not. I know it's been a long time, but would you mind looking at a couple of pictures?"

"What kind of jam?"

"A personal one."

"If it's health-related," she warns, "you know we can't release any information."

He knows, he says, but can she just take a quick look, it may be a moot point anyway. Before she can answer affirmatively or negatively, he takes the eight-by-ten sheet out and slides it onto the desk in front of her.

Kristen looks slightly different in each shot. If you examine them closely, you can tell that in two pictures she'd posed with friends who'd later been cropped out of the picture. The other pair is more paparazzi-style, though in one she's looking directly into the camera with a haunting, piercing stare.

Josh took the picture with a zoom lens, standing on a bench at school. Kristen is in a little crowd but the rest of the people all have their backs to her; she's the only one facing the opposite direction, which creates a nice contrast. She's giving him a very hard look, one of those ambiguous expressions that make you want to guess what she's thinking. You don't know whether she likes or hates you, and when you finally settle on one or the other sentiment, you still don't trust yourself.

"It's the same chick."

He blinks.

"The same as who?"

"The same detective who was in here a few weeks back asking about her."

She starts to hand back the sheet but then stops halfway. Something has caught her eye—she's staring at the picture at the bottom left corner, the only one in the bunch in which Kristen is wearing a hat. It's a baseball cap with a logo of the Sundance Film Festival across its front.

"What is it?" he asks.

When she finally looks up at him, she seems both perplexed and alarmed.

"What happened to her?"

"Do you remember her?"

"Maybe."

"Like a strong maybe or a weak maybe?"

"You work at Parkview?" she asks.

"Yeah."

"We have a doctor who volunteers a couple of times a month from there. Dr. Beckler."

A little jolt courses through him, followed by momentary panic.

"I forget her first name," she adds. It's an innocent enough remark, but the way she says it seems a little forced—too deliberate. Discombobulated as he is, though, he has the good sense to realize that she's trying to test him.

"Anne."

"That's right, *Anne.*" She continues to eye him suspiciously, however. "You know her?"

"Yes. Well," he says awkwardly, "we've had our moments in the OR."

"Oh?"

He's about to attempt to qualify the statement when he hears the door behind him jar open. Turning around, he sees a tall young woman with dark hair heading toward them. She must have been in her mid- to late twenties. Not a teenager. Instinctively, he takes back the eight-by-ten and slips it into its manila folder.

The intruder approaches. "Hi," she says in an irritatingly cheerful voice, compensating perhaps for her anxiousness. "I have an eleven-thirty appointment with Dr. Ghuman."

"Hi," the receptionist chimes back, and directs her to a set of forms. They're sitting on a counter next to a short rack that is filled with a dozen or so neatly displayed informational pamphlets. It reminds Cogan of the rack in his travel agency filled with brochures advertising various destinations, resorts, and cruises. The only difference here is that most of these brochures are for trips you don't want to take.

"She should be right with you," the receptionist says to the woman. "She's just finishing up with a patient." Then, in a much lower voice, almost a whisper, she turns to him and tells him to leave.

"I'm sorry," she says. "I can't help you."

Not knowing quite what else to do, he looks at her and smiles.

"What's your name?" he asks.

"Heather. Why?"

"You drink coffee, Heather?"

"Yeah."

"Well, I'm going to make a run over to Peet's for a cappuccino. You want one?"

"Yes, but that's beside the point."

"I'll be back in fifteen minutes," he goes on, undaunted. "I'll wait outside by my car. If you want it, just peek your head out and I'll bring it over."

"And if I don't?"

"I'll try a different approach."

"And what if I call the police?"

"They'll have to get their own coffee."

May 7, 2007—p.m. 3:10

If Madden and Burns had left the tape running for another fifteen minutes, they would have noticed Cogan's car pulling back into the clinic's lot. The parking lot security camera captured him standing next to his car, reading—or pretending to read—a newspaper for a little over ten minutes. Next, it recorded Heather leaving through the clinic's back door and approaching him from behind. Though the image on the screen wasn't terribly sharp, you could tell that he was startled; he jumped a little. "Are you her father?"

"That's what I asked him," Heather says. "Whether he was her father. And he said something like, 'Christ, you scared me.' "

Madden looks at Burns and Burns looks at Madden.

"Why'd you decide to go out and meet him?" Madden asks.

"I don't know. I guess I was bored."

"What happened next?"

"Well, when he said he wasn't her father, I thought he might be working for her father, and we talked about that. And then we started chatting, and he told me the story of what had happened. And I just got an OK vibe. You know, people think just because I dress and look like this—and I work at the free clinic—that I'm some butch lesbian who hates guys. But that's not what I'm about."

They wait for her to tell them what she's about, but she

leaves it at that.

"So you chatted," Madden says.

"Yeah, we chatted, and at some point I figured it would be OK to tell him."

"Tell him what?"

"That I remembered seeing the girl. Or at least I thought I did."

Another exchange of sideways glances between the detectives.

"Really, it was the hat," she says. "The Sundance Film Festival logo. That's what I remembered. He had a picture of her wearing it."

The girl came in around 4 p.m. on February 18, she says, suddenly more specific. Like many of the girls that come in, she may have called earlier to make sure the clinic was open and ask whether someone could see her. Or she may not have.

Physically speaking, she remembers little about her beyond the fact that she had light hair and was wearing the baseball cap. The girl may have looked a little tired, but she showed no visible marks—bruises or scratches—that would indicate that she'd been physically abused. If she had, she would have noted it in her journal. Instead, she'd only written: *4 p.m. Blond girl. Has that maybe-I-did-something-I-shouldn't-have look. Worried contraception failed. Says she had intercourse previous PM.*

"Before I went outside to talk to him, I looked it up."

The girl gave her name as Chris Ray—she spelled it with a C—and said she was almost seventeen.

"Not terribly creative," Madden says under his breath to Burns. "Ray's her middle name."

"Chris for Kristen," Burns offers back.

"Whatever," Heather says. The only reason she remembered the name was because she was a fan of *King Kong*.

"She didn't say she was sixteen. She said 'almost' seventeen, like that song. And I said something like, 'Don't worry, honey, it doesn't matter how old you are.' And then I told her that her name reminded me of *King Kong*. You know, Fay Wray, the original Kong, not the new one—or the one with what's-her-name, Jessica Lange. And we talked about that for a couple a minutes while we waited for Dr. Ghuman. She liked Jeff Bridges."

It was Sunday, she confirms—one of the clinic's busiest days, though you wouldn't know it by the parking lot, which only had a handful of cars parked in it at a given time, three of which belonged to the clinic's workers. Last year there'd been an overly publicized incident of vandalism. A couple of teenagers had been caught by security cameras spray painting and keying cars in the clinic's lot. But according to Heather, the main reason visitors—particularly the high school kids—parked down the street was to protect their "precious" reputations.

"They think that if they aren't actually parked in the lot, it doesn't really count," she comments. "If they run into someone they know, they can say they were on their way somewhere else and just stopped in to ask about birth control."

She has no idea whether Chris Ray had parked in the lot that afternoon or not. And she doesn't know what the result of her examination had been. And even if she did, she wouldn't say.

She'd said something similar to Cogan.

"Let me see the picture again," she'd said to Cogan. After she looked at it one more time, she remarked, "I'm pretty certain it was her. That's all I'm willing to say. But you didn't hear it from me. I never told you that. OK?"

"Heather," Madden says, unable to completely hide his exasperation, "Can I ask you one last question?"

"I don't know if I'll answer, but go ahead."

"When I talked to you before, when I came here last month, why didn't you check your journal then?"

"I didn't recognize her. You showed me a picture and I

didn't recognize her. What do you want me to say? I'm not even supposed to be talking to you guys."

May 7, 2007—p.m. 3:36

When he and Burns had originally canvassed the nearby free clinics, Madden had prided himself on being thorough, making sure to cross all the t's and dot all the i's. But walking back to his car now, he finds himself swearing under his breath, admonishing himself for being too perfunctory.

The diary. The damned diary. If he's made mistakes, they can be traced back to that confounded document. In hindsight, he wishes that when he'd received it, no one had apprised him of how it had been discovered or of Kristen's initial claims that her account was fabricated. He wishes someone had just handed it to him and said: "Do you think this is fact or fiction?"

He isn't sure what his answer would have been, but at least he could have read it with a more objective eye and not one that had been clouded by the thought that the author had tried to cover up the truth by turning it into a lie.

Fact: Kristen never wrote about visiting a clinic. Her narrative moved from her having sex with the doctor to her waking up in the morning with him sitting beside her on the bed, to her speaking to Carrie later that day.

I didn't tell her right away. While driving home that morning all we talked about was what a wreck I'd been and how freaked she was by it. She started getting on my case because of all the trouble I could've gotten her brother into. It was like, if I died, her brother would have been in deep shit. I had to alert her to the fact that wasn't it more important that I wasn't dead? Couldn't we focus on the positive?

The real drama in the ensuing hours and days just following the incident seemed to revolve around the petty competition between two friends. One had slept with the other's fantasy boyfriend, and in the process, both had ended up with bruised egos for different reasons. What was interesting—and indeed what gave the journal an authentic tone—was that the irony of the situation hadn't been lost on Kristen.

Observation: To live someone else's fantasy is perhaps the cruelest punishment you can inflict on someone. It's the ultimate theft, even if the prize isn't all that it's cracked up to be. The thing is, I'm the one she should hate. But she's got too much pride, so she pretends to hate him instead. She keeps telling me to go see him and tell him to his face what a bastard he is.

Madden chastises himself for being seduced by mere words, even as he tries to comfort himself with the rationalization that Carrie and other witnesses had corroborated virtually everything in the document.

"What do you think, Hank?" Burns asks.

They're both sitting in the car, strapped in with their seat belts, but Madden hasn't started the engine yet.

"I think we've got a problem," he says.

"You asked her parents whether she'd been to the clinic, didn't you?"

He thinks about the exact wording of his questions.

"I asked them if she'd seen a doctor after the incident."

"And they said she had?"

"Her father sent her to a doctor. To check whether she was a virgin."

They sit there staring out the windshield. The car is parked in the shade, under a eucalyptus tree, which has scattered its seeds and leaves over that corner of the lot. Madden notices that some leaves and seeds have fallen on the hood.

"I know this sounds weird," Burns says after a moment, "but what if she was trying to protect the doc?"

"What do you mean?"

"What if she was examined the day after the incident by these folks here and the exam report shows she indeed had sex within hours of the exam. That would implicate him, would it not?"

He's thankful Burns is there. He's more optimistic, a glass-half-full guy. He, on the other hand, always manages to read the worst into everything.

"It's possible," he says. "But what's he doing here, then?"

"True."

They sit in silence again.

"We could tail him," Madden says.

"We could."

"For a few days. See what he's up to."

"He may screw up."

"He may."

"You going to tell Pete?" Burns asks.

"Maybe not just yet."

"When?"

"When we know for sure."

"Know for sure what?"

"Know for sure one way or another."

"Fair enough."

"You're a good man, Burns."

"Today, Hank. But you know that if anything goes down on this, you're taking the heat. He's your boy not mine, and you're locked in something fierce. But if you think that taking him down is going to somehow open the sky up and make the birds chirp in melodious fashion, you are sadly mistaken. Even if he is guilty, he's not *your* doctor. And no one ever will be."

"I know."

"Then let him go."

"I can't. Not yet."

"Then start the car, man."

30/ Cooking with MSG

March 1, 2007—p.m. 1:45

Watkins would have killed him if he knew, but two weeks after the party he'd called Kristen from a pay phone on campus. Jim had lifted her cell number from his sister's phone a few days earlier but didn't work up the courage to call her until Sunday, when he felt more certain the coast was clear. Even then, he had trouble dialing. He'd get to the last digit, hesitate, then put the receiver back on its hook and stop to question his judgment. Four times he hung up before finally letting the call go through. And he probably would have hung up again if she hadn't answered after the first ring.

"Hello."

"Hello, Kristen?"

"Hey. Who's this?"

"Jim. Carrie's brother."

"Hey."

As *heys* went, it was neither positive (*hey, I'm totally psyched to hear from you*) nor negative (*ugh, it's you*). Her tone seemed completely indifferent, which only made him more nervous.

"I just wanted to check and see how you were," he went on, his voice quavering slightly. "Carrie said you were OK, but I just wanted to make sure."

"I had a splitting headache for a couple of days," came her reply, "but I'm all right now. Listen, I'm sorry about what happened. I heard you got in trouble with your frat."

The apology surprised him. It was the last thing he expected. *Damn*, he thought, *was Watkins right?*

"No, I should be the one apologizing," he said, relaxing a little. "I never should have let you drink that much."

"I guess it could've been worse. At least they didn't have to pump my stomach."

He laughed. "Yeah, I guess." It blew him away that she could have a sense of humor about the whole thing. "It was lucky you guys knew that doctor."

"Dr. Cogan. Yeah, he's cool."

They talked like that for another minute or so. First he apologized, then she. Then he said, "Hey, I gotta bounce. I'm about to be late for a meeting with my history TA. But could I call you again? You know, to check up on you."

Silence. His throat tightened, his heart pounded hard in his chest.

"Yeah, sure," she finally said. "Just no more parties. Not this year, anyway."

"No, don't worry. No more parties."

A couple of days later he called her again. This time her *hey* was more friendly—friendly enough, anyway, for him to think she might actually be glad he was calling. So after a minute or so of small talk, he asked her to the movies that coming Sunday.

He said, "Hey, I'm thinking about hitting a movie Sunday. A couple of good ones just came out. Wanna join me?"

At first, he thought she was going to turn him down. She said she'd already seen the first movie he mentioned. And when she began to offer her assessment of it, he thought it was her way of easing into a brush-off. But then, out of the blue, she said: "What time?"

"What time what?"

"Are you thinking of going?"

* * *

He met her at the theater at five-thirty, twenty-five minutes before the movie was supposed to begin. He picked the twilight show for a couple of reasons: not only did it play into his low-key, this-may-or-may-not-be-a-date approach, but it also afforded him the time to take her somewhere after the movie.

The place he had in mind was The Blue Chalk Café, off of University Avenue in downtown Palo Alto. Blue Chalk was a full-scale restaurant, with a large bar upstairs and a gaming area, off to the right when you first walked in, that was home to four blood-red pool tables and a long, solitary shuffleboard table. Though the place generally attracted an older, professional crowd, there was always a small contingent from the U., and he and a couple buddies from school sometimes went there during the week to play shuffleboard.

"Blue Chalk, huh?" his sister would call to pry the next day. "So civilized, Jimbo."

They spent a little over an hour there—enough time to play three games. Kristen had never played shuffleboard before, so the first match wasn't much of a contest. She kept sliding her rocks into the side and end gutters. But by the middle of the second game her touch began to improve and she actually would've beaten him in the third game if he hadn't come up with a great shot to knock one of her rocks out of the three-point zone.

"What'd you talk about?" Carrie would ask.

As he had hoped, the activity had helped put them both at ease. During the first game, he was mainly instructing, teaching her the not-so-fine art of shuffleboard strategy. But by the second game they'd moved onto gossip. He asked her about some of the freshman and sophomore girls—now sophomores and juniors—whom he'd thought had potential when he was back in high school. She told him whose stock was on the rise and whose wasn't and how these two computer geeks she knew had just put out a popularity index, which was totally brilliant. It was a sociological experiment. They had a computer formula for rating people and, though your looks and what clique you hung with were big factors, there were intangibles.

"We talked a lot about that popularity list," he'd tell Carrie. "Who was on it and where and all that. I hear you're ninety-seven and Kristen's ninety-two."

"I know. Doesn't that suck? I didn't even crack the top fifty."

After the third match, they called it a night, and he walked Kristen back to her car, which wasn't actually her car, but her mother's. She said she hadn't had a car since she totaled her Jetta before Christmas, and her father was going to see how she behaved before getting her another one. When she said that, they looked at each other, and he knew she was thinking about that night. But neither of them said anything.

"Did you kiss her?" Carrie would ask.

"No."

He went to kiss her. "Well, goodnight," he said, and leaned forward, but he didn't head directly for her mouth. He slowly headed toward her face and at the last second he turned a little, or maybe she did, and he only caught the edge of her mouth.

Carrie would ask, "Are you sure?"

"Why, what'd she say?"

"She said you kissed her goodnight."

"On the lips?"

"Yeah."

He'd laughed. He knew his sister well enough to know she was fishing. "She's a nice girl. I don't think she'd kiss and tell."

Carrie let out one of her whiny groans. "Come on."

"There's nothing to tell. We went to the movies. We played shuffleboard. What do you want from me?"

"Hello, I want dirt."

"Shut up, Carrie. I'm not in the mood for this high-school crap."

"Jeez. Aren't we a little cranky today."

Jim couldn't remember exactly how much time passed between that first time they played shuffleboard and the day he heard about the diary, but it was probably a good month. That Saturday, a few hours before Kristen killed herself, his sister called him around noon and said: "Did you hear?"

"Did I hear what?" he asked, still groggy.

"Kristen's mother found her journal."

"Yeah, so?"

"And hello, there was sexual stuff in there."

Jim's eyes opened wide. She now had his full attention; he was completely alert.

"What sort of sexual stuff?"

Silence. She didn't answer right away, and the longer she waited, the more impatient Jim became because he knew it was for effect. Finally, he snapped.

"Goddammit, Carrie, what sort of sexual stuff?"

"That night she got drunk at the frat—"

He felt his whole body go tense. "Yeah," he said, breathlessly, "what about it?"

"She had sex."

"It's in there? She wrote about it?"

"Totally. Remember that doctor we took her to? He fucked her."

His stomach dropped.

"What?"

"Yeah. She lost her virginity to that guy. She told me right after it happened. But I was sworn to secrecy. Now everybody's going to know. Her parents are totally going to press charges."

His head was swirling. He felt for a second like he was going to faint.

"Who knows about this?"

"I don't know. Her parents. The police. I think they're on their way over to her house."

"What?" He rolled over and looked at his clock radio. "When?"

"I don't know. What's wrong?" Carrie asked.

"Nothing."

"You sound like shit, Jim. Dad told you to lay off the booze."

"I wasn't drinking."

"Jim?"

"I wasn't. I swear."

He sure as hell felt like having one now, though. "You're at home?"

"Yeah, why?"

"Are the cops going to talk to you?"

"I don't know," she said. "Probably at some point."

"Well, stay there. I'm coming over."

"If they talk to me, Jim, I'm going to tell them the truth," she warned. "I'm not going to lie for her. I can't. I told her."

"Well, I'd like to know just what you think the truth is."

Jim and Kristen had never talked about what happened to her that night at the doctor's house. Not in any detail, anyway. But there were hints that she had feelings for Cogan. She told him about the whole knife-music thing—how he played music while he operated—and how she'd made a CD for him, which got Jim kind of jealous. He didn't want to talk about the guy, but she kept bringing him up, and one day when he met her, she was pretty down. When he asked what was wrong, she said she'd run into Dr. Cogan at the Safeway and he'd been pretty frosty.

"Are you stalking him?" he'd remarked jokingly, not really understanding why she cared whether he was frosty or not.

She glared at him. Whenever he made a snippy comment

about the guy, her expression would darken and she'd give him a hard look.

Still, there were certain questions he had to ask. He couldn't help it. He'd think them, and suddenly they'd come out of his mouth. *Is she into him? She is. I know she is.* And bam, before he could stop himself, he was asking: "You like him, don't you?"

"Dr. Cogan? As a person, yeah. He has this way about him. Like he's effortlessly in control. I just feel comfortable around him."

"But do you want to?"

"Do I want to what?"

"Never mind."

Another time, after she had told him she kept a journal, he thought, *I wonder what shit she writes about me*, and the next thing he knew he was asking: "Do you ever write about me in your journal?"

"Sure."

"Is it OK?"

"What I wrote?"

"Yeah."

She smiled. "A lot of what I write isn't OK. I spend a lot of time complaining."

"Is that why you keep a journal? To have a place to vent?"

"Oh, I don't know."

They were at Starbucks, sitting at a table, both of them drinking chai. He remembered her looking down at her hands, which were playing with an empty sugar packet. She was folding it into a little square. When she looked up at him again, she said something he wouldn't forget.

"There are things you want to keep close to you and things you don't. Writing, I guess, allows me to control that. I can keep things close and push them away at the same time."

* * *

How did Watkins react? After Jim told him that Kristen had killed herself and that the detective had come to speak to him earlier that afternoon, Watkins's fist tightened into a ball and if he wasn't going to punch him, he looked ready to punch somebody or something else.

"Killed herself?" he asked. "Are you kidding me?"

"Yesterday," Jim said, still unable to believe it himself. He'd hesitated to tell Watkins but word at the frat had already gotten out about a detective asking questions and he decided that it was better Watkins heard the story from him rather than filtered through someone who didn't know as much.

"And she had a blog?"

"No, not a blog. A journal. In a notebook. She wasn't writing it for other people. She didn't believe in that."

"How do you know?" Watkins asked, eying him warily.

"My sister told me."

He assured him—and then reassured him—that he'd stuck to the story they'd rehearsed.

"It's the doctor they're after," he told him. "They're just trying to piece together what happened that night."

"I don't believe it," Watkins said absently, sitting on the edge of his bed, staring straight ahead, speaking in a monotone. Not only did he seem stunned, but Jim also thought he detected a flicker of grief. Perhaps, however, he'd judged too hastily.

"Don't believe what?"

"That she fucked this doctor."

"It's not like she fucked him. He fucked her."

"If she wrote about it, *she* fucked him."

"What are you talking about?"

"It's too weird," he said, still somewhere else. "Something's wrong."

"You're the king of fucking weird," Jim said. "And

you're telling me *this* is too weird?"

Watkins looked over at him. "You just stick to the story," he said, his voice a notch lower but sharper now. "If this somehow gets back to us we're going to be in a deep shit, *capice*? We could be held responsible for this girl's death."

"How?" Jim demanded. "She doesn't remember anything."

"She's dead, dodo. The dead don't remember. However, they do have a habit of making other people not forget. So, you do not waver. And if they press you on something, you do not get flustered. Vigorous defensive, Mr. P. When they come at you, you come right back. Firm but not angry. Got it?"

"Firm but not angry," he repeated, not sure what else to say.

"Good. Now we're cooking with MSG."

"Hey," Kristen said, thinking she knew who was calling from the number on her Caller ID.

"Hey."

"Oh, hey. I thought you were Carrie."

"I'm at home."

"In your old room?"

"No, in the backyard. Lying on the grass."

That afternoon, he was the one who'd made the fourth call to Kristen. When Madden had asked Carrie about the five conversations she'd had with Kristen that day, she hadn't corrected him and told him, no, she'd actually only had four. She talked to Kristen so much she couldn't remember exactly how many times she'd spoken to her. But Jim remembered the conversation very well.

"I heard," he said.

"Carrie told you? About Dr. Cogan?"

"It's true then? You slept with him?"

"Yeah."

A moment of silence. He was trying not to let his anger overcome him.

"Willingly?" he asked.

"Yes. But my father still wants to press charges."

"What are going to do?"

"I don't know. I took a couple of Percoset."

Silence again.

"Jim?"

"What?"

"Remember how you told me about lying down by the fountain."

"Yeah."

Sometimes, at school, he'd go over to the "The Claw" fountain in White Plaza, in front of the campus bookstore. Square-shaped and perfect for wading on hot days, the fountain had at its center a sculpture that looked like a jagged, petrified, almost primordial hand coming out of the ground. It was a popular meeting point for students. He told her that sometimes he'd go there and lie down along the rim of the fountain and close his eyes and actually think he was invisible because people would sit down near him and say the most fucked up things. Girls talking about having sex with their boyfriends. Girls talking about having sex with girls. Wild shit.

"Well, I wish I were invisible now," she said.

"I can't see you anymore."

"I mean it, Jim."

"And I mean it, too," he said. "I can't see you anymore, Kristen. That's what I called to tell you. I don't think it would be a good idea."

"Forever?"

"Well, I'm just . . . I guess, you know, I'm disappointed."

"Because I slept with Dr. Cogan?"

"No. I mean, yeah, yes that has something to do with it. But it's more that you didn't tell me. You weren't honest with me."

"About losing my virginity?"

He hadn't thought of that.

"No," he said, "Like, more generally speaking."

"I just didn't tell you I slept with him. Everything else I said was true, even the part about how I said I wanted to lose my virginity. That was all the truth."

"Whatever. I just can't believe you willingly had sex with that dude. I mean, he's like forty-five."

"Great," she said. "My father's disappointed in me. My mother is. And now you are, too."

She was crying. He heard her sniffling.

"I'm sorry," he said. "I didn't mean it like that. That was the wrong word."

"Well, screw you. Screw all of you."

"Kristen, wait."

But it was too late. She'd hung up.

PART 4

COMING CLEAN

31/ Beckler's mercy

May 9, 2007—p.m. 4:56

Dr. Anne Beckler always parked in the same spot in the hospital's lot. She didn't have a space with her name on it, but she was the type of person who felt she deserved one, and to make up for the injustice she subconsciously made believe she'd been assigned one. So what if it was toward the back of the lot where almost no one parked. It was her space and she parked in it everyday unless someone mistakenly commandeered it. On the rare occasion that happened, she didn't treat the theft like the end of the world, but it threw her off enough to put her in a noticeable funk that left nurses whispering and giggling in its wake. The joke was that someday Beckler would discover that the car's owner was a patient and she'd refuse to operate on him until he moved his car.

Cogan, sitting in his car a few spaces over from hers, chuckles to himself, remembering the nurses making fun of her behind her back. It's all he can do to keep reminding himself that he really hates the idea of returning to Parkview to solicit Beckler in the parking lot. The encounter will likely be unpleasant. The board shows Rebuff at two to three odds and Profoundly Humbling Experience, another favorite, is getting bet heavily as they near post-time. He's put everything on the long-shot Soft Spot, and in doing so, will finally get a chance to ride his theory that Beckler isn't as bad as he thinks, that somewhere underneath that modulating fiery, glacial facade is, well, a speck of affection for him.

His phone rings just before 5 p.m.

"OK," Josie Ling, one of the OR nurses informs him. "She's gone down to her office. She should be out in a few minutes."

Sure enough, right around the five-minute mark, he sees her come out of the hospital's side entrance. She's carrying her soft leather briefcase in one hand and a large, white shopping bag in the other. When she's about thirty yards away, he opens his car door and gets out. She doesn't see him immediately, but when she does, she hesitates for a moment, panic in her eyes. Instead of greeting her with his customary grin, he holds his poker face, which he hopes will be less provocative.

After she gets over the initial shock, she's actually the one who smiles.

"Hello, Cogan," she says, stopping in front his car, just before the front fender. "What brings you to Parkview?"

"I came to ask a favor."

"Of who?"

"You."

She looks around suspiciously, as if trying to ascertain whether she's about to be the butt of some practical joke. Then she laughs.

"You've got to be kidding."

<u>May 9—p.m. 6:40</u>

"Here's what I got," Billings says, shifting the toothpick in his mouth from one side to the other. "So except for going to Safeway to get some groceries and going for a jog around eleven, he's home all day. But then, at four-fifteen, he gets in his car and drives down to the hospital."

"Which hospital?" Madden asks.

"Parkview, man. Where he used to work."

Madden looks at Burns. For the past couple of days, with Fernandez on vacation, the three of them have been taking turns tailing him, though Billings, who Cogan hasn't met and fortuitously has the lightest caseload, has been doing the bulk of the surveillance. Of the three of them, he's also the most nondescript. He's of average height and looks, has a thin frame and full head of closely cropped, light brown hair. He has virtually no distinguishing features save exceptionally good, exceptionally white teeth, which he takes exceptionally good care of, and a self-assured smile that he once admitted, after several rounds of drinks at The Goose, he modeled after Robert Redford's smile in one of the early scenes in *Butch Cassidy*. That smile, of course, rankles Madden to no end, for it represents cheap seduction—not of women—but of those in their fraternity. Billings may only be an average detective at best, but he's universally popular in local law-enforcement circles, the guy everybody wants to buy a beer.

"What was he doing at Parkview?"

Billings hands him a digital photo he'd printed out on an inkjet printer. Pointing at the photo with his toothpick, he says, "He waited for *her*." The picture's a little fuzzy from being blown up a little more than it should, but Madden has no trouble recognizing the woman with short, dark hair.

"Dr. Beckler," he remarks to Burns.

"Yeah," Billings feels compelled to interject. "I assumed she was a doctor."

Burns: "Where'd he wait for her?"

"In the parking lot."

Cogan pulled into the back of the lot and waited in his car. Right around five, Billings says, he saw this woman—this Dr. Beckler—heading toward the area where Cogan was parked. When she was twenty-five yards or so from him, Cogan stepped out of the car. He didn't go to greet her, though. Instead, he stood next to his car and waited for her to notice him.

"Could you tell whether she was expecting him?" Madden asks.

"Didn't appear that way."

When she saw him, she stopped in her tracks, clearly surprised. From his vantage point, he was having troubling seeing Cogan's hands. But from the glimpses he got, he didn't see a weapon.

They spoke for about five minutes. Their conversation didn't seem heated. She started to leave, then came back and said something. Not longer after the second exchange they both got in their separate cars and left. Cogan went directly home.

Burns: "Did she give him anything?"

"No. She had a shopping bag and a briefcase, but never took anything out of either."

Madden stares at the photo. He sees the shopping bag Billings is talking about.

"What do you think, Hank?" Burns asks.

"That's a Neiman Marcus bag, isn't it?"

Burns scrutinizes the photo.

"Yeah. What about it?"

"Nothing. I just didn't picture Dr. Beckler as a Neiman Marcus kind of gal."

<u>May 9—p.m. 5:02</u>

"I need your help, Anne."

"Is this one of your pathetic attempts at humor, Cogan?"

He shakes his head. "You know I wouldn't ask unless it was really important. And I would appreciate that if you turn me down, you keep this conversation confidential."

"I can't guarantee that."

"Fair enough."

She sets the shopping bag down.

"You better not be fucking with me."

He is in a way. He's always fucking with her. But this time there's no cum line. No, he truly needs her help. He says that he'd heard through the grapevine that she volunteered a couple of times a month at The Free Clinic. "I need you to pull a patient's chart," he says. "The name on file should be Ray. Chris Ray. I need to know what she was treated for."

"Who's Chris Ray?" she asks.

"The girl."

"*The* girl?"

"Yes."

"How do you know?"

"I know."

"You know she came in to the clinic?"

"Using that alias. The Sunday after the incident. The next day."

"Are the police aware of this?"

"I don't think they are. They definitely poked around, but it doesn't look like they tried that hard to I.D. her."

She looks at him with renewed skepticism.

"I'll give you a hint," he says, anticipating her next question. "Lead singer, *Twelve Picassos.*"

Her eyes open wide. "Heather? The admin?"

"She recognized the girl from a picture I showed her. A certain baseball cap jogged her memory. For the record, I swore I wouldn't tell you she told me."

"And you lament your betrayal with such pride. That's what I love about you, Cogan, your ability to instill trust."

He smiles. "You miss me, don't you, Beckler? Admit it, deep down, you miss me?"

She isn't biting. "What's there?" she asks.

"What's where?"

"In the chart?"

"A diagnosis."

"That what, exonerates you?"

"Maybe."

"And maybe not?"

"Something like that."

He knows she isn't going to let him get away with such a throwaway response, and the result is about what he expects: she picks up her shopping bag and starts to walk away.

"Anne, wait."

She turns around.

"Look, it cuts both ways."

He tells her the truth. There may be evidence that both exonerates and implicates him. He explains how he thinks the girl had sex with someone else that night and he believes she was treated for an STD. Having that on paper isn't necessarily going to help his cause, though.

"Because what, you've been treated for an STD yourself?" she asks.

"That's part of it."

"Jesus, Cogan. Recently?"

"No, a few years ago."

"And the other part?"

Proof, he says. It will give them the proof they're looking for that she actually had intercourse that evening. What's more indisputable evidence than an examination report dated the next day?

Beckler's face suddenly expresses alarm.

"You're not asking me to—"

"No way," he says. "I just want to know what's there. I need to know what's there."

"And then what?"

"Haven't got that far. I'm only at the part where I beg and plead with Dr. Beckler in the Parkview parking lot."

"And what does she do?"

"She says she'll help me."

"Why?"

"Because she likes the idea of this pompous asshole trauma surgeon who gives her shit all the time being indebted to her for the rest of his life."

"You're reaching, Cogan."

"I prefer to see it at as going down swinging."

She picks up her shopping bag and smiles. "It's been a pleasure as always, Doctor."

"That's my line."

"I know."

Watching her go, he shakes his head, grimacing a little. He'd thrown his best pitch and it just missed off the corner for ball four. Now she's heading to first base and the tying run (or is it the winning run?) is trotting in from third. He glances down the line for the imaginary baserunner, and to his mild surprise, there is a person. He's stationary, though. A guy in a blue polo shirt is facing the entrance of the hospital, standing next to his car, several rows down, waiting—or maybe pretending to wait—for someone.

<u>May 9—p.m. 6:45</u>

The encounter mystifies Madden. He'd interviewed Dr. Beckler. Discussing Cogan, she'd been very matter of fact, unemotional. She didn't seem to like him, but respected him as a surgeon. He remembered her saying that he was arrogant, had a reputation as a womanizer, and sometimes said inappropriate things. "But that's par for the surgeon course, isn't it, detective?"

They talked briefly about any "inappropriate" incidents in the past involving either hospital staff or patients. She remembered some small incident involving a patient, but it had "gone away." And that was it. That was all she wanted to say. Her final comment was: "Look, we don't get along. He pisses me off all the time and seems to enjoy it. But I'm not shallow enough drudge up any dirt that isn't there just because we don't get along. And I'm not going to pretend he isn't good at what he does. The beauty of the situation is that Dr. Cogan seems to be doing a fine job of digging his own grave. My assistance is not required."

Why did Cogan wait for her in the parking lot? Was he worried that she had made disparaging comments about him and simply wanted to confront her? Or was it something even more basic than that? Had he left something at the hospital? Did he want her to deliver a message?

And then it dawns on him. *Is it possible?*

He picks up his notebook and leafs through it, looking through his notes for the phone number he'd jotted down. Finding it, he sits down and punches the numbers in on his desk phone.

"What are you doing?" Burns inquires.

"What does it look like I'm doing?" he says, and just then he gets a voice on the line. "Hi, Rebecca. Detective Madden. Sorry to bother you so late in the day. Quick question. Does the name Dr. Beckler ring any bells for you?"

Anne Beckler? Why yes, she says. She volunteers at the clinic a couple of times a month. Why, has something happened to her?

"No, no. We just interviewed her previously and she mentioned something about volunteer work. Thank you."

After he hangs up, both Burns and Billings, who are standing, stare down at him with anticipation.

"What's up?" Burns asks.

Madden smiles. "Turns out Dr. Beckler volunteers at the clinic a couple of times a month."

"Interesting," Burns says. "And if you were a betting man?"

"I'd wager he was asking her to pull a file for him."

"You mean shred it."

"Maybe. Maybe not."

Billings laughs. "I think you boys are hitting the Viagra a little too hard. That woman ain't shredding shit. Whatever he was selling, she wasn't buying."

"That young lady, Heather, didn't seem too receptive on that tape we saw at the clinic, did she, Burnsy?"

"Not the least bit," he agrees.

"And yet twenty minutes later she was spilling quite freely."

"She was quite porous."

Now Billings is really amused. He's smiling gleefully. "This dude's got you spooked."

"He's not my dude," Burns says. "He's Hank's."

"Well, he's sure got the Hankster spooked. Got his demon-slayer face on. Nothing like a good medical thriller for Detective Madden."

Madden shoots him a cautionary glare. "Not today, Ace. Not now. I'm not in the mood."

32/ Nothing, but the truth

May 10, 2007—p.m. 12:33

The next day, a little after twelve-thirty, Joanie's Café in Palo Alto: seated at a table near the window of the small, country-kitchen style restaurant that's known for its good food, Cogan is having lunch with Carolyn Dupuy. Madden, in his car, parked a few doors down on the other side of California Avenue, the main artery into Palo Alto's second, less posh downtown a mile further south off the El Camino, notes the time in his notebook and writes, "Lunch at Joanie's with attorney."

The detective's wearing an A's baseball cap flipped around backwards and a pair of white Oakley sunglasses that he removes from time to time to peer through a set of compact but powerful Nikon binoculars. Whenever he catches a glimpse of himself in the rear-view mirror, he feels a little ridiculous, but the disguise is effective enough—or so Burns assured him between laughs when they passed the baton just before noon at the entrance to Cogan's neighborhood.

From his vantage, the conversation hardly appears to be a client-attorney conference. At first, Cogan does most of the talking while Dupuy listens attentively, a slight smile on her face. They initially appear to be having a light, cheerful exchange. Then Dupuy's mood suddenly changes. She seems crestfallen. If they'd been complete strangers to him, he'd have guessed he'd broken up with her or confessed to an infidelity. But they're not, which gives him pause for concern.

The conversation appears to cease for two or three minutes; they eat in silence. And then something disquieting happens. Not long after they resume talking, Cogan holds up a document and shows it to her. At first, Madden thinks it's the menu, but when he brings the binoculars to his eyes, he catches a glimpse of a headline he's all too familiar with: "Detective Doesn't Let Handicap . . ."

His heart flutters. He looks down at the passenger seat, wondering whether his mind is playing tricks on him. When he raises the binoculars again, he realizes there's no mistake; it's the article about him, and Cogan is pointing to a certain paragraph in the middle of it.

"Carolyn, I hope you understand what I'm about to tell you. I'm withholding information from you."

She blinks, clearly startled by the revelation.

"It's not related to the accusation," he quickly adds. He lowers his voice, though the din of lunchtime crowd, as well as a light breeze, is preventing his words from carrying. "I've told you the truth about my relations with the girl. I did not have sex with her and nothing will change that."

Silence. She looks down at her salad in an effort, it seems, either to collect her thoughts or check her anger.

"I don't know how to respond," she says after a moment. "I don't know how to respond to someone telling me nothing."

"Anything?" Burns asks, checking in by cell phone.

"He's over at Joanie's with the Dupuy woman."

For some reason—and he finds it irksome—he has a hard time referring to her as Cogan's "attorney." He can do it on paper, but not in conversation.

"At least he's out," Burns says.

"That's what I thought."

"Where are you?"

"Just little bit down on the other side of the street. I've got a pretty good shot." He trains the binoculars on their table as he speaks. "They're outside near the front."

"Me and Billings are over at the Mexican place. You want me to drop off a burrito or something?"

"Thanks. I packed a sandwich."

"Pete was looking for you."

"He knows how to get a hold of me."

"He asked how we were doing with the ex-girlfriends. What do you want me to tell him?"

"Tell him what we always tell him."

"We're working on some promising leads?"

"*Very* promising."

"Are we?"

"I don't know. But there's something weird going on here."

"What?"

"Hard to tell. I sure wish I had some audio, though. I'd really like to know what they're talking about."

Cogan takes a sip of his iced tea and glances out the window of the café. The dark sedan that followed him to Joanie's is now parked across the street. He can't tell exactly who's in the car, but since this morning, when he spotted Madden's partner, the black fellow, doing his best to blend in with the predominantly white customers outside his neighborhood Safeway, he's certain that the police, not some private eye hired by the family, is tailing him. The girl from the Free Clinic must have tattled on him, which is OK; he feels in control now.

"Why'd you tell me you're withholding information,

Ted?"

He turns and looks at Carolyn. She's adopted what he recognizes as her challenge posture: leaning towards him slightly, she has her elbows on the table and her hands folded resolutely in front of her face.

"Would you have preferred I not?" he asks.

"No. But it puts me in a very bad position."

"You're protected this way."

"How considerate."

"I also wanted to give you the opportunity to drop me as a client."

"Do you want me to drop you?"

"No. But I didn't want you to later regret not having the opportunity."

"I seem to remember a similar offer a couple of years ago."

The words weren't quite the same, she recalls, but he delivered them in a similar tone. One might describe it as icy. Something about Ted being Ted, live with it or move on.

"It's different this time," he says.

"What, besides the fact that I'm working for you instead of fucking you?"

"I value your friendship."

Stunned is too strong a description for her reaction, but the way he said it, so bluntly and earnestly, caught her off guard.

"You return all my calls promptly," he goes on in the same tone. "You listen to all my whining. You're consistent and reliable, and you're supportive."

He watches as her eyes fill with sadness so profound that he thinks for a moment she might cry. He knows she'd wanted those exact qualities from him at one time. He knew back then, but knowing it only made things harder.

"And I haven't billed for enough of it," she deadpans, trying to shake herself of the emotion.

"That's not it. You care, Carolyn. You genuinely want to

save me, even if you think I did it."

"You're a good doctor, Ted," she says, not denying his accusation. "Everybody says so, even the people who aren't your biggest fans."

"And what about the person part?"

"The truth?"

"Always."

"You're a better person when you're doctoring."

Now it's his turn to get emotional. He misses it then. Wexler, Kim, kvetching with Klein in the cafeteria, even the nameless interns and DocToBe Rosenbaum. But he especially misses the feeling of walking down the corridor to the trauma room not knowing exactly what's waiting for him but utterly unconcerned at the same time. He misses who he was then. She's right, he thinks, and suddenly has a vision of his brother, Phil, sitting out in the backyard many years ago, smoking pot, staring up at the stars, missing his old self, too, the guy who got left behind in Vietnam.

"You know," he said, "I haven't told my brother about any of this. He doesn't know. I was hoping it would . . . well . . . go away quickly."

"I know. Still, there's going to be a moment when we have to make our case more publicly. Pretty soon, Ted, we're going to need to do some PR."

"I think about him sometimes. My brother, Phil, the one who was in Vietnam."

"I remember you talking about him."

"Do you remember what you said that one night? About the takeaway?"

She squints a little, the recollection within reach but fuzzy. "Remind me."

"I asked him what his takeaway from the war was."

When he came back from Vietnam, his brother, who was usually pretty subdued, would get really angry sometimes, come home fuming about some random person he'd encountered, another "useless fucking idiot." When his father asked him what was wrong, he'd just say, "You wouldn't fucking understand."

He'd always wanted to ask Phil about what his father didn't understand, but he was thirteen and in some ways his brother scared the shit out of him. Years later, after his graduation ceremony from Yale, they'd gone and had a beer, just the two of them. In the bar that night, he asked him what he'd taken away from Vietnam. He wanted to know the one thing that he carried around with him after that experience. He wanted to know how it had shaken his soul. What lesson had he learned from it?

He remembered his brother smiling. "No one's every asked me about it like that," he said. But he didn't answer the question right away. Instead, he talked about what he'd experienced when he got back. How people had treated him badly. Well, no, *they* hadn't treated him badly. They'd just behaved badly. He'd hated how mediocre everybody seemed. How lazy. How misinformed. And all he could think about was that he'd risked his life for these people. He'd risked his life for these awful fucking people.

"I'll tell you, Teddy, what I took away from it. The American public isn't worth dying for. It's just not worth it."

At the time, Cogan didn't really get it. He was twenty-one, ready to take on the world, a hard-charger who was not only going out to make his fortune, but damn if he wasn't going to help people while he did it. Yet he had enough respect for his brother, and his life experience, to realize there must be some truth to the statement, and that someday he'd inevitably come to appreciate it.

As time passed and he settled into his career and life, he did. But he also began to interpret the remark in slightly different ways. Late one evening, after a particularly hard night (and day) at the hospital, he heard himself interpret it in a way that was altogether different.

"You know, I've been thinking," he said to the woman lying next to him. "If the American public isn't worth dying for, then why is it worth saving?"

"That's easy," she said. She moved closer to him and put her hand on his chest. "They're worth saving," she whispered tenderly in his ear, "so I can make more money."

"I'm serious," he said.

"So am I."

Now, sitting across from him, that same woman is smiling nostalgically.

"Remember?" he says.

"Yeah. I was happy then."

"And you're not happy now?"

"In a different way."

"Better or worse."

"Different."

He takes a sip of his drink and wipes his mouth with his napkin. It's one of the more personal moments they've shared over the last month. He's tempted to try to draw it out further, but quickly thinks better of it. Any time he's gotten too personal, it's only led to friction. Instead, he asks:

"What do you know about Madden?"

"Why?"

"Outside of work, do you know anything about him?"

She shrugs. "He goes to my church. The old one. On Oak Grove. Church of the Nativity. Or I should say, I sometimes go to his, for my attendance has been seriously lagging these days."

"No dirt? No rumors?"

She shakes her head. "He's a pretty private guy. I don't know anybody who socializes with him. He's got a couple of kids. He's married to a Hispanic woman. From Nicaragua, I believe."

From his front shirt pocket he takes out the folded up copy of the *Mercury News* article she'd given him. Opening it, he holds it up in front of him, but at an angle, pointing it toward the window, hoping whoever is watching will somehow see it. He's highlighted a few of the paragraphs with a yellow highlighter. "Read this again," he says.

She takes the article from him and skims it quickly, murmuring aloud the passages he's highlighted.

"OK," she says when she's through.

He deliberately holds it up between them again and points to one of the yellowed passages. "Do you see this part? The part where it talks about the doctor who sexually abused him."

She nods. "Yeah."

"I was thinking maybe your investigator should look into it. Take him off the girl and the family for a couple of days. As long as we're going after everyone, we might as well go after the detective. He's potentially got a built-in bias toward doctors. Who knows how far he's willing to go to destroy me."

"You think he'd do something illegal?"

"I don't know. I don't know enough about him to make that call."

"The abuse story checks out," she says. "I've had my guy poking around already. His boyhood doctor was dismissed from the hospital."

"The doctor still alive?"

"Died several years ago. Why, is this something you've looked into? Is that the information you're withholding from me?"

"No."

"You're not going tell me? Not even a hint?"

He shakes his head.

"I don't get it, Ted."

He looks down at his plate, avoiding her deadly pout. Picking at the remnants of his asian chicken salad, he says:

"I'm not trying to manipulate you, Carolyn. I just need a few days to work a couple things out. I'll tell you everything. Soon. I promise."

33/ Was what it was

May 11, 2007—p.m. 5:28

When he's "chilling" in his bed, like he's doing now, or at the gym lifting weights, or just walking alone between classes, it comes back in little flashbacks, like the ones he's used to seeing in movies: Watkins's maniacal smile, Kristen's lifeless face, the stain on the bed sheet, the pounding beat of the Chemical Brothers. They appear for an instant, solitary and fleeting.

The flashbacks don't haunt him exactly. No, he concludes, they don't rack him with guilt, because when someone kills herself, you feel worst about what you last said to her, less about what came before. But in recent days, the flashbacks have come more frequently and intensely; the thought that they're there, suddenly indelible and inescapable, makes him think of what Watkins said, that the dead don't remember—but they have a habit of making people not forget.

The other day he watched enviously as Fleischman used the video-editing program on his Mac to slice and dice footage he'd shot with his camcorder. Fleischman showed him how you dragged the marker to a certain point on the story line, hit your mouse button, dragged it to another point, hit the mouse button again, then the delete key, and presto, the section was gone, instantly eliminated.

He imagined that instead of Fleischman's footage in the computer, they were working on his. A couple of cuts later, just a five-minute sequence here, a two-minute sequence there, and everything would have been fine, the way it should have been—though, of course, there was no way to erase what happened later at the doctor's home. He didn't own that footage.

If you asked Watkins, he'd say it was just a question of how you looked at the tape. If he really had the footage there in front of him, he'd say look, s*he* initiated the action. *She* kissed him. And while she may have been out of it, she wasn't really unconscious. Not totally anyway.

He'd sometimes wanted to tell her. If he kept Watkins out of it, he thought he could somehow make it OK. He'd even suggested that to Watkins to try to get him off his back. "If she doesn't remember," he said, "why can't I make the memory for her? I'll say we hooked up. I'll make it nice. It'll be between her and me. You'll be out of it."

Watkins didn't trust him to pull it off. He'd fuck it up somehow. And furthermore, he didn't see the point. It was an unnecessary risk. Nothing happened. It was as simple as that.

He was right. But just a week before she died, he couldn't resist making an impetuous foray.

"I want to ask you something personal," he'd said to Kristen." You don't have to answer if you don't want."

They were sitting in his car in front of her house. It was early evening and still light out.

"Ask," she replied, "and I'll decide."

He put his hands on the steering wheel, gripping it tightly. "When you were a kid, how did you think you'd lose your virginity?"

She smiled. "I don't know. I guess I was of the romantic school. The long-term boyfriend thing. But I wasn't all obsessed by it or anything."

He nodded, plotting his next question, but before he

could formulate it, she asked:

"How 'bout you, how'd you think you'd lose it?"

"Uh, I don't know. Lots of ways, I guess. I wasn't picky."

He must have turned red because she laughed and said, "You're blushing. How cute. So, how'd you lose it?"

And there it was. The opening. The question he wanted, asked in just the right way.

"Oh, you know," he said, looking straight ahead, out the windshield. "One of the guys at the frat hooked me up. I was pretty wasted and he got this girl to go up to his room with me. I actually don't remember much. Just that it was kind of awkward and not all that long."

He didn't look over at her as he spoke, but even in profile, he must have appeared tense, for he heard her say:

"You don't seem OK with it."

"It was what it was."

"Did you ever speak to her again?"

Now he looked at her. He was at the edge. He was there, staring down into the ravine, ready to take the fall. All he had to say was, "I'm talking to you now, aren't I?" And he almost did.

You did, he now thought, lying in bed, staring up the ceiling, tossing a squeeze ball in the air. *You did.*

But at the last instant he'd stepped back.

"Yeah, I spoke with her," he said. "It was kind of weird. But we spoke and it was cool. We never said anything about it, though."

"And you're OK with that?"

"Yeah, as I said, it was what it was."

How would she have reacted? Would she have been upset? Would she have believed him?

"Why are you telling me this now?" she probably would have asked. And he would've had to say that with everything that had happened he thought it would be too much; it would have been overwhelming. "And what do you think it is now?" he imagined her retort.

"I'm sorry," he whispers aloud, tossing the squeeze ball in the air. "I'm sorry."

And just then he hears a knock on his door. He catches the ball and holds it in front of his face, his fist clenched.

"Who is it?" he asks tersely, concerned it's Watkins or the police. Who's worse at this point, he doesn't know.

"It's Gwen," the muffled voice comes through the door.

Gwen? What's she doing here?

He gets up from the bed, and opening the door, attempts a suave greeting:

"To what do I owe the—"

But his voice trails off when he sees she's not alone. A man, an older man, is standing a little behind her to her left. His face looks very familiar. And then he realizes why.

34/ Missing minutes

May 11, 2007—p.m. 4:58

When Cogan arrives at Meyer Library, the former undergraduate library that students still refer to by its old tongue-in-cheek acronym UgLy (the cement and glass building is neither attractive nor particularly comfortable to study in, but it does stay open 24/7), Gwen Dayton is already there, waiting for him at the top of the steps, dressed in white jeans and a blue Abercrombie and Fitch T-shirt, as tall and lanky as he remembers her, an easy spot. Understandably, she sounded a bit apprehensive on the phone, which is probably why she now has an unexpected escort, a much shorter, less attractive girl whose no-nonsense attitude and firm handshake makes him think *future FBI agent.* Gwen introduces her as Kathy Jorgenson.

The awkward greeting behind them, they set off for fraternity row, a cluster of eight or nine houses spread out across three separate streets that appear on the map as a U placed on its left side. Periodically glancing backward to make sure he isn't being followed, he listens to Gwen tell him what she'd already told Carolyn: the party that night had been at a frat that had been at one time the school's admissions office. Thus, its nickname: Rejection House.

The frat prides itself on being eclectic and has a reputation of drawing an attractive roster of guys, many of whom don't take the Greek concept too seriously and benefit from the "bad boy" mystique of having the word "rejection" incorporated into the description of their brotherhood. Out front of the white house, on the well-manicured lawn, a couple of members are throwing a Frisbee, daring a black Labrador, who's dashing back and forth between them, to intercept their passes.

"Hey, Tom," Gwen says to the one on the right. "Have you seen Mark?"

"I haven't," says Tom, a wiry guy with short, curly hair, his eyes covered with wrap-around sunglasses. "But he may be up there."

Mark Weiss, the frat president and Gwen's boyfriend, isn't there. Gwen knew he wouldn't be there because she'd talked to him earlier that day and he said he wasn't going to be there. Which is why she'd chosen this time to give him the tour he'd asked for.

"We'll make this quick," she says, leading them up the stairs. "There isn't much to see anyway."

There really isn't.

"She was sitting there," Gwen says, pointing to a spot on the floor. "She was propped up against that wall, right next to the radiator."

They're standing in the middle of the third-floor bathroom, which has an old, slightly rundown, institutional vibe to it, though it's surprisingly clean and free of the faint scent of stale beer that greeted them on the ground floor. There's two of everything. Two urinals, two stalls, two showers, two sinks, even two windows, one of which is open, drawing in a light but steady breeze of warm spring air.

Gwen set the scene, describing the people who were around Kristen. He stares at the spot. Listening to Carolyn's interview tapes and later reading the transcript, he'd imagined the scene many times. He hadn't expected a catharsis visiting the place, but seeing it now is an oddly empty experience, for there's little his imagination hasn't already filled in. Even the flaking of the silver paint on the radiator is strangely familiar.

He looks at Kathy, Gwen's friend, who's been virtually silent during the tour.

"Were you here?" he asks.

No," she says. "I'd left already. But I saw her earlier, dancing. She was drunk. But not prop-me-up-against-a-radiator drunk."

"Let me ask you guys something," he says. "And this may seem like a little bit of a weird question. But do you know of anybody at school who had an STD in recent months? You know, a venereal disease?"

They look at each other, slightly taken aback.

"I know a girl with herpes," Kathy offers after a moment. "She got it from some guy last summer in Spain. Does that count?"

Before they leave the floor, he takes a quick peek down the adjacent hallway, which is lit during the day by two skylights that, with the sun now lower on the horizon, aren't drawing in a ton of light. He might have investigated further; Gwen, however, is wary of knocking on any doors because she says many of the guys had been interviewed before, some of them several times, and they're getting fed up with all the questions, especially since their punishment, in the form of two years probation for the frat, has already been exacted by the authorities.

He scans the doors, counting four on each side of the hall. Two on each side are doubles, according to Kathy, and two are singles, bringing the total number of occupants on the floor to twelve. He remembers Carolyn telling him that thirty-three "brothers" lived in the house while another eighteen lived elsewhere on campus, which meant that not every floor was laid out exactly the same.

"Who you looking for? Maybe I can help."

In unison, they turn around to face the voice. Standing at the top of the stairwell is a guy who can only be described as a refugee from some vehemently hip jeans ad. He has pretty-boy features but a blue-collar outfit: along with the Levi's, he's wearing tan work boots and a short-sleeve over a long-sleeve T-shirt, the one on top splattered in spots with paint that's faded but visible. In his hand, he's clutching a rather large organic chemistry book.

"Oh, hey, Gwen," he says.

"Hey, C. J.," she greets him coolly.

He can't t tell whether she's disappointed to see him or just disappointed they'd been caught standing in the hallway and now had to explain their presence.

"What's up? You looking for Mark?"

"Yeah."

"He went up to the city for a dinner with his uncle. You didn't know?"

"I didn't think he'd left yet."

C. J. turns his gaze on him. "I know Miss Jorgenson, but who's this?"

"This is Ted," Cogan says.

"Ted, you a cop or something? Or a reporter?"

"I'm the accused."

"Shut the front door. You're the dude? You're the doc?"

"I'm the dude."

C. J. lets out a staccato laugh, presumably in recognition of some just-discovered irony. "So, what's up? What you doin' in our house, Ted?"

"Getting the proverbial lay of the land, so to speak."

"Very smart. I like to see that. Advance preparation is everything. Unfortunately, I'm in the midst of just such an undertaking myself." He holds up the book. "And if you'll excuse me, I've got a final to study for. Adieu ladies." He steps between Gwen and Kathy and walks down the hall, to the third door on the left.

"Hey," Gwen calls out after him. "Have you seen Jim Pinklow?"

"P-Flam?" He puts his key in his door. "No, not recently. He doesn't come by the house much anymore. I think he got a little spooked after that night. Maybe he's at the library. He sometimes hangs on the second floor, in that little alcove area."

"We didn't see him at Green or UgLy. Thanks. We'll try his dorm."

C. J. flashes a reveling grin. "You do that."

Later, looking back on the visit, that final, parting smirk will be the thing that leaves the most indelible impression. He isn't sure why at first, but then he realizes that it reminds him of his own smile, which all too often is misinterpreted as conceit or worse, gloating. C. J. knows something they don't, but at that moment, watching him disappear into his room, he doesn't think it has anything to do with Kristen. He only thinks he's the type of guy who gets laid a lot, a guy who can shift effortlessly from charm to callous indifference.

"Who was that?" he asks as they make their way down the stairwell.

"*That*," Gwen says, "was C. J. Watkins. He's a junior and, as you can see, a little full of himself."

"What's his story?"

"Kath thinks he's gay. Isn't that so, Kath?"

"I definitely get that vibe, don't you?" Kathy says.

He can't tell whether she's asking him or Gwen, but no, he says, he didn't get a gay vibe.

Gwen: "Good looking guy, though. Lots of girls like him."

"A lot of stupid girls," her friend opines.

"Oh, come now, Miss Jorgenson," Gwen mocks her good-naturedly. "Don't insult yourself like that."

"OK, I had a crush. Freshman year. For like fifteen minutes. I admit it. Guilty as charged."

Forgetting whom she's with, she doesn't think anything of the last remark—and neither does he—until Gwen makes a face, admonishing her.

"Oh, sorry," she says, mortified. "I didn't mean it like that."

He smiles, opening the front door to the frat for them.

"I know," he says. "Don't worry."

May 11—p.m. 5:21

"Hank, I lost him. I could swear he gave me the slip."

Madden's in the apartment of a rape victim, a twenty-six-year-old woman who alleges she was accosted by an upstairs neighbor. In the other room, the living room, Burns is interviewing the roommate of the victim. He's stepped into the kitchen to take Billings' call.

"Where are you?" he asks in a low voice.

"I'm over at the University. He drove over here around five and went to the bookstore."

"So you think he saw you and purposely gave you the slip?"

"I don't know for sure. But he was there in the stacks, looking at some books, and he went behind a row, and the next thing I know, he's gone."

"Where are you now?"

"I'm back at the parking lot. I went to see if his car is still here."

"Is it?"

"Affirmative."

"Shit."

"What do you want me to do, Hank?"

"What's he doing over at the University?"

"I don't know what the fuck he's doing here. I'm just following the fuck."

"Sorry, I was just thinking out loud."

"What's the name of the frat?" Billings asks. "I was going to check over there, but I don't know which one it is."

"Rejection House. It's the old admissions building, right in the middle of frat row."

"Rejection House?"

"Yes, just ask someone when you get close. Don't worry, they'll know. I gotta go. We're doing an interview. Call me after you get there."

May 11—p.m. 5:31

"No, I don't know anyone personally who had an STD," Jim Pinklow says a few minutes later in his dorm room.

Cogan: "Not personally?"

"Well, I mean I heard this story about how these two guys went to Miami a couple of years ago and got totally trashed and one of them ended up sleeping with a stripper and getting some STD from her—I think it was Chlamydia. And the other guy ended up sleeping in the bathtub in the hotel room while the other guy was having wild sex all night in the bed. That was the big joke or irony or whatever you want to call it. The guy who paid for all the drinks didn't get laid and the other guy did, but he ended up getting an STD. There was something karmic about that, you know."

"That was two years ago?"

"Yeah, these guys are seniors now. I know who they are, but I'm not friends with them or anything. That's what I meant by not knowing them personally."

Cogan looks at the kid, taking in his features. It's not immediately apparent, but when you look hard, you can see his sister, Carrie. The eyes are the same, blue and set wider apart than average. Similar builds, too. He's pretty short—maybe five-seven or five-eight—and slightly stocky. He's also tense. He isn't sure who's making him more anxious, him or Gwen, who's decided to take a stroll around the room and give his personal effects the once over. The other girl volunteered to stay outside ("Me and Jim had a little falling out after that night," she says), so it's just the three of them standing there. But it still feels plenty crowded in the small room.

"Who's this?" Gwen asks, pointing to one of three framed pictures on top of a bureau.

"Someone I met in Germany last year," is Jim's perfunctory reply.

While she quizzes him on the blond in the shot, Cogan does his own little sweep of the photo gallery, not sure what he's looking for, but confident he'd know when he saw it. He picks up one of the frames to get a better look: the shot is of Jim and two buddies, probably high school friends, standing at the top of what Cogan recognizes to be the Headwall lift at Squaw Valley with Lake Tahoe in the background. They're all wearing sunglasses, looking tan and their version of cool.

"Why do you want to know if I know someone who had an STD?" Jim asks.

"It's just a theory I'm working on," he says, putting the frame down.

"What sort of theory?"

"He thinks someone else slept with Kristen that night," Gwen says.

"Someone else? You mean, besides him?"

"Not him."

"How do you figure that?"

He ignores the question, even though it seems to be directed more at Gwen than him. In fact, Jim now seems to be speaking as if he isn't there.

"You said you were with Kristen most of the night," he cuts in. "So you'd noticed if she'd taken off for a bit? Or you would have noticed if she was with another guy?"

"Yeah, I was definitely keeping an eye on her, especially later on."

"But you didn't see her talking to anybody else?"

"Sure, some guys talked to her."

"Who?"

"I don't know. Kyle, I guess. And my friend Rob came over and was hanging with us for a bit. But he was mainly talking to me. And Brad Deering, I think."

He turns to Gwen: "Do you know those guys?"

"I think so. Kyle, for sure. I'm friends with his girlfriend, Holly."

"Look," Jim says, "I would have noticed if someone walked away with her. Even for five minutes."

"You weren't watching your sister?"

"I was kind of watching her, too. And some of the time they were together."

"But you were more concerned with Kristen?"

"Do you have a sister?"

No. He has a brother, Cogan says.

"Well, you can be concerned but not want her to be there at the same time. I wasn't all that interested in hanging with my little sister at a party. I was doing her a major favor even allowing her to come."

"But hanging out with her friend was OK?"

"She was cool. I'd known her since I was a little kid. What do you want me tell you? I've been through this like ten times before. You're the guy who should be answering the questions. My sister trusted you."

He feels his phone vibrating in his pocket. Partly out of habit and partly because he wants to diffuse Jim before he really went off, he pulls the cell out and looks at the caller ID number on the flip's external LCD. It was a local number he didn't recognize. "Sorry," he says, putting the phone back in his pocket.

"Whatever," Jim says, confused over why he'd apologized. He thought he was apologizing for asking redundant questions, not taking his phone out in the middle of a conversation. "It's a fucked-up, tragic situation. I just—it's just getting way tired, you know. There's no closure." He's rambling now. "I just keep thinking that none of this ever would have happened if her parents didn't find her damn diary. Her father's a bastard. He's always been a hard-ass. Why didn't they ask her what she wanted? Does anybody care about what she wanted?"

"I know what she wanted."

They both look at him.

"What?" Gwen asks.

"She wanted her memory to be hers. She didn't want to let anybody take it away from her."

Gwen again: "How do you know that?"

"Male intuition."

"Is there such a thing?"

"Not usually. But there's a pill you can now take."

She smiles. "An intuition-enhancer?"

"Exactly."

The conversation may have tipped into a full-blown flirt session if Gwen doesn't notice that Jim is lost in thought. From the disconcerted expression on his face, he seems to be having a little trouble digesting his conclusions. They're giving him heartburn.

"What's wrong, Jim?" she asks.

"Nothing," he says. "It's just that I never thought about it like that. For some reason I always thought she'd want to forget what happened."

"You don't write in a diary to forget what happened."

Gwen said it, but oddly the kid looks at him—really looks him in the eyes for the first time—and for a brief moment he feels a strange sort of commiseration.

"No, I guess you're right," Jim says.

<u>May 11—p.m. 5:29</u>

"He's not here," Billings says.

"Was he there?"

"I just talked to two guys out front. They said they hadn't seen him. Couple of girls and a guy went up a bit earlier. They knew them, though."

Madden is silent on the phone. He doesn't know quite what to say. The campus is big. Cogan could have gone anywhere. By the same token, the bookstore is big. He may have never left the bookstore.

"Hank, what do you want me to do?"

"Just go back to the car."

"What if it's not there?"

"Call me if it's not there."

"I'm sorry, man."

"Hey, it happens," he offers half-heartedly, unable to hide his disappointment. "But you really think he gave you the slip on purpose?"

"I was watching him closely. I looked down at a book for a sec, and when I looked up he was gone. What does that strike you as?"

"What book was it?"

"What book was what?"

"Were you looking at?"

"I don't know. Some whale book. One of those coffee table books with pictures. Save the whale and shit."

"Save the whale, huh?"

"Yeah, save the fucking whale."

May 11—p.m. 5:43

He walks them back to the library, where they'd left their books. They pause in front of the modern-styled building, and he begins to make his farewells, thanking them both for the tour, when Gwen tells her friend she wants to speak to him alone, she'll catch up to her in a minute.

After Kathy goes inside, she says, "I'm sorry for not telling you she was coming."

She's speaking more softly, which gives him pause for concern. He isn't quite ready for another frank conversation.

"No, it was the sensible thing to do," he says. "It would look funny if we were walking around alone together."

"I want you to know that I've never said anything to anybody about what happened between us."

"Ditto."

He hopes she might read the brevity of his response as a red light, but she only sees green.

"You know, I perjured myself."

A smile breaks onto his face.

"That's funny?"

"No," he apologizes. "Just the way you said it. The legalese."

He says it reminds him of something one of his patients had once told him about downloading music on the original Napster. Everybody was calling it stealing. But technically, the crime was copyright infringement, not theft. The language made the act seem less egregious.

"OK, so I lied," she says. "I didn't tell your lawyer you called me after that night. I was going to. I told her about you asking for my phone number—"

"I know. I heard the tape."

"So, are you going to use it against me? Will it come out? Because it's been going well with Mark. We're supposed to live together over the summer."

Oh, so that's why you're here, he thinks. *That's why you agreed to meet me.*

"Gwen, we're doing everything we can to keep this from going to trial. If they get me on this, they're going to bring me up on murder charges. Do you understand that?"

"Can they do that?"

"There's something called foreseeable harm. Ask your buddy at the law school about it. If they can prove that I had sex with Kristen, they can argue that crime led to her taking her life."

Just then a girl walks past them and says hello. Gwen's disposition changes completely.

"Hey, Steph," she says, smiling cheerily, as if exchanging greetings at a cocktail party. "I'll be up in a minute. We're on three in the usual place."

She waits for the girl to drift out of earshot before resuming the conversation.

"I'll do what I can to help, Ted. I don't know why, but I don't believe you did it. I guess because I saw you there with her, and how you acted. But I'd like to stick to our agreement. I think it would be best for both of us."

"That would be my preference as well—ideally."

The last word falls heavily. She nods, her eyes downcast, her mouth in a calculated, stoic pout, not so different from the one he'd received from Carolyn earlier. She hadn't quite gotten the response she was looking for, and she looks more beautiful for it. This is not the same girl whom he remembers putting her clothes back on in his room, parting demurely. "Thank you," she'd said. "That was nice. I'm going to go now. I hope you don't mind."

Polite, straightforward, subdued yet passionate, a careful risk taker above the fray with a rocket body: That's Gwen Dayton, the abbreviated version he knows. There isn't a manipulative bone in her body, and yet there the angle is, now jutting out at him, tempting him to make promises he can't keep. Luckily, before he does, like a warning alarm, his phone goes off again.

"This is Cogan," he says, not bothering to check the Caller ID.

A male voice informs him that he's calling from the Kinko's on Colorado. He has copies waiting for him at the front counter.

"I didn't make any copies."

"I don't know what to tell you, sir. There's an envelope here with your name and phone number on it."

"What's inside?"

"You want me to open it?"

"Yeah, open it."

"You sure?"

"Yeah."

He hears the muffled sound of a tear, and then:

"It says 'Clinic Visit Form' at the top."

Jesus. Beckler. Did she come through? Is it possible?

"There's a name," the guy goes on.

"Chris Ray?"

"Yeah, that's it."

"OK, put it back now. Thanks."

"What is it?" Gwen asks after he flipped his phone closed.

"Nothing. Someone made a mistake."

"You sure?"

"Yeah."

He looks at his watch and seeing the time, wheels around abruptly, scanning the area for his shadow; he'd completely forgotten about him. His eyes dart from one person to the next: most of them are students who are either on the move or chatting in small groups of twos and threes in front of the library, just as they're doing. A biker whizzes by, and then another. It's going on six; rush hour has begun.

"I gotta go," he says, and in his exuberance, almost kisses her on the lips. "Just do me one favor: If Jim says anything to you, please call me."

"I will."

He touches his hand to her cheek. "And smile. It's going to be all right."

35/ Redhots and rose petals

May 11, 2007—p.m. 5:45

Jim had never had a gun, let alone a weapon of any kind, knife, spear, bow and arrow, baseball bat, pointed at him in his life, which is why it's so easy to answer the question he's now being asked.

"Tell me, Mr. P., you ever had a gun held to your head before?"

C. J. Watkins is standing behind him, indeed holding a gun, a Walther PPK, directly to his right temple.

"No," Jim gasps through Watkins's neck lock.

"How does it feel?"

"Cold."

"Good," says Watkins. "That's the way it's supposed to feel. Now that we've got that all straightened out, we're going to talk about what just transpired in this room a few minutes ago. Why were you speaking to the Daytona 500 and that dude who looks an awful lot like the doc we read about in the papers? I saw them go into the house, and guess where I found them: on the third floor."

"They came to see me," he struggles to say.

"What'd they want?"

"They wanted to know whether I saw Kristen go off with anybody that night."

"What'd you say?"

"I said I was with her the whole time."

Jim feels Watkins's arm muscles flex against his throat as he tightens the lock. "Don't fucking lie to me."

"I'm not."

He can barely breathe.

"You better not be. I'll come back here and put a slug between your eyes. You understand?"

"Yes."

Finally, Watkins releases him. He tumbles on to the bed, first gasping then coughing uncontrollably. At one point, his gag-reflex kicks in and he makes a horrible vomiting sound, but nothing comes out.

"You all right?" Watkins appears genuinely concerned. "Sorry, kid, I didn't mean to hurt you."

"What the fuck?" His breathing finally starts to return to normal. "Are you crazy? Is that thing real?"

" 'Course it's real. For an airgun."

"Shit, man. It looks real."

Watkins holds it up in front of him, admiring it.

"The Walter PPK. German craftsmanship at its finest. The firearm of choice of Mr. Bond, James Bond, and the CIA."

"Where'd you get it?"

"My father gave it to me."

"Your father gave you an airgun?"

"Well, I sorta borrowed it, really. He's got a collection. He buys 'em on eBay. Replicas of legendary guns."

"Doesn't he know it's missing?"

"I strongly doubt it. He's got a lot."

"What'd you say he did?"

"Real estate."

"In Florida?"

"Florida. The Carolinas. He's got some property in Colorado, Wyoming. You want to hold it?" he said, extending the gun out to him.

Jim shakes his head no, averting his eyes from the weapon. "What do you need that thing for anyway?"

"You spend any time in East Palo Alto?"

"No."

"Well, you spend any time in EPA you're going to need a piece. Even if it's just for show."

"What's in EPA?"

"Whatever shade of brown I want."

"Charming."

"Don't you worry about what's in EPA, Mr. P. You worry about what you're going to do about the present predicament."

"You tell me," he says, because he knows he's going to tell him anyway.

Watkins smiles at his pre-emptive strike.

"How much do you think he knows?"

Jim considers lying. But as soon as he hesitates, he knows he's lost; Watkins won't believe him and he'd soon be in another headlock. Fuck him, he thinks. The doc knows a lot. We're fucked. We're going to get caught. But it's not my goddamn fault. I wasn't the scumbag, STD-infected motherfucker. So let's see what you do with this:

"He asked me whether I knew anybody who had an STD."

Watkins doesn't say anything at first. He just stares at him in what appears to be veritable shock, and Jim smiles inside. Then Watkins explodes. Clenching his fist and stomping his boot, he shouts, "Dammit. Dammit fucking all."

"I don't know how he knows," he decides he'd better interject. "She—Kristen—must have said something to someone at some point. I don't know. I told him I didn't know anybody. He seemed to buy it."

"Fuck me," Watkins says. "Fuck me with a drain pipe. Did he say anything else?"

"No. Those were the two main things. He wanted to know whether I'd seen her with anybody else and whether I knew of anybody who had VD."

"What'd he ask first?"

"About the VD."

"And what was his tone?"

"What do you mean?"

"Was he being pissy about it? Or was he just asking?"

"Just asking. I swear, I don't think he knows who was involved. He's got a clue, but he's just fishing."

Watkins starts pacing back and forth in the small space that's afforded him, muttering a mix of profanities while hosting his own question and answer session. "How much does he know? If he's asking specific questions like that, too much . . . and who knows what Mr. P. really told him . . . did he walk out of here with the answer he was looking for? Depends on how P. said what he said . . . subtle nuances to take in to consideration . . . how much time?"

It goes like that for several minutes. It's pretty disconcerting to watch. Watkins pacing and ranting, waving around the gun a little too liberally even for a fake, lost in his own world. And then he stops all of a sudden, pivots toward him and asks:

"How long was he in here?"

"I don't know. Not long. Maybe seven, eight minutes max."

"Did he touch anything?"

Jim starts to say no, but then he catches himself, and exclaims excitedly, "Yeah, he did actually." He goes up and goes to the dresser. "This photo," he said, reaching for the frame.

Watkins grabs his wrist, stopping his hand short of its destination. "Show me where. Did he touch the frame or the glass?"

He doesn't know exactly where. Maybe both. He wasn't really watching. He just remembers him picking it up and looking at it.

"Do you have a magnifying glass?"

"No."

"Well, go to the bookstore and get one."

"Right now? I've got a final to study for."

"If you don't go right now, it may be the final final you study for."

"What's this all about?"

"Me being a fucking genius," he says. "I've got a brilliant idea."

"What sort of idea?"

"I knew a girl once, back in Florida. She had this guy who liked her a lot."

"So?"

"So he sent her a pizza. A special pizza that had all these funky toppings on it."

"Like what?"

"Like rose petals. Like candied hearts. You know, those little Redhots. Sappy shit."

Jim's still puzzled.

"What's that got to do with us?"

"You'll see. Just go get the magnifying glass."

36/ The pizza

May 11, 2007—p.m. 9:24

The call comes in late, around 9:30 that same Friday. Madden's at home, helping his son set up a model roller-coaster in the basement, when his wife knocks on the door to tell him his cell phone is ringing. She hands him the phone at the top of the stairs.

"Detective Madden?" he hears a woman's tense voice ask.

"Yes."

"This is Samantha Pinklow," she says, a little out of breath. "Carrie's mom. I'm sorry to disturb you, but you said if anything came up we should call."

He feels a little butterfly flutter in his stomach. "Yes, Mrs. Pinklow, what can I do for you?"

"Someone delivered a pizza to our home a few minutes ago."

"OK," he says, not knowing quite what to make of that.

"For starters, we didn't order a pizza."

"So you don't know who delivered the pizza?"

"No. It just . . . well . . . appeared."

Carrie, she explains, peeked out the front door to check why their dog was barking, and there it was, a large pizza box, sitting on the welcome mat. There was no note, no bill, nothing except the box. They thought maybe it was a wrong delivery.

"Is there a pizza inside?" he asks.

"Yes, but it has an unusual set of toppings."

"Excuse me?"

"Can you please come over. We didn't touch it. Carrie, she's hysterical."

"Mrs. Pinklow, what's on the pizza?"

"Horrible things," she says. "Please come. And hurry."

About ten minutes later, Madden is on his haunches, looking down at the mystery pizza. Standing next to him is Bill Kroiter, who'd turned up a little before he had after getting a similar call from Samantha Pinklow.

Holding the lid open with a ball-point pen, Madden stares down at the custom-made pie. He's seen some strange things in his time, but this has to be one of the odder pieces of evidence he's going to have to book. Indeed, it's a pizza—cheese with tomato sauce all right—but instead of pepperoni, mushrooms or peppers, this pie has a set of toppings you'd order from a hardware store, not a pizza parlor. He counts a total of six toppings on eight slices: Two Xacto knifes, mirroring each other on opposing slices; wax lips with six staples punched into them haphazardly; five pieces of clear, broken glass of varying sizes; scattered red rose petals (on two slices); a few little mounds of a powdery substance that could be detergent or Ajax, and what appears to be pieces of computer memory modules. Three or four sticks have been broken up and sprinkled on a portion of the pizza, whose container bears the markings of Round Table Pizza, a west coast chain.

The message is as clear to him as it is to Bill Kroiter: Remember to forget.

"She say whether it was warm when they first opened it?"

"I don't think they checked," Kroiter says. "But I bet it was ordered hours ago."

Madden nods. He looks at the pie again, then back up at

Kroiter. The guy looks keyed up yet haggard at the same time, with bright, eager eyes that have dark moons under them. Before Cogan had been arrested, he'd been calling Madden almost daily for updates. But in recent days they hadn't spoken, and he hadn't seen him in-person for three weeks, maybe longer. The wait for a more final resolution seems to have taken a heavy toll on him. He probably hadn't been sleeping and he guesses his marriage is suffering. If the marriage was strong before a tragedy of this magnitude, it could be sustained; it might even get stronger. But if there are weak links—and Madden has heard there are—chances are they wouldn't make it another year, especially with their remaining kids off at school. He feels bad for him.

"Well," he says, "I'll bring it in and have one of the guys canvass the Roundtables in the area, and we'll see if we can track our delivery boy down."

"Somehow I doubt he paid with a credit card," Kroiter remarks and just then Carrie appears in the doorway, with her mother at her side. She has an anxious look to her and her eyes are puffy from crying.

"Hi, Carrie," Madden says. "You OK? Got a little scare, huh?"

"Yeah," she says quietly.

"You have any idea who might be behind this?"

She shakes her head.

"Anybody been bothering you at school? Anything like that?"

Again, she doesn't respond audibly; she just shakes her head.

"Well, we're going to a whack at seeing if we can find out where this came from and who might have delivered it."

"I saw him," she says suddenly.

They all look at her.

"Saw who?" he asks.

"Dr. Cogan. A few days ago. At the Borders in the New Varsity."

"You saw him?" repeats Madden, a little dumbfounded. "Did he say anything to you?"

"Yeah, we talked."

"You talked?" Now he sounds truly flabbergasted. Why hadn't she told them right away?

"Yeah, it was casual. Like a conversation."

"What'd you talk about?"

"Lots of things, I guess. About Kristen. About that movie *Thomas Crown Affair*. About why he got divorced. Stuff like that."

She says everything nonchalantly yet she knows very well the impact her words are having.

"Did he threaten you?" he asks.

"No."

"You sure?"

"Yes. I mean, it was just an accident we were both there. He even said something about how he wasn't supposed to say anything to me."

"You think it's him?" Kroiter says, asking what they're all wondering.

Madden doesn't answer right away. He's tired and doesn't know what to think except that he finds the whole situation extremely disconcerting. It never ceases to amaze him what people are capable of doing when they're in a tight spot—so sure, Cogan could have sent the pizza. But it just as easily could be a couple of kids from Kristen's high school pulling a stupid prank. Or more likely, someone who wanted them to think Cogan had sent the pizza.

"I don't know, Bill. I just don't like the blatancy of it."

"I know what you mean," Kroiter says.

37/ The Mother Teresa of hackers

May 12, 2007—p.m. 2:06

The next day, he calls Burns at home to tell him he'd booked a menacing pizza the night before. It was disturbing the peace in front of Carrie's home.

"What the hell?" Burns says after he finishes the recap. "You think he sent it?"

"If I were a betting man?"

"Yeah."

"Gotta say it doesn't feel like his style. It's a little too creative. But I got a partial off one of the pieces of glass and it's a likely match."

"So it's him."

"Maybe. The thing is, it's the only print we found on any of the contents in the package. There's nothing on the razors, the computer chips. I got a couple of nice thumb prints off the outside of the box, but I bet they're from one of the guys at the pizza shop."

"So you're saying that whoever put the package together was being too careful to leave even a nice little partial."

"Seems odd, doesn't it?"

"The whole thing seems odd," Burns says.

There are other facts to consider: In the last forty-eight hours none of them had logged Cogan in the vicinity of a Roundtable and he'd been at home yesterday at 8:30 p.m., the last time Billings checked up on him. But they didn't have him nailed down at the delivery time, which was a problem.

Even so, Madden thinks it doesn't make sense. What would Cogan hope to accomplish by sending a menacing pizza to the girl's home? There were other, less obtuse ways to spook her. Like through the media. Two short articles had appeared in the local editions of the *Mercury News* and *The Chronicle*, but the case had yet to attract major publicity. Dupuy had told Crowley that her client preferred it that way—both for his sake and the families involved. But at a certain point, they would have to resort to more hardball tactics, go to a scorched-earth approach. "I will sensationalize this thing if I have to, Dick," she'd warned.

"Maybe Kroiter delivered it," Burns suggests. "You think of that?"

He actually had. But the same question applied. What did it gain him? More heat on the doc perhaps. Yet, at the same time, if his ruse were uncovered, it would totally jeopardize the case. The guy would have to be nuts. That wasn't totally out of the question, but still, it was a stretch.

"Where are you now?" Burns asks.

"I'm outside a Starbucks. The Santa Cruz Ave. one in downtown Menlo. He's inside with those kids."

"The next-door neighbor?"

"Yeah, and his friend."

"What are they doing?"

"I'm not sure. They've got a laptop. They're hanging out. Maybe they're playing a game. I can't tell."

"How long you going to keep this up, Hank?"

"It's going to break, Burnsy. I got a feeling. It's going to break soon."

"How soon?"

He knows what Burns is really asking. He's tired of the flying-under-the-radar act.

"We'll talk to Pete and Crowley on Monday, OK? We'll

lay out what we've got and see how they want to proceed."

"Hank?"

"What?"

"You think he purposely gave Billings the slip the other day? You get any indication he knows he's being followed?"

"No. But that doesn't mean anything."

"Why?"

"Because for all we know, he wants us to follow him."

May 12—p.m. 1:40

"OK, here's the deal," Josh says, placing the empty envelope next to Cogan's laptop on the small, square café table. "She says she wants you to put the thousand bucks in the envelope, then I walk over to Fed Ex and send it to the address on the envelope. When she sees the receipt, she'll hack in."

Lifting an eyebrow, Cogan looks at the name. If it weren't neatly typed, he would have thought it was misspelled. Diafongon Babdo is the name and he or she lived in Mali, Africa.

"You're serious? I'm mailing a thousand bucks to someone in Mali?"

"She sponsors some kids over there," Josh explains. "This is the teacher at the local school. She says over there a thousand dollars is the equivalent of twenty thousand here, maybe more. It's really a lot of money. You'd really be doing someone a lot of good."

"She doesn't want anything?"

"She wants you to pay for her coffee."

"That's it?"

"That's it."

"What is she, the Mother Teresa of hackers?"

"Something like that. Except she's an atheist."

"I'll be damned," he says, truly awed that such a person,

especially one so young, exists. "And she thinks she can do it?"

"She knows she can get in. She's done it before. She just doesn't know whether she can find the info you're looking for."

He glances in her direction. The virtual teammate he only knows by the call handle Vas (short for Vaseline) is sitting in the flesh at a table on the other side of the café with Steve, who would be assisting her in her little extraction. The Starbucks they're in is one of the largest in the area, and being a weekend afternoon, is more crowded than usual. Between the cherry-colored, wood-paneled columns and all the patrons, he's having a hard time getting a good look at her. Petite, with a wide face, dark-rimmed glasses and brown, medium-length hair that's pulled back in a ponytail, she reminds him of the actress Janeane Garofalo—from a distance anyway. She's older than the boys, but only by a year; she's a junior at their high school.

Some of the patrons are shoppers taking a break from store browsing, but a fair number are high school and college kids who've made the place a hang out. Where's his shadow? Madden—yes, it has to be Madden this time—is sitting outside in his car, wearing an A's baseball cap turned around backwards and sunglasses. He's drinking his own coffee and reading a newspaper. How long will he remain out there? Or better question: How long will they be in here?

"She's not going to get in trouble?"

Josh laughs. "Ted, I'm telling you, she's not going to even use her computer. It's untraceable. Don't be a wuss."

"It's traceable to some poor schmuck."

"Schmucks," Josh corrects him. "She's going to use every computer that's logged onto the Net in here."

This Starbucks, like most of the others in the area, offers broadband wireless Internet access, and a handful of customers, he among them, have laptops perched on their tables and are surfing the Web. With a little luck and a lot of help from a rogue program that Vas and a friend had created as "a goof," each one of them would soon be sharing a piece of their bandwidth to hack into the University's allegedly iron-clad network, and then hopefully, the student records at the infirmary, which he'd confirmed were computerized.

"I hope you're right," he says and just then he hears a chime alerting him that he has an instant message.

Vas, using the handle slipandslide84, had typed: "Fingers tap-tap-tapping, she says, w8ing, w8ing, w8ing . . . zzzzzzz."

"Well?" Josh says.

He stares at the screen for a few seconds, then types:

"Diafongon? Male or female?"

"Chk," the reply comes back with an emoticon of a winking baby chicken with a bow in its hair and puckered lips.

He sends his own smiling emoticon back, then, turning his chair a little to shield his hands from the cop, he pulls out a folded sheet of paper that contains ten one-hundred-dollar bills. He slips it into the envelope, and hands it to Josh.

"He's going," he types.

"R&R," she writes back.

May 12—p.m. 3:20

Madden starts to get impatient after an hour. He's gone through two newspapers and is twenty pages into a Tom Clancy novel Burns left in the car a few days ago. Looking out the window, he thinks: *You know I'm out here, wasting my time, and you're taking pleasure in it. I can see that little smirk every time you glance out the window. What are you up to, you son of a bitch?*

He gives it another ten minutes, then flips the baseball cap around so it's facing forwards, gets out and walks around, stretching his legs. There's a little jewelry store on Santa Cruz, and he goes in and looks around. Then he goes to nearby Draeger's, a gourmet supermarket, and buys a turkey-and-cheddar bagel sandwich. It's almost one. They've been sitting there for close to an hour and a half.

"I've had enough," he says to Burns when he calls on the radio to check in.

"You going home?"

"Thought I'd pick up a coffee first."

"At the deli?"

"No, across the street."

May 12—p.m. 3:22

The updates arrive sporadically. Vas informs him of her progress with short, cryptic messages. She seems to be composing them with flare, even borderline silliness, for her own amusement rather than out of necessity. He isn't surprised, given her reputation as a witty trash talker in their online league.

"U ever married?" she writes.

"Was," he responds. "Few years back."

"Carry your bride across the threshold?"

"Forgot. By the time I remembered, too late."

"I just did it. np."

She's in, Josh says, quietly interpreting. No problem.

A little later she writes:

"Foo. At H but wrong1. Hopped wrong bus."

She'd found the University's hospital directory, Josh translates, not the school's student clinic.

Just before one, at about ninety-minute mark, she sends good news:

"Parking the car. In lot. Like lot a lot. Is it a lot to ask to like a lot a lot?"

Shortly afterwards, his phone goes off. It's Steve calling from across the room.

"She's in the database," he says giddily, "but there's no

way to search it for specific terms, only names of students."

"OK, start going down the list I gave you and look for those keywords." He'd given Steve a list all the members of the frat, plus a handful of medical terms and names of antibiotics, including Azithromycin, doxycycline, and metronidazole. "Call me back if you find anything," he says, and just as he finishes the sentence, he sees Madden standing in line, getting ready to place an order. Even though he knows he shouldn't be surprised to see him, his eyes open wide as if he's the last person he'd expect to encounter.

"What's wrong?" Josh says, observing his alarmed expression.

"Nothing."

"I've seen that guy before."

"Yeah, he's the cop who arrested me."

Now Josh is the one to be fearful.

"You're kidding. What's he doing here? Should we tell them to stop?"

"If he was here to stop us, he would have done it already."

A few moments later, Josh looks over at the line, where Madden, at the front, is paying for the coffee he's collecting.

"Don't look," he warns the kid. "Don't pay any attention. I'll handle it."

"Is he coming over here? I think he's coming over here."

Indeed, he's moving in their direction. But before he gets too far, he stops at the condiment table, and loads his cup (it appears to be a standard American coffee) with a shot of milk and sugar. He puts the lid back on his cup, flips the drink tab open, and takes a few more steps in their direction. When he's about fifteen away, he stops and takes a sip of the coffee, looking over the top of the cup as he drinks. Their eyes meet. Expressionless, Madden brings the cup to chest height.

"What's he doing?" Josh whispers, his eyes locked on the table in front of him.

Cogan doesn't answer. He's concentrating on holding the stare, willing himself to match Madden's. The contest lasts a good ten to twelve seconds. And then it's over. Madden takes one more sip, turns away and walks out the door.

"Relax," he tells Josh, "he's gone."

"Did he see us?"

"Sure."

"You think he knows?"

"No. He just wanted to send a little message."

"What's the message?"

"He's nobody's fool."

"Is that good or bad?"

"Hopefully, it's irrelevant," he says, then types, "Anything?" into the instant message box.

"Patience, grasshopper," comes the reply.

<u>May 12—p.m. 3:56</u>

There are a couple of false alarms—one guy was treated with a certain antibiotic for an illnesses that turned out not to be a STD and some guy named Phil Dunham was treated for Pediculosis Pubis, more commonly known as crabs.

By the time they get down to the names that start with M and N, he's increasingly pessimistic they're going to find anything—until the following message flashes across his screen.

"Trichomoniasis. Chlamydia. Azithromycin. Good?"

They'd hit the motherload: a possible match.

He types: "What's the name? Who is it?"

Instead of an answer, his phone rings instead.

"Ted," Steve says a little breathlessly.

"What?"

"It's Jim. It's Jim Pinklow. Carrie's brother."

"You're kidding."

"No. We're taking a screenshot now. She'll print it for you later."

The little bastard. Of course he didn't see anybody else go off with her. Because he'd gone off with her himself.

"Ted, you there?"

"Yeah."

"You want us to do the rest?"

"No, log off. Let's get out of here."

38/ Screaming in whisper

Feb. 17, 2007—p.m. 11:12

They may have found his name first but he actually had sex with her second. Watkins had given him the opportunity to go first, but he hadn't been ready; he wasn't aroused. And that had proved quite unfortunate. He thinks about that sometimes, thinks that if he'd gone first, maybe Watkins, that contaminated bastard, wouldn't have gone at all. And then maybe it would have been OK. But that's not how it went down.

In the little flashbacks, the one thing he remembers most vividly is Watkins's voice after it was over. He wasn't shouting but screaming in a whisper.

"You gotta pull yourself together, man," he said, kneeling over him, uncomfortably close to his face. "I can't have you go catatonic on me. We've only got a few minutes. You're not going to pass out on me?"

He was sitting on the floor, with his back propped up against Watkins's double bed, his head in his hands. He still had his shirt and socks on, but nothing else. There, above him on the bed, lay Kristen, passed out. Though he couldn't see it from where he was sitting, he knew what was there next to her: on the bed, right below her, was a large stain of blood.

He lifted his head a little and peered up at Watkins. He

felt dizzy. "Was there this much blood after you fucked Becky Goffman?" His voice fell heavily on the word "fucked"—a little too heavily for Watkins's taste.

"No, moron," he hissed. "There wasn't this much fucking blood. But she could be on the rag for all we know."

"You think?"

"What's the difference? We gotta clean her up and get her out of here. Let's go, pledge. Get your goddamn clothes on." Watkins grabbed him by the front of his shirt and lifted him off the floor.

"OK, OK," Jim said.

"Here," Watkins said, going to a small refrigerator he had in the corner of the room. "Chug some of this." He handed him a bottle of spring water, then went to his bureau and fished out a couple of pills—one from a big bottle of Aleve and another from a smaller, unlabeled bottle. "Now take these."

"What are they?"

"Clarity."

After Jim had taken the pills and put his clothes back on, all of a sudden he felt C. J.'s hands around his throat. His back went thud against the wall as Watkins pushed him up against it.

"If I go down for this, P-brain, because of your inability to cope with the situation at hand, I will kill you. Do I make myself clear? I'm not going down for this shit."

"No one's going down," Jim managed to say, and Watkins loosened his grip. "No one," Jim repeated.

"I know," said Watkins, his smile returning. "Now find her underwear. I'm going to go out for a minute. Don't answer the door unless you hear three knocks." He went to the door and grabbed a big blue towel that was on a hook on the back of it. He took a peek outside. Seeing the coast was clear, he slipped out.

Jim quickly found her underwear. It was on the ground in between Watkins's little nightstand and the bed. He picked it up and balled it up tightly in his hand, not quite sure what to do next. The boombox on the floor was still putting out music—the Chemical Brothers and their funky techno beat. He thought about turning it off, but then he thought Watkins might get mad if he did. A wave of nausea swept over him and he went and sat in a chair in the corner of the room.

How had it happened? How had it come to this? One minute they were playing a stupid game of Truth or Dare. There had been a few silly questions, then Watkins had dared her to make out with him. He remembered her pointing at Watkins. "You," she said. "You're like 30." But she leaned into him anyway and Jim watched incredulously as their mouths locked. He felt himself smiling, but it was tinged with pain.

Then it was his turn. She came over and half fell onto the bed next to him. He helped her right herself and then she leaned over and kissed him—a sloppy, wet kiss that ended with her passing out on the bed next to him and Watkins laughing. "Potent, Mr. P., potent."

He didn't know why he let it go further than that. Why, when Watkins stripped off her clothes, did he do nothing, and watched instead, almost fascinated as he forced himself inside her? And why, when Watkins said, "Get in there, Mr. P.," that he'd done as he said and pulled down his own pants down and climbed on top of her?

He had made some feeble attempts at foreplay. Yes, it seemed ridiculous. But he'd gently kissed her and stroked her face, as if that would make it real. And once, when her eyes had opened briefly, he thought it was real. But then he heard Watkins laughing. "What are you doing, Casanova?"

He had trouble getting in her at first, but then Watkins wiped something on her—some sort of gel—and with one wiggle and a thrust he went in, he was fucking. It wasn't how it was supposed to happen. But there it was happening. He was fucking.

Three knocks. Watkins was at the door. Jim quickly got up and unlocked the door and Watkins slipped in and locked it behind him. He had wetted half the towel, and though it was soaked, Jim didn't think it would be enough to take out the stain. They needed something more powerful, a chemical. They needed the Chemical Brothers.

"OK," Watkins said, "I'm going to clean her up. I want you to make sure there's no blood on her clothes. Not a drop. Understand?"

Watkins turned on the small light next to his bed.

"What about the stain?" Jim asked.

"Don't worry about that. I'll get rid of it. First we clean her up and get her out of here."

39/ A lesson in pitching

May 13, 2007—p.m. 12:05

Sunday. Noon. At first Madden doesn't see the guy standing over by the visitors' dugout. He'd been concentrating on catching for his son, who'd inexplicably been having trouble with his control the last two games, walking nearly a dozen batters in each. He hadn't been missing badly, but he was consistently off the plate—and he isn't doing any better in today's practice session. Frustratingly, whenever he makes a comment to his son, even if only to voice his encouragement, it seems to have an adverse effect: the boy starts overthrowing, pitching the ball high or worse, in the dirt, skipping it past him.

"Keep your left elbow and shoulder up."

Chico turns toward the voice, which belongs to a lone spectator who, hands in pockets, is standing just behind the protective fence on the first-base side.

"What?"

The guy steps out from behind the fence and saunters into what would be the first base coach's box on game day. By the time he speaks next, Madden, to his dismay, realizes who he is.

"On your way to the plate," Cogan says, "remember to keep your left side up. You're letting it dip. Pitch it again."

Chico does as he's told, this time decidedly more conscious of his mechanics. But the result is the same: the ball goes high and outside.

"See, you did it again," he says, moving onto the field toward the pitcher's mound. "Here, let me show. You mind?"

Before Madden can object, Chico relinquishes his mitt and ball and Cogan is standing on the mound facing him.

"OK, body straight and relaxed," he says. "Stand tall. Your head doesn't move, your weight is centered, then you take a small step back to the left at a forty-five degree angle."

Madden stands behind the plate, mesmerized, half-wondering if what he's watching is real. Cogan's voice is almost hypnotic. He does everything in slow motion, going through each piece of the delivery from the pivoting of the right foot parallel to the pitching rubber to the follow through of the right wrist to the left ankle. Then he starts to speed it up, offering a different tip with each follow-through:

"Remember, the lower half moves first."

"Always throw from the far right side of the rubber to get a better angle on the hitter."

"Location up and down, in and out. Keep the hitter off balance."

At first, Cogan doesn't throw the ball. But on the third or fourth simulated pitch, he lets the ball go and tosses it to him. With each successive pitch, he throws the ball a little harder, and soon the pitches are coming in nearly as fast as his son's, only they're coming in over the plate, belt high.

Ten warm-up pitches later, Cogan turns to Chico and says: "Who's your favorite pitcher?"

"Maddox," Chico is quick to reply.

"Excellent choice. Mine was always Seaver. Tom Seaver."

Cogan then covers his mouth with the mitt and whispers something to his son.

"Get ready, Dad," Chico says gleefully. "He says he's going to bring it."

And before Madden can object, Cogan is in his motion and the ball is in Madden's mitt. He tosses it back, staring at

Cogan hard, pissed that he's challenging him like this in front of his son. He gets down a little deeper in his crouch and holds the mitt out in front of him, bracing for the impact.

Whap. Cogan hits the target almost dead center.

One after another they come in, pop, pop, pop, only now there are no mantras recited between pitches. Cogan has an intense look on his face that's at once full of emotion and emotionless. He's truly pitching.

After he's thrown about a dozen fastballs, he hands the mitt back to Chico and tells him to try again. Chico gets on the mound, and, imitating Cogan's motion, pitches the ball to Madden. It's a little high.

"Good," his new coach says. "Now think about everything I just told you and then stop thinking about it."

Chico stands on the mound, looking upward for a moment. Then he gets set and goes into his motion. Whap, the ball hits his catcher's mitt. This time, though, he didn't have to move. "Nice, Chico," he says, throwing the ball back.

The next pitch is the same; it cuts through the heart of plate. And the next. Out of the next ten pitches he throws, eight are strikes and the two that are balls are close enough to induce a batter to swing.

Having felt he mastered the lesson, Chico now wants Cogan to show him how to pitch a curve.

"Another day," he says. "I've got to talk to your father alone for a minute.

But I'll write down those pointers so you remember them."

He takes out a plain white envelope and begins to write on the back of it. Madden approaches the mound. He feels like a manager about to make a pitching change. But instead of taking the ball from his son, he gives him his catcher's mitt.

"Go see how your sister's team is doing," he says. "I've got to speak with Dr. Cogan."

"But the game hasn't even started yet."

It's true. Off in the distance, well behind the right field fence, he can see the girls standing in a line, waiting to take their warm-up shots at the goalie. Kick-off is still a few minutes away.

"Please, Chico. It's the last time I say it. Thank Dr. Cogan and go."

"Thank you, Dr. Cogan."

"No problem."

His son trundles off in the direction of the nearby soccer field. When he's a safe distance away, he said to Cogan:

"How did you know I was here?"

He holds up his hand. "Just a sec." He's still writing. "There you go," he says, handing him the envelope. On the back of it he'd written, "4 Steps to Proper Pitching" and listed the four steps.

"Thanks," he grumbles.

"How old is he?"

"Eleven."

"He's got a good arm."

"Yeah, his coach thinks so, too."

"Did his coach teach him how to pitch?"

"Not really. Not like you just did. I take it you played."

"Long time ago. In college."

"Well, thank you. He's been having a lot of trouble with his control."

"My pleasure."

An awkward silence.

"So you didn't answer me. What are you doing here?"

Cogan smiles. "I followed you over from your church. I came to tell you it's over, detective."

"Excuse me."

"Your case is shot. I don't know who's got you in his pocket. I don't know whether it's the DA or the girl's father, but you missed some crucial details."

"I know."

"You know?"

"Thanks to the number you pulled over at the Free Clinic, we know that Kristen visited the Clinic the day after you allegedly had sex with her."

Cogan is perplexed. Madden can see he really thinks the fix is in. "So you know she was treated for an STD?"

"No, we didn't. We hadn't tried to obtain a release of her medical records yet. Frankly, we were waiting to see what you'd do with the information before we proceeded along that route."

Cogan laughs. "You were going to wait. How long were you going to wait?"

"Not long."

"But long enough to see what trouble I could get myself into."

"We didn't know what you were up to. We didn't know if you were trying to cover something up. Tell me, how did you become aware she was treated for an STD?"

"Carrie told me."

This time, the ball went right through his mitt, and hit him square in the chest. Or at least it felt that way.

"Carrie told you?"

"Well, in a manner of speaking. And how 'bout this? How 'bout I have proof Jim Pinklow, one of your star witnesses, was treated for the same STD. He's your rapist not me."

"What's your proof?"

"You're holding it," he says nodding at the envelope he'd given him with the pitching tips written on the back of it. "The examination reports are in that envelope. Kristen used a fake name, but I'm sure if you do a little investigating—I know that must be hard for your crack staff at the Robbery/Homicide Unit, being so busy following me around—I'm sure you'll be able to put two and two together."

Madden opens the envelope and unfolds the papers. There are three sheets. The first is a short record of Jim's student clinic history, with references to a treatment for

Chlamydia, while the last two are copies of Clinic Visit forms, both with the name Chris Ray at the top. Chris Ray's date of birth, he notices, is similar to Kristen's but a few months off—it made her seventeen not sixteen at the time of the examination. Her visits were spaced exactly fourteen days apart, two Sundays from each other, and indeed, the first one fell on the day after the alleged incident. The two pages are filled with medical jargon.

Page one:

PMH: 17 y.o. white female here for initial pelvic exam. Reports first intercourse last PM. No BCM used. LMP two weeks ago. Pt c/o small amount of bloody vaginal discharge and vulvar soreness this AM. Denies abdominal or pelvic pain. Past medical history significant for only splenectomy post MVA six months ago. No meds, no allergies. Pt desires emergency contraception.

Physical exam: BP-116/78 pulse-88 Temp-98.2

Pelvic exam: Several 2-3 cm violaceous ecchymotic areas noted on perineum. Vulva with slightly edematous labia and moderate erythema, no lesiona, no excoriations. Hymen with tear at 5 o'clock. Vagina with erythema and serosanguinous drainage, no lacerations. Cervix slightly friable. Uterus normal size, nontender. Adnexa normal size nontender.

Wet smear- moderate RBC's, few WBC's, no hyphae, no trichomonads, moderate active sperm, no foul odor. Urine pregnancy test- NEG.

Impression: Normal pelvic exam except ecchymotic perineum. ??Trauma with IC. (Pt denies sexual or physical abuse.) Candidate for emergency contraception.

Plan: Pap smear, VDRL, Chlamydia and GC tests pending. Condom use stressed. Offered counseling referrals related to potential abuse. Given 2 Ovral pills stat, with 2 more to be taken in 12 hours. Risks and benefits of emergency contraception reviewed. Advised return to clinic in 2 weeks for follow-up STD and pregnancy testing.

Page two:

F/U history: Pt c/o vulvovaginal itching and irritation with moderate discharge. Denies fever, dysuria, abdominal or pelvic pain. Denies intercourse since last visit.

Physical exam: Perineum clear, no ecchymosis. Vulva with moderate erythema, no lesions. Thin drainage at introitus. Vagina with erythema and copious foamy discharge. Strawberry cervix friable with moderate mucoprurlent discharge at os. Uterus normal size, nontender. Adnexa normal size, nontender, no masses.
Wet smear- moderate RBC's, moderate WBC's, numerous trichomonads, no hyphae, no clue cells. Urine pregnancy test-NEG.

Impression: Trichomonal vaginitis
Cervicitis R/O Chlamydia vs. GC

Plan: Azithromycin 2 gms. stat. No ETOH X 48 hours. VDRL, Chlamydia and GC tests pending

When he's through skimming the documents, he asks Cogan: "There's another follow-up visit. Where is it?"

"I don't have it."

"How'd you get these?"

"Not important. But what you're going to do about it is."

"The other day, when you were in Joanie's with your attorney, did you know I was outside?"

"Maybe. Why?"

"So you're attorney was in on it?"

"On what?"

"The whole *Mercury* article gag?"

"No, she didn't know. She doesn't know anything. She doesn't know those documents exist. But she will soon."

"So what were you asking her?"

"When?"

"When you were showing her the article."

"About your bias."

Madden feels the hairs on the back of his head stand up. "What bias is that?"

"Your pre-determined bias in this case. Against me."

"I don't know what you're talking about."

"You were molested by a doctor, detective."

"I wasn't molested, Doctor, I was raped."

"My point exactly."

He stares at him heatedly. A wave of paranoia. Suddenly, he's scared he's being set up.

Is he wearing a wire?

Suppressing an urge to frisk him, he asks: "How long have you had these documents?"

"Not long."

"You like pizza?"

"What?"

"Did you have pizza delivered to Carrie's home two nights ago?"

"A pizza? Why would I want to have a pizza delivered to Carrie?"

His disbelief seems genuine. Too genuine.

"A pizza was delivered to her home," he says. "And you spoke to her earlier in the week."

Cogan shrugs. "What, was it poisoned or something?"

"No, not exactly."

"Well, I don't know anything about a pizza. All I know is that I've got a meeting with my attorney tomorrow morning at nine. I'm going to give her those documents. And if the charges against me aren't dropped within twenty-four hours, I take it all to the press."

With that he walks off the mound. Nearing the first base line, Madden calls out him.

"Doctor."

He turns around. "What?"

"I'm not in anybody's pocket. There is no conspiracy here."

Cogan smiles. He looks at the ground and contemplatively kicks at the dirt a little. After a moment, he says, "You know, detective, before this all happened, I used to get some really difficult patients. And I mean difficult from a behavioral not a medical standpoint. There are some patients you really don't like. But I still treat them to the best of my abilities."

"I'm not on a personal crusade. What happened to me happened a long time ago."

"Maybe. But you still dislike me. You have from the beginning."

"Like you said, whether I like you or not has nothing do with how I do my job."

Another smile, this one broader.

"You have a good day, detective."

40/ The dog gets mangier

May 13, 2007—p.m. 9:30

During the NFL season, The Dutch Goose attracts a healthy crowd on Sunday right through the ESPN late game, which starts at five-thirty on the West Coast. However, in the spring, Sunday evenings are quiet, and by nine, the place has pretty much cleared out except for a handful of hopelessly single over-40 males and hard-drinking, heavy-smoking women who step outside every half hour or so to take their drags. Madden, even with his tie loosened and his hair mussed, doesn't exactly fit in with this amiably sorry bunch. But he's doing his best to.

"I don't go to the movies all that often," he says a little too loudly with the hint of a slur creeping into his speech, "but here's one that has special meaning for me tonight."

They're playing a little game with the bartender, Eddie, a gentlemanly Irish guy in his early forties who's almost as bald as him. Someone recites a line from a movie and Eddie has to guess which movie it's from. Unfortunately, it's now his turn.

"Houston, we have a problem," he says.

"Oh, that's lame," says a rather weathered, buxom, bottle blond named Peggy who's sitting next to him up at the bar. She's wearing a black V-neck T-shirt that leaves enough cleavage exposed to reveal a small tattoo of the cartoon character Taz, the Tasmanian devil, on the upper portion of her left breast. Earlier she'd suggested that if he played his cards right she might show him her Yosemite Sam.

"*Apollo 13*," says Eddie.

"Yeah, that was a good movie," Peggy remarks hoarsely. "Tom Hanks. He had to lose a lot of weight for *Survivor*."

"Hello, Hank." He feels a large arm over his shoulder and looks up to see Pastorini standing next to him.

"Oh, hey, Pete. Welcome to my impromptu retirement party."

"Twenty-four years a dick," Peggy says.

"Fourteen," he corrects her.

"Oh, shit, sorry." She lets out a loud, raspy laugh. "Twenty-four was the age of my last boyfriend, what a useless prick he was. Except for the sex, of course."

"Of course," Madden says, raising his glass as she leans into him suggestively.

"How many has he had, Eddie?" Pastorini asks.

"He's working on his fifth," says the bartender.

"He's fine," Peggy says.

"He's pretty snockered," says Eddie. "I was going to call him a cab. But then he said you were coming."

Pastorini: "Come on, Hank. Let's have a little chat."

His boss, whom he just notices is looking very hip-hop dressed in a navy-colored, velour Adidas sweat suit, now has him by the arm and is tugging him gently, trying to get him off the barstool.

"Where's your bling bling, Sarge?"

"Hank, a word."

"Careful, big boy, he's got a bum foot," the blond warns.

"I know he's got a bum foot. And if you don't shut up, I'll give you one, too."

"Touchy, touchy," she says. "Someone had too much caffeine today."

With some further encouragement from Pastorini, he manages to stand up. Swaying a little, he declares: "Pete, I'm drunk."

"No shit. Eddie, bring us over a couple of Diet Cokes, would ya? No ice."

Pastorini leads him to one the booths and deposits him onto the banquette side. Shortly, Eddie arrives with the Diet Cokes, which look awfully like Guinness Stout because he'd served them in pint glasses.

"Drink that," Pastorini orders. "Then I want to see those documents."

He takes two big gulps of the Coke. It tastes much better than the beer.

"What happened, Hank?" he goes on. "Everything seemed fine when I spoke to you this morning. You told me you had a partial thumbprint from the pizza that was his."

He isn't sure whether it's the beer or the reminder of all that had gone wrong, but he's hit with a wave of nausea. He closes his eyes, and when he opens them again he's staring down at a sea of initials, names, and assorted other words that have been carved into the table. For some reason his eyes fall on the words "The Clash." He's totally mystified by what it means. *Clash of what?*

"I let it get too personal, Pete. I told myself I wouldn't. But I did. I'm a friggin' disgrace."

"Stop that."

Leaning back, he manages, after a brief struggle, to pull the envelope—Cogan's envelope—out of his front pants pocket and hand it to Pastorini. It's still folded in three, and unfurling it, Pastorini reads what he sees written.

"Four steps to proper pitching," he says, puzzled.

"No, no, inside. Look inside."

Pastorini takes out the copies and looks them over. While he pursues them, Madden drinks the rest of the Coke.

"How did he get these?" Pastorini asks.

"I told you. I don't know."

He stares down at the table, running his finger over one of the grooves of a carved letter. It was the first B in Bob. It said "Bob + Liz." He wonders where they are now.

"Hank."

He lifts his head.

"What?"

"What did he say to you?"

"He said I'm a pathetic excuse for a detective. And you know what, Pete? He's right."

"Hank, I'm not listening. You're drunk and you're talking gibberish. I refuse to listen."

"Well, you'd better. This case was a dog from the beginning, Pete. I told you it was a dog. And you wouldn't listen to me. And now it's the ruin of me."

"You're overreacting."

He shakes his head melancholically. "She forgot. It slipped her mind."

"What?"

"That's what Carrie said when I asked her why she didn't tell me about Kristen saying something about how Cogan should see a doctor. 'I forgot. There was a lot of stuff going on in my head,' he says, mimicking her high-pitched voice. 'And you never asked me anything about that stuff.' And you know what? She was right. Isn't that a hoot, Pete? I never asked. You know why?"

"Because of the diary," Pastorini said impatiently. "I know, you told me."

He lets out a little belch, and seeing his Coke is finished, takes the one that's sitting in front of Pastorini.

"I see why you like this stuff," he says after he'd gulped down half his drink. "Very refreshing."

"So let's recap, Hank."

"Yes, let's."

"We've got a bunch of inadmissible, illegally obtained evidence, a victim who's suddenly highly lacking in the credibility department, an insecure detective who he thinks he's full of shit, and a key witness who very possibly may have had sex with the victim while she was in a severely debilitated state."

"Sounds about right," he agrees, raising his glass in a mock toast. "Your dog is looking mighty mangy at this point. What do you say we put him out of his misery?"

"Not a chance."

Just then he feels his phone vibrating. He takes the Motorola out of its belt clip and hands it to Pastorini.

"It's my wife," he says, flipping it open for him. "Can you talk to her? I don't think I'm in any condition to talk to her. She's called twice already."

Pastorini takes the phone.

"Maria, it's Pete." A beat, then: "No, I've never seen him like this. But he's all right. I'm going to get him home shortly. I'm going to drive him, so don't worry."

Handing the phone back to him, he says:

"We're right back at square one, Hank. Nothing's changed except that we have another bad guy to take down."

"I'm the bad guy."

"No, you're not. This guy's the bad guy," he says, holding up Jim's student clinic report.

"Maybe. But it's too messed up. I already fucked it up. Crowley's going to have our collective asses when he sees the bad press. I'm done for."

"Let me handle Crowley. You work on getting a confession."

He laughs. "And I thought I was the only one at the table who was intoxicated."

"I'm serious."

"I don't think you understand. We're never going to get to the bottom of this, Pete. You know why? Because there is no bottom."

"We get the girl to play ball again. We do another Open Wide."

"With her own brother? Are you insane?"

"Well, we get the doc to play then," Pastorini counters, realizing his mistake. "He's got a vested interest. If you're going to let him off the hook, at least make him earn it."

Madden considers that. He'd considered it earlier, when he was sober, and it had seemed like a poor option. And now that he's drunk, it still seems poor.

"And what? What kind of leverage does he have against the kid?"

"I don't know," Pastorini says. "That's up to you to figure out. All I know is that he sure seemed to do a number on you, so he must have something going for him. Now drink the rest of that and let's go."

41/ Bart's journal

May 15, 2007

To whom it may concern:

Pretty soon I'm going to meet Dr. Cogan at the little park near the Linear Accelerator. I suppose it's an apt place for our meeting because ever since that night I've felt like a particle that's been split in two and I haven't been able to quite put myself back together the way I'd like.

Dr. Cogan called me yesterday and said he wanted to meet privately with me. He had something he wanted to show me, which he couldn't talk about over the phone. I'm not sure what it could be, but it couldn't be good. But after talking it over with Watkins, we decided I should go meet him, and that if the doc accuses me of anything, I should admit to nothing. Watkins knows the park and suggested it at as a meeting point.

I didn't sleep much last night. I'm really tired and I haven't been able to study for my first final on Thursday. I'm not so worried about dealing with Dr. Cogan. Him I can handle. But Watkins has really been getting on my nerves. For the record, he nearly choked me to death the other day. And he's been harassing me ever since. It's really the psychological torture that's getting to me. I don't think he understands that I need to study. I don't care what he does to me, but I cannot fail those exams. I cannot fail.

As such, I have a bad feeling about today. I hope it goes all right, but there's clearly some reason not to be optimistic. So if something bad should happen, please look in the folder marked Simpsons Episodes. In the Season Three folder you'll find a folder called Bart's Journal. It's really mine. And while it may not answer everything, it will hopefully show you how sorry I am that this all happened and how much I really cared for Kristen even though my stupid ego helped kill her.

Sincerely,
Jim Pinklow

42/ Taking one for the team

May 15, 2007—a.m. 9:40

Wells Fargo bank parking lot, Sharon Heights Shopping Center, Tuesday morning. Inside a white van, a technician is doing the first of several sound checks he'll do that morning.

"It's sunny," Madden says as they await the technician's verdict. "So we're going with the sunglasses. The microphone's in the frame."

Madden points to a spot near the left hinge of a pair of thick-framed Ray Bans, which are sitting on top of a little ledge next to half drunken cup of coffee. The sunglasses had a neoprene eyewear restraint, a Crokie, attached to the ends of each arm.

"They're not the most stylish model, but with the Crokie on it, you can just leave them dangling from your neck. If the sun's in your eyes, feel free put them on. They're real, working sunglasses."

He goes on to explain that their receiver will be able to pick up the audio from the transmitter at a distance up to fifteen hundred feet, but they would park the van closer than that. They also have a second, more powerful transmitter attached to the bench, so if he's able to remain in its vicinity, they'll be very well covered. Another factor in their favor: there's little wind today.

"You've been on the flip side of this," the detective says

unapologetically, "so you know the deal. You've got a limited amount of time before the surprise factor wears off. Those first thirty seconds are crucial."

He nods, remembering all too well his bungled conversation with Carrie.

"You want to go over the script one more time or are you OK?"

"I'm good," he says.

"OK. Well, as I mentioned, Mr. Burns, whom you've met, will be walking his dog toward the southwest corner, over by the drinking fountain."

He shows him a crude diagram of the park that he'd drawn himself on a piece of paper. At the center he put three X's next to each other to mark the central bench. A single X with a circle around it marked Burns's position next the drinking fountain, which is depicted as a small square. The two benches on the perimeter of the park are also marked by three X's. And finally, his position, just outside the park, on the south side, is marked by an X with a circle around it. Technically, both his position and Burns's are equidistant from the central bench, but Burns will be out in the open while the van will be parked on the road behind some trees and bushes, semi-concealed.

"He's not going to be that close because we don't want him that close," he continues. "But you'll be able to see him. And if everything's good, he won't do anything."

Cogan: "And if it's bad, if you're not getting audio, he picks up the dog and holds him up?"

"Correct."

"What kind of dog is it?"

"I don't know exactly, but it's little," Madden says. "And it's white."

"Is it a police dog?"

"No, it's a lap dog. It's his girlfriend's."

"So he isn't doing anybody much good."

"No, but he's well trained."

"OK," the technician says, picking up the sunglasses and handing them to him. "We're all set for now. They're all yours. We'll do another test when you get closer."

He slips the Crokie over the back of his neck and lets the glasses fall to his chest.

"How do I look?" he asks

"You look like you," Madden says. "Which is how you want to look."

With fifteen minutes to kill before they set off for the park, he sits in his car with Carolyn, talking more about the future than the present.

"What are you thinking?" she asks.

"Just wondering what the hospital's going to do. They could still force me out. If I leave, I'd like to leave on my own terms."

"I don't think now's the time to be worrying about that."

"What do you think she'll do when it comes out?"

"Who?"

"Carrie."

"You mean, do I think she'll recant? I suppose it depends on how sure she is she saw what she says she did. She'll be offered plenty of therapy and counseling, I'm sure."

"What if she continues to insist she saw me?"

"She can insist all she want," she says. "They still won't have a case."

"How would you react?"

"If what?"

"If you found out you had sex with somebody you didn't think you did?"

"I don't think you should assume Kristen didn't know. Ultimately, that may have been why she killed herself."

"But let's just say you had no idea. It happens."

"I suppose going forward I'd have a very hard time trusting people, guys in particular. I have a hard enough time already, but it would be magnified tenfold."

He nods.

"What's up, Ted?" she asks when he doesn't respond verbally. "What's bothering you?"

"Nothing. I was just so focused on getting a result, I hadn't spent much time thinking how this would all pan out if I got the result I wanted."

"Well, get it first, then you can think all you want."

"You're not mad at me, then?"

"We were on different timetables. I think we always have been. When you want to go faster, I want to go slower. When I want to go faster, you want to stop. That's just the way it is."

He smiles. "Damn shame, isn't it?"

"I would have gotten you off. I said I would."

"I needed more than to get off."

She laughs.

"What?"

"Listen to us," she said. "How silly would that sound if someone heard that out of context? Me promising to get you off, you needed more than to get off."

She laughs again, and this time he laughs with her. They have a good chuckle, then suddenly, he remembers the sunglasses.

"Shit, is this on?"

She looks at him, mortified. A moment later they hear the van's side door slide open and watch Madden step out and knock on the driver's side window. He rolls it down for him.

"Yes, it's on," he says. "And we're on. If you could come with me, please, Ms. Dupuy, we'll be on our way."

Right from the beginning, things don't go according plan. The audio is fine, but the problem is Jim doesn't enter the park from either of the two entrances they thought he would. The park is almost a perfect circle, predominantly covered by neatly-trimmed grass, with an asphalt bike/walking path following its perimeter and a circular cement area in the middle that from the air would like a bull's-eye. You can enter the park from all sides, but the majority of people enter from the south and west entrances because they abut the access road, where you're allowed to park. The other option is the north entrance because it connects to Sand Hill—four-lanes wide here—the road that takes you up to the 280 freeway and into the hills and is a popular with bikers. As it happens, Jim comes in through the east entrance, which is really the start (or end) of a separate bike path for recreational riders and pedestrians than runs parallel to Sand Hill. That area, right outside the east entrance, is more of a "naturalist's" spot, a woodedarea that appeals to dog walkers.

When Cogan sees Jim standing by the entrance, he waves him over. But the kid won't move; he motions for him to come to him. It goes back and forth like that for a couple of turns until he reluctantly gives in and hesitantly leaves his position at the center bench and starts walking toward him.

To his left, about sixty yards off, he sees Burns and the dog, which is on the ground, sniffing a shrub. He's half - expecting him to give him some sort of signal to stop, but when none comes, he assumes everything is all right: They won't have the bench transmitter but the body-worn one must be working fine. Picking up his gait, he forces himself to walk more confidently.

"Hey," he says when he's close enough.

"Hey," Jim says.

He gestures toward the bench. "You don't want to sit down?"

"Nah. I've been sitting a lot lately. Let's get this over with. What do you want to show me?"

"Some documents I think you'll find interesting."

He hands him an envelope that contains copies of the

copies he'd given Madden.

"The first person is actually Kristen," he says, watching Jim's expression grow more disturbed the longer he scans the pages. "The second one, as you can see, is you. And for some reason, you appear to have both contracted Chlamydia at exactly at the same time."

Jim looks up and scouts the area, and sees Billings off to the right.

"Who gave these to you?" he asks in a low voice.

"Someone who doesn't like you," he says.

"Who?"

"I know what happened, Jim. You had sex with Kristen that night at the party. She was passed out and you had sex with her."

"She was not passed out."

"We have a witness. A witness has come forward."

"Who?"

He's supposed to say "one of your fraternity brothers," but before he can, something hits him on the back right side of his head and pitches him forward. He's out before he hits the ground.

Both Madden and Carolyn hear the thud in the van.

"What was that?" he says, speaking into his walkie-talkie.

Burns: "What was what?"

A moment of silence, then they hear Jim's voice again.

"What are you doing? Are you out of your mind?"

All kinds of noise on the line: Sounds of rustling, the microphone getting bumped and jostled.

Burns: "I don't have a visual."

Through the rustling, heavy breathing, then another voice: "You dimwit. He could be wired."

Jim: "Is he?"

Madden: "Burns, I need a visual now."

The other voice: "You're a lucky bastard."

Burns: "Come again, Hank."

Carolyn: "Get him out of there."

Jim: "Fuck, dude, not with the gun again."

Madden: "Burns, he has a weapon."

The other voice: "I told you I'm not going down for this, Mr. P. And I meant it."

Burns: "Please repeat."

All the voices were overlapping, confusing Madden. "Get him out," he shouts and just then he hears Jim say:

"Go fuck yourself."

Madden doesn't wait to hear what C. J. Watkins says next. Nor does he wait for Jim to pull a boxcutter from his pocket and say, "I've had enough of this shit," or for Watkins's gun to go off. No, by then, he's already flung the van door open, has jumped out, and is running.

The sound of the shot, though muffled by the silencer, brings Cogan back to consciousness. Lying on his side, he can't move at first and his vision is blurred. The first words that come into his head are probable concussion, and opening and closing his eyes groggily, he sees, at a strange angle, flashes of the bottom half of someone, and down on the ground, the backside of a body. He hears groans and forces himself to roll over a little to the right and get up on his knees.

"Ah, just in time," he hears a familiar voice say, and looks up to the see C. J. Watkins standing over him, holding a gun by his side. That seems odd, but what seems odder, is that he has surgical gloves on his hands.

"Do you mind holding this for a second?"

Before he can respond, Watkins takes his right wrist, jerks it upward, causing him to fall on his side again. He presses the gun to his palm, holding his hand over his fingers.

"Sorry, dude," he says. "But sometimes you gotta take one for the team."

* * *

Madden is a terrible sight coming out of the bushes, propelled forward wildly, his platform shoe tosses out in front of him like an anchor attached to a Bungee chord that yanks him ahead in short, awkward bursts. When Burns, looking a little bewildered, sees him, he drops the dog leash and starts running, too. He may have had better form, but Madden, aided by a downhill incline and a twenty-yard head start, manages to reach the east entrance first. There, in the shadows, he sees a figure aiming a gun at a figure lying on the ground.

"No!" someone cries out and almost simultaneously he extends his gun out in front of with both hands and shouts, "Freeze."

But instead of freezing the figure turns towards him. At that second, he only sees the gun swinging towards him at an angle perpendicular to the ground. And just as he's about to come into its line of fire, he squeezes the trigger on his gun.

Later, he'll wonder whether C. J. Watkins intended to shoot him.

The figure that Watkins was aiming his gun at was not Cogan, but Jim, who'd been shot once in the neck. After the shot rings out, Cogan gets to his knees again. From that position, he watches Burns kick the gun away from Watkins, who's sprawled out on the ground. Burns, his gun trained on the kid, says: "Jesus, Hank. You nailed him."

Cogan manages to stand up. He checks his own wound first: the back of his head is throbbing and bleeding from where Watkins had hit him with the butt of his gun.

"Are you hit?" Burns asks.

"No."

He takes one look at Watkins, and thinks the guy's going to box if he hasn't already. His eyes are closed and his face is ashen. He has on his familiar double T-shirt, and even though the outer, short-sleeve shirt is a dark, olive color, he can see that Madden's bullet struck him a few inches north of the solar plexus and had probably hit his heart. Moving past him, he turns his attention to Jim, who's on the ground a little off to the right. He'd been hit in the left side of the neck and is bleeding profusely. There're already a large puddle welling up on the ground next to him, but he's still alive—his eyes are open, looking up at him beseechingly. Cogan puts his hand over the wound and holds it there as tightly as he can. Jim's trying to say something, but he can't. A sound comes out but it's more of a cough.

"We've got to get him out of here," he says.

"Hank, you all right?" Burns asks Madden, who's standing there with his gun by his side, in a state of shock. "Hank?"

"Madden, get over here," Cogan shouts. "Gimme a hand."

Just then Carolyn shows up, looking decidedly out of place in her business suit. "Oh my God," she says.

"Get over here, Madden," he repeats.

Finally, the detective comes out his stupor. He puts his gun back in its holster and comes over.

"Jesus," he says, staring down at the boy.

"We need to scoop him and get him out of here right now. He's lost a lot of blood. If we take the freeway, we can get him to Parkview in five or six minutes. With the traffic on Sand Hill it'll be faster than taking him to the University's Medical Center."

Whether it'd be faster or not was debatable, but in a crisis you go with what's familiar and while Parkview's a couple miles further in distance, he knows just where to go and who to call.

"Shouldn't we wait for the paramedics?" Madden asks.

Instantly, Burns is on his police radio, asking for two ambulances for two shooting victims.

"Not if you want him to die. Get his legs and let's go. Carolyn, help us."

With him having to hold his neck tightly from front to back (he thought he felt an exit wound), they have a little trouble with their positioning at first. But after a few awkward steps they begin to master the art of the six-legged race and get him moving at a pretty good clip toward the van.

"What should I do with him?" Burns calls after them.

"Stay there," Madden tells him. "Just stay there."

When they get up to the van, the technician is standing outside it, the expression on his face that of someone who's gotten a little more than he bargained for. He already has the side door open wide and the engine running.

"I heard everything," he says. "It's all recorded."

"Do you know how to get Parkview Hospital?" he asks.

"I think so."

"I'll drive," Madden volunteers.

As carefully as they can, they load Jim into the van and lay him out on the carpeted floor. He tries to keep his head stable and applies pressure to both sides of the wound the whole time, but every once in a while, his hand slips a little, and blood seeps between his fingers. If it's a complete dissection of either the jugular or the carotid, the kid is fucked—he'll either box or be permanently brain damaged. The wound is a little in on the neck, more toward the trachea, so it very well could be the artery, but there are so many vessels in that area, he wouldn't be able to tell unless he opened him up.

He asks Carolyn to dial a number for him. When she's through dialing she holds the phone up to his ear, though she has some difficulty keeping it there as the van careens onto the freeway's on ramp.

"Who's this?" he says.

It's Catherine, one of the emergency room nurses.

"Catherine, it's Ted. Ted Cogan. I want you to listen carefully. I have a nineteen-year-old male who's been shot in the neck and has a vascular injury with significant blood loss. We're going to need blood and fluid and a vascular surgeon prepared."

"Are you serious?"

"Yes, I'm serious. Do it now. We'll be there in five minutes."

After he hangs up, he turns his attention back to Jim, whose eyes are open but he's having trouble breathing. All the swelling from the gunshot is probably compressing his airway.

He touches his wrist. He's getting stridorous—or clammy, in layman terms—and his pulse is thready and racing. With heavy blood loss, the body constricts its blood vessels, diverting blood to the vital organs.

"Jim, can you feel my hand? Blink if you can feel my hand."

He blinks, which is a good sign.

"Can I do anything?" Carolyn asks.

"Touch his ankle," he says.

"Jim, can you feel that. Blink for me if you can feel her hand."

Again, he blinks.

"OK, we're almost to the hospital. Hang with us for a little longer, buddy. You've been shot in the neck but if you can feel your hands and legs, that's a good sign. I want you to relax as much as you can. You're going to be in good hands in a few minutes."

He's dying. He can see it in his eyes. He can hear it in his breathing. He's going to box and there's nothing he can do about it except ask him not to.

"Don't you box on me, Jim," he says half under his breath. "Do you understand? You will not box."

They're all there: Doctor Kim, Wexler, and the two interns whose names he always forgot. They're waiting for them when they arrive, along with the attending physician, a guy named Mark Franklin, who's at the head of the pyramid that morning. They get Jim on a gurney and wheel him right into the trauma room, where a nurse immediately starts ventilating him while Wexler cuts his clothes off and another nurse jams a large bore IV into one arm, then the other. One intern draws blood and the other prepares to feed a Foley catheter into his urinary tract, so once the fluids come, they'll have a receptacle to drain into. Until they know what type of blood he has, they'll fill him with uncrossed match blood.

When the IV's are in, he feels and then sees Kim hovering over his shoulder. The resident puts his hand over his, the one he's using as a ligature, and says:

"It's OK, Ted. I got it."

And with that he steps back and becomes a spectator. Drained, he stands next to Madden in the back corner of the room, watching them follow the procedures he knows all too well. The adrenalin subsiding, he starts to feel his head again and by the time Franklin says, "OK, let's get some neck film and get him up to the OR," he's feeling a little woozy.

And then they're gone. Down the hall they go, but only when they get in the elevators does he notice Beckler standing in the hallway, staring at him, aghast. He realizes then what a mess he looks, his hands and shirt covered in blood.

"Hello, Anne," he says, leaning against the wall for support.

"Christ, Cogan. What happened? Josie said you were down here."

"Oh, you know, a little accident."

"Little?"

Madden walks up to him and puts a hand on the back of his shoulder.

"You OK, Cogan?"

"He's got a nasty cut," Wexler says, taking a closer look at the back of his head. "You're going to need some stitches, my friend."

"I'll take care of it," Beckler offers.

He pushes himself away from the wall. "This should be good," he says. "I always thought you were a good closer, Beckler. Did I ever tell you that?" He puts his arm around her shoulders and leans on her a little as they walk together down the hall.

"You know, I owe you big time," he says. "They got the guy. The real guy."

"The kid back there in trauma?"

"Yeah, though I think it's a little more complicated than that."

He explains that the cop didn't shoot him, another kid did, and he's not sure why.

"If I did anything, Cogan," she says. "I did it for myself. You know, they were already lining up your replacement. And the leading candidate just happens to be someone I like less than you."

"Do I know him?"

"Her."

"Ah, I see."

"However, I can't deny that experiencing you in a humbler state made a favorable impression. I saw a glimmer of evolution there, Cogan."

He smiles as they stop in front of a vacant examination room. His head is still throbbing but the dizziness is gone; he's totally lucid.

"How 'bout a coffee, Anne? You'd never have coffee with me. Ultimately, I think that was the source of all our problems."

"Do me a favor, Cogan."

"Anything."

"Shut up."

43/ Business Class

May 18, 2007

When you're hit in the neck with bullet and your carotid artery is completely severed, you have little chance of survival. Jim was lucky: in his case, the artery was only partially dissected. The bullet sheared a small chunk of the vessel's wall off, leaving a hole a quarter inch in diameter, while also damaging his larynx. To expose the injuries, the surgeon made a "hockey-stick" incision with the long limb of the scalpel parallel to the anterior border of the sternocleidomastoid muscle. He opened the wound in layers, retracting the sternocleidomastoid muscle laterally to expose the common, internal, external carotid arteries and the jugular vein, and repaired the damaged segment in the common carotid with a vein patch.

All this was done in less than half an hour, yet Cogan knew that such vascular injuries to the neck brought with them a high probability of stroke. So when Kim gave him word later that day Jim had survived but had suffered an acute stroke to the left side of his brain, he wasn't surprised. It would be several days, even weeks, before they'd fully understand the scope of the damage, but when Jim woke two days after the operation, the right side of his face, arm, and leg were seventy to eighty percent paralyzed and he was experiencing serious memory loss.

The brain contains a number of different kinds of memory, including short-term, long-term, declarative, and non-declarative. In Jim's case, his long-term and declarative memory, which holds conscious memories of specific information and events, were most affected. (Non-declarative memory is a learned habit such as riding a bike or driving a car that once learned is not forgotten). When he woke up, he did not recognize, for example, his family. "Jim, do you know who I am?" his mother asked. The injury to his larynx and paralysis in his face prevented him from responding verbally, but he was able to indicate with a perceptible shake of his head that no, he didn't know who she was. A few days later, when she asked the same question, he scrawled the word, "Mom," on a notepad with his left hand. But the only reason he was able to do it was because she'd told him a few days earlier she was his Mom.

The doctors said that with time and therapy he would improve. Some memories might never return, his right side might never be quite as strong as his left, and his personality might be altered. But the brain had a way of rewiring itself, and stroke victims, especially younger ones like him, had gone on to lead healthy, productive lives.

"We feel very fortunate that Jim is alive today," his father says, reading from a statement to a group of a dozen or so reporters who've gathered in the hospital courtyard five days after the shooting. "He continues to make positive progress with each passing day. Regrettably, at this time, he remembers neither the shooting nor the incidents leading up to the shooting. We therefore cannot comment on the allegations that have been made."

Crowley, unusually tightlipped, also reads a short statement from the podium: "All charges against Dr. Cogan have been dropped. At this time, however, no additional arrests have been made and we cannot comment on the most recent allegations, as an investigation is ongoing. We ask that you direct all your inquiries into the shooting death of Mr. Watkins to Commander Gillian Hartwick of the Menlo Park police department."

Commander Hartwick takes her turn closing ranks, too. "After a thorough investigation, it has been determined that Detective Henry Madden discharged his weapon in self defense after the assailant, Christopher James Watkins, turned his weapon on him. Let it be said that that this is the first time detective Madden fired his weapon while on duty, and while his actions were unavoidable and necessary, he regrets that they caused the loss of human life."

Cogan says precious little publicly. He won, and when you win, it doesn't do you a whole lot of good to stand at the top of summit, beating your chest and raining down insults on your former detractors, who are scurrying around at base camp, looking for a sleeping bag and a tent to crawl into to take cover from shit storm they see coming. He doesn't need Carolyn to tell him that, but she does anyway.

"Humble, compassionate, and no names," she advises.

And so in his statement, which turns out to be the longest of the bunch, he doesn't disparage anyone—the police, the DA's office, the hospital administration, Jim, Carrie, Kristen, or her father. Instead, he speaks a language the authorities are comfortable with, the language of the clean and well swept, of the tidy little ledge high above the amorphous, mucky bottom.

"I was falsely accused of a crime I didn't commit," he says from the podium, glancing at his typed notes as he speaks. "It might be trite to say that I knew that the truth would prevail, but for those of you who supported me during this difficult time, I say you were right, the truth did prevail, though I'm sorry it had to end the way it did."

"Until all this happened, I was in the business of saving people. Some of them were good, some bad, and some were a little of both. We have rules in our business. A strict set of guidelines we follow to minimize risk. However, usually the best of us, when it comes down to it, rely on instinct and sometimes end up having to ignore the rules."

"All along, I felt, in my heart of hearts, that Kristen was one of the good ones. When I asked myself why she wrote the untruths she did, the only answer I could come up with was that she wasn't lying. She believed in the fiction she created. It was her story, the way she wanted it, and no one was going to take that away from her. I'm only sorry now that I couldn't have made her realize things weren't so bleak that she would feel the impulse to take her own life. For that I would like to apologize to her family, who have had to endure a nightmare far more horrific than mine these last several weeks."

Privately, of course, the authorities inform him they have a good inkling what's down in the muck. They're with him: The two frat boys raped Kristen. But to prove it is another matter. Sex is one thing. But rape is an altogether different beast. And now, with one of them dead and the other barely knowing who he, let alone Kristen, is, well, that made things awfully challenging, even with the journal cum love letters they found on Jim's computer.

Even Kroiter has had enough. The stakes have changed, the enemies have multiplied, and earlier that morning, standing on his welcome mat, frustration overcame him. "Get the fuck off my lawn," he bellowed to a TV crew. "Neither my wife nor I has anything to say. So leave us alone."

A week later, on June 6, several arrests are made. Joseph Greene and Dwight Johnson, proprietors of Miss Tiki's Beauty Salon in East Palo Alto, are booked and charged with promoting prostitution and underage prostitution, along with twelve women, who are brought up on prostitution charges. In a separate raid, Lincoln Barkley and Jaime Pulido are both charged with two felony counts of possessing and selling illegal firearms and drug trafficking.

The arrests are part of an orchestrated effort by both the Menlo Park and East Palo Alto police departments to demonstrate that they're responding swiftly to the shooting with material action and to reinforce the notion that C. J. Watkins is the troubled youth they claimed. Unfortunately, the image they sketched in the days immediately following his death didn't always jibe with the photo of the clean-cut kid that was being circulated in the media, sandwiched between adjectives like bright, charming, and popular. The dark-side argument needed a beefier foundation, and in one sweeping, well-coordinated operation, they silence the small minority of critics who contend Madden acted hastily in slaying Watkins. Behold, they intonate none too subtly, the real C. J. Watkins was having sex with prostitutes, buying and selling amphetamines and other designer drugs to students, and fraternizing with gun dealers.

However, part of their PR problem stems from Madden's refusal to go along with the media's attempts to portray him as a hero. So long as Carrie, the doctor, and the victim/suspect aren't talking, Madden, the handicapped detective with a chip on his shoulder, is the most logical lens through which reporters and television producers can tell their stories. The most hungry and accommodating of them brazenly promise a sympathetic profile, an expanded, spicier version of the last article, a piece that he can "always look back upon and be proud of, something his kids will show their grandkids."

Imagine their surprise when they hear he wants nothing to do with it. He tells Pastorini and Hartwick that's the last thing he wants, another puff piece celebrating the hurdles he's had to overcome. Sitting in the sergeant's office, he says, "What I have to say wouldn't translate well, Pete. The department wouldn't like it. It's not sound-bite friendly."

"What do you want to say, Hank?" Pastorini asks.

Madden doesn't respond at first. But after some reflection, he says:

"Between you and me, Pete, shooting that kid and—"

He falls silent, suddenly embarrassed.

"What?" Pastorini urges.

"Well, saving the doc there in the park and rushing Jim to the hospital—that whole thing, the whole combination, just set something off in me. Afterwards, I thought about what Cogan did. Here's this kid who could have destroyed his life, and without even a second of hesitation, he goes all out to save him. I don't know, Pete. You go through all your life looking for some sort of revenge and suddenly you realize what you really should have been looking for was the exact opposite. It threw me for a loop."

Pastorini looks at him, a little dumbfounded. "Did you apologize to him?"

"No. I thanked him, though."

"For what?"

"For being a good doctor."

"Very touching," says Pastorini.

Madden smiles. "Hey, Pete."

"What?"

"Say Open Wide."

"Why?"

"Just say it."

"Open Wide," Pastorini says.

Madden smiles again.

"Say it again."

"Open Wide."

Madden's smile broadens.

"I'll be damned. Hey, Billings," Pastorini shouts through his half open door, "Get in here. I want you to see something."

The next day, Cogan opens the newspaper and spots a short article with the headline, "Detective Still Mum on Shooting."

About half the piece is a rehash of earlier profiles of Madden, describing his physical handicap, as well as his childhood sexual abuse—both of which, according to Commander Hartwick, the detective has long ago put behind him.

"While Detective Madden is a private man," the commander is quoting as saying, "the main reason he doesn't want to discuss the shooting is that he feels strongly that Dr. Cogan and the team of doctors and nurses at Parkview Hospital who saved Jim Pinklow's life are the heroes here. What they did was truly remarkable. All he had to do was to pull the trigger of a gun."

And for a time, Cogan does feel remarkable. He knows the feeling will fade, but while it lasts, he feels a quiet satisfaction that he hasn't felt in quite some time, not since he pitched a three-hit shutout his senior year, the only complete game of his college career.

One morning he gets a call from a hospital administrator. She's calling to ask him what day he'd like to start again. Not if, but what day.

"Monday, I guess, is fine," he replies. "I'll take my usual shifts if that's possible."

"Absolutely. But you might want to take your first few weeks a little slower. You know, work your way back into the swing of things."

She sounds more like a flight attendant than the impatient underpaid staffer he was used to.

"No, you're right. Can you just put me on for three days? I'll see how I feel after a couple of weeks."

And so months of contemplation, fantasies of a triumphant departure, and nerve-racking debates over possible career paths are erased in a single instant by an inconsequential bureaucrat with a nice tone of voice who happened to ask one question instead of another. Not if, but *what* day.

"It just seemed all right," he tells Carolyn that Monday,

calling her from his old office, which he found exactly the same way he'd left it.

"How does it feel to be back?" she asks.

"Well, it's the same plane, but I'm flying business class instead of coach. That's what it feels like."

"Now there's the secret to life."

A month passes. Then two. And soon it's as if he'd never left. July and August come and go and he doesn't hear from Carrie. He's vaguely disappointed, for although part of him thinks it will be best to forget her, he feels she owes him some sort of explanation and an apology. Madden had given him that—maybe not in precise words, but the sentiment was there. They'd had a drink together at The Dutch Goose and somewhere between beer one and two he agreed to become an assistant coach for Morey's, his son's Little League team sponsored by Peninsula Building Materials.

Madden didn't think he'd hear from her.

"Her parents sent her away somewhere," he said. "They haven't told us exactly where. I think it's some sort of Bible school."

He turned out to only be half right.

"Carrie was here," Josh calls Cogan up at work one day to tell him. "She stopped by a little while ago, around four, to say goodbye. She looked good. She left a package for you. She's moving back East."

When he gets home, he finds a medium-sized padded envelope in his mailbox. Inside, there's a note:

Dear Dr. Cogan:

I hope this finds you well. I read in the paper that you had gone back to work and got your job back, which I was glad to hear. As for me, I'm off to boarding school in Connecticut. My father was able to pull some strings and get me in for the fall semester. It's not top tier or any-

thing but it seems pretty nice, and the people I met when I visited this summer seem cool. You always said Kristen would be better off on the East Coast, and I guess, in a strange way, I'm taking your advice.

I think about everything that's happened and I think about you sometimes, but I don't really know how to put into words how I feel. I'm pretty mixed up, which is part of the reason my parents decided it would be best if I got a fresh start somewhere else. I'm grateful to you for saving my brother's life but I also keep thinking that none of this would have happened if you hadn't done what you did to Kristen. I could, of course, say the same thing about my brother. It makes things awfully complicated when you don't know exactly who to blame, especially when maybe we were all a little to blame. But I do know what I saw. Which is why I thought you should have the disc they found in Kristen's computer the day she died. She made it for you, though I'm not sure if and when she was going to give it to you. The list of song is below. I don't know if you'll want to play it while you're operating, but maybe you should. I think you'll like it. I did.

1. *Split Screen Sadness—John Mayer*
2. *Blame it on the Tetons—Modest Mouse*
3. *All Apologies—Sinead O'Connor*
4. *Anthems for a Seventeen-Year-Old Girl—Broken Social Scene*
5. *Open Your Eyes—Snow Patrol*
6. *Honestly—Zwan*
7. *Maps—Yeah, Yeah, Yeahs*
8. *Kiss Me Deadly—Lita Ford*
9. *Believe Me Natalie—The Killers*
10. *We Will Become Silhouettes—The Postal Service*
11. *Float On—Modest Mouse*
12. *Can We Still Be Friends—Todd Rundgren*

Lastly, I've enclosed something else that Kristen's parents wanted you to have. They finally got her journal back from the police the other day. It was too painful for them to keep and they were going to destroy it at first, but then they decided you should have it. If you read it, you'll understand why they don't think I was lying. I know what I saw, Dr. Cogan, and I'll never forget it.

Yours truly,
Carrie Pinklow

44/ Under Monet's water lilies

Sept. 7, 2007—a.m. 7:38

"Hey, hey, there he is," Klein greets Cogan a couple of mornings later in the cafeteria for breakfast in their usual spot. It's just after seven-thirty and there are only a handful of people scattered about the room. "You seem rather chipper, old boy."

"Got six hours last night. Straight."

"Impressive," Klein says enviously. "No action?"

He shakes his head. "A double MVA early on but that's it. Real quiet."

"You hear about Franklin?"

"No, what?"

"He has this guy come in the other day, in the middle of the day. He says he's been shot. He tells him he's got a bullet high in his chest, right here."

Klein points to a spot just below his right clavicle.

"OK."

"So Franklin sees the skin's bruised there, but it's not broken, which seems weird. But he looks at the film and sure enough, the bullet's lodged there. Only he can't find an entry wound. He looks everywhere and he can't find it. And so he says, 'Excuse me, sir, but I can't find an entry wound. Where did you initially get shot?' Well, of course, the guy knows he's looking for the entry wound but he doesn't say anything until he asks. And he gives him an 'Oh-by-the-way-I-forgot-to-tell-you.' "

"Gotta love those. You know you're going to get right to the real heart of the problem when a patient says, 'Oh, by the way . . .' "

"Never fails."

"So where'd he get shot?"

Klein leans forward a little and whispers: "Right in the asshole."

"No shit."

"Yeah. It turns out this guy was fucking some dude's wife and the guy comes home and pops him right in the ass between the cheeks. And the fucking bullet rattles around inside him, doesn't hit anything vital, and lodges in his shoulder. Is that amazing or what?"

He winces, thinking about it. "I don't know whether to call him lucky or not."

"Oh, he was lucky. Hey, what's with the sunglasses?"

"Patient gave them to me. I told him I was going down to Costa Rica on vacation and he gave them to me."

Klein takes a closer look at the Ray Bans, which are dangling from Cogan's neck, attached by a Croakie.

"Not bad," he says. "You going with anybody?"

"Carolyn."

"A little bonus action, huh?"

"Separate rooms. Just friends."

"Yeah. Uh-huh."

"She can't date a former client for six months."

"What happened to her guy?"

"Got the boot. Seems he's been a little too preoccupied these days with his business."

"And suddenly you're Mr. Attentive?"

"Let's just say that I have a newfound appreciation for the people who were there for me in my hour of darkness. And that appreciation is manifesting itself in different ways. One happens to be attentiveness. She's a good woman. I want to give her a chance."

"I see," Klein says, not taking the assertion as seriously as he should. "Teddy C., version 2.0. Must be a popular download."

"It helps that it's free."

"You slut."

Klein takes a bite out of his cinnamon-raisin bagel. Cogan waits for him to finish chewing, then says: "I've got something for you."

"Cool. What?"

He puts Carrie's clear, generic CD-R case down on the table in front of him. The case doesn't have a label, so Klein can see the disc inside. She labeled it *Knife Music II* with a black Sharpie.

"This is from Carrie, Kristen's friend."

"You saw her?"

"No, but she sent me a little care package and this was in it."

"That's kind of creepy. Kristen made a mix for you, didn't she? It was pretty good if I remember correctly."

"Yeah, it was. And this one's good, too. But that's not the most interesting thing. There was something else in the package."

He puts the journal down on the table next to the CD-R. Monet's water lilies adorn the cover of the hardbound notebook. A little yellow Post-it, inserted at about the midway point of the notebook, is sticking out of the top.

"Is that what I think it is?" Klein asks, a hint of edginess in his voice.

He nods. "Kristen's diary. Open to the page the Post-it is attached to."

"Why?"

"Just open it."

He does as he's told.

"Now I want you to read to me starting from the second-to-last paragraph on the page."

"What's this about, Ted?"

"Read it, Klein."

After a moment's hesitation, he lowers his voice and says: "The full weight of a man on top of me isn't something I'd ever really felt before. A grown man. It was something. I didn't feel pinned, though. Or claustrophobic. He was tender. He kept kissing me on my neck and then on my boobs. I felt his boner on my leg. I kept waiting for it to come but he took his time, which is good I suppose. But as each minute passed, I got more nervous. And then, like that, I felt it—"

Klein looks up at him, a pained expression on his face. "Ted, this isn't cool. People can hear." He glances around, seeming to hope someone might come to his aid. But the place is practically empty.

"Don't worry. Keep going."

Again, Klein takes a moment before continuing. "It wasn't as painful as I thought, but it was definitely like a sharp jab," he reads, his voice wavering. "He went slowly at first and then he was pumping harder and I could feel him going deep inside me and it hurt but I did my best to relax and find the joy in it because that's how I wanted to remember it. It's funny how when you're doing something—you know, doing something real important—you actually end up projecting yourself into the future and thinking back on something while you're already still there. But it kind of crystallizes the moment. I remember his warm breath on my neck. He was breathing hard, but he wasn't looking at me. He kept grunting. I wasn't sure what I should be doing. So I said, 'Fuck me. Fuck me like you mean it,' because I'd once seen a woman do that in a movie. And that got him grunting more, which I thought was a good thing. Then I heard him whisper in my ear, 'I'm going to count down from ten and when I get to one I'm going to come.' And then he started counting. Ten . . . nine . . . eight . . . seven . . ."

Klein stops at seven and looks up at him.

"There are only two guys I've ever told about that," Cogan says. "You and Reinhart. I think it was at this very table that I told you. I believe you were talking about the lack of sex you and your wife were having and I suggested a way for you to spice things up a bit."

"Look, I don't—"

"And when I read that you know what I thought? I thought the Rhino weighs a good seventy-five to eighty pounds more than I do. But you and me, Kleiny, we're about the same weight and have the same tenor of voice. And well, you have more gray hair, but in the dark, that's pretty hard to notice."

Klein doesn't say anything. He's now looking down at the diary, his lower lip quivering.

"Why, Klein? You were my best friend."

"I'm sorry," he says, tears welling up in his eyes.

"Why?"

"Because I didn't fucking know she was sixteen years old, that's why. I thought she was older."

"I don't understand. What's that got to do with anything?"

Klein looks at him beseechingly. He doesn't want to explain, but he knows he has to.

"Tell me, Klein."

"OK, don't shout. It was a mistake. I made a mistake. It was stupid. After being out with you guys that night for my birthday, I came home and Trish was asleep. Typical. So I called you and I heard that you had women there. And I thought it was the usual types you hang out with. I didn't know. I thought you had two there and shit, it was my birthday, my wife was goddamn passed out, so I got in my car and went over. When I got to your place, the lights were off. I went around through the side gate to the backyard like I sometimes do and the sliding-glass door was open a crack. I went into the house, and then I saw that there was someone in the guest room. And I sat down at the edge of the bed. And when I did, she woke up and took my hand. She took my hand and put it under the covers. And she was naked. I'm sorry. I can't tell you how sorry I am."

He's crying now.

"And you had intercourse with her?"

Klein doesn't answer. He's blubbering.

"Tell me," he says.

"I did. I fucked her. You won't tell Trish, will you?"

"Jesus, Klein."

"I'm sorry," he repeats.

"I don't get it. You were going to just stand by and watch me lose my career and possibly get convicted of rape and manslaughter. What did I do to you to deserve that? What?"

"Nothing," Klein says. "You were just you."

"What the hell does that mean?"

Klein wipes his nose.

"I've always envied you, man."

"For what? For the women?"

"Sure, there were the women," Klein says. "But it wasn't just that. There's an effortlessness to you, man. You're good looking, people like you, and you're always on your game—and people respond to that. They want to be around that. *I* wanted to be around that. But sometimes, you know, I would start to hate you for having those qualities because I knew I didn't have them. And then I would hate myself for hating you because you were my best friend."

"Fuck, Klein. It's one thing to be jealous and another to let my life go down the toilet. The punishment doesn't fit the crime."

"I know, Ted. But I couldn't have handled it. I had a wife. I had kids. You were single. I knew you could handle it. I knew you could get off. And look, you're better for it. You're a better man."

"Better, yes, but more forgiving, no."

"Please don't tell Trish. I'll make it up to you."

"How, Klein?"

"I'll figure out a way. I will."

"I'm afraid it's too late," he says. And with that, he gets up and takes both the CD and diary and puts them in his bag. He gives Klein a napkin to wipe his face.

"It's over, right?" Klein asks.

He doesn't answer. He just takes a moment to stare at him in utter disdain. Then he turns his back on him and walks away.

"Ted," he hears Klein call after him pleadingly. "Ted. Tell me it's over."

"For him," says Madden as he enters the room and moves toward Klein, holding a pair of handcuffs. He'd been standing just outside the cafeteria, listening to their whole conversation through an earpiece.

"Unfortunately for you, Doctor, it's just beginning."

www.knifemusicbook.com

Made in the USA